M000196368

VERY LIKE A QUEEN

ALSO BY MARTIN LAKE

Novels

A Love Most Dangerous

The Flame of Resistance: The Lost King Book 1

Triumph and Catastrophe: The Lost King Book 2

Blood of Ironside: The Lost King Book 3

Outcasts: Crusades Book 1

The Artful Dodger

Land of Blood and Water

Short Stories

For King and Country

The Big School

Mr Toad's Wedding

VERY LIKE A QUEEN

MARTIN LAKE

LAKE UNION PUBLISHING

This is a work of fiction. Names, characters, organizations, places, events, and incidents are either products of the author's imagination or are used fictitiously.

Text copyright © 2016 by Martin Lake

All rights reserved.

No part of this book may be reproduced, or stored in a retrieval system, or transmitted in any form or by any means, electronic, mechanical, photocopying, recording, or otherwise, without express written permission of the publisher.

Published by Lake Union Publishing, Seattle

www.apub.com

Amazon, the Amazon logo, and Lake Union Publishing are trademarks of Amazon.com, Inc., or its affiliates.

ISBN-13: 9781503953277
ISBN-10: 1503953270

Cover design by Kathleen Lynch

Printed in the United States of America

In memory of Sandra Lawson

Prologue

December 1539

To be a queen of King Henry VIII of England is to place your life in peril.

His first wife, Catherine of Aragon, despite being daughter to the wealthiest monarchs in Europe, was denied, denigrated and divorced. Mary, the only child of the marriage, was declared a bastard.

His second wife, Anne Boleyn, was accused of treason, adultery and incest. She was beheaded. Their daughter, Elizabeth, once the apple of Henry's eye, was also declared a bastard.

His third wife, Jane Seymour, gave birth to a son and died a few days later. She was buried with much pomp and circumstance, as befitted the only wife to provide an heir to the throne.

I am Alice Petherton and I am not Henry's queen. I have no intention of becoming one.

I am his lover, his mistress, his favorite. That is sufficient for me. I am firmly resolved to keep my health, my head and my life.

It is two years since I became King Henry's lover. I did so because Richard Rich, one of the most powerful men in the Kingdom, was set upon taking me, using means more foul than fair. When a powerful man threatens a lovely young girl, who can she turn to? The most powerful man in the land, of course.

The King provided a haven, but it turned out that even this was far from safe. Six months after becoming his favorite, I fell victim to his rage and was banished from his presence. Richard Rich saw to it that I was removed from Court and left alone, penniless and defenseless in the most dangerous streets of London.

Sometimes I wake in the middle of the night sweating with terror at the memory of what happened to me next. The loathsome touch of Richard Rich would have been far sweeter than the fate I suffered.

It does not do to dwell on such memories. Suffice to say that I escaped from a place I still cannot bring myself to speak about.

After I escaped I enjoyed perhaps the happiest time of my life, dwelling quietly in the country at the home of the Cooper family, who took me in and treated me almost like a daughter. I thought that I had left the world of power and danger and intrigue behind me and was settling into a life of peace and friendship. I thought wrong.

The King had become so morose and ungovernable that I was summoned back to Court. Within days I was back in his bed. The summons was none of his doing. It was the work of Sir Thomas Cromwell. A man who many in the Kingdom think the devil incarnate.

But I like him. He is my friend and my mentor.

Chapter 1
What Is Love?

December 1539

"For goodness' sake, Sissy Cooper, stop that awful noise," I said.

Sissy looked up at me in alarm. "I was only humming, Alice. It was a little song."

"Well it's a very irritating little song. And you're humming out of tune."

"Sorry. It's just I don't notice when I'm doing my needlework."

I shook my head in exasperation and turned back to my book. I could not find the right word. The verse was almost finished and I was pleased with it. But I needed a word to describe how the maid felt when she first saw her lover. No word was right. Some sounded too ridiculous, the ravings of a lovesick child. Others sounded too cold, too austere to describe a real, true love. I wanted the woman to be a woman, not an ice-maiden. And I did not want her to spout words like some scholar who had read of love in dusty volumes but never experienced it.

I put down my pen. Was the difficulty because I had never truly felt love in my own heart? I frowned as I thought back on these last two years. Oh, I had known plenty much of lovemaking. Despite his age and injury, King Henry was boisterous and demanding when he felt in the mood for pleasure. But how much had I known of love?

The King sometimes told me that he loved me. But this was in rare moments, the times when he let his guard down. When he was hot with lust and intent on wooing me, when he was distracted by some passing thought and forgot he must ever play the King. And sometimes, after we had just made love, when for a moment he was a little more besotted with me than normal.

But had I loved him? That was the question. Had I loved any man?

Unbidden, the image of Art Scrump came to my mind, the only other man I had ever allowed in my bed. But I dismissed the thought of him at once. He had beguiled me, then betrayed me. Best not to uncover that nest of baby birds and hissing vipers.

I thought back to the King. Had I loved him ever? Did I love him now?

It seemed a silly question as I asked it, a foolish notion altogether. Of course I did not love him. I was his mistress, his bedfellow; that was all. And he was my protector, my shield. My master in every way. Paymaster, bed-master, lord and master.

Could a servant truly love her master? Could a hound? Yes, a hound could. But a kitten? Now there was a different matter entirely.

"How are you getting on with your writing, Alice?" Sissy asked shyly.

"Not very well."

"Ah, I'm sorry. You write such lovely songs."

"They're not songs, Sissy. They're poems. How many times do I have to tell you?"

She bit her lip, her face contrite. "I'm sorry. It's just hard for me to understand. When you read them they sound a bit like songs."

"But they're not songs."

"Why not though? I bet Mary could set them to music. Then they'd sound much better."

I opened my mouth to remonstrate but thought better of it. Sissy would never understand the difference between poetry and songs. To be honest, I wasn't sure I did either.

"Where is Mary?" I asked.

"She's with Susan in the sitting room. They thought you'd best be left in peace to get on with your songs."

"Poems, Sissy, poems."

"Yes, Alice." Sissy put down her needlework. "It must be nearly dinnertime. Shall I go to the sitting room and tell them you've finished?"

I glanced out of the window. The sky was a murky, mud-grey color. I hated this time of year. The lovely colors of autumn had flown and dull, dank days had settled on Greenwich Castle with all their sullen misery. Heavy, brooding clouds blanketed the sky without even the relief of rain. On a few days the wind had whipped up and blown the sky clear. But within hours the clouds had crept back, darker, more determined. It lowered my spirits.

"When will Christmas come?" I wondered aloud.

"Not long now," Sissy said. "Only three weeks, I think."

"So it is." My spirits lifted a little at the thought.

Sissy got to her feet. She wore that quiet, determined look that she had developed of late. "It is dinnertime, Alice," she said. "They'll be waiting to serve."

Waiting on me, I thought. Even after a year I could not quite reconcile myself to the fact that I was mistress of Greenwich Castle.

It was not much of a castle, to be honest. It consisted of a suite of apartments with a romantic-looking tower attached. A child with a peashooter could have easily conquered it. But I had half a dozen servants who were efficient and attentive. I had Sissy Cooper, my maid and friend. And most wonderful of all, I had Susan Dunster and Mary

Zouche as my companions. Like me, they had been Maids of Honor to Anne Boleyn and Jane Seymour. They were my best friends and my staunchest allies.

"Come along then," I said to Sissy. "Let's join the others."

Susan and Mary were already in the dining room when we arrived.

"Are you hungry?" I asked with an attempt to sound disapproving of the fact that they had entered before me.

"Starving hungry," Susan said, not noticing my tone, or choosing not to. "This dreary weather leaves me nothing to do except eat."

"You should take up a pastime," I said. "Like Mary or I have done."

"I have pastimes enough, thank you." She narrowed her eyes, making herself look mischievous and deceitful. "I am quite content to scheme and plot."

"Scheming and plotting may get you in trouble," I said.

"It hasn't so far," she replied with a chuckle. "It's all been rather good fun."

I laughed with her, never able to stay angry with my friends, nor even pretend to. I could never manage my friends and closest servants like a lady should. They could play the game in front of visitors and for that I was thankful. But when we were here all alone, they seemed to forget that I was their mistress and the most powerful woman in the realm. And so did I.

But Mary and Susan were the most loyal of friends. Nobody could ask for better. And loyalty was no small feat in a Court as dangerous as King Henry's.

Dinner was served and was delicious as always. A hearty beef stew with little onions and pickled red cabbage. Fresh white bread with butter as rich as cream. A syllabub and raspberry preserve on the side.

The wine was even better, a soft red from the Loire Valley. The Valley of Kings, Sir Thomas Cromwell calls it, the loveliest place on earth. How appropriate for the mistress of the King to drink a wine from such a desirable place.

We talked lightly over dinner. The latest gossip, of course, concerned Anne, the sister of the Duke of Cleves, and the King's betrothed. She had already set out from Flanders, no doubt wondering if her fate would be as awful as those of King Henry's first three wives.

Other princesses had certainly pondered it. One, the Duchess of Milan, had refused the marriage proposal saying that she did not have enough heads to run the risk.

My friends thought my nose would be put out of joint at the thought of the King taking a new wife. Not a bit of it. I had long worried that he might ask me to sit upon the poison throne. Thank goodness his advisers would not countenance such favor alighting on the orphan of a family that had only narrowly scrambled into gentry. I don't think the King desired it much either. He thought it far better to keep me as his mistress, to take his pleasure whenever the itch in his loins demanded.

I swear that I must have fairy blood in me, the gift of second sight. The instant I thought about the King's lust the door opened to reveal my Page, Humphrey.

"Henry wants you," he said. "He's just come down from Hampton Court. Right hungry he is, so I'm told."

"I'll box your ears if you talk in that fashion," I said.

I caught a glimpse of Sissy looking distraught at my words. She was more and more moonstruck every day, following Humphrey with her eyes whenever she couldn't follow him in person.

The horses seemed lethargic as they made their way down the winding drive towards Greenwich Palace. It was only half a mile distant from my home in Greenwich Castle but the horses could barely be encouraged into a trot. I forbade the drivers to use a whip. I hated whips, with good reason. So we were at the mercy of the beasts and today they seemed intent on moving slowly. Perhaps I was as foolish a mistress of my horses as I was of my servants.

At length we reached the Palace and I made my way towards the King's privy chambers. His groom, Gregory Frost, was waiting for me. "What the devil kept you?" he demanded.

"I haven't got wings," I said with a smile.

"Well you're no angel, certainly." He gave me a wry look. I don't know when we had grown quite so familiar but there was no returning to the more formal situation of our first acquaintance.

"What mood is he in?" I asked.

"A joyful one, heaven be praised," he said with a knowing smile. "As always, of course."

"Of course. I just wished to know how rapturous was his joy."

"You'll find out, Alice," he said. "He's in his sitting room."

I followed Frost through the suite of rooms and into the King's sitting room. He was lounging in a chair with his hands behind his head, as if in the most lovely of summer daydreams.

He was casually dressed, wearing a plain silk shirt, a doublet embroidered with whirls of scrollwork and a surcoat trimmed with rabbit fur. He wore his favorite felt hat, adorned with only an ermine fringe upon the top.

It was only a fortnight since I had seen him last but his face appeared a little more rounded and his chin looked fleshy. But his sharp eyes still glittered brighter than stars, counteracting the toll of years upon his flesh. For once they were not watchful. In fact the King looked content and self-satisfied. His lips, so much thinner than the rest of his person, had composed themselves into a smile.

"Ah, Alice," he said. "You've arrived."

"I came as soon as I heard your summons," I said.

He nodded and waved his hand for me to join him.

"I have had a busy fortnight," he said. "Much coming and going of ambassadors. Many tedious meetings with Master Cromwell. He is like a nervous chicken at the moment, skittish as a capon when a fox is close by."

I smiled at his words. I could not imagine Sir Thomas Cromwell being either skittish or nervous.

"I see Thomas Cromwell as more of a goose," I said. "All inquisitiveness and righteous anger."

The King slapped his thigh. "Oh, I like that, Alice. I must tell him what you say."

"I'm not sure I should want that," I said quickly.

"I don't see why not. You can't try to tell me you're fearful of him. Not you, Alice. You're a rarity in the Kingdom because of it. You know you have him eating out of your hands."

"If you say so, Your Grace."

"I do say so. I witness it with my own eyes."

I gave him a smile which hovered on the border between reassuring and teasing. "I hope you're not jealous, Majesty?"

He laughed. "What need do I have of being jealous? You and Thomas Cromwell are the two people who I trust most in all the world."

I smiled more broadly despite the chill his words caused in my heart. The more the King spoke of trust, the more his courtiers thought of the scaffold.

He picked up his cup and swirled it gently in his hand, staring into it with a thoughtful expression.

"Have you seen the portrait of the Lady Anne?" he asked. "Anne of Cleves?"

"I have not, Your Grace."

"Then I think you should see it."

A strange light came into his eyes. I followed his gaze. Hanging on an easel was Master Holbein's portrait of a young woman.

"Go on," said the King. "Take a closer look."

I went over to the portrait. I got a shock when I examined it closely, and it was all I could do to hold my tongue.

"She is very pretty," I said eventually.

There was a silence.

"Go on."

I studied the portrait once more and tried to calm my feeling of apprehension. "She looks like a princess," I said. "And every bit like she should be a queen."

He murmured appreciatively.

"She has a very gentle look, Your Grace," I continued. I was warming to the subject now. "As though she will be both capable and obedient. And her lips look very kissable."

The King laughed. "And what about her eyes, Alice? What about her eyes?"

I peered more closely at her eyes. He wanted me to say that they were enticing eyes, come-to-bed eyes.

Indeed they did look like she was ready for bed but only because she appeared exhausted. In fact, everything about her looked tired and dull; she appeared to have as little vitality or wit as a cow munching grass.

I started to say something, anything, about her eyes, but I found myself quite lost for words.

When the King spoke again his voice was quieter, suspicion flaring. "You seemed somewhat startled when you first saw her face."

"Because she is so lovely," I lied.

It was not that, of course. I was shocked because Anne of Cleves looked so much like Jane Seymour. That same bland, bovine look; that same sense of vacant obedience.

Anne was prettier than Jane; who wouldn't be? She lacked Jane's sharp little eyes and that thin, pursed mouth that had always made the Queen look like she was sucking a lemon.

I imagined that Anne would also lack Jane's vicious determination, a trait that Jane had managed to hide from everyone except her closest companions. I wondered whether to point out the similarity between the two women but something kept me from doing so. Best not to go there. At least not unless the King did.

So here we had the King's newest bride. She would, I believed, be perfect for him.

Henry, you see, yearned for two different types of women. He desired the fiery, the sensual, the dazzling woman who offered him a love which was both delicious and dangerous. But he also wanted the obedient, the tractable, the docile woman who was content to do as he commanded.

Anne of Cleves had a placid, dull face coupled with eyes which the King presumably considered to promise an inner fire. He must have believed he'd finally found a woman who possessed all the qualities he wished for.

It would be a remarkable woman who could do that. Or a remarkable dissembler.

I studied the portrait once again. I did not think that Anne of Cleves looked clever enough to be a dissembler.

The King gave a prodigious yawn. *To my duty*, I thought, and turned to him with a teasing smile.

Chapter 2
Summoned by Thomas Cromwell

"How much longer will this take, Master Holbein?"

The King's painter stared at me. "As I have told you repeatedly, Mistress Petherton, it will take as long as it will take."

I stared ruefully at Susan, who was dozing by the fire.

"But you have been here two days," I said, "and have not even picked up a chalk or a brush."

He sighed and took a step towards me. "I tell you again. Producing a great picture is more about the eyes than the hands. I use my eyes far more than I use my brush. This is what I am doing now."

I stared at his hands. Great big ugly hands, with sausage fingers. They looked more suited for chopping wood than for painting or drawing.

In fact, Master Holbein looked more like a tradesman than an artist. Big round face, heavy jowl, large nose. A tradesman, a butcher probably, his face suggesting he was more akin to the beasts he was slicing than to the customers he was about to serve.

Yet his eyes, his eyes were very different from a tradesman's.

Deep, deep eyes which seemed set somewhere far within his soul; eyes which regarded you much as a mirror might regard the person staring into it. Not praising, not condemning, merely observing. Hoping to catch the essence of the person they were staring at. I could well see that Master Hans Holbein would employ those farseeing, clever eyes far more than his pudgy sausage fingers.

He placed his hands upon his hips and gave a little twinkling smile.

"I was overjoyed when the King commanded me to paint you," he said. "It is well-known that Alice Petherton is the most beautiful creature at Court."

"You flatter me, Master Holbein."

"Not at all. And rumor does not match up to the reality; you are far more beautiful. Yet now that I have seen you I wish I had never been asked to paint you."

My mouth opened in anger but before I could speak the artist held up his hands to placate me.

"It is because I begin to despair at ever being able to paint you at all, Mistress Petherton." He stepped closer, regarding me. "Every person's face changes a little with their mood," he said, "but most have a predominant look and that is the one I search for, the one I seek to capture on canvas."

He shook his head. "But you, Alice. Your face is not like this. It changes all the time. It is . . . now what is the English word?" He muttered to himself for a moment and then shook his head. "I cannot remember."

He reached out for my chin and moved it slightly one way and then the next. "I look at you and think I have found your one true beauty. Then you have a pleasant thought and your beauty changes. Your friend, Fräulein Dunster, says something to make you laugh and your appearance changes once more. A little later a melancholy thought strikes you and it changes yet again. And then, when you get bored and a little tired, as you have done this afternoon, your face grows full and sensual as though you want to go to your bed. And then you seem a different creature altogether."

He clicked his fingers. "Effervescent. That is the word I wanted. You are effervescent, Alice Petherton, and I doubt I will ever be able to capture your beauty with chalk or brush."

"Then you shall be punished by the King for your failure."

The artist laughed. "Oh, Henry may box my ears a little but that is all. He has an artistic temperament himself and he would do no harm to a fellow artist."

Don't be too sure of it, I thought to myself. He did me harm enough six months after I became his lover. I banished the thought from my mind. Just as he had banished me from his bed.

"And how do I compare to Anne of Cleves?" I asked.

Holbein pursed his lips and then shrugged. For the briefest moment he seemed a little troubled. Then he smiled.

"As I said, you are the most beautiful creature at Court."

"But surely I will be eclipsed by the King's new wife?" I put an innocent look upon my face. "I have seen the portrait you painted of her. She looks very pretty."

"She is indeed. King Henry loves beautiful women and he desires a beautiful wife. The Lady Anne will delight the King and grace the Court."

A shadow passed over his face. "Alas, she is not as beautiful as you, Alice. I suppose every king hopes his new wife will be more beautiful than his lover. But it is a foolish hope. Lovers will always outshine queens."

He tapped the chalk thoughtfully upon his lips and looked more intently at me. "She is not as effervescent as you, Alice. Not so difficult to catch and hold."

"If you doubt you'll ever be able to capture my looks, just how long do you intend to stay and stare at me?"

"As I said, for as long as it takes. Four days, five, maybe a month."

I looked at him in astonishment.

But at that moment he leapt towards his easel. "Do not move," he cried. "Hold that look."

I needed no admonishment for I remained amazed as he worked feverishly at his easel.

"There," he said at last. "I have the first sketch."

I shifted in my seat. "May I see it?"

He shook his head. "I do not like to show my sketches to my models. It changes how they choose to pose in the next sitting. It makes them compose their faces to suit what they have just seen."

He stared thoughtfully at the picture. "You really are beautiful, Mistress Petherton. If you were a model from Florence and I were Botticelli I would paint you in the nude. And I would delight to do so."

"You forget yourself, sir," I said.

But inwardly I hugged myself. I thought I might like to be painted naked.

He chuckled. "You must forgive we artists for our honesty."

"That's as may be. But I don't have to forgive your impertinence."

I glared at him but he grinned at me without the slightest sense of concern. I guessed he had seen through my pretense of anger. We are both the King's favorites, in truth. Both his creatures who only prosper for as long as we please him. And for as long as he deigns to favor us.

"See," Holbein said. "Your look has changed as many times as moments since you spoke. You are like a river in springtime. The waters flow and ripple, the sun sparkles on it, the shadows of the clouds flutter over it. A river in springtime."

He clapped his hands loudly, taking pleasure in his own words.

"What's happening?" cried Susan, roused suddenly from her doze.

"Anything could have happened," I said tartly. "Much good you are as a chaperone, Susan Dunster. I could have been molested by Master Holbein and you would have slept through it."

Susan shrugged. "It is extremely tedious to sit here while this man stares at you. He is like a cow in a field. Or a bull. It is small wonder that I have to rest my eyes occasionally."

The artist turned to her and grinned. "You would be easier to paint than your mistress," he said. "You have a predominant quality and that makes it simpler to capture your essence."

"Predominant quality?" I said, intrigued. "And what is Susan's predominant quality, pray?"

"Shrew," he answered. "Clever, witty, seeing to the heart of things and commenting with a tongue as sharp as a filleting knife."

I smiled at this and was interested to see that Susan was not at all annoyed by his words. Indeed she seemed rather pleased with them.

"You like to be a shrew?" he asked with some surprise.

"Better than being a dupe or an ass," she said.

Holbein looked baffled.

"A dupe," she said, "is someone who allows others to delude him by deluding himself first. An ass, Master Holbein, is someone who allows his or her master to ride them with little reward or thanks." She gave me a knowing little smile.

"Hush your tongue," I said. "I know well what you are suggesting."

"As do I," Holbein said. "And I know who you speak of." He gave a huge grin, content to be both ass and dupe. As for me, I was not at all sure how I felt about it. An ass lodged in the most palatial of stables is still an ass.

The door opened and Sissy poked her head in, her face anxious.

"Sorry to disturb you, Alice," she said. Noticing Holbein, she gave a little clumsy curtsy. "Mistress Petherton, I should say. But there's a messenger come from the Palace to say that the Lord Privy Seal demands your presence."

"What of it?" I said. "You seem troubled."

Sissy looked round as if there were someone close by who was listening and watching. "The messenger is Sir Richard Rich. He has a carriage waiting to take you down."

"Take you down," said Susan. "Never truer words spoken in innocence."

I could not help myself. I shuddered at the mere mention of the name. Richard Rich was the person I hated most in all the world. And feared.

"I do not wish to travel with him," I said. "Not even for half a mile."

"He's very insistent," Sissy said.

Holbein picked up his cloak and offered me his arm. "The weather is clement, Mistress Petherton. Let us say that I chose to walk you down to the Palace to seek out a setting where I might paint you."

"Outdoors?" I said.

"It is all the rage in the Italian cities."

"That's very kind of you, Hans. I accept."

"Anything to keep you from proximity with that viper, Rich."

"Take care of what you say, Master Holbein," I said in alarm. "That viper has teeth and they are charged full to the brim with poison."

Sir Thomas Cromwell may have been the most hated person in the Kingdom but Richard Rich was close behind. It was said that in his climb to power he had trod not on steps but on the corpses of men he helped topple from the King's favor.

And Rich was not content with helping destroy such men. As Chancellor of the Court of Augmentations, he worked hand in glove with Sir Thomas to abolish the religious houses and thereby enrich the Crown. I always thought that Thomas did it for love of the King. Rich, I believed, did it purely out of malice and to enhance his own wealth and position. His standing rose higher day by day, only surpassed by his insufferable arrogance.

At that moment the door was flung open and Sir Richard Rich strode into the room. He looked around at the furnishings as if taking an inventory. Sissy took a backward step, pressing herself against the wall.

I thought of protesting at his intrusion but decided against it. I knew all too well how vicious was his spite.

"My master, Baron Cromwell, commands you to attend upon him," he said. He sniffed and put a kerchief to his nose. "It is very stuffy in here." He took another step, still sniffing. "Do you not find it putrid, Master Holbein? A smell of earth or mud. Or worse."

He turned and looked at Sissy, opening his eyes wide in a pretense of surprise. "Ah, you must be the milkmaid your mistress has taken into service. That explains it. Pray move yourself downwind, Miss Barnyard, or I shall be overcome."

Sissy looked from his face to mine, her lips wobbling, tears beginning to fill her eyes.

I stepped towards him, my anger so strong it conquered my disquiet at his presence.

"How dare you speak in such a fashion to my servant? If you cannot be civil then be gone. At once."

I did not wait to see his reaction but went to Sissy and touched her on the arm.

"Do not trouble yourself with Sir Richard's words, Sissy," I said. "It is but a jest, though a clumsy one. You must always remember that he loves the smell of freshly raked muck."

Rich smiled at my retort, a smile as bleak as famine. He turned his dead-fish eyes upon me and I recalled the time I had almost pierced one with my bodkin.

"Your wicked tongue will be the death of you, dear Alice," he said.

The threat hung upon the air like fog.

"When I have men like you to assist me to my grave?" I said.

I paused a moment. "Surely not, dear Sir Richard."

He did not respond, merely stared at me with those empty eyes.

"Baron Cromwell waits upon you."

"Then please hurry back to him and say that I will attend upon him as soon as possible."

"He wants you urgently. You must come at once."

"What can be so urgent that I cannot delay for a few minutes?"

"Who knows," Rich answered. "Maybe Lady Anne of Cleves has arrived and demands that you be banished from Court. Maybe the King has tired of you and has commanded Cromwell to dispense with you. One way or the other."

He gave me a smile so terrifying that I felt sick to my soul. If anybody else had spoken such words I might well have ignored them. But when Richard Rich uttered threats it was wise to take heed. They might be bluster, they might be intended just to alarm. But it was best to take heed and be warned.

"You must come at once," he repeated. "You can come with me in my carriage."

"I have decided to walk," I said. "With Master Holbein. He wishes to find a place to paint me."

Rich looked astonished at my words. "You would keep my master waiting while you dawdle along with this foreigner?" He shook his head. "I must insist that you come by carriage." He pointed out of the window. "Besides, it's starting to rain. Not the sort of weather for a jaunt."

He was right, a sudden storm had blown up. The low, dark sky began to empty, fierce rain mixed with sleet. It might turn to snow any moment.

I swallowed hard, defeated by this. "How large is your carriage? My maid must come with me and Master Holbein will want to return to the Palace if I am gone from here."

"Space for three," he said. "You must choose between the milkmaid and the dauber."

"No need," said Holbein. "I can ride with the driver."

"But you'll get drenched," I said.

"In your service, I am happy to," he said. And his eyes went to Rich.

Chapter 3
Thomas Cromwell

Baron Cromwell, the Lord Privy Seal, looked up briefly, indicated a seat with his pen and continued to scribble upon a manuscript.

I watched him as he wrote. His focus was astounding. He was like a hound stalking a quarry, oblivious to everything else apart from what he was working on. Or so he appeared to the casual observer.

I knew, in fact, that some vital part of his mind was aware of what was going on around him, warily keeping watch. It was, no doubt, one of the reasons he had survived and thrived at the most perilous Court in Christendom.

He had been King Henry's principal minister for many years. He maintained his position because of his intelligence, his capacity for endless work and his total loyalty to the King. That and the fact that he had enriched the Crown beyond the King's greediest hopes.

Many people hated Sir Thomas; many more feared him. As had I, at first. But he had taken a liking to me. Perhaps it was because I pleased the King so greatly. Perhaps it was because he loved me a little, though I was never sure if it was with a lover's or a father's eye.

Or perhaps it was because he saw something of himself in me. Most people would have been horrified by such a thought. I was rather pleased.

He put his pen down at last and read over what he had written.

"I shan't be needing you for the moment, Richard," he said, though without looking up.

Rich appeared discomforted by his master's words. But he knew better than to argue, and with a little scowl he backed out of the room.

"I wish you had not sent Rich to collect me," I said once the door had closed behind him.

"You need have no fear of Master Rich," Thomas said, waving his hand dismissively. He assumed that his favor kept me safe from the viper. He may have been right, although I never felt it.

"Draw up a stool, Sissy," Cromwell said. "Your mistress and I may be some while."

He folded his hands, rested his chin upon them and regarded me.

"The King is not well," he said.

"I am sorry to hear it," I replied. "He was in good health when I saw him yesterday."

"Today his leg is causing him agony. Perhaps yesterday, when you saw him, he indulged himself too much."

I thought back to what we had done the previous night. "Not overmuch, Your Grace."

He sniffed again. "The King is not getting any younger. Your task is to entertain him, not kill him."

"He is a hard man to deny."

"I know that. None know it better. But when you don't deny him he gets overtired and his blasted leg begins to pain him. And it is not only the King who suffers then."

He rubbed his head unconsciously. I suppressed a smile. Of late, whenever he was displeased, the King had taken to boxing his First Minister upon the head.

"And when he is in a foul mood," Cromwell continued, "I have no latitude to deny him anything. Not even when it is for his own good."

I sighed. "So what would you seek to deny him at the moment?"

Cromwell picked up a pile of papers, banged them against the desk to straighten them and placed them back again in precisely the same spot.

"Envoys from Emperor Charles have arrived in Court. The King insists on seeing them at once and on his own."

"Is that so unusual?"

"It is when we don't know them. I don't like the uncertainty of newcomers."

"Then it seems to me that you must persuade the King to allow you to be with him when he sees the envoys."

"I've tried. But the French ambassador, Charles de Marillac, has arrived at the exact same time, though I doubt this is coincidence. Marillac says he wishes to present a scholar sent by King François. The King commands me to attend Monsieur Marillac while he meets with the Germans." He jabbed his pen fiercely in the pot. The ink splashed out across the table.

I smiled. So the German envoys see the King while the French ambassador must content himself with the Minister. Henry must have decided it was the Emperor's turn to be placated and the French King's to be insulted. The three monarchs believed they were demigods, but they acted like schoolboys.

"May I ask why you summoned me, Your Grace?" I said.

"The King wants you to come with me to meet the French scholar."

I sat back in my chair in surprise.

"Apparently the Frenchman is an old friend of the King's and he wants you to entertain him." He gave a little chuckle. "I'm sure you'll be more pleasant company than the Duke and I."

"The Duke of Suffolk?"

"Norfolk. There is still unpleasantness between the French and friend Suffolk."

And that over a woman, I thought to myself. Schoolboys, one and all.

"There is another reason the King wishes you to attend upon Ambassador Marillac," Thomas continued. "The King is considering employing him as tutor to the Lady Elizabeth. You know the child well and the King wants your opinion of whether a scholar will be able to handle her."

"Handle her?" I said. "You make her sound like she's a difficult young woman. She's only a child."

"The King's words," he answered. "And let's not forget that Anne Boleyn was her mother."

I raised my eyebrows at this comment. Thomas gave an enigmatic smile.

"When will the French gentlemen arrive?" I asked.

"They're here now. We must meet them shortly."

I put a hand to my breast.

"But I'm not suitably dressed," I said. "I was sitting for a portrait for the King. I can't possibly meet the Ambassador like this."

I pulled back my cloak. Thomas's eyes opened wide in surprise.

The portrait was intended to be seen by the King only and my gown was cut very low.

Cromwell frowned. "I asked Sir Richard to tell you about the meeting most explicitly. I wanted you to have time to dress yourself appropriately."

"I didn't know that I was to receive such important visitors."

"But I told him." His gaze turned towards the door where Rich had exited.

"Then he kept quiet on purpose," I said. "To make me look a fool."

Cromwell shrugged. "There's no time to do anything about it now. We must go."

"Please wait a moment, Thomas. Let me think."

My mind raced.

"Sissy," I cried. "I left my new red gown in the King's lodging when we went hunting last week. Go and fetch it."

Sissy ran to do my bidding. I turned towards Sir Thomas. "I shall have to change my garments here."

"Of course. I will leave you in peace." He rose from his chair. Before he left the room he paused and studied me a moment.

"What is it?" I asked.

"The way you tap your fingers on your chin when you think. I've seen you do it before and it reminds me of someone else who did the same. But for the life of me I can't recall who."

His face took on an anxious expression. Thomas Cromwell survived because his intellect was colossal. Any hint that he could not recall something must be deeply troubling to him.

"I will return in ten minutes," he said. "If you've not beautified yourself by then, you will have to do." He smiled. "And you are beautiful enough in any case."

Fifteen minutes later we were seated in the smaller of the two Presence Chambers. The Duke of Norfolk was already there. He looked angry at being made to wait.

"Where have you been, Thomas?" he snapped. "And what is she doing here?"

"I have been about the King's business, Your Grace," Cromwell answered smoothly. "And Alice is here because the King desires it. He wants her to meet with his old friend and entertain him."

I smiled sweetly at the Duke. His face gave not so much as a flicker of a response. A year or so before I had the passing thought that the Duke reminded me of an owl and once I had entertained the notion I could not dismiss it. The long, sharp, cruel nose, the hooded, wide-awake, watchful eyes which I swore never blinked, the way his stillness would suddenly erupt in a flurry of outrage, his arms flying and his manner all swift action. Yes, very much the owl. I felt sure that one day I would see his head turn completely round.

"What is the name of the King's friend?" I asked.

"Bunbun," Norfolk said.

Cromwell peered at his papers for a moment. "Bourbon," he said. "Nicholas Bourbon." He gave the Duke a smile as broad as it was sly. "He was a good friend of your niece, I believe."

"Mary?" Norfolk said. "Is Bourbon another from her stable of French riders?"

"No, Your Grace, not Mary. Your other niece. The one who lost her head to the King."

Norfolk cleared his throat and did not answer. Anne Boleyn had been his protégé and, in the end, he became her nemesis. It was Norfolk who presided over her trial. He was the great survivor. Anne, sadly, had not proved to be.

A knock came on the door and two men entered the room. The younger was dressed in a light-blue doublet with a grey jerkin made of soft leather. He wore a large, sleeveless robe over this, trimmed with fox fur. His hat was unusual, being higher than any I had ever seen before and brightly colored. A long golden chain hung about his neck. Presumably this was Charles de Marillac, the Ambassador.

The other man I assumed to be Nicholas Bourbon. He was a little older, in his mid-thirties I guessed. He was dressed much more simply than the Ambassador, in a doublet and tan-colored jerkin with a small felt cap upon his head. He looked drab in comparison with the splendid Marillac.

But I could not take my gaze from him. His face was smooth and unblemished with a small, well-trimmed beard. His warm, kindly eyes sparkled and shone. They seemed to be farseeing and very, very wise.

He glanced towards me and all at once my insides fluttered as if being tickled by a thousand feathers. His eyes were the color of hazelnuts ripening on a tree and seemed to speak of summer and warmth and pleasant meals by gentle rivers. I felt my face redden. I knew that I should look away. But I chose not to and stared back at him as if I had not been moved in the slightest.

The Ambassador said something in a light tone and Monsieur Bourbon turned to look at him. It was my first glimpse of his profile. He had the finest nose I have ever seen on a man, of perfect length for his face, neither too big nor too small, straight and true without bump or blemish. It was the nose of a man who studied the stars or looked upon distant vistas, a man who sought unflinchingly for the truth.

I blinked, astonished at myself. What was I thinking? I was like a young girl made giddy by her first sip of ale at a village fete. I forced my gaze away and looked at the Duke of Norfolk. I knew that looking at him would guarantee to put all thoughts of gaiety from my heart.

Norfolk lounged in his seat, head resting on one bony finger, his customary look of disdain upon his face.

"Welcome, Your Excellency," he said, larding the words with a tone he made thoroughly unwelcoming.

Charles de Marillac swept off his hat and gave a low and courtly bow. His companion did likewise and I saw that he held his hat tight, as if ill at ease.

"King François sends his greetings to you, my dear Duke," the Ambassador said, "and you also, my most dear Baron Cromwell."

Norfolk gave a contemptuous sniff by way of reply. "This must be Monsieur Bunbun," he continued, waving his fingers dismissively at the Ambassador's companion.

"Bourbon, Your Grace," the Ambassador corrected. "Monsieur Nicholas Bourbon." He smiled but it was a smile which was more angry than good-humored.

Norfolk stared at him with no trace of emotion. "Forgive me, Monsieur. I find it hard to get my English tongue round Frenchie names."

Thomas stared at him with furrowed brow. I wondered why for a moment and then realized. The Duke was normally a supporter of closer ties with France. This strange and blatant disagreeableness was, to say the least, questionable.

"There is nothing to forgive," Bourbon said. "The fault, alas, lies with the arrogance of the men who built the Tower of Babel. Were it not for their folly the world, no doubt, would all speak French."

Monsieur Bourbon's English was excellent, though the purr of his French accent danced amongst his words. My breath quickened to hear him speak.

"I doubt it," said the Duke. "I hear that God's tongue is English."

"I think you are misinformed, your Grace," said Cromwell. "The Good Lord speaks Hebrew, or so my Jewish friends tell me."

Norfolk scowled but said nothing. Presumably he could not think of a reply cutting enough.

"And you, dear lady?" Marillac said to me. "To whom do I have the pleasure?"

"My name is Alice Petherton," I said.

Nicholas Bourbon's lips gave the most fleeting of smiles and he regarded me with open curiosity.

"The King's strumpet," said Norfolk. "Why she's here, God only knows."

If I thought my face had been red before then I was very much mistaken. I blushed what I was sure must be a furious crimson, not with pleasure but with shame and bitter anger.

Both Frenchmen nodded graciously. It was as if they had not heard the Duke's foul comment.

In the meanwhile, I still blushed red as sunset and thought my face would surely burst into flame. But at that moment, Nicholas Bourbon stepped towards me, reached out for my hand and took it to his lips. It was barely a kiss; his lips made only the lightest of touches, the grazing of a rabbit on a clover leaf. But I felt his breath upon the tips of my fingers, as warm as honey in sunshine.

I looked into his eyes and was lost.

"It is a pleasure to meet with you, Alice Petherton," he said. "The greatest of pleasures."

"I am here to entertain your honors," I said.

I could barely hear my own voice. The whole of the room had dissolved into mist around the two of us. I knew that the others were still here, might even be looking at us, but the only things I could see, hear and feel were Nicholas and myself. The rest of the world was fading into twilight.

I saw him straighten, saw his eyes twinkle and then, yes, I swear I saw his own cheeks begin to color.

"Well if you're here to entertain," came a voice like grit, "pour us some wine."

The glow which surrounded me disappeared like a bubble of soap.

"Yes, Your Grace," I said to Norfolk.

The Duke was staring at me with even less humor than he normally managed. Sir Thomas looked amused and for once did not bother to hide it.

I walked across to the cabinet and poured four glasses of wine. I took a quick mouthful from one while I thought nobody would notice. I was a fool because, of course, Sir Thomas was watching. He gave me a swift look of reprimand, a warning which I acknowledged with a nod.

And he was not the only one who noticed. Thankfully the Duke and Ambassador were engaged in glaring at one another. But Nicholas Bourbon had been watching me. I did not know how to read his look.

I placed the glasses on a tray and took them over to the men, making sure that I gave Nicholas the glass I had sipped from. Then I returned to my seat.

"Take a little wine, Alice," said Sir Thomas, with a slightly ironic tone. "We may be here awhile and a sip or two will refresh you mightily."

I thanked him and poured myself some. I was careful to heed his advice, though, and did not take much. And all the while I drank deeply of the face and form of Nicholas Bourbon.

Servants arrived with refreshments and the Duke bade the visitors join him in the repast. I needed no command and presided over the meal, telling the maidservants who to serve first and which were the choicest items to offer.

After a little while the Duke called loudly across the chamber.

"I hear that you are acquainted with King Henry, Monsieur Barber. How so?"

Nicholas Bourbon's eyes twinkled at the insulting misuse of his name. It seemed to me he was too big a man to let such petty insults rankle.

"I came to England five years ago, Your Grace. It was a little after I had angered the Dean of Theology at the Sorbonne and had been thrown into prison."

I gave a little gasp of horror. From the looks I received, it did not go unnoticed by any in the room.

"King François was kind enough to order me released," he continued, "but his command was obstructed and ignored. Eventually I was given my freedom but thought it best to remove myself from the threat of any more unwelcome attention. So I came to London."

I frowned at his words. I could not imagine anyone daring to disobey the command of our King.

Nicholas inclined his head to the Duke. "Your Grace, I was given assistance and friendship by your niece, Anne Boleyn. I owe her a lot.

I sometimes suspect that she played a part in securing my release from prison."

Norfolk scowled. He clearly hated it whenever Anne was mentioned.

"And, of course," Nicholas continued, "I was treated most kindly by His Majesty, who introduced me to many men who have remained my friends. Master Holbein, in particular, who I am told still paints for His Majesty."

"He does indeed," I said, speaking out of turn. "I have been with Master Holbein this afternoon. He is endeavoring to paint a portrait of me."

"And I can think of no better artist to paint you, Mademoiselle. Although even the redoubtable Hans will find it impossible to capture the full delicacy of your beauty."

I giggled like a schoolgirl and just managed to transform it into a laugh of polite dismissal.

"Pass me some meat, girl," said the Duke. I stared with wide-eyed insolence at him and gestured to a servant.

"Attend to His Grace," I said in as forceful a tone as I could. "He requires some meat." I was not going to let our visitors think I was a mere servant here to fetch and carry.

"And why were you in prison, Monsieur Bourbon?" asked Sir Thomas, swift to move things back to the conversation. "What raised the ire of the dangerous theologian, Dean Béda?"

"I had flung some barbs at him in a collection of my poems."

"Poems?" I said. "You write poetry?" I spoke in a casual manner although I was thrilled to hear it.

"Of quality enough to get me thrown into jail," he answered with a smile.

We gazed at each other in silence.

"Poetry and religion," said the Ambassador lightly. "They cause us much comfort and much sorrow. And I must say that I feel sorrow at the delay in the arrival of King Henry. Will he be here soon?"

"He won't be here at all," said the Duke. "I am deputizing for him."

The Ambassador looked surprised at his words. But he swiftly concealed this and his face changed to display insult and outrage.

"I am deeply dismayed," he said, rising to his feet and gesturing Nicholas Bourbon to do likewise. "I am the Ambassador of His Majesty, King François of France. I expect to be seen by the King of England when I attend the Palace."

"You invited yourself," said the Duke. "What did you expect?"

"A little more courtesy," he said, rounding on Norfolk. His voice was cutting.

"My dear Ambassador Marillac," Sir Thomas said in a placating tone, "there is good reason for His Majesty's absence. He is unwell and not able to move around easily. His old jousting wound is playing him up today. It is the inclement weather, I'm afraid."

He lowered his voice and made it even more familiar. "Besides, this is not the first time that you and I have met alone, without the King."

He shot a little glance at the Duke, who reacted to this information with surprise and a disquiet he could not quite conceal.

Thomas smiled and turned back to the Ambassador. He did not see that the Duke's look of surprise had instantly changed to one of determined calculation and cunning.

I did, and my heart grew cold at the sight.

Chapter 4
Wanton Madness

Sir Thomas did not speak to me as we walked from the Presence Chamber to his own office.

When he closed the door he gave me a disapproving look.

"You made something of a fool of yourself in there, Alice. You were supposed to entertain Monsieur Bourbon, not lose your heart to him."

I was flabbergasted that he had noticed. But then I cursed myself. Of course he would notice; not a fly landed on his webs without him being aware. I had been stupid and astonishingly careless.

"You are the King's mistress," Sir Thomas continued. "To look at another man is wanton madness. You endanger yourself by doing so."

I was about to reply but stopped myself. There was nothing I could say, for he was right. I was grateful that he had reminded me. And then I wondered if others in the room had noticed. I felt sick at the thought.

"And you did not deal with the Duke as well as you might," he continued. "He is a dangerous man when roused and he had clearly decided to put you in your place. You should have been content to remain there."

"My place is in the King's bed as the Duke so crudely reminded us." I folded my arms and gave him a defiant look. "It is not to serve the Duke of Norfolk's appetite with meat and titbits."

"Oh, but it is if he commands it, Alice. Norfolk is the premier Duke of the Kingdom and you do well to remember it."

I did not reply for a moment, seething with a mixture of fear and anger.

"I will heed your kind advice," I said at last. "But may I also proffer some in return?"

He looked at me in surprise and then nodded.

"It is that you take your own advice in relation to the Duke."

He frowned, confused.

"You reminded Ambassador Marillac that you had occasionally seen him alone. Those words discomforted the Duke."

Sir Thomas rubbed his hands together gleefully. "I did that on purpose. One to add to my score, I think."

I shook my head. "Do not be so sure, Thomas. I saw the Duke's reaction when he got over his initial surprise. He means to turn your boast against you."

He shrugged his shoulders. "He can try. But if he thinks that I ever saw the Ambassador on my own without the prior agreement of the King, he will find nothing to prove it."

I looked at him thoughtfully, sifting his words. "Not finding proof does not mean that you didn't see him without the King's approval."

Sir Thomas smiled and did not answer.

At that moment there came the sound of three sharp knocks on the door. It was flung open and Ralph Sadler stepped into the room, carrying a pile of papers.

Ralph was a protégé of Sir Thomas's and worked as his secretary. He was the only man allowed to enter the chamber without waiting for Thomas's command.

He beamed at me and put most of the papers on the desk.

"A request from the Archbishop of Canterbury," he said, handing one of the papers to Sir Thomas.

Thomas took it to the window to peruse it better.

"You deal with this, Ralph," he said, handing him back the document. "I must away to the King. His meeting with the Imperial envoys should be over by now. I need to know what was discussed."

Sir Thomas turned to me. "You may return to your apartment, Alice."

I curtsied, gestured Sissy to do likewise and made for the door. Ralph hurried ahead and held it open for me.

"Oh, and Alice," Thomas called. "If the King does ask you to his bedroom tonight, be mindful of his injury."

"I will, Your Grace." But as I walked along the corridor I thought only that I would much prefer to entertain Nicholas Bourbon.

Sissy held her peace until we were alone in a carriage.

"What's all this about you and the French ambassador?" she asked, eyes agog. "You lost your heart to him?"

"Not the Ambassador, Sissy. Monsieur Bourbon, the man who accompanied him. He's an old friend of Queen Anne's and the King asked me to entertain him."

"But you lost your heart to him?"

"Of course I didn't. Sir Thomas was jesting." I turned to look out of the carriage window to hide my face from her.

"But you didn't deny it to Sir Thomas," she said.

"Again, that was a jest."

Sissy did not reply. But a little later I felt her hand creep into mine.

"I hope it was only a jest, Alice. You don't want to anger the King. Not after what happened before."

I did not answer for a moment. I recalled the time I had dared to argue with the King, to plead for the life of an innocent man. I paid a heavy price for it. The King dispensed with me for six months and I had been forced to live in squalor and worse. It had been a terrible time. The only real good that came out of it was that I met Sissy, when I stayed at her family's farm.

"Thank you," I said. "I appreciate your concern."

Susan Dunster was not so easily mollified. We had spoken briefly when I returned to the apartments but I told her little of my meeting.

So I was the more astonished when she burst into my chamber a few minutes before supper.

"What on earth were you thinking?" she cried. "A Frenchman!"

"What did Sissy tell you?" I said. I rounded on Sissy, who retreated behind Susan, biting her lip in anxiety.

"Don't blame Sissy," Susan snapped. "I got it out of her."

"What right have you to interrogate Sissy?" I began.

"Every right when I suspect she is hiding something that concerns your welfare."

"You are not my chaperone, Susan, nor my guardian."

"No. But I am your friend. And I don't want you to endanger yourself again. Sissy did right to tell me what happened. If the King finds out you were mooning over this Frenchman, you may be banished from Court again. Or worse. The King's temper is getting fouler by the day. Even Sir Thomas has to walk on eggshells."

I did not reply; I knew that she was right. I took her hands in mine.

"But if you'd seen him, Susan. If you'd seen Nicholas Bourbon. He is the most beautiful man. The most beautiful you could imagine."

"You won't be able to look at him if your head is chopped off by an ax."

I swallowed hard. She had a way of speaking, did Susan. Blunt was not the word for it. I sighed. Her words were wise and best heeded.

"You're right," I said, finally. "I suppose." Even to my own ears my voice sounded petulant.

Then I gave a smile. "He was very, very beautiful," I wheedled.

Susan sniffed and folded her arms. "Tell me then. You won't rest until you have."

I clapped my hands with joy and patted the settle. Susan sat down with a determined scowl still upon her face.

I ignored this and thought of how to tell her.

"He is like Apollo," I said at last. "Like Apollo might have looked when he took human form."

"Or Narcissus, perhaps?"

"Apollo," I said firmly. "His skin is fair and unblemished, his nose is as straight as a rule with perfect nostrils and not one bump. His cheek has a little red glow and his mouth is small, with fine red lips. But his eyes. Oh Susan, you should see those eyes. They are so warm, so wise, so kind. Yet they have a sparkle in them, more than a sparkle. I could dance forever in front of those eyes. I could drown in them."

Susan's eyebrows arched and she gave a mocking look. She turned towards Sissy. "Quick, hurry for a pail of water. We must quench Alice's fire before she destroys us all."

I slapped her on the hand playfully. "Don't be such a spoilsport."

"But you are the King's lover. He will not tolerate any straying on your part." She took my hand in hers and stared into my eyes. "I'm serious, Alice, and you should be too. Don't forget how quick he was to dismiss you when you had the temerity to oppose him."

"But he was in a rage, then. He behaved like a spoiled child, nothing more."

Susan snorted in disbelief.

"Even if that were the case," she said, "he didn't lift a finger to help you when that villain Richard Rich threw you to the wolves. He completely washed his hands of you, forgot all about you."

"He didn't know what was happening. He punished those who did me ill when he found out."

"Only so that he could enrich himself at their expense."

"I got two manors to my own name," I said. "And these apartments. Which you benefit from, might I add."

"I know all that. But I also know that the King is fickle. You are not the only mistress he has enjoyed, and where are they now? And he still keeps a stable of fillies at Farnham Castle."

"He doesn't go to them anymore," I said.

"He doesn't go there often."

I did not answer. I had found out only three months before that the King had occasional recourse to other young women who he kept hid away in Farnham.

"I'll be careful," I said. "In any case the King will not wish to concern himself with me when the Lady Anne arrives from Cleves."

"If she ever comes."

I shrugged. "There's no reason to think she won't. There's only delay because her brother is haggling over the dowry."

"Well, let's hope she's worth every penny then." She gave me a shrewd look. "I hear rumor, Alice, I hear rumor."

"Tut-tut to your rumors, Susan." I stepped towards the door. "Come, supper will be ready."

I took a deep breath. I had received two warnings about my folly, from Sir Thomas and now Susan. I determined that I would forget all about Nicholas Bourbon. Beautiful he may be, but that was not sufficient to outweigh the risk.

We strolled along the corridor to the dining room. Every time I did so I marveled at my good fortune. To be mistress of Greenwich Castle felt like being a fairy princess. I could ignore the whispers of unpleasant courtiers, ignore the fawning of friendly ones. Here I was content to be just myself with my friends. Not a princess at all, I decided.

We heard the sound of a recorder as we neared the dining room. Mary was sitting by the fire playing a new tune.

"That's lovely, Mary," I said. "Is it one of your own?"

"It is," she answered. "But I cannot concentrate on it as I wish."

Strands of her golden hair had escaped from her bonnet and fell artlessly across her brow. It set off her fine grey eyes to even greater distinction. She seemed distracted and rather tired.

"Are you unwell?" I asked, touching her forehead to check for any sign of fever. To my relief, there was none.

"I'm quite well," she said, putting her recorder by. "It's just that I have had many disturbing dreams these past few nights. I awake a little troubled."

"Perhaps they are presentiments," said Susan with a pointed look at me. "Perhaps they warn of impending disaster."

"Whatever can you mean?" Mary asked.

So Susan related all the matter of Nicholas Bourbon, with great relish, may I say. She did not embroider it for she had no need to. First she related what Sissy had told her. Then she repeated, word for word, what I had said concerning how wonderful I thought Nicholas Bourbon was. I blushed to hear my words repeated.

Even worse, as she spoke of him my desire was rekindled. I reminded myself how very dangerous my position might be. I took a deep breath and strengthened my resolve to forget all about Nicholas Bourbon. It was well I did so, for at that moment, my page, Humphrey, appeared.

"You've been summoned by Henry," he said. "You're to go at once."

My heart flew to my mouth but I managed to hide my concern. Or so I thought. Sissy burst into tears and flew into Humphrey's arms.

He looked over her shoulder at me, bewildered. "Best hurry, Alice; the King's said to be bellowing for you."

Chapter 5

Much by Way of Education

The carriage raced down the hill towards Greenwich Palace, the horses skidding on the ice in their haste. The Palace was dimly lit under the cloudless night sky. The starlight sparkled on the frost, which was even now riming the lawns and paths. It looked beautiful, but I feared that the fairy palace might harbor within a very angry, brooding beast. I took deep gulps of the cold air, hoping to calm myself. Then I plunged into the Palace and headed for the King's privy apartments.

Gregory Frost was waiting for me in the antechamber. He looked mildly surprised.

"Are you truly an angel, Alice? Have you wings that you got here so swiftly?" He gave a little dry chuckle at his own wit.

"Fast horses," I answered. "Is the King within?"

He tilted his head towards the door and quietly pushed it open.

The King was sitting by the fire, his embroidered coat flung upon a chair. He looked tired and drawn as if he were recovering from some debilitating illness. His foot was raised, resting on a padded stool close to the fire.

"Are you well, Your Grace?" I asked, trying to keep any sign of nervousness from my voice. I failed completely.

The King crooked his finger towards me. "I am better, Alice, thank you." I curtsied and he touched my cheek. "I can hear the worry in your voice, my child. It is a great comfort to me."

He patted a place next to him and I sat.

"It's this damned leg," he said. "Will it never heal? I sometimes think it has been poisoned by that witch, Boleyn."

I tensed slightly at these words.

"I know you were fond of Anne," he said. "But she was a witch, my dear. As well as being an adulteress. And an incestuous one at that." He shook his head at the memory.

"Is there anything I can do to ease your discomfort?" I said to change the subject. Any mention of Anne brought out the distemper in him.

"Later perhaps, when we have talked about your meeting with the French ambassador."

I nodded, cursing myself for my earlier foolishness. *He knows*, I thought. It wasn't only Sir Thomas who saw my infatuation for Nicholas. The Duke of Norfolk must have noticed and poured poison in the King's ear.

My mind raced, wondering how I could put things right. Then the King spoke again and his voice sounded normal, without the slightest trace of suspicion.

"Have you eaten, my dear?"

I glanced at him in surprise, and allowed myself to hope that he'd heard nothing.

"I was just about to, Your Grace," I said. "And then I received your summons."

"You must eat," he said. "As must I."

I glanced over towards the sideboard where there was enough food for a company of guards.

"Will you serve me, Alice?" the King said, sounding very sorry for himself. "I find it wearisome to move and I cannot abide to have Frost here any longer. His long face is making me feel worse than ever."

"Gladly," I said, hurrying to the sideboard. "I am delighted to serve you."

"More than to do the same for the Duke of Norfolk, I hear."

My hand froze. I closed my eyes for a moment, forced them open and picked up a plate.

"What did you hear, Your Majesty?" I asked as casually as I could. *And from who did you hear it?* I was desperate to add but did not dare.

"Thomas said that the Duke demanded that you serve him and you refused. Well, not so much refused as commanded a servant to do so." He gave a false little laugh. "That was very clever of you."

I piled up his plate with food and took it over to him, with a glass of finest claret.

"And yourself," he said. "Get a plate for yourself."

I placed a slice of pork and an apple on the plate. I knew I would have trouble eating more.

"The Duke doesn't much care for you," the King said when I sat beside him.

"He doesn't much care for anybody except himself," I said.

"And me, Alice. He cares for me."

"That goes without saying, Your Majesty."

He frowned at my words. "But why doesn't he care for you, I wonder?" he said, almost to himself.

He tapped me on the knee. "I think I have it. I think the Duke lusts after you, Alice. And he became jealous at your interest in a younger man."

A chill seized my heart.

"Your Majesty?" I asked, my voice trembling. "A younger man?"

"Me, you ninny. The Duke is jealous of your liaison with me. And who wouldn't be? For you are the fairest flower in all the land."

Oh, thank God.

He chuckled to himself but then frowned and gave me a puzzled look. "Why are you calling me Your Majesty? That is a title I no longer require you to call me."

"I don't know, Your Grace. Probably because that is how you were referred to all afternoon, with the French ambassador."

"Ah yes, Marillac. A shrewd young man, very shrewd. I have to watch him like a hawk. He has all the intelligence his fool of a master so signally lacks. I am the rightful King of France and that buffoon François squats upon my throne."

He grumbled to himself a little and I took the opportunity to skewer a piece of chicken with my knife and put it to his lips. He nibbled at it for a moment and then plunged it into his mouth before giving me a tiny, conspiratorial smile. I guessed that his leg was not paining him as much as he pretended and that I would soon have occasion to help him forget it.

"What did you think of my friend, Monsieur Bourbon?" he asked.

My heart nearly stopped.

"He seemed quite pleasant," I said with a dismissive, disinterested tone. "Very earnest. Rather dull."

"Yes, well he's a scholar. A teacher in fact. Loves facts and theories. But I wouldn't call him dull. Earnest, yes. He loves to debate theology, which I enjoyed doing with him when he was here last. But not dull." He picked up his glass and sipped at the wine. "I wonder whether he might be a tutor to little Elizabeth. What do you think?"

"I think that is an excellent idea," I said. "Lady Elizabeth is a very clever little girl. I think she would benefit from his stern intellect."

The King nodded. He always liked people to agree with him. Not that anybody dared disagree. Except for two men, perhaps. Thomas Cromwell, if he absolutely could not avoid it. And, even more rarely, Thomas Cranmer, Archbishop of Canterbury. And only then after an agony of prayer and indecision.

I had learnt to my cost that I dare never again take such a terrible risk.

"Then you shall take Monsieur Bourbon to see the girl," the King said. "Elizabeth is fond of you. She might trust someone that you recommend."

I was stunned at this news. Overjoyed, excited and scared, all at the same time. My heart became an acrobat, flying high with joy one instant, plummeting to the depths the next.

"Did you hear me?" the King repeated. "I said that Elizabeth might trust someone you recommend."

"That may be so," I answered, grateful to concentrate on something other than Nicholas Bourbon.

The King, no doubt, thought that his little daughter would be suspicious of any tutor that he wanted for her. Henry's younger daughter might have been only six years of age but she was more astute than many an adult. As astute as her father, in fact.

"What of her governess, Katherine Champernowne?" I asked. "I've heard that s Catherine he is a most accomplished tutor. Is there something amiss that you wish her replaced?"

"She teaches her well, according to all accounts. But I have heard lately that Elizabeth is beginning to play the little mistress to her governess. The child needs the firmer hand and mind of a man, I think. Not too firm, for she is young. But Monsieur Bourbon is of gentle nature and could offer her much by way of education."

I said no more, although I thought that the idea of a man teaching such a young girl was ludicrous. But then I thought again. Although he had denied Elizabeth all right to the throne and rarely saw her, the King was fond enough of her, fonder of her than of his eldest child, Mary, at any rate. Perhaps he realized that Elizabeth needed more than Kat Champernowne could offer. The King knew Nicholas Bourbon reasonably well. Maybe he was just what Elizabeth needed.

I felt a little wriggle of excitement curl through me at the thought of this. And then I smiled. *Goodness, Alice*, I thought. *You'll be getting envious of the child at this rate.*

The King drained his cup of wine and yawned prodigiously.

"I am tired," he said. "I desire we go to bed."

I looked at him with some anxiety. "Of course, Your Grace. But may I caution you to be a little more circumspect while we are at our exercise. I do not wish to harm your leg."

"You won't, my dear. I shall lie back in complete repose while you undertake the more vigorous duties. It is the prerogative of youth to entertain. And the prerogative of Kings to be entertained."

I smiled and prayed that his leg had stopped suppurating.

Chapter 6
A Husband for Lady Mary

The next morning I awoke feeling nauseous. The wound from the King's leg had broken open during our lovemaking and the smell had permeated every corner of the chamber. I slipped out of bed and opened the casement to let in fresh air. Winter had come early this year and the air was so bitter cold it almost took my breath away. But it served its purpose, clearing the stench from the room and the sickness from my stomach.

The King awoke and saw what I had done. He guessed the reason for it, I am sure, but he was delicate enough not to comment on it. Delicate for his own feelings chiefly, but also for mine, a little.

Gregory Frost attended the King and speedily sent for the King's physicians to attend to his leg. In the meanwhile Sir Thomas Heneage, the Groom of the Stool, arrived and patiently bided twenty minutes in the royal retiring room while the King performed his private functions. Or rather, did not. A servant was summoned and took away an empty stool bucket. The King, no doubt, would wax more miserable today because of this failure.

The physicians spent the next thirty minutes draining and dressing the wound on the King's leg. The sight of it was so distressing and the smell so vile that I excused myself, saying that I wished to bathe.

It was a constant surprise to me that the King allowed me to use his bathroom. He was a fastidious man in most matters and it would, therefore, be natural to assume that he would wish to keep his bathroom for his sole use. But perhaps it was his fastidiousness which explained it. The King was a man of the senses. He loved the smell of good food and the bouquet of a fine wine. He certainly would not tolerate a lover who was not clean and fresh. As I settled into the warm water I recalled how he delighted to place his nose close to my skin and breathe in the scent of me. I bathed every day in order to please him.

We breakfasted in his Dining Chamber. Suddenly his mood lifted and he gestured to Frost to come closer. "Gregory," he said, "send for the Lord Privy Seal."

He turned to me and rubbed his hands in glee. "I had almost forgot, Alice. We have a surprise visitor today. I wanted to see him in Greenwich as it is quieter than Whitehall. Best to keep such visitors from the prying eyes of foreign envoys. And my courtiers, come to think of it."

"A surprise visitor, Your Grace? How exciting."

"Not a surprise to me, of course. I summoned him." Here he looked around as if the walls might have ears. "My visitor is Philip, Duke of Palatinate-Neuburg."

At that moment, there came a knock on the door and Sir Thomas Cromwell entered. He was all bustle and tapped a roll of papers on his knuckles. I smiled, for it almost looked as though he were slapping himself for some misdemeanor.

"Your Grace," he said, bowing to the King and giving me a quick nod. "The Duke arrived late yesterday evening. He informed me he is most fatigued by the journey. The weather was inclement to say the least and the journey across the channel extremely rough." He shrugged his shoulders as if these dangers were of no importance.

"Where is he now?" the King asked.

"He awaits in the Presence Chamber. I thought it best to put him there, out of the way. Wriothesley is with him."

"Good."

I felt unease at this information. Thomas Wriothesley had returned from diplomatic duties only recently, yet already his presence was everywhere.

More to the point, he was ever in the company of Richard Rich. I feared that Wriothesley would come to prove equally a villain. Why the King and Sir Thomas favored such men was beyond my understanding.

"Let us go and see the Duke," cried the King, getting to his feet by hauling on my shoulder. I staggered under the weight, but Gregory Frost came to my rescue and hoisted the King by his other arm.

"Stop manhandling me," the King said, pushing Frost away. Unfortunately he still leaned his vast bulk upon me.

We stepped into the King's Presence Chamber, where a fire roared dangerously high. A chair had been placed inches in front of it and slumped upon this was a figure wrapped in a costly riding cloak. Duke Philip was handsome enough, although he looked tired and drawn. Three men stood in a group on the far side of the room, watching him.

Philip saw the King and sprang to his feet, all trace of weariness gone. He threw his cloak to the floor and held out his hands.

The King looked slightly disconcerted at this but took his hands nevertheless. "Welcome to England, dear cousin," he said.

"The pleasure is mine entirely," Philip said, enunciating the words very carefully. It appeared that these were the only words he knew, for when he said something more it was in German.

The King could not speak this language and so decided to speak in Latin. It left the Duke bemused and he spoke once more in German, more slowly but with greater emphasis. We were all relieved when Sir Thomas gestured to one of the other men in the room.

The large and prosperous-looking man strode over to the King. He was tall and stocky with a mighty beard and hair which cascaded from his cap. He wore a coat of bearskin. Were it not for his pleasant face he might well have been one.

"Your Majesty," Thomas said, "this is the merchant, Derick Berck. He speaks excellent English and will translate for us."

It soon became clear why the King had invited the Duke to England. With great enthusiasm he formally offered Philip the hand of his daughter, the Lady Mary, in marriage. This took me somewhat by surprise. I was even more surprised that the Duke was willing to accept a girl of so few prospects. After all, the King had declared Mary illegitimate and she had little favor and less hope. She was also a very devout Catholic and the Duke, I had heard, was Lutheran.

What would attract him to Mary? I wondered. It could only be money. Money which the King was willing to spend in order to rid himself of the child he liked least, who he resented, and, perhaps more importantly, who he felt most guilty about. If he could ship her off to the depths of Germany he would breathe easier.

The interview was concluded after half an hour. The King looked relieved. He could not abide delay and slowness, and the necessity of translating had proved irksome to him.

But when we returned to his privy chamber he pronounced himself pleased.

"You did well, Thomas," he told Cromwell. "And this marriage will be even more galling to the Emperor than mine to Anne of Cleves." He rubbed his hands in delight. "He'll be enraged that the daughter of his aunt is marrying a Lutheran. He will be mortified." He chuckled to himself for a little while.

Sir Thomas looked on benignly. He had long been an adversary of Emperor Charles and no doubt was delighted at the thought of wrong-footing him.

"Come, Alice, you're a young woman," the King said. "What is your impression of Duke Philip? Will he please Mary, do you think?"

I was surprised that he asked me. Or rather I was surprised that he cared a jot about Mary's feelings or desires.

"He is a handsome man," I said, "and not many years older than your daughter. And he seems to have a light and good-spirited temperament."

"Maybe a little too good-spirited," said the King. "I have heard that money trickles through his fingers like rain through a pauper's coat. Well, he'll not get a constantly open purse from me. I shall do right by Mary, but no more."

I suppressed a smile. No monarch knew better than he what it was like to have money trickle through the fingers. He was said to be more profligate than any king who had sat upon the throne. It was rumored that he had spent more than ten of his predecessors together.

"Do not fear that Philip will be a drain upon you," said Sir Thomas. "If anything, I mean to make sure that he pays for the privilege of marrying into your family."

The King grunted happily. "We will send the Duke to see Mary at Hertford. And I'd like you to go with him, Alice. You can report back to me how Mary receives him."

"I am honored at your trust in me," I said.

The King appeared to have a sudden thought. "I believe that Mary and Elizabeth are both at Hertford House."

Sir Thomas nodded. "That is so, Your Grace."

"Then in that case I will send Nicholas Bourbon to see Elizabeth at the same time as the Duke journeys there. Bourbon can travel with Alice and she can tell me how both my daughters like the foreigners."

Sir Thomas gave a little cough. "I wonder if we are not asking Alice to do a little too much," he said. "Let her go with Duke Philip by all means. She will be able to give you a woman's perspective on how Mary receives him.

"But maybe send someone else with Monsieur Bourbon when he travels to see Elizabeth. If we delay a little, I am sure that I will be able to find someone other than Alice to accompany Bourbon. A learned man; a tutor perhaps."

I realized why Thomas said this. He was trying to keep me at a distance from Nicholas Bourbon.

"You don't think that Alice can judge a man like Bourbon?" the King asked, sharply.

"I did not say that, Your Grace. I just worry that she will not have the opportunity to fulfil that task *and* observe the Lady Mary's feelings towards the Duke."

The King frowned a little at this. He never liked to be gainsaid.

"If you think that observing two children and two men will prove too much for Alice," he said, "then perhaps she should go with Bourbon. I can always send Wriothesley or Rich with the Duke. It might be more appropriate."

Again Sir Thomas coughed discreetly. "I would advise that Alice go with the Duke," he said. "She is more expert in love than in letters."

The King looked at him suspiciously. "Have it your own way, Thomas," he said.

"Thank you, Your Majesty." He paused. "I am reluctant to send Rich at the moment. There is much work for him concerning certain larger abbeys. I need him here and would advise you send Wriothesley with the Duke."

The King's eyes displayed a flash of anger.

"Thank you for your advice, Thomas," he said. "But I'm sending Rich."

"But . . ." Thomas began.

"But nothing. I'm sending Rich."

I looked daggers at my friend. His determination to keep me away from Nicholas Bourbon meant that now I had to journey to Hertford with that monster, Rich.

Sir Thomas inclined his head and made a note in his ledger.

I hoped that he would be able to come up with a plan to prevent this eventuality.

"And now to other matters," said the King. "Alice, take a cup of wine."

And then he stared pointedly at Thomas.

Chapter 7
Hidden from the Bride

Thomas acknowledged the King's look, put down his pen and gazed at me in a most curious manner.

"The sister of the Duke of Cleves is only a few days distant from Calais," he said. "However, the authorities there say that the weather is inclement, too dangerous for a crossing. The minute it improves she will take ship for England."

He coughed, picked up his wine, thought better of it and replaced it on the desk.

"His Majesty and I have discussed your situation," he said briskly. "The decision has been made that you are to leave your apartments immediately."

I nodded but could not answer. I glanced at the King who was busying himself by staring out of the window, more than happy to leave Thomas to give me such unwelcome news.

I had expected this, of course, but I was surprised that it upset me as much as it did. I had grown accustomed to being the mistress of Greenwich Castle. The King had called upon me less and less over the last few months and I had allowed myself to grow complacent. I'd begun to feel like I was a princess indeed; almost that I had rights to the Castle. These thoughts were, of course, the height of folly. But who can control folly when it suits so wonderfully?

"It will not do for His Majesty's new bride to run the risk of meeting you," Sir Thomas continued. "Nor indeed of ever knowing of your existence."

A terrible fear seized me. Was my life in danger? Fortunately, before I could even make a move to throw myself on their mercy, to weep and wail, Sir Thomas gave me a reassuring smile.

"You are to be given apartments in the King's new palace in Surrey," he said. He leaned forward, his eyes twinkling. "At Nonsuch Palace."

I allowed myself to breathe. The exhalation was astonishingly loud, but luckily it sounded like a sigh of pleasure.

"You may well be pleased," said the King, turning his gaze upon us once again. "Nonsuch is the finest palace in England. In Europe. In the world."

"Even Marillac, the French ambassador, admits as much," Cromwell added smugly. "François's châteaux of Chambord and Fontainebleau will be eclipsed by Nonsuch."

"I am honored to be accommodated at the new palace," I said. It did not feel that much of an honor; Nonsuch was still a building site by all accounts. I supposed, though, it was better than being banished from Court or having to fend for myself in London. Or worse.

But then another thought came to me. I turned towards the King. "Of course, if Your Majesty prefers it I could go to one of my own manors. Buckland in Kent perhaps, or Luddington?"

"Luddington's too far," he said. "And Buckland is too close to Dover. I don't want you to be seen by my bride. Not even for a moment. Nonsuch it is."

I bowed my head graciously. I would have to get used to the dust and clamor of building work.

"You will be able to take your household with you," continued Sir Thomas. "His Majesty has graciously consented to that."

"And a pension of ninety pounds a year," the King added. "From my purse."

"You are too generous, Your Grace."

"Am I? Shall I cut it then?" He laughed loudly. I was not able to sense how much true humor there was in that laugh.

"When shall I leave Greenwich?" I asked. "It will take me a few days, no longer."

"That will be good," said Sir Thomas. "Who knows when the weather will improve enough to enable a safe crossing of the channel? Anne could be in England sooner than we think."

"But I want you to go to Hertford first," said the King. "To see Mary about taking Duke Philip as husband."

"I look forward to it," I said. I paused and gave a thoughtful glance. "And you are quite decided that Sir Richard Rich must go to Hertford as well? When Sir Thomas has such need of him?"

The King looked at Thomas, who tapped his fingers on the desk but did not look up. He opened a ledger and began to read it with great intensity.

"This feels like a conspiracy between the two of you," the King said icily.

"It is not, Your Grace," I said quickly. "I suspect that Thomas hopes to spare me the anguish of traveling with a man who has given me so much grief in the past."

The King's eyes flickered with sudden realization. "Well, of course, I also don't want you to suffer upset," he said.

He glared at Thomas. "But unlike the Lord Privy Seal, I am confident that Rich holds his King in awe and would not do anything to harm you."

Thomas licked his lips anxiously, aware that the King was waiting for him to make answer.

"Of course I know that Rich is in awe of Your Majesty," he said. "It is merely that I was seeking to avoid Alice experiencing the slightest twinge of anxiety."

"Would you experience such a thing, Alice?" the King asked. "Are you anxious that my puissance is not sufficient to protect you from a man like Rich?"

For a split second I did not know how best to respond. I did not wish for either Thomas or myself to seem to doubt the King. And then it came to me.

"No man in his right mind would dare to disobey you, Your Majesty," I said. "It is just that sometimes I doubt that Sir Richard is always of right mind."

I could almost hear the silence in the room.

Sir Thomas glanced up at the King. "So shall Thomas Wriothesley accompany Alice?" he asked, smoothly. "Rich can be found useful work elsewhere."

The King nodded once and stroked his beard thoughtfully.

My stomach flew like swifts in joyful flight. I did not like Wriothesley overmuch, but I did not fear him as I did Rich.

"And is Monsieur Bourbon still to see the Princess Elizabeth?" I inquired casually.

"Yes," said Sir Thomas. "You will all travel there together. But you are to concern yourself solely with the Duke and Lady Mary. I thought you understood that already."

"I do, Sir Thomas. What makes you think otherwise?"

He gave me an annoyed look, which I returned with my most seductive of smiles. He stared at me a few moments longer but then, despite himself, a little grin took his mouth. The King was not the only man I could charm.

He turned towards the King. "We must talk about the relations between the Emperor and the King of France," he said.

The King sighed. "Must we?" He stared at Sir Thomas, who did not answer. "If we must, Thomas. If we absolutely must."

He gave me a weary smile and indicated that I should leave.

The King commanded that I stay at the Palace rather than return to the Castle. As evening drew on, I sat in the window of his Study with a book in my hand. It was the eighth book of Ovid's great work. I had been engrossed by the tale of the Minotaur, incarcerated in an endless labyrinth. At the back of my mind was the memory of my own imprisonment.

I felt terrified of the Minotaur, but the more I read the more I felt pity for him as well. To be shunned by mankind was a dreadful punishment. Even worse was to be banished to that place of damnation by a man the poor creature believed was his father. Did the Minotaur weep for his father? Did he howl for his mother, who had nourished and protected him until his bestial rages grew too terrible to contain? Did he feel betrayed by both his parents?

I placed the book in my lap while I mused on these matters. I was heartily pleased that no such creatures walked in England nowadays.

But then, of a sudden, I recalled the evil people I had known. Timothy Crane, the brothel keeper, and his cruel assistant, Thorne. My lover, Art Scrump, who had sold me to them to buy off his creditors. Sir Edmund Tint, who abused me. Were they not as evil and bestial as the Minotaur? Worse, for they were human and had human attributes. Worse, because they knew exactly what they were doing and reveled in it.

And, of course, there was Richard Rich, the villain. He always turned up, ever haunted me. Thank goodness I would not have to journey to Hertford with him.

I gazed out of the window. The sky was grey as swarming rats, heavy, broiling and threatening. The daylight grew dimmer and took on a ghastly, ghostly yellow tinge. It was like the face of a sick man who had suddenly grown much worse. It disquieted my spirit, felt menacing and dire.

I picked up the book again, thinking to lose myself in more ancient perils. But I put it down again almost instantly, fascinated by the ominous sky.

And then I saw them. Flakes of snow had begun to fall.

I threw the casement open, heedless of the cold. More and more flakes descended. They became an endless stream, most plunging down without pause, a few caught by tiny breezes, tumbling and eddying, as if they were reluctant to fall any lower. But fall they did.

The world grew hushed. Birds and beasts hid themselves away; men hurried home to shelter. The snow was the most silent of all. Not a murmur came from it as it fell, not a drip or skitter as it softly hit the earth. It fell like mute tears upon a maiden's face, come from nowhere, streaming endlessly.

I thought my heart might break.

If only I'd had my notebook with me. I might have captured the moment forever.

I rested my chin upon the windowsill and watched. The paths were the first parts of the gardens to be dusted by snowflakes. And then the bare, brown earth took on a fragile coverlet. The grass resisted longest. It grew moist and wet, yet still showed green. At last the snow began to settle even on this, extinguishing the green, hiding the leaves. The whole of the parkland became mantled in snow.

I strained my ears to listen. Not a sound. Even the Palace seemed to have grown quieter.

I felt better now, like I used to when I was upset as a child and my mother pushed the bedcovers close about me to make me warm and safe. *Was I warm and safe?* I wondered. I was to be sent away from Court. But what would really happen when Anne arrived from Cleves?

I sighed and shut the window. No good would come of thinking on this. Events would run their course whether I wished them to or not.

The important thing was how I responded to them. How I managed the dance.

And in the meanwhile I was to travel to Hertford with Nicholas Bourbon.

Chapter 8
To Hertford and the Princesses

The Court moved to Whitehall Palace the next day. I never much cared for the place. It was vast and chill, vainglorious and bleak. I was relieved to set out on our journey a couple of days later. It was a clear, sharp morning and I was grateful that I had thought to wrap up as warmly as I had. The thick mink coat kept out even the most bitter of winds and I snuggled into it with pleasure. Sissy was less well protected and shivered and sniffed as we walked towards the waiting coaches. I felt a pang of guilt.

"Get one of my cloaks from the luggage," I told her.

"Are you cold then, Alice?"

"It's not for me, it's for you. You can wear two cloaks. It will be a long, cold journey."

She nodded gratefully and wiped her nose with the back of her hand.

I glanced towards the east where the sun was just rising. Above the countless roofs and spires of London the sky was turning a delicate rosy pink. It looked beautiful and my heart felt giddy and light. For a moment I imagined myself in the country, where I was brought up, or at Sissy's home in Stratford. I thought of the Coopers' farm, of their sheep and cows munching endlessly in the fields, of searching for eggs with Sissy's littlest sisters, of the birds welcoming the dawn with astonishing songs.

But then my thoughts were interrupted by the myriad cries of people selling their wares to the waking city. Few birds in London, save birds of prey. Yet even this shrill and raucous clamor could not completely disturb my pleasure. I did not care for Whitehall Palace, and to escape from London and courtiers and King would be wonderful.

And even more wonderful was to muse upon who I was traveling with.

As if the thought were child to the deed, Nicholas Bourbon appeared from the other side of the carriage. He doffed his hat and gave a low and courteous bow. He was well prepared for the journey, wearing a deep-brown fur coat tied at his waist by a thick red sash. I was glad, for I worried that, being a man from the warm south, he might feel our English cold more bitterly than most. A fine scarf was knotted artlessly around his neck.

"Miss Petherton," he said. "It is a pleasure to see you this morning."

He stepped closer, took my hand in his and brought it to his lips. He kissed my fingers for only the briefest moment, but I was stirred by it and felt my cheeks turn pink as the morning sky.

"And you, sir," I said quickly. "I trust you are prepared for your meeting with the Princess?"

He gave a little, quirky smile.

"How can I prepare for such a meeting? The Princess is said to be a paragon of intellect, of as good a wit as a man thrice or four times her age. I am told that I must decide whether I can usefully be her tutor. In reality I suspect that it will be the Princess who makes the decision."

I gave a little laugh. "I think you may be correct there, Monsieur Bourbon. Elizabeth is one of the cleverest children I've met."

"I am led to believe that she can read and write in several languages and can debate on many matters."

"That's true," I said. "But as well as her undoubted intelligence, she has something more."

"What is this something more?"

"Wisdom, Monsieur Bourbon. The Princess is imbued with great wisdom."

He considered this for a moment and then nodded.

"Wisdom, what we in France call *sagacité*, is something we are born with or not," he said. "A grace given or withheld by God. It is not something that can be taught or forgotten."

Elizabeth was one of the most watchful children I had ever known. It was as if she realized already that being suspicious might be the only thing which would keep her alive. Maybe it would prove a more useful gift than all the learning in the world.

But I did not tell Monsieur Bourbon this. Nor did I tell him that Elizabeth had been legally proclaimed a bastard and had no hope of attaining anything in life other than neglect and frustration. Unless, of course, she was wise enough to make an ally of her little brother.

The guards by the carriage straightened to attention.

Monsieur Bourbon turned to see what had made them do this but I had no need to. I knew full well who our other traveling companion was. And I disliked him every bit as much as I liked Nicholas Bourbon.

Thomas Wriothesley was in his mid-thirties but he looked much older. He had a long face, shaped rather like a shovel. His cheekbones were so prominent they looked as though he'd been in a brawl and come out much the worse, yet his cheeks were deeply hollowed as if he were suffering from some mysterious illness.

His eyebrows were the only feature of his face that seemed healthy. They arched permanently, as though he were constantly asking questions.

I felt sure that was the case. He was a loathsome, inquisitive man and I disliked him almost as much as his fellow snake, Sir Richard Rich.

"My dear lady," Wriothesley said, stooping to kiss my hand. His breath was foul and clammy. It felt like my flesh had become covered with a sticky and unpleasant film.

"Good morning, Master Wriothesley," I said, resisting the temptation to wipe my hand on my cloak. "I trust you are fully prepared for your mission?"

"Fully prepared, Mistress Petherton, apart from want of sleep."

I turned my face away and looked at the horses. I did not wish to appear the slightest bit interested in his life or health.

"I toil long for Baron Cromwell," he continued. "The years of working through the night have meant that I now am a stranger to the blissful state of sleep."

"I would have thought you toiled for the King and not for the Lord Privy Seal."

Wriothesley gave me a bleak smile. "That is what I implied."

"Toiling for the King is not a duty, Master Wriothesley," I said. "Surely it is a more blissful state than even slumber?"

He did not bother to hide his malicious expression.

"You would know this, of course," he said, blinking his eyes once, like a newt.

He turned towards Monsieur Bourbon. "You are the Frenchman?"

"Nicholas Bourbon," he replied, "potential tutor to the young Princess."

Wriothesley sniffed and drew himself up to his full height. "The Lady Elizabeth," he said. "She is a bastard and therefore not a princess."

"Thank you for educating me," Nicholas said. "To whom am I talking?"

"I am Thomas Wriothesley, lately ambassador to the Holy Roman Emperor. I have an important embassy to Lady Mary, the eldest daughter of the King."

"The daughter in whom the Emperor takes a very great interest?" Nicholas said. "They are cousins are they not? And she is a most staunch Catholic. The Emperor must like that in her."

Wriothesley shrugged. "Lady Mary is a strong-willed young woman. For many years she foolishly persisted in denying that her father is head of the church in England."

"Strong-willed and brave then," Nicholas said.

Wriothesley stared at him as if he were imprinting his face upon his mind. It was a look which might make many a man quail, but it appeared to have no effect upon the Frenchman.

"I wish you well in your embassy," Nicholas said. "The King has betrothed the girl to so many men she may not take you seriously."

Wriothesley gave a smile like the baring of teeth.

I was pleased to see that Nicholas's barb had gone home.

At that moment, Duke Philip arrived. I was astonished to see that he was dressed in the flimsiest of clothing. Fine and extravagant they may be, but they would not keep him warm on the journey he was about to make.

I need not have concerned myself. A moment later, I realized he dressed in this manner only to appear a strong and vigorous prince to any bystanders. His servants were surreptitiously stowing warm furs and blankets in his carriage together with stone hot-water bottles. I felt envious.

But then I glanced at Nicholas Bourbon; I would be warm enough if he traveled with me.

"I go with the Duke," said Wriothesley, airily. "The rest of you are to go in the second coach."

My heart flew like a bird. To be rid of Wriothesley and in the company of Monsieur Bourbon was a very pleasant outcome.

But then fate, or rather Duke Philip, intervened. He was horrified at the thought of my traveling with a man and insisted that Nicholas travel in his coach.

Nicholas agreed immediately, although he gave Wriothesley a searching and not altogether friendly look. He took a step towards the Duke's coach, came back, took my hand and kissed it.

The journey should not have been a long one for it was only twenty miles to Hertford Castle. I assumed that we would reach it at about noon. I had not reckoned with the Duke's weak stomach. The swaying and rolling of the coach took their toll upon him. *So much for the strong and healthy prince*, I thought.

We stopped after only two miles for him to leap out of the coach to be sick. It was the first of many such stops. I thought that there would be nothing left of the man for Mary to see. The poor thing looked more woebegone with every mile.

It was two in the afternoon before we arrived at the Castle. Wriothesley and the Duke hurried off to see the Lady Mary. Wriothesley made it clear that I was not to join them. I demurred at this, saying that the King desired that I be at the meeting between his daughter and her suitor.

"The King felt it more appropriate that you do not attend," Wriothesley said. "You are to concern yourself with his younger bastard only."

I gazed at him for a moment, wondering if he was speaking the truth. It had been the King's idea that I come to observe the meeting between Mary and Duke Philip. Perhaps since then he had changed his mind or had it changed for him.

Or it might be that Wriothesley was lying for his own nefarious purposes.

"As the King desires," I said.

My heart grew lighter at the news. It would mean that I could spend more time with Nicholas. In any case I had no wish to watch as poor Mary was paraded like a prime heifer for yet another customer. The poor girl had been betrothed to half the royalty of Europe with

Henry wriggling out of the deal the moment it no longer suited his policies.

The less I was a party to such cruel games the better I liked it.

We waited in an antechamber for ten minutes. I found it hard to keep my eyes from Nicholas. And, for once, I found it hard to engage in idle talk.

Eventually the door opened and the Lady Elizabeth entered. She was dressed in a simple gown with no ornament and little fancy work. I was surprised; this was no fit clothing for a daughter of the King. No doubt the preparations for the King's own marriage had strained the Royal finances in recent months. His two daughters had clearly borne the burden of all the economies.

Elizabeth gave a tilt of her head and began a charming little speech of welcome to Monsieur Bourbon in French. I could speak a little of the language but not well enough to follow everything that was being said. Elizabeth was indeed a very intelligent girl. She was six years of age yet she acted with a confidence far beyond her years.

At the end of the speech, Monsieur Bourbon clapped his hands enthusiastically and cried out, "Bravo, *ma chère Princesse*, bravo." I joined in the applause.

Elizabeth blushed and looked round at her attendants to see their response. They smiled and cooed but did not applaud. Sensible policy, no doubt. A child of Henry Tudor should not be given too much adulation. A prickly vanity was the family's sixth sense.

One of the attendants came forward to welcome us. But before she had time to speak, Elizabeth extended her hand towards her. "This is my governess, Kat Champernowne," she said. "It is Kat who teaches me to read and write, in English, Flemish, Italian and Spanish." She gave Nicholas Bourbon a shrewd look. "And French."

Bourbon nodded graciously towards the governess. "You are to be congratulated, madam. You have taught Princess Elizabeth exceedingly well." But I saw that he blushed a little nonetheless and looked discomforted.

"She is not Princess Elizabeth," said another lady. "Her title is now Lady Elizabeth."

"I stand corrected," Nicholas said. "But any woman of sweet nature, young or old, may be likened to a princess whatever her birth or title."

"Maybe in France," the woman answered. "Not in England."

"Thank you for reminding us, Margaret," Kat Champernowne said with a sniff.

The woman stared at her defiantly for a moment but then looked away.

I saw Elizabeth take note of this and smile. Watchful child indeed.

"You will dine with us," Kat continued. "We have delayed our meal until your arrival."

"That will be delightful," Nicholas said. "I hope you have not been too troubled by our tardiness."

"We have a little," said Elizabeth. "I'm hungry." And she led the way to the dining room.

Chapter 9
Myths and More

Because we had arrived so late at Hertford Castle there was no chance of us returning to London that night.

I was accommodated in a bleak little chamber with a tiny anteroom little bigger than a cupboard for Sissy. After leaving my belongings there, I wasted no time and hurried down towards the warmth and comfort of the sitting room. I was too chilled to read for a moment and put my book down in order to warm my hands at the fire. A few minutes later I was delighted to see Nicholas Bourbon enter the room.

"You like to read?" Nicholas asked, picking up the book from the table beside me.

"I do, my lord."

"I am not a lord, Mademoiselle Petherton," he said with a little smile. He studied the book. "Ovid's *Metamorphoses*. You enjoy this book?"

"Yes. I mean no . . . Or maybe . . . I'm not really sure." I chided myself for my indecisiveness; he must have thought me a fool.

"What I mean," I continued in an attempt to rescue my position, "is that I don't think it is a book to like or dislike. It's too big to bear such an epithet."

He smiled once more, and this time I worried that he might be smiling at me with condescension.

"You are right, Alice. Such works are so mighty in nature that our petty likes and dislikes pale in comparison with them." He gave me another smile and now I realized it was not mocking but warm.

"Which of the tales has most moved you?" he asked.

"The one concerning the Minotaur," I answered. "I think about it a lot. It's a sad story. I feel terror at the thought of the Minotaur. But he could not help his rages nor his nature, so I also feel pity for him."

"You feel pity for a monster that devours maidens? That drinks their blood and devours their flesh?"

"I live at Court, Monsieur Bourbon. I am familiar with such activities."

He looked at me in astonishment.

A fierce shiver seized me. It was partly made of fear that I had said such dangerous words. And partly made of joy that I had confided my thoughts so wildly. That I had entrusted my safety to him. I put a finger to my lips.

He stared at me for a moment longer and then put his own finger to his lips and smiled. My throat drained of all moisture and I had to swallow. I began to feel quite giddy.

He placed the book back on the table.

"I have never seen the sad side of the Minotaur before you spoke of it," he murmured. "I had always sympathized with the young people who were sacrificed. I was glad that Theseus slew the monster."

"He did so only with the aid of Princess Ariadne," I said. "He would not have succeeded without her help."

Nicholas nodded. "That is true. And it is therefore a bitter thing that he deserted her on an island and returned to Athens. That is not the action of a gentleman."

I laughed at his quip. And I was pleased that he thought this.

We fell silent. It was a pleasant silence, a warm and thoughtful one.

But then a log split in the fire, the noise like the cracking of a whip, making me jump. It spat sap and made the fire blaze furiously for a moment. Nicholas bent and picked up a poker to push the log back. The flames licked greedily at it, waxing prodigiously.

"Although I feel sorrow for the Minotaur," I said, "I feel still more sympathy for Pasiphaë, the monster's mother. She had a cruel fate. It was no fault of hers that the sea god made her fall in love with a bull."

"But she did a deceitful thing," Nicholas said. "When she asked Daedalus to make a wooden cow that she might hide within it and thereby make love with the bull."

I shuddered at the thought of this.

"That is true," I said. "But her punishment was bitter. To give birth to the monster Minotaur."

"Her punishment was made crueler by the actions of her husband," Nicholas said. "She loved her child, despite his dreadful nature. Her deepest grief must have come when her husband imprisoned him."

I nodded. She must have felt rage at her husband for this act. And guilt that her own sins had led to it.

Nicholas stood up and walked a few yards back and forth across the room. He seemed agitated, as if he had to move or he would begin to suffer. I watched him in some surprise. At last he stopped his pacing and came back and sat with me.

"I can sympathize with the Minotaur in his imprisonment," he said. He looked out of the window and his face grew troubled. "I was imprisoned for fifteen months and thought that I would never be released."

I felt a swift flood of sympathy for him. How could I not?

A lump as hard as stone filled my stomach. I felt again the wild fear, the sense of powerlessness, the desperation of being imprisoned in the brothel. I observed once more the cruelty of my captors. Thankfully I had learnt to blot out the pain. But not my bitter anger.

I blinked away the tears. I wondered if I would ever banish the memory of those terrible days.

I looked at Nicholas as he stared out of the window. I was pleased that he was doing so, for it meant he had not seen my own distress. I guessed that in his mind he too had returned to prison. Perhaps he was less successful than I at putting it behind him.

I took his hand and made my voice calm. "It must have been awful for you. What was the cause?"

"None that I could see," he said. "But plenty that my enemies could."

He turned his face towards me and forced a wry grin. "I wrote a poem, 'In Praise of God Almighty,' which my enemies said proved I was a follower of Martin Luther."

"And are you?"

He smiled and did not answer. Then he said, "I have never met the man. I cannot be a follower of a man I have not met."

"But you are a follower of Christ, no doubt. Yet you've never met him."

He looked surprised and a little confused.

"That is different," he said at last. "And it is not to be spoken of."

He folded his hands in his lap. His eyes were bright with surprise and, I think, admiration.

"I am glad you were released," I said at last.

"As am I. Even King François could not procure my freedom. My enemies defied him for many months."

I shook my head in wonder. I could not see anyone defying King Henry for even an hour.

"So what was the cause of your release?"

"I wrote to Jean, the Cardinal of Lorraine. He was one of the King's friends and an influential adviser. He was also a firm friend of poets and thinkers. I think it may have been he who obtained my freedom."

"I must say I'm astonished that your King could be disobeyed in this manner. Nobody in England would dare defy King Henry."

"Few would dare to defy King François. It was my misfortune that I was imprisoned by one who did." He gave a little shrug and then looked a little anxious.

"You will not tell of this?" he asked. "It will never do for anyone in England to think that François cannot command in his own realm."

"Of course not," I said. I felt a thrill of delight that he had told me such sensitive information. *Was it because he trusted me*, I wondered, *or did he wish to share an intimacy?*

Chapter 10

The Hunger of the King

I returned to Whitehall Palace the next morning considerably flustered. I could feel Sissy watching me the whole while. I brushed aside her attempts to talk and stared out of the window.

How could I have been such a fool?

I had allowed myself to become enamored of the Frenchman. I had allowed my heart to trip and almost fall. What had I been thinking? I was the King's mistress. He would not countenance any other man in my bed. It would be the death of the man and the ruin of me. I closed my eyes and rested my head against the window. It might even be the death of me.

I shuddered. It felt like someone was walking over my grave. And I knew that the walker's legs were huge and heavy, one of them oozing with a suppurating, stinking wound which made its owner wild and dangerous.

I breathed a prayer that I had come to my senses in time.

I had expected to give my report on the Princesses to Sir Thomas but I was summoned immediately to the King. My heart plummeted.

Had some spy seen my behavior with Nicholas Bourbon and reported it to him?

Surely that could not be. I had been circumspect and modest in all my public dealings with Monsieur Bourbon.

A cold fear seized me. Did the King have the power to peer into my heart? Could he read my every thought and emotion? I steadied myself against the wall of the corridor and took a deep breath. *That's nonsense, Alice*, I thought. *You've been reading too many tales of heroes and monsters. Henry is the King, not the Minotaur. A human, not a god. I'm going to meet my master, not my maker.*

I walked into his chamber as boldly as I could manage. Too boldly it seemed.

"You seem full of the joys of spring," the King said sourly. "And yet we are in the grip of deep winter."

His leg must have been paining him.

"I am pleased to return to London," I said. "To be in your presence once more. To be at your call."

I knelt at his feet and he patted me on the head.

"Sit here, my dear," he said, indicating a space beside him.

I did so and tried to calm the clamor of my heart. A deep rumble emanated from his chest. I breathed a sigh of relief; the sound was a sign not of anger, but of content. Perhaps my return to his presence was as pleasing to him as I pretended it was to me.

He sipped at a cup, his eyes watching me shrewdly from above the brim. "Tell me, Alice, what did the Lady Mary think of our friend the Duke?"

I swallowed hard and wondered how best to answer. *The truth*, I thought. The King might not be able to read my thoughts but he could always scent dissembling.

"I did not see their first meeting, Your Grace."

He looked surprised. "Why so?"

"Master Wriothesley said that you commanded me not to attend their initial encounter. Because of this I accompanied Monsieur Bourbon to the Lady Elizabeth."

"I said no such thing at all," he said. "I wanted the opposite. I wanted you to see Mary's reaction with a woman's eyes. What good are Wriothesley's eyes in matters of the heart?"

I said not a word but raised my eyebrows to signify my agreement.

"Do you think this was Thomas Cromwell's doing?"

"Not at all, Your Majesty," I said quickly. "The Lord Privy Seal was most insistent that I see the Lady Mary on her first meeting with the Duke."

"Who then? Who could have ordered such a thing?" He drummed his fingers angrily on the arm of the settle. "Frost," he bellowed.

A bare instant later the door opened and the King's groom appeared.

"Your Majesty?"

"Send Thomas Wriothesley to me. But leave him waiting outside to kick his heels."

"Your Majesty." Frost slid away on silent feet.

"I was able to see Lady Mary with the Duke later in the day," I said.

"And how then? How did she view the Duke?"

I tried to marshal my recollections. In truth, it was hard to tell exactly how Mary felt about anything, she was so adept at hiding her feelings. I remembered that she had given a fleeting smile at one of the Duke's jests, a glance away when he spoke to her, a curious little peeping at him whenever his attention was elsewhere. More the actions of a child of twelve than a woman in her twenties. I hesitated for a moment and thought it safest to describe her behavior exactly.

The King listened and then frowned. "But what does that mean, Alice? What do these gestures and looks mean?"

I could not help myself. I laughed aloud with pleasure and clasped his hand. "Oh Henry, you are lord of all you survey yet still you cannot see into a woman's heart." I shook my head. "You are truly the King of men."

His eyes narrowed a moment as they did at any hint of criticism. Then he laughed as loud as I had done and kissed me on the lips.

"You are right, my darling. I am an innocent where women are concerned. They are an enigma to every man, myself included. Even you, dear Alice, are a mystery to me."

"Of course, Your Grace. How else could I make you desire me so?"

"It's not your mystery I desire," he said. "But there again, perhaps that is part of it."

He fell silent and looked at me fondly.

"I am an innocent where women are concerned," he repeated. "That is why I have been so trapped and traduced by sorceresses in the past. The Spaniard, the incestuous whore." He sighed, a huge sigh, and felt sorry for himself.

"So, what of Mary's looks and gestures, Alice?" he said at last. "What do they signify?"

I took a deep breath, unhappy at having to express an opinion to him. Such words were always remembered by the King and had a habit of coming back to haunt one. But there was nothing for it but to come up with some answer.

"I think it safe to say that the Duke did not displease Lady Mary," I said. "It may be that she even found him pleasant and interesting."

"But love, Alice? Were there signs of love?"

I pursed my lips. "Maybe it is a little too soon to speak of love."

"Nonsense, woman. Love happens with the flight of an arrow, the waft of a wind. Look at me and you. It happened in an instant. Less than an instant. You only had to look into my eyes and you were lost."

I nodded in agreement, although my memory was that it was my eyes that were looked into, his heart that was lost.

He tapped his fingers on the settle arm once again, but this time in thought and not in anger. I had learnt to read his gestures better than a book.

"So love between Mary and the Duke is possible?" he said at last.

"It is, I think." And then I stopped myself and looked at him in surprise.

"What's the matter, girl?" he said.

"Forgive me, Your Grace, but I am somewhat bewildered."

"Why so?"

"I thought that marriages between the children of princes were matters of politics and diplomacy. I am a little surprised that you consider Mary's heart in this matter. Surprised and pleased."

He appeared uncomfortable and shuffled in his seat. When he eventually spoke it was in a low voice, as if he feared that someone might overhear.

"I have not always been the fondest of fathers towards Mary."

He sat in silence while I marveled. I had never heard him admit to any mistake on his part, nor any confusion or misjudgment. Certainly not to ever being wrong.

"I loved her at first," he continued. "But when her mother proved so defiant, the child grew cold and distant. I reacted in a way that maybe I should not have done. I banished her from my home and plucked her from the center of my heart. And she proved every bit as willful and contrary as her mother towards me. She defied me as a child should not do to her father. And not to her King."

He sighed again. "But now she has rendered obedience to me once again. She has bowed the knee, acknowledged that it is I, not the Bishop of Rome, who is head of the Church. Acknowledged that my marriage to her mother was invalid and that she is a bastard."

He gave me a wan smile. "She is a good child now, and I find that I view her fondly and wish the best for her. No more talk of marrying her off to the Emperor. Nor to the King of France or his strange and melancholy offspring. I want her to marry for love."

His words made me suspicious. I wondered if he was telling the truth, or if it was solely political advantage which made him consider marrying Mary to the Duke. I would have to ask Sir Thomas when next I saw him.

"No doubt people will think I am marrying her to the Duke to annoy the Emperor and strengthen my position with the German Princes," he said.

Ah, I had no need to ask Sir Thomas after all.

"But that is only part of the reason." He gave me a wistful smile. "I would that I had married for love. I hope with all my heart that Mary and Elizabeth do."

I did not answer for a moment, puzzling over his words. Perhaps he means it, I concluded. Or at least as much as he means anything without an ulterior motive.

"And your son?" I said at last. "Shall he marry for love?"

He shook his head. "That luxury is not given to kings."

I squeezed his hand. "They have other luxuries," I said.

He stood and helped me to my feet.

"Let me taste those luxuries once again, my dear."

"But Thomas Wriothesley, Your Grace? You summoned him."

"Let him wait."

He had to wait a long while.

The King had always been a hungry, demanding lover. He was the master of his bed just as much as he was master of his Kingdom. No matter that he was an aging man and one who suffered dreadfully from the injury to his leg. He rode me at full tilt, as though hunting for stags or competing at a tournament. He could do neither of these at the moment. His council had persuaded him not to take part in any more tournaments, and even hunting was beyond him.

So the only riding still left to him was of his mistress. He was unusually exuberant and demanding this morning. He wanted energy and tricks aplenty. If it had been with any other man I would have felt cheaply used. But his high good humor and his youthful joy and pleasure at the act of love swept me along with the chase. I cannot say that our lovemaking was truly enjoyable. But it was engrossing.

It was towards the end of our romp that I suddenly thought of Nicholas Bourbon. Once the thought of him had entered my head I could not shake it loose. His face appeared before me, handsome and amused. I blushed at the sight of it, ashamed at what I was doing in front of him. Nicholas put his fingers to his lips and shook his head slightly as if to tell me not to speak, not to worry. I looked away and saw the King below me, his face all red and sweaty, his breath coming quick. How I longed for it to be Nicholas and not Henry inside of me. And then I climaxed; a long and unsettling one. I glanced up. The vision of Nicholas had disappeared.

"Thank you, Alice," the King sighed as I slumped on the bed beside him. "You make me feel like a youth again."

"You are youthful in all important ways," I said.

It was a barefaced lie, but lately the King appeared to accept lies and fawning as truths. A year ago he would have acquiesced in my falsehoods but he would have known them to be merely the flattery of a young mistress. Now he seemed to believe anything he thought congenial. In bed and out of it.

"Time for dinner," he cried, struggling to rise. I helped him upright and he swung his legs out of bed. My heart ached for him at that moment. He seemed so old and ill, so wounded.

But, kingly as ever, he took a breath, mastered the pain and climbed to his feet. Normally he would have summoned gentlemen to dress him; but lately, after our bouts of love, he had preferred me to do this. I enjoyed it, I must confess. Somewhat more than undressing him, come to think of it.

I helped him into his dining room. Here was another change. For most of his life he had eaten surrounded by nobles, advisers and servants. Increasingly he preferred to dine with a few companions or even alone.

He rubbed his hands with glee at the feast set out before us. I glanced at the vast array of dishes and wondered if we were to dine alone or with a dozen other people. It made no difference to the King or his cooks. He sat at the table and commanded his servants to fetch him helpings of this or that dish. When a quarter of the food had been piled up before him, enough for three men, he held up his hands.

"Enough, enough," he cried. "My physicians tell me, Alice, that I must restrict my meals until I am able to exercise again."

"I know, Your Grace," I said. "But you have done wondrous exercise this morning."

I don't think he heard me. Feasting seemed his chief pleasure nowadays, apart from the one he had just indulged in with me. I admired the courage of his physicians in seeking to curtail at least one of his two appetites. I doubted that they would have dared to deny him my attentions.

It was only when we had finished that he clicked his fingers. "Thomas Wriothesley," he said. "I had forgot him."

I hadn't. I delighted to think that the odious man had been kept waiting for two hours now.

"Help me to the Presence Chamber," he said. "We'll see him there."

Wriothesley came into the room all swagger. Then he paused, somewhat thrown by seeing me there, one foot hovering uncertainly just above the floor. Perhaps his long absence from Court meant he did not understand my position. His master Richard Rich should have informed him, of course. But then scoundrels keep important secrets even from their brother serpents.

"The Lord Privy Seal has informed me of your report upon the meeting of Lady Mary and the Duke," the King said.

Wriothesley's eyes flickered. He was surprised by this, presumably believing the King had summoned him to give the report himself.

"Naturally," he said, swiftly recovering his composure. "I assume that I am here to add my voice to my written words."

The King shook his head. "No. You are here to explain why you told Alice Petherton not to be at the first meeting between my daughter and Duke Philip."

Wriothesley's eyes went from the King's to mine. I stared back at him coolly.

"But Your Majesty," he stammered. "I did so on your direct command."

The King raised one eyebrow. Wriothesley quailed as though the eyebrow were a bow in the hand of an accomplished archer.

"It was a most express command," Wriothesley added, his voice now very small.

"Written in my hand?"

"No, Your Majesty."

"Given to you by the Lord Privy Seal?"

"No, Your Majesty." He swallowed visibly. "By the Duke . . ."

"The Duke of Norfolk?"

Wriothesley nodded. He had no more breath left for words.

"Norfolk?" bellowed the King.

Wriothesley almost threw himself to the floor but seemed to think better of it.

"Yes, Your Majesty," he said. "The Duke of Norfolk."

The King turned to me, his face suddenly composed and calm. "Well, that's most peculiar."

He waved his hand in dismissal of Wriothesley. The man looked round in consternation. Gregory Frost ushered him gently towards the door as if he were a child who had been beaten by his father.

"Most peculiar," the King repeated. He scratched his chin thoughtfully.

"The Duke of Norfolk doesn't much care for you, Alice," he said. "Why is that, do you think?"

"I have no idea, Your Majesty. I'm sure he has his reasons. The Duke is a complex man."

"Hmm. He's a complex man whose very soul shudders for power. Not much complexity in such a naked craving. I've never much cared for him, if truth were told. But he's clever and loyal. I could no more do without him than I could Sir Thomas."

He yawned and stretched. "No matter. The Duke hates his wife, so I'm not surprised that he dislikes you."

"He loves his mistress though. Or so it is said."

The King looked at me with narrowed eyes. He gave a cold, strange laugh. "Perhaps it is not that Norfolk dislikes you after all. Perhaps he likes you too much."

Clearly, the King's suspicious mind had grasped hold of the word *mistress*.

I shuddered and shook my head. "I very much doubt that. Towards me the Duke is as affectionate as a bird of prey." I touched the King's hand. "In truth, I like him no better than he likes me."

"But if he loves you, Alice?"

I shook my head again. "As I said, he seems to me to be cold and ruthless, Your Grace, with interest only in the kill, not in life and love."

The King laughed. But I saw his mind filing the suspicion away just the same.

"You have not asked me about the Lady Elizabeth," I said. "How she liked the Frenchman?"

I felt myself all flustered as I mentioned Nicholas Bourbon. But I wished to divert the King from his foolish suspicions. I knew that if I did not, his mistrust would grow to encompass not only the Duke but me as well.

Besides, it thrilled me to talk of Monsieur Bourbon. I wanted to talk of him to anyone, to everyone, if only the merest mention. Even though I knew it was perilous to talk about him with the King.

"Well what of it?" the King asked with no real interest. "Did the child like the man?"

"She did, I think. She spoke a good deal with him, in French as well as Latin."

"If she's so damned clever maybe she has no need of an additional tutor. I could save myself the expense."

"Katherine Champernowne is a very good tutor," I said. "But her native tongue is not French and there are limits to how well she can teach the language. I noticed that Monsieur Bourbon struggled a little with understanding Elizabeth's pronunciation. If you would have her become more fluent in that tongue then maybe you should engage the Frenchman."

I bit my lip, realizing that I was in danger of pressing Nicholas's merits a little too much.

"Or another one," the King said. "Bourbon comes with good credentials but he does not come cheap."

I thought it best not to reply.

"Besides," the King continued, "the man has been recommended to me by Ambassador Marillac. I wonder at this enthusiasm. Perhaps Bourbon's a spy."

My heart juddered at his words. They could place Nicholas in untold danger.

"Perhaps another Frenchman then," I said, trying to keep my voice light and disinterested. "A man of your own choosing. Or an Englishman who can speak the tongue better than Kat Champernowne."

"Or none at all. I'm not sure I want Elizabeth any more accomplished at foreign tongues. She'll be more proficient than I am. I don't want her talking about me to the French unless I understand what she's saying." He laughed indulgently at the jest. But, as always with the King, his humor masked a hidden thought, a deeper suspicion.

"I'll ask Sir Thomas to decide on the matter of a tutor," he said. "He'll enjoy the ferreting."

He drank deeply from his wine and took my hand.

"Now, my dear, to other matters. You realize that my new bride is even now in Calais."

"Waiting for the weather to improve enough to make the crossing," I said.

"Indeed." He looked at me. "What think you of her?"

"I have not met her, Your Grace."

"Nor have I. But her portrait." He sighed. "She seems to me to be the epitome of what a queen should be. Do you not think so?"

"She is very . . ." Here I paused, thinking for the best words to describe her. "Very pleasant, very kind looking."

"Not beautiful?" The King looked genuinely surprised. "I think she is beautiful."

"Beautiful, without question, Your Grace."

"A different beauty from yours, of course. But equally lovely, wouldn't you say?"

"Maybe lovelier," I said. "The courtiers who have seen her say that she is radiant."

He nodded and a little smile came across his face. "Anne is radiant. That is exactly the word for her. A princess and a saint. She will for a certainty give me a second son, a playmate for Edward."

How he craved that. He was terrified that Edward would die in his youth, just as his own brother and his bastard son, FitzRoy, had. He needed a second son, a second string, as security for his legacy. I sometimes wondered if he repented pronouncing both his daughters bastards and excluding them from the throne.

Who would be King if Edward died? I thought. This was a constant concern of the Court, although only the closest of friends dared discuss it openly. Any question concerning the royal succession would be construed as treason. Had I been braver, I might have asked Sir Thomas Cromwell or Archbishop Cranmer. Not that either of them would have been careless enough to discuss it.

Contemplating all of this, another thought came to me. I had been the King's lover for two years now and never sign of a child. I looked at the King and felt a sad pity. No doubt he was too old to father another. His hope now seemed rather poignant.

He gave a little cough to clear his throat, reached for my hand and squeezed it gently. "You do see that I must send you from Court," he said.

"I do, Your Grace." I gave a sorrowful look, not sure whether the emotion was a true one or a false.

"I am sorry for it, Alice, but there it is."

"I am sorry, also, for I adore you. But I quite understand."

He beamed happily at my words. He so loved to be adored.

"I am sending you to Nonsuch Palace. None such palace." He bent and kissed me on the brow. "None such mistress."

I smiled but did not answer for a moment. Then I put my finger to my chin as if a sudden thought had come to me.

"I so appreciate your sending me to Nonsuch Palace," I said, "but I am a little concerned about it."

His face suddenly became all suspicion.

"My concern is this," I said hurriedly. "You have wisely decided that I must not be seen by your new bride. Yet will you not want her to see Nonsuch? She most certainly will desire to see it."

I paused and sighed. "I do not know how I am to stay there without being seen by Anne."

He frowned and rubbed his chin. "That is an excellent point, Alice. I had wondered this myself, of course, but Sir Thomas seemed happy with your being lodged in Nonsuch so I put aside my concerns."

"It is good that we are of one accord in this matter," I said. "I wonder if you have come to the same solution as I have."

He waved his hand for me to continue. He had clearly paid no attention to our previous conversation on the issue.

"I could go to my manor at Luddington. It is little further from London than Nonsuch. But Queen Anne will have no inkling of it, no desire to visit in the slightest."

The King clapped his hands. "Clever girl, Alice," he said. "I have thought exactly the same for some time now. And who knows, I may one day come to visit you there."

Chapter 11
News and Worse

It was bitterly cold on the river. The wind howled from the east, buffeting us so savagely that I thought we might be thrown overboard. It was only eight or so miles from Whitehall to Greenwich and would normally take a couple of hours. But the wind had caught us and there seemed little hope of getting there in that time.

"There'll be more snow on the morrow," said the burly waterman, a youth with massive arms, which he used to propel the boat with much strength but little skill.

"More snow," I muttered. "Surely there's no more snow in the heavens."

"It don't come from heaven," he said. "It comes from Muscovy. There aren't no angels in Muscovy."

He spat into the river but the wind caught it and blew it into my hair.

"You brute," cried Sissy, brushing it away with her fingers.

"Mighty sorry, miss," the man said. "No offense intended."

I scowled at him but could not bring myself to answer.

We passed by the Tower of London and heard the roaring of the beasts of the Royal Menagerie.

"I hope my Uncle Ned's tucked up nice and warm tonight," Sissy said.

"Me too," I said. Ned Pepper was Beast Keeper and lived in the Tower close to the animals. *Too close*, I thought, remembering how his daughter had been killed by a lion. That had ushered in the most terrible time of my life. It led to my dismissal from the King, my abduction and imprisonment. It might well have ended in my death if I had not been saved by Ned Pepper and his keepers, healed by Ned's wife and daughter. "Me too," I repeated.

The wind dropped soon after and the waterman began to make better progress. "At least the tide's not against us," he said.

"How much longer before we get to Greenwich?" I asked.

"Before dark," he answered. "Or I hope so at any rate."

The light was just beginning to fail when we finally turned the corner of the river. I looked at Greenwich Castle on the hill overlooking the Palace. The ancient, sturdy walls of the Castle contrasted with the more ornate and insubstantial walls of the Palace below. The Castle was small, a keep with a fortified gatehouse and one crumbling tower. But it looked like it had sprung from Malory's *Morte d'Arthur*. I often chose to think of myself as Guinevere, even though I knew that Henry was no King Arthur. But might Nicholas Bourbon prove a Lancelot?

A little sigh of sorrow escaped from me. I had come to love the strange old place and would miss it when I left. I usually accompanied the King when he traveled to his other palaces. But when he was at Greenwich Palace he was content to let me stay up in the Castle. It was almost as if, by housing me a short distance away, he fooled himself that I was his secret mistress. The result he did not intend was that I had almost come to see myself as mistress of the Castle.

We alighted at the Palace, the waterman effusing apologies at the delay and for spitting in the wind. I condescended to forgive him then, thinking fondly of my waterman friend, Walter Scrump. The man's face showed his relief. I was no secret to the watermen of London, certainly. But there again it was said that they knew as much about the King's business as even Thomas Cromwell.

A Palace carriage whisked us up the winding drive to the Castle. I hugged myself with anticipation. Susan and Mary would be there to welcome me; the fires would be roaring and supper waiting. An evening of chatter awaited. What more could I desire?

We were given a warm welcome by our friends. Mary had composed a new song and sang it to us while supper was being laid out on the table. It was beautiful, a song of blooming days in April, of a squire who loved a princess and pined to death when she married a prince.

We took our seats in front of the fire. "You can dine with us tonight," I told Sissy. "The servants will have eaten already so there will be little left for you."

I knew I should not do this with my maid, but Sissy had been my friend before she insisted on becoming my servant. If it were not for the kindness of her and her family I might never have recovered from my ordeal in the brothel.

I watched Sissy as she took a seat at the table and happily tucked a napkin around her neck. Neither of us could ever be sure of her real status. When I had need of comfort and good cheer, I told her she was my friend. When she annoyed me, I reminded her that she was a servant. She accepted either position with happy content and slipped from one to another like a child running in and out of a puddle.

"Will you sing the song again after supper?" I asked Mary. "I thought it was delightful."

"I will if you'll read us your latest poem."

"And tell us all about Princess Mary and her German lover," said Susan. "I can't see Mary ever having the warmth to enjoy a husband, but God knows she deserves a bit of good luck in her life."

"This might be her good luck," I said. "I think she was a little enamored of the Duke."

"Not as much as you were of Monsieur Bourbon," said Sissy, her eyes wide and shining.

I felt my cheeks redden as she said it.

My friends looked at me in astonishment.

"What?" said Susan.

"The handsome Frenchie," Sissy said. "He likes Alice and I'm sure that Alice is keen on him." Before I could stop her, Sissy was in full flow, telling them all about our journey to Hertford and how we had been closeted together in the library for an hour. It was as if she was giving a second rendition of Mary's song of the squire and the princess. I should have stopped her but I did not know what to do for the best. To make too much of it would only serve to make my friends more suspicious and me appear guilty.

At last she finished. Mary turned towards me, openmouthed and silent.

Susan was not so quiet.

"You must be out of your mind. Whatever were you thinking, Alice? If the King finds out he'll rage as mad as a bulldog in a pit. He'll have the neck of this Frenchman, and I shudder to think what he'll do to you."

"Think about the last time you angered the King," Mary said. "Remember what happened to you then."

I had no need to be reminded of that.

"There is nothing for the King to find out," I said.

"Nothing?" cried Susan. "You were alone with the Frenchman for an hour. Even the most docile of men would wonder at that. The King could never be described as docile and he's bloated up with suspicion. He drinks and eats rumor and secrets. He sees treachery in every act he's not set in motion himself."

"He's not quite that bad—" I began.

"Not that bad? Tell that to Thomas More; tell that to Anne Boleyn, her brother and the musician Smeaton. Tell that to the poor fools he's sent to the stake because he feels they're over-enthusiastic about the religious changes he started in the first place."

"He won't find out, Susan."

"He might," said Mary. "The Court is full of vicious gossips. And not everybody loves you."

"But how will they know? There is nothing for them to know."

"There doesn't need to be anything to know," Susan said. "And if even Sissy has her suspicions then imagine what bastards like the Duke of Norfolk think. Or Sir Richard Rich?"

My heart grew cold at mention of these names. My friends were right. I had been an utter fool. I knew it all along but I believed I'd been clever enough to hide the stirrings of my heart. I swallowed the lump filling up my throat. Richard Rich would stop at nothing to cause me a second downfall. And he was a friend of Thomas Wriothesley, so news of my behavior with Nicholas might already be with him.

"Even if there is some validity in your fears," I said as gamely as I could, "we must remember that the King's attention is focused on Anne of Cleves. He means to go and meet her the moment she steps foot in England. He will forget about me soon enough."

They listened to me in silence but their faces looked dubious.

"And I am to be sent away from here, to my manor at Luddington."

"You see," said Susan. "The King's banished you once again. It's the slippery slope, Alice."

"It's nothing of the sort," I said. I spoke loudly, trying to convince myself. "He doesn't want his new queen to see me. Where's the surprise in that? We discussed it before my trip to Hertford."

Susan mumbled to herself for a little longer but she could see the sense in my words.

"So there's really nothing to worry about," I said. "The events of the past few days are over and done."

At that point, a servant entered the room.

"Sorry to disturb you, miss," he said. "But a Monsieur Bourbon has called to see you. I asked him to wait in the parlor."

Chapter 12

A Visit from Monsieur Bourbon

Naturally Susan and Mary insisted on coming with me to greet my visitor.

"You must send him packing at once," Susan said. "And you must impress upon him that it is folly for him to have come here."

I opened the door to the parlor. Nicholas Bourbon was standing by the fire, a book in his hand. He glanced up as I approached and I felt more warmed by his eyes than by the logs blazing in the hearth.

"Alice," he said, taking my hand and kissing it.

He gave a gracious smile to my friends.

"You're to leave," snapped Susan. "Immediately."

"But I have only just arrived." He turned to me with a bewildered expression. "And I came at your request."

"My request?" The breath fled from my body.

"Yes. A message came to me a little while ago. I was told that you desired to see me most urgently."

"Who told you that?" demanded Mary.

Nicholas shrugged. "A messenger. I did not think to inquire of his name."

"But who did the message come from?" Susan asked.

"From Mademoiselle Petherton. I have just told you this."

He turned to me once again. "Have I done something wrong in responding to your message?"

"It was not my message," I said, biting my lip with anxiety. "You have been duped, Monsieur Bourbon, and I do not know by who."

He gave a gentle smile. "I am glad to have been duped in this fashion. I am glad to see you again, Alice."

"Well you can be glad all by yourself," said Susan. "You must leave at once. And don't go by carriage. You must leave on foot."

He shook his head in astonishment. "But why is this? What is happening here?"

"I don't know," I said. "Your very presence here is a danger to me. And the fact that someone saw fit to inveigle you here makes it seem even more dangerous."

"Inveigle?"

"Trap you," Susan said. "Lure you. Fool you and take you for a fool."

He held up his hands to stop her torrent of abuse. "I did not know. I am, as you say, inveigled."

"It's not your fault, Nicholas," I said. "Please don't blame yourself."

If looks could kill then Susan would be a murderer. But I did not know who would be the victim, Monsieur Bourbon or myself.

"I will go immediately," Nicholas said.

I glanced out of the window. The snow was falling faster than ever. Straight from Muscovy, as the waterman had said.

"It's terrible weather out there," I said. My resolve was beginning to falter.

"It will hide me all the better," he said with a gallant smile. "I welcome such a tempest if it serves as a shield for you." He gave me a long, lingering look and I felt my legs begin to shake.

"You must make sure to keep warm," I said. I reached out and touched him on the arm. "I'll ask one of the servants to provide you with a thicker cloak."

"You'll do no such thing," said Susan. "The cloak will be traced to you. You might as well go straight to the King and confess your guilt."

"What guilt?" Nicholas said. "There is no reason to feel guilty." He spoke to Susan but all the time he looked at me.

I tried to speak but only a little moan came to my lips. Fire burned in my belly and I could see nothing other than his face. He took my hand. I should have pulled free but I did not. His hand was warm and soft, like a child's but with the strength of a man. I felt his lips upon my fingers, a gentle breath, a kiss of southern sunshine, a caress of wine and romance. And then his eyes looked into mine once more.

I am lost, I thought. *Lost forever.* And I did not care one jot for any disgrace or doom or danger. I was lost and my heart sang with a fierce joy.

He turned and strode from the hall. My legs gave up the struggle and I had to cling to the back of a chair.

"You little idiot," Susan said. But there was scant anger in her voice. It was full of love and care and pity.

"But who could have sent him such a false message?" Mary asked.

"I can think of only one man," I said. "Richard Rich."

Chapter 13

To Luddington Manor

We left Greenwich early the next morning and took a boat to the Tower, where a large carriage was waiting for us. It was one of the King's own carriages, well upholstered, with masses of blankets and cushions to keep us warm and comfortable. Not all of us, of course. There was no room in the carriage for Humphrey. He would have to ride on one of the four horses pulling the carriage. Sissy fussed over him, making sure that he had a flask of wine before joining us in the coach.

Ned and Edith Pepper came down from the Tower to see us off and to bring a hamper of food for the journey. We did not need any; the carriage was crammed with food and wine, but I thanked them most profusely, nonetheless.

Edith pressed some pies into Sissy's hand. "Give these to your mother if you get the chance to go over there," she said. "Mincemeat pies. For Christmas."

Tears filled Sissy's eyes and Edith gave her a huge hug. "Now you make sure you look after Alice," she said.

"She does," I said. "I couldn't ask for better."

Edith smiled and then gave me a hug. "And you make sure you look after yourself," she said in a very serious tone. "Just make sure."

I followed Susan and Mary into the carriage while Sissy tucked blankets around us to keep us warm. I pondered Edith's words, wondering at how serious she had sounded. I guessed she remembered still the terrible state I'd been in when she first saw me. *No need to worry, Edith,* I thought. *I'll tread much more carefully in the future.*

Ned passed in four stone bottles, hot with water. "They'll help keep the chill off," he said. Then he nodded to the lead driver and we set off.

We soon left the streets of London behind and headed west. The carriage slithered along the icy surface for the whole of the morning. At this rate it would take an age to reach Luddington.

I spent the first hour of the journey thinking about Nicholas. Of course my friends had been right to warn me about the dangers of any friendship with him. And of course I had been right to agree that he leave the Castle.

It was very honorable of him to have left, I thought. But then another thought came. *What if he'd got caught in the snow?*

It was so cold, so terrible a storm. My heart lurched. What if he had been unable to make it back to shelter? Maybe he had been caught out of doors in the worst of the storm. What if he'd laid himself down to die? I very nearly stopped the coach there and then and commanded it to return to Greenwich so I could search for him. Then I collected myself. Nicholas was strong; he was wise. He did not have far to go to reach the river and he would have found a place in one of the inns by the Palace. *He will be all right,* I told myself. *He will be safe.*

The snow began to fall once more and we moved ever more slowly. We made only half the progress we should have done by the end of the day and were hardly any distance from London when we had to stop for the night. The inn was large but not pleasant. The food was execrable and the innkeeper a villainous-looking rogue. He sized me up in a twinkling and then had a good long look at my carriage. No doubt he was in league with thieves and vagabonds; in fact several of the men drinking in his inn looked as though they were merely on a refreshment break from various nefarious enterprises.

I was grateful that Sir Thomas had insisted that I be accompanied by four armed horsemen. The innkeeper scrutinized them as well and scratched at his tangled beard as he did so. After a little while he spat on the ground and rubbed his foot in it with a sneer of contempt. It seemed to me that the four men had proved enough to daunt him.

The next morning we set out on the road once again. Sissy was overjoyed at the thought of going to Luddington as it was only a few miles from her home in Stratford.

"Perhaps we could go over to our farm one day," she said hopefully.

"That would be delightful," I said. I smiled to myself. Sissy would be able to preen and boast when she brought three ladies from the Court to see her family. I was not sure of the wisdom of allowing Humphrey to come though. I did not think her parents would take kindly to his interest in Sissy. Nor the way they mooned over each other.

"Do you think you'll ever see the King again?" Sissy asked.

"I don't know," I said. "And to be honest I don't much care. In fact, I'm glad to be leaving behind all those grand palaces. I'd much rather be at one of my own manors."

Not that I had ever seen either of them, of course.

They came to me as payment for the cruel treatment meted out to me by their owner, Sir Edmund Tint. As far as I knew he was still imprisoned somewhere.

The snow had stopped by now and we made better progress for the following two days. But our good fortune did not last. The weather turned so foul that the next day we did not get close to Luddington and we had to stay at one last inn. The innkeeper made a great fuss of us, told us that it was the eve of Christmas and then, with a fulsome smile, charged us double what he should have done in recognition of that joyous Christian feast.

As we started out the next morning Sissy leaned closer to me.

"It's Christmas Day, Alice."

"I know, Sissy. And a merry day to you. I don't know if there's a church in Luddington for us to worship."

"I'm not worried about that," she answered. "It's just that we can't be sure the manor at Luddington is fit for us to stay in. And seeing as it's Christmas, I was wondering whether we could go to my house instead of the manor."

I smiled. "But will your parents welcome Susan and Mary, as well as you and me? Is there room?"

"We'll make room, Alice. We will. The little ones can squash up in bed."

I kissed her on the cheek. "That is a wonderful suggestion."

"And the driver and guards can stay in the inn on the river," she added.

I kissed her once again.

The desire to revisit the Cooper farm and enjoy all the boisterous blessings of that loving, lively family quickened my heart.

Chapter 14
Christmas with the Coopers

Sissy's brothers and sisters were the first to see us as we pulled up in front of the farm. They ran towards us as we got out of the carriage, their voices high on the cold late-morning air.

The girls leapt into Sissy's arms, screaming with delight.

The boys were more restrained, the eldest, Edward, most of all. He looked at me out of the corner of his eye and flushed so red it looked positively dangerous.

"Mother," cried Sissy, untangling her sisters from her arms.

Hannah Cooper was standing in the doorway, wiping her hands on a kitchen cloth. She smiled broadly, yet her eyes were full of tears.

Sissy ran and hugged her, as fierce in loving as her sisters had been with her.

"It's good to see you," Hannah sobbed. "So good to see you."

I turned and glanced at Humphrey, wondering what he would think of this. He beamed in delight. Ah yes, I remembered. Humphrey's mother was the only person he seemed to truly love. Until, of course, he met Sissy.

Humphrey, for all his strut and swagger, was an enthusiast for love.

Robert Cooper heard the noise and hurried out of the cowshed. He yelled with joy, picked up Sissy and swung her round and round until she grew dizzy and begged him to stop.

She staggered a little and kissed her father repeatedly. Then she stopped and glanced over at Humphrey. She bit her lip a little nervously.

Robert followed her gaze.

"Hello, young man," he said. His eyes had grown narrow and thoughtful.

Humphrey hesitated for only a moment. He hurried over to Robert, his hand outstretched.

"Humphrey Buck, at your service, sir."

Robert took his hand and shook it cautiously.

"I used to be Page to the King," Humphrey continued, "but now I'm chief servant to Alice Petherton. Well, butler to be more accurate. Steward even. Yes, steward about sums it up."

"He's a Page," said Susan, "but he thinks he's a knight-errant."

Humphrey shot an angry glance at her but instantly changed it to one of boyish good humor, presumably well aware of the need to make a good impression on Sissy's family.

"Very droll, Susan," he said with a good-humored chuckle, "very droll."

He turned back to Robert. "I am very pleased to make your acquaintance, sir. Sissy has told me many lovely tales about you."

"She has, has she?" Robert said. "I'm glad that she's found a friend that she can be so familiar with."

"Oh yes," said Humphrey, "we're the best of friends."

Sissy blushed. Robert noticed and frowned.

"Come in out of the cold," Hannah called. She gave Sissy a knowing and shrewd nod. I guessed this was but the prelude to an interrogation concerning Humphrey.

As I was about to follow, Robert held up his hand to detain me.

"It's good to see you again, Alice. We hoped that we would." He paused and then looked at me more closely. "And are you recovered? From what happened to you?"

"Completely," I said.

It was true, or partly true at any rate. I might not have forgotten about my ordeal and doubted I would ever do so. But I was not going to let Crane and Thorne's treatment of me keep me cowed and scared. I refused to be haunted by them.

But these were not thoughts to burden this kindly man with.

He smiled in relief.

Hannah touched me gently on the arm. "And Sissy? Has she been a good girl? Has she given you good service?"

"I could not ask for better," I answered. "She is an excellent maid and an even better friend."

She sighed with pleasure. "Let's get you all settled," she said.

We had arrived in time for dinner. Christmas dinner. It was a feast such as only the Coopers could lay on.

A rich, fat goose had been roasting since dawn. Robert hurried out to slaughter a couple of chickens, plucked and jointed them in minutes and threw them into a skillet.

Meanwhile Hannah set her daughters to work preparing more vegetables.

Humphrey came and whispered a question in my ear.

I nodded. He beamed with delight and hurried out to our carriage.

He returned in minutes carrying two of the larger hampers, placed them on the floor and threw them open. They contained the provisions we had brought for our journey, finer fare than any the Coopers would have known.

There were three bottles of fine claret, one of Malmsey and one of sack. "There's more in the carriage," Humphrey said. "I'll get them in a tick."

Robert came over and joined the children in peering into the hampers. They would certainly have never seen anything like it.

There was a large venison pie, a little battered from the journey but still good, two beef and oyster puddings, three game pies, a leg of salt pork, pickled herrings and two pheasants still bearing feathers. And there was a fat, fresh capon.

"The bird will do for tomorrow," Humphrey said airily.

Sissy looked at me anxiously, wondering at how I would respond to his impertinence.

"As you recommend," I told Humphrey, with as serious a face as I could muster. "After all, you are my steward."

He grinned more widely than even he normally managed.

"And the piece of resistance," he cried. With a flourish he pulled out a rich mincemeat and fruit pudding.

"We've got a pudding already boiling up," Hannah said. "But another won't go amiss."

The meal was wonderful. Much better than any of the fine feasts we were used to, because it was served and eaten with an abundance of love and good spirits.

Robert was particularly pleased with the wines and repeatedly proclaimed his wonder at their taste. Humphrey was assiduous in paying attention to him, but in very nearly as unobtrusive a manner as an experienced Court servant.

Finally, after more than an hour of feasting, we placed our knives on our empty plates and beamed at each other.

"Merry Christmas," said Robert. Then he put his hand to his face. "Do you know, I forgot to say grace."

"I think God will have heard it," Mary said. "Silent though it might have been."

Robert beamed at her. She was very pretty and he was merry with wine.

"See that you don't forget yourself again, Robert Cooper," Hannah told him with an amused look. But I didn't think she was referring to the saying of grace.

We stayed the night and woke to a day of wild wind but clear skies.

Hannah wasted no time in insisting we stay a second night and we gladly agreed.

We spent that day gathered round the fire, eating yet more food and drinking yet more wine. Thank goodness we had brought so many provisions with us.

Early in the afternoon Robert insisted that we go for a walk along the riverbank. Scores of swans sailed up and down, looking for all the world like they had also decided to take some winter exercise. Most were breeding pairs. Someone told me once that swans mate for life. Lucky swans. I thought of Nicholas and sighed.

That night, Humphrey asked to speak with Robert in private. I exchanged glances with Susan and Mary. Hannah began to hum a little song to herself as she washed the dishes. Robert gave a nod and led Humphrey outside.

Sissy, love her, did not notice them leaving the room.

They returned minutes later and Robert clapped his hands.

The room fell silent. Hannah looked at her husband, a slow smile working its way across her face. He nodded and glanced at Sissy.

"I have an announcement to make," Robert began. "Humphrey Buck, Alice's steward, has asked me for Sissy's hand in marriage."

The little girls squealed in delight. Sissy appeared dumbfounded, her mouth dropping open and remaining so.

"And he said yes," cried Humphrey.

"He said *later*," Robert continued. He drew himself up to his full height and beckoned to Sissy to join them as he continued to address us.

"Humphrey has given me details of his family and of his excellent prospects. From what he has said and, I must add, from my own observations, he and Sissy are fond of each other."

Sissy blushed and hung her head. Humphrey put his hands on his hips and looked round in triumph.

"So I am happy to give my blessing," Robert said. "When they are a little older. In a year or so. When they have both grown up a little more."

Sissy giggled with joy.

"I'm very pleased," said Hannah. She held out her arms for Sissy.

"And so am I," I said. "I think they will be good for each other. I think they will make one another happy."

"It's no more than we deserve," Humphrey said. "Everyone deserves to be happy. Especially Pages."

"I thought you were a steward," Susan said dryly. "Demoted so soon?"

Humphrey opened his mouth to reply but for once words failed him.

Chapter 15
The Flanders Mare

January 1540

I loved spending time with the Coopers and at my own manor in Luddington. The manor house was smaller than I had imagined but it was very comfortable. There were two rooms downstairs, one for dining and entertaining and the other a sitting room. Upstairs there were three bedrooms, the largest with a view over a pond to the rear of the house. There was a scullery to prepare food, a stable, various storerooms and a large cottage garden. The manor came complete with a gardener, a stable boy, a cook and a madcap housekeeper who spent most of her time gossiping with Susan.

It was altogether very pleasant.

But I missed the excitement and glamour of the Court.

So it was with mixed feelings that I received a summons from the King early in January, commanding me to return to Greenwich Palace immediately.

I was sad to have to leave this pleasant haven. But I was excited by the summons. Delighted, surprised and intrigued. What could he want with me, so soon after sending me away?

"I expect that the new Queen wants you as a Maid of Honor," Mary said.

Susan gave a sniff. I think she had rather different ideas as to the reason I had been summoned.

"Where we going?" Humphrey asked. "Hampton Court, Whitehall?"

"Greenwich Palace," I said.

The only thing which dampened my pleasure was that my lovely rooms in the Castle were close by yet I would no longer be able to stay there. Never mind, I would be back at Court again. Back at the center of things.

And then I thought, *perhaps I will be able to see Nicholas again.*

The weather was much improved and we made better time than we had on our journey to Stratford. Whether because of this, or my excitement at returning to Court, I felt little fatigue from the tedious days of travel and almost skipped into the Palace.

To my surprise I was not taken to the King's privy chambers upon arrival but led along familiar corridors to the study of the Lord Privy Seal.

The room was dark, darker than I remembered it. It was a dreary, overcast day, and what little light there was had been shut out by a curtain pulled close against the cold. A small fire burned in the grate. It gave little heat and less light, although the scent of it was sweet. Sir Thomas often placed pinecones in his fires, for he loved the smell they gave off as they roasted.

The brightest light came from the candle upon his desk. It was made of finest beeswax, with a good wick well trimmed. Sir Thomas was not getting any younger and his eyes were beginning to lose their sharpness. He had become most particular about his candles. This one cast a strong glow upon his desk and lit up his face as he bent at his correspondence.

"Welcome, Alice," he said dryly. He put down his pen and looked at me. "I am pleased that you were able to return so promptly."

"As am I. It is good to see you, Thomas. I trust you had a pleasant Christmas season."

He smiled and shrugged.

"And how is the King?" I continued. "Is he happy with Anne?"

Even in the dim light I could see the transformation upon the Lord Privy Seal's face. His normal look when we were together was one of wry good humor. Now his face twisted as if he were in pain. He gave a swallow and his hands lifted a little from the desk as if he were at a loss how to answer.

"The King is not happy with the woman from Cleves," came a voice from the darkest corner of the room.

I gasped. I had not realized there was anybody else in the room. Sir Thomas looked even more woeful, a certain sickness about the jowls.

The owner of the voice heaved himself to his feet.

"Your Majesty," I said, rising swiftly and doing a curtsy. I quickly took stock of what I had said to Sir Thomas, fearful that something might have been unfit for the King's ears.

The King lumbered towards us and sank into a chair. The candlelight played upon his features with fits and starts. It gave his face a most alarming aspect: light and shade, present and gone, open and concealed. Very like the man, I realized. Very like indeed.

"The King is not at all happy with the German female," he repeated. He shot Sir Thomas a venomous glance. I had occasionally seen them in fierce debate but never had I seen the King give his counselor such a look before. Almost imperceptibly, Sir Thomas's head bowed. He looked subdued, submissive. Abject.

"I am distressed to hear such a thing, Your Majesty," I said.

"Not as distressed as I am to feel it," he replied.

I said nothing, waiting to hear more.

"I like her not, Alice," he cried. "I like her not at all. That knave Holbein played me false." He thumped his hand upon the table. I felt a sudden panic for my friend Hans.

"He painted Anne to look a handsome woman," the King continued, "a woman pleasant of face and form. She is none of those things. Holbein deceived me with the portrait."

Holbein frequently embellished pictures of the King, but this was never a cause for royal complaint. The artist was most careful to make him look taller, more imposing, more youthful and more vigorous. The mural which Holbein had painted for Whitehall Palace pictured the King, true enough, but without a blemish or hint of weakness. The most accurate thing about the painting was that it caught exactly the King's aggression and prickly need to challenge. The King's potency and power.

"And it was not Holbein alone who betrayed me," he continued with bitter tone. "Lisle, Thomas Seymour, Lord Clifford, even the Lord Admiral. Damn them all. Every last one of them informed me that the German wench was beautiful." He gave a hollow laugh. "Beautiful. She has the face of a horse and the figure of a cow."

He turned towards Sir Thomas, his finger jabbing at his chest. "The face of a horse, Thomas. And what does she smell like?"

Thomas looked like a schoolboy facing the worst of all bullies. "Smell, Your Grace?" he stammered.

"I've told you. I've told you already."

He boxed Thomas on the ear and then turned to me. "She smells of the barnyard, Alice. Of noisome animals, sweltering in the heat. By the gods, the weather's cold enough not to allow for such a stench. Yet she stinks of sweat, rancid flesh and worse."

"She had undergone a long and difficult journey," Thomas whispered.

"Then she should have bathed. She should have made herself clean before she saw me."

"But you met her in surprise, Your Grace. When you appeared to her she did not even know who you were."

"That's another thing, Alice," the King said, choosing to ignore Sir Thomas's words. "I approached her, slipped my arms around her and gave her a kiss. And she had the temerity to push me away and look horrified."

He glared at me, expecting me to answer.

I swallowed nervously, wondering which eggshell path to take.

"That was a most remiss deed," I said. "To push you away and look so ill upon you. Would that Master Holbein had taken a portrait of you to show Anne in Cleves. Then, for certain, she would have realized she was being embraced by her King and not some jackanapes of a courtier."

The King frowned, his lips working in silent mumble. "You think she might not have realized it was me?" he said at last.

"I was not there, Your Grace. But it might perhaps be so."

He picked up a paper knife and weighed it in his hand. Then he looked up and smashed his palm upon the desk.

The candle shook, the room was plunged into a chaos of careering light.

"That might have been so. That I might well concede. But she continues to smell and she remains ugly."

He pointed a finger at Sir Thomas. "You got me into this predicament, Cromwell. You get me out of it before I have to marry her."

Sir Thomas raised his hands in the air, a supplicant. "I am not sure that is possible, Your Majesty."

"Make it possible. And make it quick. I cannot bear to be in her presence."

"I shall try . . ." Thomas began.

"You will not try; you will succeed," the King cried. "God's teeth, your master Wolsey failed to annul my marriage to Catherine of Aragon. Do you remember that, Cromwell? Do you recall?"

How could he fail to recall it? I wondered.

Over the past months, Thomas had spoken much about his old master, Cardinal Wolsey. Wolsey was of common birth yet possessed abilities so stupendous he rose to become the King's most trusted minister. The King would make no decision without him and invariably followed his counsel.

Wolsey served the King well. And he did the same for himself. He was showered with gifts by King and supplicants and became the richest man in England, wealthier than many nobles, wealthy enough to build Hampton Court Palace. It looked like his star would never set.

But when the King, hot for Anne Boleyn, commanded him to find a means to annul his marriage, Wolsey failed. His enemies saw their chance; he was accused of treason, and fell. Most of his friends were swift to desert him. Thomas Cromwell was one of the few who did not.

"I remember the Cardinal's failure like it was yesterday," Thomas answered.

"Yes, Wolsey failed me, Thomas. Even though he was said to be the cleverest man in all Europe. Even though he was a giant compared to you."

He held Thomas's gaze for a terribly long time.

"And do you know why he failed me?" he asked in a voice of ice.

Thomas shook his head.

"Not because of his intelligence, not because of his wisdom, not because of his famous capacity for hard work. No, Wolsey failed me because he chose to. Because he did not agree with what I wanted. Because he no longer felt enough love for me. Nor enough fear."

The only answer was Thomas swallowing.

Then the King turned to me. His face was a mask of cold anger.

"And you, Alice Petherton. Don't presume to disobey my wishes in the future. You will go where I tell you and not sneak off to some place too distant to return within the day."

I nodded my head, too terrified to speak, too terrified to remind him that he had agreed for me to go to Luddington.

"You'll go to Eltham," he continued, "where I can keep closer watch upon you. Where I can have you to hand."

I nodded eagerly. "Of course, Your Majesty." I took a breath. "I trust, I very much hope, that nobody from Court will tell, and that the Lady Anne will not find out I am there."

Thomas looked down at the desk, clearly horrified at my words. He must have felt it too obvious a disagreement, too obvious a challenge.

The King rubbed his nose angrily. "You may be right. My servants are no longer to be trusted." Here he stared at Sir Thomas, whose head sank further still.

"Where do you suggest?" the King asked me. "No doubt you have your answer already framed."

"Perhaps at my manor in Kent," I answered. "Buckland. It is not too far from London for Your Majesty's convenience, but none of my servants there would dream of traveling to London to spread gossip."

The King sniffed and rubbed his nose again.

"Well, Cromwell, what do you say to that?"

Cromwell lifted his head. Already, now that the King had seen fit to ask his advice, a look of relief and hope began to chase away his earlier distress.

"I think it is a very good suggestion, Your Grace. But, as you say, Alice must not leave anywhere without your direct command. She must be available at a moment's notice should you require it."

"Whether I require it or not is no concern of yours. Your only concern is to get me out of marrying the mare from Flanders."

He smashed his fist upon the table once again. "Damn it, man, what are you doing gaping at me like that? You should be working,

working day and night to find a way of getting rid of the monstrosity you've sought to burden me with."

Sir Thomas looked at me with pleading eyes, hoping I would interject.

"It is getting late, Your Grace," I said quietly. "The weather is inclement. I hope you are not thinking of leaving the Palace this afternoon." I paused and gave him a long look. "And if it pleases you I should also like to stay here for the night."

He gazed at me, his eyelids flickering with suspicion. Then he sighed. "You are wise," he said. "Very wise. But I would not have you seen by too many watchful eyes."

"I could go to my old chambers, Your Grace."

He shook his head. "You can stay here in the Palace. I may invite you to sup with me later." Then he gave one of his now-rare captivating smiles.

I could see the relief flood over Sir Thomas. He turned to me with a look which was part gratitude, part wild hope and part abject despair.

I shuddered to see it.

Chapter 16

New Wife, New Queen

The next morning the King changed his mind about my going to Buckland. I had obviously proved much too pleasant company during the night and he wanted me closer at hand than the furthest reaches of Kent.

"I'm being sent to Knole House," I told Sir Thomas later that day.

"Far enough from London to be hid away, but near enough to be spirited back." He nodded sagely. "The King has made a wise choice. It's one of his smaller houses, mansion more than palace, and only twenty miles from Greenwich."

He looked rather better than he had the previous day and I told him so.

"It seems that your company soothed His Majesty's temper," he said.

He touched me briefly on the hand. "I am grateful for that, Alice. And for the fact that you supported me yesterday."

"As much as I dared."

He tilted his head. "That is the most any of us can do."

I sat at his desk even though he had not invited me to. His eyes avoided mine for a moment. Then he looked at me as if he wanted to say more but could not bring himself to ask.

"I have never seen the King so angry," I said.

"Nor me," he said eventually. He gave a huge sigh. A lifetime of weighing his words was not so easily shrugged off, but now it seemed he had made up his mind to unburden himself and the floodgates opened.

"The King is in a rage about Anne," he continued. "He feels that in this matter of the marriage he has been personally attacked. Worse, he feels he has been taken for a fool."

"By you?"

He nodded glumly and pushed his hands through his hair.

"Did you have any idea of her appearance?" I asked.

"None whatsoever. I took Holbein's portrait to be an accurate one. He is usually scrupulous and exact."

"He can flatter," I said. "He has been known to make the King look younger and more regal."

"The council told Holbein not to use such artifice on this occasion. He produced likenesses of a number of princesses, Anne's younger sister included. He performed his task admirably."

"In that case, why does the King think Anne looks so much worse than her portrait?"

Sir Thomas leaned back in his chair and groaned. "The portrait is accurate, face on. There is no disputing that; the likeness is uncanny. But Anne possesses a very large nose. I doubt even King François of France has a longer one. And while it is acceptable for a man to be so endowed, it is, alas, not so for King Henry's bride.

"Holbein realized this and painted Anne full-face rather than in profile. I think he did it partly in order to please the King, but mainly in order to flatter the lady. Hans is ever the gentleman."

I sighed in relief. The blame could not be laid entirely at Holbein's door. He might lose his position as Court Painter, but that would be the worst of his punishment.

"And her odor?" I said. I was almost reluctant to raise the subject but could not control my curiosity. "What of that?"

"She had spent days in travel, crossing choppy seas, and then riding miles on rough and icy roads. She was nervous and ill at ease." He shook his head wearily. "One of her gentlewomen says Anne is given to nervous sweats at such times."

"But she can bathe. You know how much the King values hygiene."

"Apparently the court of Cleves has no such fastidiousness."

"Then somebody needs to tell her of her duties in this regard."

Sir Thomas nodded thoughtfully and scribbled a note upon his papers.

"I think she is a kindly soul," he murmured at last. "And I think she will prove a dutiful wife. All she has to do now is learn English and take a greater interest in books."

"And smell fresher and cut off half her nose," I said.

He groaned and lowered his face to the desk.

"Courage, Sir Thomas," I said. "You have retrieved worse situations before."

He raised his head. "You're right, Alice. Or I hope you are. The King wants me to see if I can revoke this marriage. Alas, even my old master, Wolsey, failed in his attempt to do similar in regard to Queen Catherine."

He pulled out a handkerchief and dabbed around his mouth. It seemed that Anne was not the only one who suffered nervous sweats.

"But the King had the Pope to contend with on that occasion," I said. "He is Pope in his own Kingdom now."

"But an isolated one. He is in a mighty fret about the new friendship between King François and the Emperor Charles. He needs the friendship of the Lutheran Princes, and they will not be happy if he is seen to insult the Duke of Cleves."

I saw now the terrible quandary Sir Thomas had found himself in. He would have to tiptoe his way across quicksand. And do it with the King upon his back, bellowing and beating all the while. My heart went out to him, but I did not doubt that he would find a way through.

"You have your work cut out for you, Sir Thomas, but I know you will be more than equal to it. Go to it with good heart."

"And you go to Knole with equal good heart, Alice. And if the King seeks you out to comfort him, then do your utmost best. For all our sakes."

My first sight of Knole House was enchanting. The snow was thick on the ground and the huge tracts of woodland surrounding it were silent save for the occasional cry of crows. There was a hush about the place very different from the other palaces I had been to.

"It looks beautiful," Sissy said.

"It does," agreed Mary. "It looks like somewhere that fairies might dwell."

"It looks drear and miserable to me," Susan said. "But let's get inside. I'm frozen half to death."

It would be a wonderful place to come with Nicholas, I thought.

As I climbed out of the carriage I glanced up at the array of windows above. Most were filigreed with frost, which meant that the house was cold inside. One wing, however, showed no such sign. The windows were clear and bright lights shone from them. A servant opened the door and bade us welcome.

"I am Robert Bench," he said. "I'm steward here and have been so for forty-one years."

I looked at him in surprise. He did not appear to be such an age. Most men of his years were slumbering in front of fires or sleeping still deeper in their graves. Robert Bench was slim and sprightly with a bright gleam to his eye.

"I was steward for five Archbishops of Canterbury before Thom Cranmer saw fit to give up ownership and pass this house to the King."

He pulled a wry face and gave a conspiratorial wink.

"In truth, wily Thom handed it to the King moments before he was about to demand it. Good dealings for the Archbishop. Bad for us poor servants that were given away, lock, stock and barrel."

He paused and stared at me with pin-sharp eyes. "Do you know the King?" he asked.

I gave him a cool glance. I could not be sure whether his question was innocent or knowing. It seemed that he placed undue emphasis on the word *know*.

"I know him very well indeed." I touched him on the shoulder. "While I stay here it would be best if you say nothing to embarrass yourself or me in relation to the King."

He gave a knowing grin. "Understood, Miss, understood."

"Make sure of it." I hurried along the corridor with Bench struggling to keep up.

The day after arriving at Knole House we heard the church bells from nearby Sevenoaks tolling exuberantly. My friends and I rose from the dining table and opened the window to listen.

A moment later Robert Bench entered the room, bearing a letter.

"It's Tuesday, is it not?" I said to him. "Do the bells in Kent toll on a Tuesday?"

"It's not for any religion," Bench said. "The messenger who brought this letter told me that the King is to wed the German lady today."

He passed me the letter with the Great Seal still affixed. It was from Sir Thomas Cromwell.

I scanned it quickly, reading the unquiet behind my friend's matter-of-fact words. It seemed that he had tried and failed to find a way of stopping the marriage without incurring the direst diplomatic and political damage. The King had finally accepted this with terrible bad grace and Thomas had fallen foul of the King's fiercest rage.

Thomas concluded the letter by asking me to join him in praying that a son would soon be born to Anne. He must have thought that the production of another son was the only thing that would reconcile the King to his new bride. The only thing which would reconcile the King to his chief adviser.

Since the death of my mother, most of my prayers had been but empty words. I neither felt nor believed in what I was asking of God and doubted even more that He would hearken to me.

On this occasion, I resolved, I would pray most dutifully. For the sake of the King, for Anne and for poor Sir Thomas. I would go to the Chapel today and offer up prayers for the birth of a healthy son.

But as the weeks drew on I realized that this was not an event to hold one's breath for. Rumor reached me that the King so loathed his wife that he could not rise to the challenge of having relations with her. They slept in the same bed, it is true. But Anne snored the night away unmolested while Henry chewed on the sheets and damned his fate, his bride, and Cromwell most of all.

The worst of the gossip said that Anne was so innocent she thought she would conceive merely from close proximity to the King. When she was told that somewhat more was required and given all the details, she was said to have turned quite faint.

"I would faint," Susan said, "or cut my throat. How you can bear the King to touch you, Alice, is quite beyond me."

It was beyond me sometimes too. But whenever I was close to him I saw the beauty within the great beast of appetites. I was fond of him, foolish though that might seem. It was something I never admitted to my friends.

I barely even admitted it to myself.

Chapter 17
The King Grows Lustful

March 1540

The news from Court was that for the whole of January and February the King appeared to have reconciled himself to marriage, treating the Queen with the utmost courtesy, encouraging her to learn English, even talking with her once or twice a week.

But I heard from Sir Thomas that behind the facade things were very different.

The King lived in near constant rage and he vented this upon his councillors, poor Thomas most of all. Yet, to my surprise, he seemed to have reserved his most terrible fury for those of his people who had loyally followed his religious reforms most enthusiastically.

I often puzzled over what had prompted his change of heart; perhaps it was his painful leg. Mary believed he had always been less enthusiastic for the new religious ideas than he pretended, using them as a cloak to divorce his first wife and later, to enrich himself beyond belief at the expense of the abbeys and churches. Susan put it down to the fact that he was a monster. I wondered if it was just his way of punishing Thomas Cromwell.

Of all the King's advisers only Archbishop Cranmer was more Protestant than Thomas. Most were lukewarm concerning the new ideas. A few, like the Duke of Norfolk, were opposed. Religion had become a battlefield. And battles cause casualties.

Whatever the reason for the King's backtracking, it astonished and infuriated his Protestant subjects and they debated it in town squares and pulpits. I cared not for all this hot air, but some were willing to face imprisonment or worse for their beliefs.

The King was more than willing to accommodate them. The prisons began to fill up and there was talk of men and women being tortured to confess to goodness knows what.

Thank goodness we're at Knole House, far from Court, I thought. *At least we're safe here from the constant fear and fury.*

The next morning I was summoned to attend the King at Hampton Court Palace.

Despite my misgivings, it was a joy to see the mellow red walls of Hampton Court again.

I had spent much of my time as Maid of Honor there and it had been the first place that I ever had a bedroom of my own. It was tiny, a miniscule room at the turn of the stairs which appeared to have been forgotten by the rest of the Court and servants. Someone once told me that it was a sickroom where people were placed when they seemed a danger to the rest of the Court. It did not worry me in the slightest. My room was my hideaway, my own little palace and home.

I had to move out of there when the King recognized me publicly as his mistress. It was not grand enough for my new position; I moved to a much larger, more splendid suite of rooms.

But it was my little chamber that I always remembered whenever I thought of Hampton Court Palace. My little chamber where I'd been happiest and most at peace.

I had no idea why I had been summoned. I hoped I would get a chance to find out from Sir Thomas before my meeting with the King. Unfortunately, that was not to be the case. As soon as I entered the Palace I was immediately ushered into the King's privy chamber.

He was sitting with his foot upon a settle. He must have been suffering a lot from pain, for it was clear that he had been unable to make his way to the table to dine. His chair was surrounded by half a dozen small tables, each of them with the remnants of his latest meal. It looked like a graveyard after the plague had visited, bones and flesh and skin piled on every plate. I counted the corpses of at least five fowl of various sorts together with assorted animal bones and veritable shoals of fish bones, mussels, clams and oysters.

Oysters. Had he eaten them as an aphrodisiac? Was this the reason I had been summoned to his side?

"I cannot stand her," he bellowed the moment he saw me.

"Who, Your Grace? Who can't you stand?"

"That creature. That simpering, foul, barnyard of a woman."

I smiled gently. "Ah. You're referring to Queen Anne."

"You've heard then? Even in that distant place you've hidden yourself away in?"

Still blaming me for decisions he no longer likes, I thought. But there was no time to consider this. I must try to tame the whirlwind.

"I've heard that she does not please Your Grace," I said. "I am sorry for it."

"Not as sorry as I am, Alice." He bent towards me and I almost reeled from his hot, stinking breath. "Tell me, my dear, am I not a handsome man? Am I not a prince of good looks and good demeanor?"

"You are, Your Grace. None better in all the world."

"Then why am I saddled with Anne? Why am I wedded to a Flanders mare? Why am I yoked to a woman who cannot arouse me to my duty to provide a son for my old age and for the Kingdom?"

"I have heard that she is untutored in the ways of love," I said.

"That's another thing," he cried. But then he fell silent and glared at me with suspicious eyes.

"Anyway," he said quickly, "you'll meet her yourself in a moment. Then you can tell me what you think of her."

He paused and then said, "If you don't already know."

At that moment, the door opened and the Queen of England entered.

She seemed surprised to see her husband with another woman standing by his side. But she quickly recovered and gave me a warm smile.

I scrutinized her swiftly but with complete thoroughness. She looked remarkably like Holbein's painting. Oval face, no skin blemishes, small mouth with thin lips, exquisite eyebrows and deep-set, hooded eyes which definitely made her look either tired or alluring.

And then she turned her face. Ah, the nose. Poor woman.

All this time, the King's eyes were glancing from her face to mine, quick as an archer releases arrows. I had no idea why he was doing so but I thought that it boded no good.

"I do not understand that I have had the pleasure," the Queen said in slow, thick English.

I curtsied. "My name is Alice Petherton, Your Grace."

She smiled for a moment and then the smile was replaced by the smallest of frowns.

So, it seemed that someone had whispered to her about me after all.

She turned to the King. "It is good for you to have such a lovely lady as Fräulein Petherton visit you when you are in pains from your wound."

"You've never met before then?" the King demanded. "You two? You've never met before?"

We shook our heads. The King glared at us once again, suspicion burning deep in his glance. He held my eyes for a moment. I did not blink. He did the same with Anne. Neither did she. I could not imagine what sort of suspicions he was harboring about us.

Then he grunted and pointed to two chairs. "Sit, dear ladies," he said. "I relish your company."

Anne gave a sudden smile and turned towards me with relief and thanks. My heart went out to her. I guessed this was the first time he had given her such a compliment.

The King ordered small beer in deference to the Queen, who preferred it to wine. We sat in the room for an hour, grinding through conversation made slow by Anne's poor English and her evident desire to say only the right thing in front of the King.

It seemed clear to me that she was well aware that the King did not care for her as a wife. Her anxiety to please was sad to observe.

But then I wondered how it might compare to my behavior in his company, or anyone's behavior, come to that. In the King's presence all were eager to please, to flatter and to agree. Few felt the absence of anxiety. My mind thought of every noble and courtier I knew and I amended that statement. *None* felt the absence of anxiety. High or low, those of confident or nervous disposition, everyone trembled in his presence.

After an hour the King turned to the Queen. "Time is passing, Anne," he said. He gave her a pointed look.

She rose immediately and curtsied. "I take my leave," she said. "I hope Your Majesty has a lovely rest for a while."

She glanced at me. I was already on my feet, one step ready to head for the door.

"Not you, Alice," the King said.

I could see the surprise and hurt upon Anne's face. But she hid her emotions in an instant, turned once more to the King and gave him a wide and thoughtful smile. Then she nodded to me and hurried to leave the room.

"Sit," the King told me. "And pass me some wine. I do not care for any more small beer."

He buried his nose in the wine glass and quaffed the contents in one swallow, holding it out for me to fill once more.

"So," he said. "What do you think of her?"

My mind raced. Of late, conversation with him had become like a walk in the deepest of forests. It was so easy to get lost there, so easy to fall prey to wild and savage things.

Best to be honest, I thought, *or relatively so.* Most of his courtiers would have agreed if he said black was white. But his words were too often a trap for the unwary and I'd learnt that it was better to speak my mind rather than dissemble too much. His anger might flare but he'd forget it sooner rather than later.

"I think she is quite pleasant company," I said.

"Yes, but you don't have to try to bed her," he snarled. "She is ugly is she not?"

"As a woman I would not call her ugly." I thought I was on fairly safe ground here. He could not argue with how a woman might judge another of her sex.

"What would you call her then? Beautiful? That's what all my cursed councillors and courtiers said."

"They were, perhaps, being gallant to her and dutiful to you."

"Well it did me no good. It did her a power of good. But not me."

He stuck his lower lip out like a child deprived of a toy. He really did think he was hard done by in the matter of his marriage.

"Come on then," he demanded. "If you do not think her ugly, do you think her beautiful?"

"No, Your Grace. I think she has a homely face, not beautiful, perhaps not even pretty. But it is pleasant enough to look upon and without blemish."

"Without blemish? What about her nose? I could batter down a castle wall with that nose."

I could not help myself; I actually giggled.

The King gave me an astonished glance.

"That is a most amusing comment, Your Grace," I said. Tears had come to my eyes and I dabbed them away with my kerchief.

Then his eyes narrowed, good humor flowed into them and he threw back his head and laughed.

"It is, isn't it?" he said, slapping his leg with pleasure. "Most amusing. I have made you weep with laughter."

His own laughter trickled to a halt and he sighed with pleasure. I looked at him with pity then. I realized that it had been a while since I had seen him enjoy himself so much.

"Your woman's eyes may be right," he said at last. "The more I see of her the less ugly she appears to be. Plain, I think of her now, more often than not."

He took another gulp at his wine. "Plain should not be acceptable for the King of England but it seems that my advisers are intent on making me miserable in this manner."

"Perhaps you will come to think more kindly of her," I said.

"More kindly, yes," he agreed. "But how can I do my husbandly duty when there is nothing about her to excite my passion?"

At that he suddenly leaned forward, his face crammed full with hurt and spite.

"I'm glad that you have not met her before," he said. "I did not want to believe it but I feared it might have been you."

I took his hand. "What do you mean, Your Grace?"

He shook his head, as if he could not believe the thoughts contained there.

"You must understand that Anne is not skilled in the arts of love," he said, picking his words with a care most unusual for him.

I nodded.

"Some even claim she is innocent of all knowledge of the act of procreation. But I am not so sure. She has heavy, drooping breasts, Alice. It's a sure sign of sexual congress, I believe. I am not convinced she is the virgin I'd been promised by her brother."

I thought it wisest not to comment on this, uncertain where his tortuous thoughts might take us.

"But virgin or no, she has no appetite for love. And no skill at it, I warrant." He paused and took another swallow of wine.

"But then, a week ago, she started to use new tricks to try to arouse my manhood." He squeezed my hand here. "The poor fellow has been shy of showing itself to her, dismayed by her looks."

He glanced away and gave a forlorn sigh. Then he turned a gimlet eye upon me.

"I was astonished at her whorish wiles. At first I thought that my suspicions had been correct all along. That she was not a virgin at all but had fornicated with half the men at her brother's court, learning the lewdest tricks.

"But then I bethought me, why now? Why has she decided to use these skills now, when she could have used them from the beginning? Why now, after two months of cold, unstirring nights?

"And then it came to me. She had not learnt these tricks in Cleves. Someone taught her these wiles here. Someone must have told her that she needed to arouse my manhood better, needed to inveigle me into entering her."

"You mean she went to someone for help?" I said.

He shrugged and squeezed my hand tight. Tighter in fact than was comfortable. "I thought for a while, Alice, that it might have been you."

"No, Your Grace, it was not."

I was genuinely horrified by his words. I would never have done such a thing.

"Calm yourself, my darling," he said. "I thought it only for a moment. Doubted you for only an instant. Besides, the fact that you two had never seen each other before this afternoon proves it could not have been you."

So he had doubted for rather more than an instant, I thought. Doubted enough to set up this little masquerade of meeting with the Queen purely to test me.

"And then another thought occurred to me," he said.

If before his voice had been tinged with suspicion, now it dripped with paranoia. "It occurred to me that it was not Anne who sought out advice. That someone in the Court knew I had not been able to perform. And that this someone decided to take steps to help Anne arouse me."

I swallowed hard. Now here was threat indeed.

"And have you any idea who that someone might be?" I asked. If there was such a person.

He gave a shrug. "Who indeed? It could have been any of my loyal servants. It may be that they did it for the best of motives, to help get a second son for the Kingdom.

"It might, however, be that they had their own purposes in mind. To make this farce of a marriage a little less of a failure. To protect their own position, perhaps."

His words hung in the air, an ax held high by the executioner moments before he strikes.

"You cannot mean me, Your Grace?" I whispered.

He looked at me in confusion. "Of course I don't mean you. Don't be such a fool. I mean it will be one of my advisers, one of the men closest to me."

And then it all became clear. He was talking about Thomas Cromwell.

"I have set my hounds to work," he said. "Sir Richard Rich and Thomas Wriothesley. They'll find out the culprit, mark my words."

I'm sure they will, I thought. *Whether innocent or not, they'll find out a victim. I must warn Sir Thomas.*

"Do you have any idea which of your advisers it might be, Your Grace?" I asked tentatively.

He shook his head. "It could be a dozen men. The Duke of Norfolk, perhaps. He would love nothing better than to jest that I am not a lusty lover. Thomas Cromwell, whose idea it was for me to marry the woman. The Duke of Suffolk, out of kindness of his heart and old, old friendship. Even the Frenchman perhaps."

"The Frenchman?" I asked in alarm, thinking of Nicholas. He was the only Frenchman I ever had cause to think about.

"Ambassador Marillac," the King said. "His master would love nothing more than a successful marriage between England and Cleves. It would put the nose of the Emperor quite out of joint."

Relief flooded through me. The King was not suspicious of Nicholas.

"I thought the King of France and the Emperor had lately become friends," I said.

"Oh, you do keep yourself informed, Alice." The King looked at me with a mixture of suspicion and admiration.

"Your Grace's worries are mine."

He gave a curt little laugh. "It seems that the King and Emperor are no longer friends. So François and Marillac now have good cause to wish my wife better educated in life and love so that our marriage becomes a happy and fruitful one."

I was anxious to turn the King's suspicions as far as possible from Sir Thomas and saw my chance.

"It is said that the French are experts in the arts of love," I said.

The King gave me a strange look. "So it is, Alice, so it is." He tugged at his beard in thought. "Perhaps we have the truth of it after all."

He smiled. "And now, talking of the arts of love." He gestured his head towards his bedroom door. "Help me up, my dear. You have been too long a stranger."

"I will remedy that, My Lord," I said.

And remedy it, I did.

Chapter 18
Unattainable

I returned to Knole a week later, quite worn out by my entertainment of the King. Troubled by his wound he might have been, but he could still be aroused to ardor. By me at any rate, if not by his Queen. It had been a demanding time, in many ways. Now for some well-earned peace and quiet. I was relieved when the carriage turned into the drive and Knole House appeared in the distance.

The first occasion I had traveled here had been in the depths of winter. Now it seemed that spring had come early. The sky was clear, a soft and milky blue with only the littlest fluffs of clouds sailing across it.

As I stepped out of the carriage, I turned my face towards the sun. It was shining bravely and I could feel its heat upon my face, a gentle warmth which seemed to reach out to caress me.

Susan and Mary hurried from the house with warm smiles of welcome.

"It's so wonderful to see the sun at last," I said. "I thought this winter would never end."

"It's early yet," said Susan. "Time enough to return to winter's grip."

"Don't be such a killjoy," I said. "I think it will be a beautiful spring."

Sissy glanced up at the sky and gave a deep sniff. "I think you're right, Alice. It will be a lovely spring and a very hot summer."

The door to the house opened and Robert Bench hurried across to welcome us.

"My beautiful young ladies," he cried, kissing my hand and Sissy's, which made her coo with delight.

"Back to join the beautiful old lady that is Knole as she prepares herself for spring." Bench beamed with pleasure and pointed out the daffodils which sprinkled the lawns on either side of the courtyard.

"They're lovely," I said. "Enchanting."

"And in the most sheltered places, wallflowers bloom and roses bud. I think we have a wonderful year ahead of us."

"See," I said to Susan. "You're in a minority."

She shrugged. "For once I'm happy to be in the wrong. I hate the winter." She stared at the flowers. "I wish I could live in Rome or Florence and spend the whole year in warmth and sunshine."

"That's not possible is it, Alice?" Sissy asked. She looked shocked at the very notion.

"It is indeed, Sissy," Bench said. "I accompanied a gaggle of bishops when they went to Rome to argue the case for the King's divorce. Rome is a wonderful place, full of ruins and beautiful nuns."

I rolled my eyes at his words. I had come to learn that there were few women he did not find beguiling.

"Full of ruined nuns if you had got your hands on them, Robert," I said.

He shrugged and gave an enigmatic smile. "You and your young ladies would beautify the city," he said. Sissy giggled and held her hand to her mouth.

"We stayed there four months, Sissy," Bench continued, "throughout the winter. And every day was blessed with sunshine and with warmth. Winter is a stranger in Rome."

"And you will be a stranger to Knole if you don't organize my luggage," I said. I'd had more than enough of old men with too great an interest in love.

He laughed, gave a deep and courtly bow and gestured to servants waiting in the doorway.

"Dinner is ready," he said. "Roast venison from our own forest."

"Lead the way," I said. "I am in need of sustenance."

I spent the afternoon walking around the gardens with Susan and Mary. It was every bit as glorious as Bench had promised. Although still the middle of March it felt more like May. Daffodils dotted the lawns to the south of the House and violets were showing bravely in their beds. The rose bushes which lined the garden walks were indeed displaying tight little buds. I sniffed at them but as yet they had no scent. Catkins quivered in the gentle breeze and several trees were showing the red tips of leaf buds.

Even the insects were fooled by the weather. Caterpillars crawled across leaves, munching as they went, and bees flew hither and thither in search of nectar. A sleepy bumblebee made its slow progress from wallflower to wallflower, hovering above each one before settling a little while for some food.

The trees were loud with the song of birds: doves, thrushes and blackbirds. On the fields beyond the parkland a flock of sheep drifted slowly in search of grass. The new lambs were already plentiful, leaping and bouncing amongst the older animals, who seemed not to even notice them.

"This is paradise," I said. "I never want to leave here."

"Do you prefer it to your castle, Alice?" Sissy asked.

"It wasn't my castle, Sissy. But yes, I much prefer it."

And not only for its beauty. Knole had been chosen because it was far enough from the capital to hide me from prying eyes. If the King wished to see me I would have to go to him. He was too full of state affairs to go to all that trouble more than very occasionally, more than on idle whim. I felt I truly was mistress of Knole House and of myself.

"It's going to be a wonderful year," I said. "Nothing will spoil it, I feel certain."

After breakfast the next day we sat in the morning room, which overlooked the duck pond. Mary was playing on her recorder and Susan studying a book, her brow furrowed in concentration. I had been reading as well—*The Canterbury Tales* by Geoffrey Chaucer. I had stumbled upon it in the library a few weeks before and I was reading it for its description of an equally lovely spring. I felt sure that today's season was more entrancing than that of a hundred or so years previous.

My eyes kept wandering from the page to stare out of the window. Already the duck pond was proving an area of contention. Various wildfowl were niggling at each other for possession and a pair of geese were hurrying towards it. The ducks already on the water eyed them apprehensively, as well they might. The geese were hissing in rage as they marched.

Out of the corner of my eye I saw a horseman cantering down the drive. He turned at the gatehouse and disappeared from view. I wondered idly who it might be—somebody lost no doubt, or a messenger from a nearby town. I felt confident that it would not be a summons from the King. He had only just dismissed me and, besides, he was too busy enjoying himself with sowing dissent between the Emperor and the King of France.

I returned to my book. I read about the Knight and liked him not at all. Too keen to go to war and deal out death, he seemed, and rather tediously prim and proper. I liked his son, the Squire, much better. Equally brave, at least when he was trying to impress the ladies, and full of life and love. It seemed to me that with his handsome looks and skill in dance and song he would make a more amusing companion than his father. And that was leaving aside the fact that he was a passionate lover.

The door was flung open by Robert Bench. Just behind him I glimpsed Sissy, so agitated she was hopping from foot to foot.

"You have a visitor, my lady," Robert said in a grave and suspicious tone. "Not from Court, for he's no Englishman."

He could not say more for Sissy cried out, "It's Mr. Bourbon, Alice. He's come to see you."

My heart became a fluttering bird. Mary ceased her music and Susan put down her book and stared at me openmouthed.

"I will receive him," I heard myself say, and marveled at my words. I heard Susan's intake of breath, a gentle tap as Mary placed her recorder on the table and, louder than these, the excited squeal of Sissy.

Mary put her hand upon my shoulder. "Is this wise?" she said.

"It is not," Susan answered for me.

"Nonetheless," I said, "I will receive him."

Robert Bench stepped into the room. A moment later so did Nicholas Bourbon.

He stared at me in silence and I gazed back at him. He was flushed from riding, his lovely face as rosy as an apple. He seemed thinner than when I had seen him last; it did not suit him and I wondered if he had been ill. I searched his face for signs of weakness and saw that it was shining and intense. He came and knelt upon the floor in front of me and took my hand and kissed it.

"Miss Petherton," he said, "I have come with every haste to see you. I am delighted to find you radiant as a star."

I gave a little gasp. I thought I might expire.

Nicholas took my arm as we stepped out into the garden. Susan and Mary followed behind as chaperones, with Humphrey and Robert further back in case I should have need of strong men to protect me. I had no idea where Sissy was, though I did not doubt that she was close by and watching every move intently. Alone of all my household, she seemed pleased about my visitor.

"This is a beautiful house, Alice," Nicholas said. "Far more suitable for you than the Castle at Greenwich."

"I liked the Castle," I said. "But yes, Knole is more beautiful and I like it better."

We stopped and he sniffed at one of the rosebuds. "No scent," he said thoughtfully. "In France the blooms would be open already and the air heady with perfume."

"Is it warmer in France then?" I asked.

"Much warmer, Alice. More alive and full of joy. England is a realm of gloom and despondency compared."

"You're unkind," I said. "England can be beautiful and joyful."

"Not lately," he said. "And I am not referring only to the weather. I fear the Kingdom is in torment."

I did not answer. I had not really considered this before, but the moment Nicholas said it I realized he was right. People were confused about the religious changes, the Court was in a constant tumult of anxiety, the King's councillors were forever sniping at each other. And the King was acting more arbitrarily with each day. He was an angry bull, pawing at the ground, no one knowing which way he'd charge but sure that charge he would.

Gloom and despondency was right. And torment, probably.

"Let's not talk of such matters," I said, squeezing Nicholas's arm. "Let's enjoy the good weather while we may."

"Alas," he said, "I will not enjoy it much longer in England."

It was as if a hand of ice had seized my heart.

"What do you mean?" I whispered.

"I am to return to France. I will leave in a month or so. The sister of the King requires me to be a tutor to her daughter."

"But you're Elizabeth's tutor," I said.

He shook his head. "The position has not been confirmed by the King. I have spent much time tutoring her but received not one penny for doing so."

"Then I shall ask him," I said. "You must not leave us." I could hear the desperation in my voice. I thought that I might burst into tears at any moment. Although I had not seen Nicholas for months, the thought of him being so far away was painful.

He stopped and kissed the tips of my fingers.

"I have no reason to wish to stay in this miserable country," he said. "Save only one."

"Only one?"

He nodded. "That is you, Alice. You are the only reason."

I did not answer. I could not.

He turned and led me along the path. My mind was in a whirl, thoughts flying like autumn leaves in a gale.

"I am the mistress of the King," I said at last in a small voice.

"I know," he said. "And as such you are unattainable. No matter how much a man may desire you, it is a forlorn desire. You are beyond reach. I have come here to look upon you one last time."

He gave a smile full of sadness, desperation and longing. My legs felt like jelly and I wondered if they would hold me up. I placed my fingers on his lips to silence him.

We strolled and talked together for the rest of the morning and Nicholas dined with us a little after noon. It was a simple enough meal but his presence made it feel like the most wonderful feast I had ever attended. Even the ever-suspicious Susan grew charmed by his wit, his polished manners and his clever conversation.

He told us how there had been trouble between the King of France and the English ambassador, and that the Duke of Norfolk had been sent to Paris to try to make amends. That the Lady Mary had become quite enamored of Duke Philip, who had gone back to Germany anticipating a speedy return for their marriage. That the King's marriage with Anne was still not progressing well. He almost said something further but he stopped himself out of respect for me. No matter how hard Susan pressed him he would not say a word more.

It was late afternoon before he announced that it was time for him to return to London.

I asked my friends to stay inside while we said our good-byes.

I stood beside him in silence. My stomach was churning like a water mill when the river is in spate. My throat felt tight and tiny and I doubted whether I would be able to speak without bursting into tears.

"I don't want you to leave," I said.

He took my hand and stared into my eyes. His were as full of sorrow as I was sure mine were, and full of kindliness and compassion as well. And then I saw something more. His eyes, his wonderful warm eyes, showed that he felt a deep, deep longing for me. He had said as much this morning, but now, just as he was about to depart from my life, his eyes told me even more strongly.

"I don't want to go," he said. "But it would be dangerous for you if I were to stay longer."

He glanced back at the house as if suspecting that the walls had ears. "News would reach the King somehow," he said. "And your position would become fraught. Maybe even perilous."

"I know," I said. "But that does not alter how I feel."

He gave a sad little smile. "Then I must be the stronger of we two. I must leave, Alice. And I must leave right away."

The groom approached with Nicholas's horse. Then he stopped, raising the horse's hoof in order to see it better.

"He's thrown a shoe," the groom said, straightening up. "He can't go anywhere without re-shoeing."

"Then have you another horse I can use?" Nicholas asked.

The groom looked him up and down. "All our horses are palfreys, my lord, suitable for the ladies only. There's none big enough or strong enough to carry you far."

"Then can you shoe my horse?"

The groom shook his head. "The smith in Sevenoaks is dead of the pox so I'll have to send to Tonbridge."

"How long will that take?" Nicholas asked.

"My stable boy can take a pony to fetch the smith. I doubt he'll come here straight away, not with him getting all Sevenoak's customers. It will be close to nightfall I reckon."

I could hardly believe it. "Then you'll have to stay," I said, my heart giddy as a newborn lamb.

Nicholas nodded. "My father was a farrier. If I'd followed his trade I could have shod the beast myself. All I could do was write a poem about the task, not perform it."

"You must be a terrible disappointment to him," I said, jesting.

He smiled. "Not as disappointing as when I tried and failed at the craft. He was relieved when I said I would not be able to follow in his footsteps."

"So am I," I said. "Otherwise I would never have met you."

And with that we returned to the House.

That night I listened until the noises of the House had one by one fallen silent. I felt queasy inside, my stomach cold as a river, my head as hot as coals. My heart trembled as much as the candle flame upon my bedside table.

A breeze sighed through the trees. Somewhere a twig beat upon a window pane: knock-knock, knock-knock. An owl hooted once, twice; then I heard the slow beating of its wings as it swept after some doomed prey.

And then there came a gentle tapping upon the door.

I looked at it in trepidation. It opened and Nicholas Bourbon slipped into the room.

He said not a word and nor did I. I gazed at him as he came and knelt beside my bed.

"I adore you," he said. And he reached out for my hand.

Gently he undid the fastening of my hair and let it cascade upon my shoulders. He kissed me, upon my cheek, upon my neck. And then his lips reached for mine. Oh, how warm and soft and tender they were. I moaned with pleasure and did not care that I did so, that I showed him how much I wanted him.

He pulled away and looked into my eyes.

"Are you sure?" he asked in a whisper.

"I'm sure," I answered.

A little smile glimmered on his lips. He reached out and, with trembling, tentative hands, undid the fastenings of my nightgown.

His fingers were softer than any man's I'd touched. He smoothed the gown along my shoulders and down my arms. I felt him drawing the fabric lower, felt it catch for a moment before he shook it free of my breasts. He took a breath as he beheld them and then he cradled one in his hands, gently and soft.

I sighed as he did so and stared into his eyes, allowing him, asking him. He pulled the nightgown lower, revealing my belly. I moved a little and he slid it over my hips and down my legs. It snagged on my feet and he fumbled for just a moment to free it. And then I was naked before him.

He gazed upon me, his eyes feasting, his lips open in joy and wonder. And then, with one swift movement, he drew his own nightgown above his head and showed himself to me, all naked.

I moaned at the sight of him, at his pleasure and his arousal.

We kissed, deep and long, our tongues making little forays into each other's mouths. He tasted beautiful, his breath sweet and hot.

I reached up and touched his cheek. His beard was soft to the touch, the petal of a rose. My fingers moved across and stroked his lips, exploring their warm softness. And then they were on my lips again. I moaned in ecstasy.

Then his lips journeyed over me. They kissed my neck, my shoulder, along my arm and then my breasts. He was so delicate, so unlike the King. Yet he knew what he was doing, knew what he wanted.

His mouth caressed my nipples and I felt the heat of it make them spring up like flowers in sunshine. I had never known them to grow so large and hard. I thought I would swoon from pleasure.

Then his mouth moved onward, his lips licking at my belly, at my hips, at the crease in my legs. And then he was between my legs, in my most private parts. I groaned aloud, my head moving from side to side, abandoned to my pleasure. How long we remained like that I do not know. I came at last, a long, rippling motion, and then he moved and his face was above me.

I nodded and I felt him enter me. He did it slowly, so slowly I thought I would die of longing. And then he was there, full and hard, filling me up, making us one, making us whole.

He was a graceful lover, moving with my movements, sometimes leading, sometimes following, most times dancing in mutual rhythm, as though we were one person and not two. Even our breath paced together, and our hearts seemed to journey with but one beat.

And then I came again, so low, so deep, so slow and yet intense I thought I'd never want to feel anything else again. It seemed as though I were being drenched in warm honey, from my face to my shoulders, down my breasts and belly, to my aching private parts, my thighs, my feet, my toes.

I heard him come, saw the little smile of content and triumph on his face, felt his spasm and release within me. Saw him close his eyes with pleasure and with release.

He settled closer on me. I felt his chest rising and falling upon my breast.

"I love you," I said.

"And I love you," he echoed.

I burst into tears.

Chapter 19
"What have I done?"

I awoke next morning with the sun shining bright through the casements. A wonderful spring morning, full of joy and promise. But then I sat up in bed, my hands pressed to my breast.

What have I done?

I turned and stared at Nicholas. He was still asleep, his face sweet and untroubled. I watched his naked chest rise and fall with his breath, rise and fall, rise and fall. He looked so beautiful, so wonderful.

What had we done?

I shook him awake. His eyes flickered open and then he saw me. His mouth opened in a smile and he blew a little kiss at me.

"The King," I cried.

He shook his head, still half lost in slumber.

"The King," I repeated. "The King, the King."

He sat up in bed, his eyes now wide open, his face tight with alarm. He looked towards the door.

"No, he's not here," I said. "But if he finds out . . ." I seized his hand, held it so tight I felt the bones shift beneath the flesh.

Nicholas put his hand to my lips, whether to silence me or calm me I do not know.

It could not stop my jabbering thoughts. Some screamed that I was a fool, others told me to hide, some pitied me, some admonished. And in the midst of all this cacophony three figures flickered in and out of consciousness: Nicholas, the King, and Richard Rich.

I thought I would be sick.

"What will we do?" I asked.

Nicholas turned to me as if he could hardly believe my words. He looked every bit as shocked and frightened as I felt.

Then it was as if a sudden thought had struck him.

He kissed my hand. Stared at me searchingly. "We could leave," he said.

"What?"

"We could leave. Now, today. Leave the country. Go to France."

"He'd stop me. The King would stop me."

Nicholas shook his head. "How could he know?"

I began to weep. "He'd know," I said. "He'd know."

I bowed my head. It was all over. Everything was over.

I leapt out of bed, held my hand out towards him. "Come quickly. Be silent. Bring your nightshirt."

Hand in hand we crept down the corridor towards the room which Nicholas had been given for the night. I dreaded to see anybody awake, dreaded to see a servant or Robert Bench. And then a door opened a fraction; a face peered out.

"Go back to bed," I hissed.

Sissy closed the door.

"Can we trust her?" Nicholas whispered.

I nodded.

We hurried along the corridor and into his room.

"We must make the bed look like you've slept in it," I said. "Go, lie in it."

He lay down, while I directed him to roll and stir, to cram the signs of a whole night's sleep into minutes.

I turned and looked around the room. Saw the candle on the bedside table, unlit.

I reached for a flint, lit the wick and watched it catch. "Let it burn halfway," I said. "Have you a book?"

Nicholas gestured towards a chair.

I picked up the book, opened it near the middle and dropped it on the floor. It would look like he'd dropped it as he fell asleep.

"My God," he cried suddenly. "You can't be found in here." He gestured wildly. "And not like this."

I looked down. I was naked. In my terror and haste I had forgotten that I was naked.

He struggled into his own nightshirt, his fingers clumsy with fear and haste.

"You must go," he said.

"Like this?"

He nodded. "You must be quick."

I took a step towards the door and froze. Footsteps pattered in the corridor outside, came close and then stopped. I held my breath. The handle turned and the door opened. A hand reached in, held out something for me. My nightdress.

I snatched it, threw it on and stepped out into the corridor. Sissy was already at her room and slipped inside, giving me only the swiftest glance.

I almost wept in relief and gratitude.

I risked one more glance at Nicholas and then hurried along to my own room.

I closed the door behind me, closed my eyes. My heart was hammering, my arms and legs shaking.

I took a step towards the bed, slumped down upon it. At length my hand reached out, touched the spot where my love had slept. It still felt a little warm, or perhaps it was only my imagination. But we had loved, we had loved, and I sighed.

Nicholas left as soon as his horse was shod. It was a grievous parting but we both knew it would have been perilous for him to stay longer.

I then had no word or sight of him for eight days, whereupon I received a letter from him. It was friendly and warm, but contained no intimacies. That would have been too great a risk for both of us. I cherished the letter and dreamed of a time when we might be together once again. And I made sure that the letter was very well hidden.

Nicholas did not mention returning to France and I became hopeful that he would be able to stay as tutor to Princess Elizabeth and ignore the summons of the French King.

I tried to banish such hopes from my mind, fearing that they were hopeless and would never come to pass.

I wrote back immediately. Wished him well in his endeavors and made it clear that this letter would be an end to our correspondence. I hoped that he would understand the reason but worried that he might not. Late one night, in great distress, I burned the letter he had sent to me, sitting up until the last fragment had been consumed. I knew then that I would never see him again.

Chapter 20
A Sketch of Katheryn Howard

April 1540

On the eighteenth of April a familiar figure arrived at Knole. It was Hans Holbein, leading a string of mules laden with easels, wooden panels and paint.

I was delighted to see him and ordered the servants to make ready a room. He was less interested in where he was going to sleep than in where he was going to paint. Robert Bench listened to his requirements—a room with large windows, preferably facing north—and led us to a bright chamber overlooking the gardens.

"This will do well," Holbein said, giving Bench a gruff nod in thanks.

"Now that you're happy, let us go and dine," I said. "Robert, please arrange for a place at table for Herr Holbein."

I was just about to follow Bench from the room when Hans placed a hand on my arm.

"Before we join your friends," he said, "I have a gift for you. From a mutual friend."

He laid a large leather wallet on the table and pulled out a sketch on a piece of pink paper.

It was a portrait of Nicholas. I picked it up with the utmost care and gazed upon it. My heart fluttered wildly and I thought I might weep with joy. It was wonderful. It was of his face, a side profile, and it was beautiful. Hans had captured the image of my love so well I might have been looking at him in the flesh.

"It is for you," he said. "I will, one day, complete a portrait of him."

"I had no idea that you knew each other," I said. I reached out and touched the image, as if I were touching his soft skin.

"We met when Nicholas came to England some years ago. We have remained good friends since."

I bent my head and almost kissed the portrait but, just in time, pretended that I was merely looking at it more closely. Perhaps not quite in time, for Holbein chuckled with good humor. I cursed myself for my carelessness.

But then he touched me gently on the hand.

"I gave you this in secret," he said. "I think it should remain a secret. Nobody else must know."

He did not need to tell me this. I recalled the fact that I had burnt the letter Nicholas sent me. I hoped, not for the first time, that he had done the same with mine.

"And you will keep it secret?" I asked.

"People used to go to priests to tell their sins and woes," Hans said. "Nowadays great men dare not do so. But when they sit for me they forget themselves. They talk, they muse, they unburden their hearts." He patted his chest. "I have more secrets locked within than I dare to tell you. Fear not for yours, Alice."

I stared at him, wondering just how much he knew. I was tempted to inquire but thought it best not to. Some things are too dangerous to share. Nicholas trusted Hans. Whether I chose to or not, I would have to do the same.

Master Holbein had been drawing all morning and I was getting stiff. He had dawdled and achieved little when he first started to sketch me back in December, but now that April was here he seemed to be charged with new energy. I wondered if this enthusiasm to finish stemmed from him or from the King. Though why the King would want my portrait painted so swiftly was beyond me.

"It's because he is still fond of you," Hans said.

"But he's married," I said. "He won't be able to display a portrait of me now."

Hans laughed. "He is married for the moment. But he is desperately seeking for ways to end the contract. Our poor friend Thomas Cromwell is daily cudgeled and cursed into finding a way of dispensing with the Queen."

Not dispensed with fatally, I hoped. A divorce, a settlement and then Anne could safely return to Cleves.

I gave a miserable sigh. The fact that the King wanted my portrait finished suggested that he intended to take me back once he had ended the marriage with Anne. Only a few months ago I would have been sanguine about this, perhaps even pleased. But not now. Not since Nicholas. It would feel like a betrayal. Of him and of myself.

I wondered what Nicholas would think about it. I bit my lip. Part of me dreamed that he would throw all caution to the wind, gallop to Knole and forbid me. But, alas, such brave romance is folly in these days. And above all, Nicholas was not a fool.

Holbein's voice interrupted my thoughts. "I've been engaged to paint a portrait of one of the Howard litter."

"And who hired you to do this?" I asked, although I was not in the slightest bit interested.

"The Duke of Norfolk."

My ears pricked up at this news. Thomas had written only this week to say that the Duke had inquired about my health. I found this astonishing, and somewhat worrying.

"One of the Duke's litter?" I asked in a voice I tried to make disinterested. "Which one?"

"This one." Hans pushed a sketchbook across the table to me. It was of a young woman, or more accurately a child. She was a pretty little thing with a turned-up nose and sleepy-looking eyes. It looked as if she was desperate for her bed, or had just climbed out of one. A sudden feeling of disquiet came to me.

"She's almost as much trouble to paint as you are," Holbein said. "A fidgety, impertinent little madam. She squirms in her seat and when I ask her to sit still she goes into a prodigious sulk." He stuck his bottom lip out. "Like this. What do you call it? A bout?"

"A pout. But I've never seen one quite as horrible as yours."

He chuckled. "A pout. She does it all the time. But then the pout stops being childish and becomes something more."

"What do you mean?"

He shrugged. "It is, perhaps, not wisdom to say."

I looked at him thoughtfully, intrigued by his words.

I picked up the sketch once again. "One of the Howard girls?" I said. "Which one in particular?"

"One of the Duke's nieces. Katheryn, she's called."

"I've never seen or heard of her."

Holbein came and stared at the picture. "That's not to be wondered at. Her father was Edmund, a wastrel so dire he was scorned and spurned by the rest of the Howards. If Baron Cromwell had not secured him a post as controller of Calais he'd no doubt have spent his days wallowing in the gutter."

"Edmund Howard," I said. "I've heard of him. As I recall the King did not much like him."

"Little wonder," Holbein said with a snort. "The very air he breathed was wasted on him. Coins slipped through his fingers and reputation through his arse. He was so impoverished he had to farm out some of his litter to the Dowager Duchess." He tapped the sketch. "This one included."

"Poor child," I said. It must have been awful to have been torn from her family like that. "I hear that the household of the Duchess was not the most fitting of places for young people."

Holbein laughed. "Do not be too sorry for the girl, Alice. She took full advantage of the fact that the Duchess did not give a fig for her wards."

I glanced at Katheryn's picture, wondering in what manner she had taken such advantage. There was something rather willful about the set of her chin. Again I felt a feeling of disquiet come over me. But I could not think what it might portend.

"You're right, Hans," I said. "She does have an impertinent look."

"Not a shred of brains but a certain low cunning. And most of that between her legs."

I looked at him in surprise. "But how old is she?"

"Fifteen years, so I hear; perhaps only fourteen. But she is more worldly-wise than a woman of twice her age."

Holbein was as adept at mastering his own face as he was of mastering pen and brush. Most of the time he wore it bland and composed, presumably so as not to appear to be judging the dangerous men he was painting. His face was just as bland now. Except for his eyes. They were twinkling, wearing a knowing and amused glint. He would rarely volunteer any information which was very dangerous, but he loved to hint at scandal.

"Why did the Duke commission you to paint her?" I asked.

"I'm sure we will find out soon enough."

I'm certain we will, I thought. It was clear that the King had no further interest in or use for Queen Anne. I daily expected him to summon me back to Court, but so far no summons had come.

Perhaps this little minx, Katheryn Howard, was the reason.

In that instant I understood why Norfolk had commissioned the portrait of his niece. He was planning to use her for his own ends. She was a jewel put on a table to attract the King's greedy soul. Or a piece of meat to feed to his appetite. The poor child.

But why on earth was the Duke tempting the King with this piece of bait?

And then it came to me. Norfolk had always disliked me. I was not family and not in his control. And I was also the friend of his arch-rival, Thomas Cromwell. Perhaps he feared that some of the words I whispered in the King's ear had been dictated by Thomas.

So now he meant Katheryn to supplant me, to become the King's new mistress.

To my utter surprise I felt a little twinge of jealousy. It lay curled in my mind like a worm on fresh-dug soil. I tried to shoo the thought away. After all, there was no reason for me to be concerned at this news. Being Henry's mistress was certainly no great pleasure.

I had embarked upon the path only to save myself from Sir Richard Rich but soon found out that the King's love was far more dangerous. The peril had increased of late, as the pain in his leg grew insupportable and his health declined. Poor man; the only features which flourished now were his greed and his temper. Both were growing monstrous, both seemed barely within his control.

I almost pitied Katheryn. I felt certain that her uncle would feel no such emotion.

After all, he had played this game before with another niece, Anne Boleyn.

It had done him no good. Anne did not feel beholden to any man, and Norfolk found himself the suitor of his niece rather than her master.

Surely the Duke realized this? Surely he realized that for Katheryn to be the King's mistress was a game not worth the candle? Could there be something else? Could he have a deeper, darker purpose?

I found myself tapping my fingers upon my chin, my thoughts darting and delving. Who had mentioned me tapping like this when deep in thought? Oh yes, Sir Thomas. How would Sir Thomas react to the news of Norfolk's plan?

The breath caught in my throat. *Perhaps this is the reason. Perhaps Norfolk means to destroy Thomas.*

My friend's influence was suffering because of the Cleves marriage. Norfolk must believe that now he had the opportunity to vanquish him. And I saw now how he planned to do it.

Having this chit of a child replace me as mistress was not Norfolk's plan at all. This was not prize enough for that spider of a man. He meant to throw the dice a second time, to repeat history.

He intended to replace an unloved Queen with one of his own choosing. Katheryn Howard.

I hastily put the sketch of Katheryn back on the table.

What would happen to Sir Thomas if that were to happen?

I shook my head. I could not believe that Sir Thomas was in danger of eclipse. He might be suffering the anger of the King, but that would pass. He was far too useful, far too able and valuable. And besides, the King felt too much respect for Thomas's intellect and loyalty.

A knock came on the door and Humphrey entered.

"Sorry to disturb you, Alice," he said, "but I thought you might want to hear the news."

My heart leapt to my mouth. I gave a quick glance at Holbein, indicating to Humphrey that I might want to hear it in private.

"Master Holbein will want to hear as well," Humphrey said.

"Very well," I said slowly.

"It's about Sir Thomas Cromwell."

Holbein put down his brush. We were both of us in debt to the Lord Privy Seal and both counted him as our friend.

"What has happened to Sir Thomas?" I asked in as level a voice as I could manage.

"He ain't Sir Thomas any longer."

My hand went to my mouth. So my fears were justified after all. He'd been stripped of his honors.

"Everyone's talking about it," Humphrey continued. "The King has made Sir Thomas an earl. The Earl of Essex."

I took a step towards him. "Are you sure?"

"A messenger came from Sir Thomas just this minute." He passed me a document.

Holbein came and looked over my shoulder as I read it. Humphrey was right. The King had made Sir Thomas an earl. Not only that, but he had promoted him to the post of Lord High Chamberlain.

"And I thought he had fallen out of favor," Holbein murmured.

"As did I. As did Sir Thomas himself."

I read the document again, wondering at the news. Thomas had written the letter in his own hand. I could read the exhilaration and joy in his script. I could almost smell the palpable sense of relief.

"An earl," I said.

"It is a great honor, yes?" Holbein said.

"A very great honor. Especially for a man of Sir Thomas's background. His father was a rogue, a man who kept an inn and was often in trouble with the law."

Holbein frowned. "Strange, therefore, that his son has often destroyed his enemies by use of that instrument."

"Ale or the law?" I said with a light laugh. "Let us toast the one with the other."

Although, in these dark days it appeared that only the liquid still retained its power and majesty. The law had been trampled in the dirt.

Chapter 21
"Come with me"

May 1540

There was much for me to enjoy about my manor in Buckland.

The King had sent me here at the end of April. I wondered if it was so that he could move Katheryn Howard into Knole in my place. I could not quite make up my mind how I felt about that.

No matter. My friends and I celebrated my birthday in good fashion. I was twenty years of age. No longer the mistress of a castle but mistress of a pretty little home.

Buckland was as lovely as anywhere I could imagine.

It was pleasantly situated in a little valley with a river flowing to the sea only a mile or so distant. On a clear day I could see Dover Castle on its hill. Sometimes I would walk upon the Downs and gaze over the channel towards France. Sometimes tears would form. If only I could go with Nicholas to his home. But it could never be.

The farm was large and prosperous, with a herd of placid cows, pigs roaming in dense mixed forest, acres of land under plough and orchard after orchard of fruit trees: apples, pears and quinces. There were beds of strawberries and greengages and, on a slope which caught the best of the sun, even a crop of hardy grapes. Surrounding the farmyard were neat cottage gardens rich with vegetables: onions, carrots, cabbages and kale. Blackberry bushes scrambled up the walls of outbuildings, and the beds close to the house overflowed with flowers.

I grew to adore this paradise and should have been happy as any creature on God's earth. But in truth I was not content. I might have been if Nicholas had been here but this seemed next to impossible.

And, to my continual amazement, I missed the King. Or, to put it more exactly, I missed the thrill of being summoned by the King.

But most of all I missed the Court: the glamour, the ostentation, the sheer excitement. It was a bear pit where good men fell and rogues were raised up in their place, a place of masquerade where nothing was as it seemed on the surface. It was a carnival of fools and I was fool enough to miss it.

May was glorious but I did not enjoy it as I should have. I prayed for something exciting to happen, anything to break up the serene, dull days.

Towards the middle of the month I watched as a horse came trotting up the path towards me. I blinked in surprise and ran out of the door.

"Nicholas," I cried. "Oh Nicholas."

His face was beaming. He leapt off his horse and gathered me in his arms.

He held me close but I held him closer, clinging on to him like I had never done with anybody before. I could feel the rise and fall of his chest against mine. I did not want to move ever again.

"What are you doing here?" I asked.

He did not answer for a moment. My heart began to hammer ever more furiously.

"I am heading for Dover," he answered. "I am returning to France."

My joy at seeing him vanished as fast as rain on parched earth. I did not answer for a moment, could not frame the words. I pulled away from his grasp, glanced up at his face.

"So you are going to be the tutor of King François's niece?"

He kissed me on the forehead. "It is not a summons I dare refuse."

My hand dropped from his arm. "Of course not." I could hear how dead my words were.

The silence grew intolerable. At length he leaned towards me, his voice low. "Your friends have seen us."

"Let them," I said. "I do not care."

"But I do," he said.

"No word of your being here will get out," I said. I could barely hide the desperation in my voice.

"You think that but you don't know for certain." He tilted my chin and looked into my eyes. "Not for certain?"

I shook my head miserably and cast my eyes to the ground.

"So," he continued, "today is but a farewell. I could not pass by without seeing you once again. But I dare not stay. It is unwise. It is unsafe."

I swallowed hard and did not answer.

He took a careful look at the house and then bent and kissed me swiftly on the lips. Before I could say anything he stepped away and climbed back upon his horse.

I could barely see him through my tears but I watched him until he disappeared from view.

I heard a footfall behind me.

"What was that all about?" Susan asked.

"He came to say good-bye. To say good-bye forever."

She pulled me to her, held me tight, so very tight. And I sobbed in her arms.

I could not sleep that night. My mind was in turmoil. I went over my meeting with Nicholas, over his words, saw once more the folly of all my doings with men. I was raw with pain, with doubt and with self-recrimination. I could no longer cry; I had run dry the well of my tears. I could barely breathe, doubted I could live.

And then the casement of my window moved. It opened quietly and a figure clambered in.

"Alice," Nicholas whispered.

I stared at him in disbelief. Shook my head, as if I were seeing a ghost.

"You did not really think I could go without spending one last night with you?" he asked.

I could not answer.

He took me in his arms, kissed me hard upon the lips. "I could not risk staying longer this morning. It was too dangerous."

I pulled him closer to me. Pulled him down upon me.

Later, when we were silent and content, I leaned up on one elbow and looked into his face.

"How did you know which was my room?" I asked.

"Susan gestured towards this window," he answered. "As I climbed onto my horse. I took a guess that she was not inviting me to visit her tonight."

Thank you, Susan, I breathed silently. *Thank you.*

"Come with me," Nicholas said when we woke the next morning.

I gazed at him in silence, barely able to understand his words.

He sat up in bed and took my hands in his. "Come with me, my darling."

I shook my head. "I don't understand."

He gave a little rueful smile and tilted his head to one side.

"You're teasing me now."

"No, I'm not. I don't understand what you mean."

"Come with me. To France."

I thought of all the times I had walked on the Downs and gazed across the sea to the coastline opposite. I remembered all my dreams of being with him, my hopes, my fantasies.

I held my hand to my breast. "I cannot," I said.

He frowned; a look of doubt clouded his face. My heart ached at the sight of it.

"You cannot?" His voice took on an edge I had never heard before. A tone I never thought I would have heard from him.

I shook my head. Tears filled my eyes.

"I am the King's mistress."

He shrugged. "Then stop being his mistress. Come with me to France."

I closed my eyes and felt the tears squeeze through my lids.

"Oh, how I would love that, Nicholas. I cannot tell you how much I would love that."

"Then do it," he cried. "For God's pity, woman, I know he has not asked for you in months. In any case, there is rumor that he is besotted with the young Howard girl."

I felt him move closer to me, felt his arms encircle me and hold me tight.

"I dare not," I said at last. "Even so, I dare not."

He pulled away.

"Dare not?" His face looked confused; his voice sounded full of doubt.

"Dare not," I said. "The King is an angry and dangerous man. Even if he has lost interest in me, he would never forgive the slight to him. He would hunt me down. Wherever I went."

"And do what?"

I shook my head. "I don't know."

The tears flooded from my eyes then and I threw myself into his arms. But even as I did so I felt him draw back a little.

Oh no, I thought, *don't do this. Be strong for me, please. Be stronger than this.*

He unlocked himself from my arms, placed his hands upon my shoulders and stared into my eyes.

"You truly believe this, Alice? You believe that King Henry would be so angry he would send men to hunt you down?"

I nodded.

Nicholas glanced away, looked at the window, looked at the door.

Ask me again, I pleaded in my head. *Ask me again.*

But he did not.

Instead he bent his head to his hand. I saw his fingers slowly wiping his brow, as if he were sifting his thoughts like so much chaff and grain.

Then he looked up at me.

"I meant it," he said. "I hoped you would come with me. I meant what I said."

But you mean it no longer, I wanted to say. But the words were too painful, too cruel for me to utter.

"I know you did," I said at last. And I thought my heart would crack.

Chapter 22
The Portrait

Nicholas left for France within the hour. I knew this was the safe, sensible thing to do. But it hurt terribly. I tried to manage my disappointment and pain but I could not. He barely noticed my reaction, it seemed. Or perhaps he chose to disguise it. Yes, it would be better if that were the reason.

I spent the rest of the week by myself, shunning my friends, nursing my grief. I took solace by taking solitary walks in the woods or by the stream that ran along the garden. Butterflies often followed me and I hoped that they were the fairies that my young friend Lucy Burton so believed in. Keeping me company, watching over me. Comforting me in my aching, ceaseless hurt.

The month of May, my birthday month, which had opened so fresh and vibrant, now seemed the stalest, cruelest, most wearisome of any month in the year. I was glad to see it draw to a close. I hoped that June at least would bring me some little pleasure.

"Master Holbein is here," Sissy cried, rushing into my chamber one afternoon. Her face was glowing with excitement. "He's got your picture, Alice."

I looked at her in surprise. My picture. The last time I had sat for him had been at Knole in April. So much had happened in the last few months that I had forgotten all about it.

"Where is he?" I asked.

"He's in the sitting room setting up the picture. Humphrey's helping him."

My heart was in my mouth. Now that he had brought it I wished to see what he had painted. Master Holbein was the most famous painter in England, perhaps in the world. I had seen many of his works and marveled at how accurate they were. He caught his subjects exactly. Every feature, every shape and shade of color, every beautiful aspect and every ugly one.

And he seemed to capture more. He seemed to find the essence of the person he had painted, some indefinable core and truth about them. It was as if he saw their outward body and, at the same time, their inmost soul.

I ran my fingers through my hair and got to my feet. Susan and Mary hurried to my side. They seemed as keen as I to see the painting.

I led the way into the sitting room. Master Holbein stood by an easel which held a picture, for the moment covered with a linen cloth. He nodded gravely when I approached.

"You've finished it?" I said.

"A while ago. I would have preferred to have you sit for me while I completed the finishing touches. But I had plenty of sketches to work from. And my inner eye." Here he tapped the middle of his forehead.

"I did not think the King would command that you finish it," I said. "Not now that he is married." I did not add, *and now that he has taken a new mistress.*

"He didn't. And nor did he pay me."

I was surprised at his words. Surely he hadn't completed the portrait at his own cost?

"Sir Thomas Cromwell paid for me to complete it," he said. "He told me that if you had no use for it I was to give it to him."

"Well let me look then," I said. Now that the moment had come I felt oddly nervous and wanted to get it over and done with.

"Don't forget that the sitter is never used to seeing herself like this," Holbein said. "Most people's mirrors are not of good quality, and when a person looks in one they always compose their features in a way quite unnatural."

"So this portrait is more natural? More lifelike?"

"It is as I saw you," he said.

He pulled off the cover and revealed the picture.

I gasped in surprise.

I could see that it was me. But I did not like it. Not one little bit. I peered closer, my eyes devouring the features greedily. My face appeared to be much more serious than I ever felt, my features set and stiff. It was as if I were dissatisfied with the world. Almost as if I was sneering at it.

"You are not pleased?" Holbein asked.

"I don't know what to say," I answered at last. "I can see the likeness; I can see it very well." I stepped closer and spoke almost to the painting rather than to him. "It's just that I didn't think I looked like this."

"It is to the life," he said, his tone a little injured, a little defensive. "Hans Holbein is famed for painting to the life."

"I do not doubt it, Hans, my friend." I placed my hand lightly on his arm. "It's just that I'm a little surprised at how I look."

"I warned you." He stepped beside me and scrutinized his work. "It is accurate," he said in a voice now thoughtful and reflective. "To the life."

I gnawed my lip.

"How does it look to you?" I asked my friends.

For a while no one answered.

Mary spoke eventually, and when she did she sounded thoughtful and hesitant.

"It is very like you, Alice," she said. "Master Holbein has caught every one of your features remarkably." She stepped closer and peered at the painting. "Remarkably."

Despite her words she did not seem at all impressed.

I glanced at Holbein. He was watching us all in silence, offering no further comment of his own.

"What do you others think?" I asked. I tried to sound lighthearted. "Sissy?"

Sissy frowned. "It's nice, miss," she said. "And Master Holbein has got lots of you right, lots of you. It's just . . ." She faltered a little.

"Just what?"

She took a deep breath. "It's just that you look less friendly than you really are, less jolly. More, more . . ." She fell silent and gave me a pained look.

"More high-and-mighty," Humphrey said. "Yeah. More high-and-mighty."

I turned to him in something close to horror. This was not a phrase he ever used as a compliment.

"You see, miss," Sissy hurried to say. "When I look at you, in your skin, I see a princess. But in the painting you look like a queen."

"A queen?" I said.

My hand darted to my neck as it always did, involuntarily, when I was compared to a queen. *I must stop doing this*, I thought. *It must make me look as alarmed as I feel.*

"A queen?" I repeated. I glanced at Holbein, who shrugged and then gave a little nod.

"What do you think, Susan?" I asked.

Susan walked towards the painting and seemed almost to square up to it, as if ready for an argument or confrontation.

"Everyone's right," she said. "As Mary said, every feature is painted with the greatest accuracy. And Humphrey and Sissy are right as well."

"To say I'm like a queen?" I said, dismayed. "High-and-mighty?"

She turned to me and nodded. "Haughty and disdainful," she said. "Implacable. Very like a queen."

"Oh, my God," I cried, my hand to my mouth.

"Well you asked," she said.

I turned from her to my portrait. I stared at it for a while longer, stared at it with growing despair.

"I'm not disappointed at what any of you say," I said at last, forcing the words from my mouth. "Nor at what Master Holbein has painted. I'm disappointed with myself."

I turned and stared out of the window. If I were to put words to my appearance in the portrait I might have said distant and aloof. But high-and-mighty? Haughty and implacable?

I felt a little inward shudder.

Silence settled upon the room. Out of the corner of my eye I could see that none of my friends were looking at the picture. Instead they glanced nervously amongst themselves. I turned once again to look at the painting. To see how others saw me.

"It is extremely accurate," Holbein said, breaking the silence at last. "And you will recall that I said you were hard to capture." He stepped very close to his creation and peered at it before turning to me with a little shrug. "I have caught you, Alice, I do not doubt it. But I have not captured you."

I felt the tears begin to form in my eyes.

"You look very pretty," Mary said in a tone a mother might use to console a bitterly disappointed child.

"Thank you," I said. And I fled from the room.

Chapter 23
Ten Fingers, Twenty Pies

June 1540

It was on the first Sunday of June that I received the letter from Sir Thomas. *It's a strange letter*, I thought, as I read it for the twentieth time. And not just because of the surprising request with which the letter concluded. The request to see me.

The letter appeared full of joy at his recent elevation to the Earldom of Essex. "I am quite restored to the King's favor," he wrote. "I am the indispensable man." I could almost see the twinkle in his eye, and the air of smug self-satisfaction.

Yet it seemed to me that his joy had something excessive about it. It seemed too feverish, too hectic, too ardent.

I tried to dismiss the thought from my head. After all, it was no wonder that he reacted with such delight to his return to Royal favor. He was devoted to the King, like a dog. He had been wounded by Henry's recent cooling towards him and had mooned around Court like a rejected cur. Now he was back in the sun again, it was understandable for him to be full of joy and frolics.

And yet.

And yet there was something febrile about the letter. As if the hound, though restored to his master's favor, still feared that a rival was biding in the kennels.

I had no such fears. There were rumors that the King had become besotted with the little Howard trollop. I had last seen him in the middle of March. He had been demanding and passionate in bed on that occasion. But since then I had heard not a word from him. Sir Thomas was not the only one that the King could pick up and discard on a whim, willy-nilly.

I heard that the King's ardor for his new toy had waxed prodigious with the coming of spring, an ardor fed and watered most assiduously by the Duke of Norfolk.

I wondered how Queen Anne felt about it. How she dealt with the insult.

As for me I was, in the main, heartily relieved. I had grown frightened of Henry's eternal foul temper and his black suspicions. Only two short years ago he had seemed a different man, a younger man, sometimes even a kindly one.

I chose to believe it was the terrible wound in his leg which had changed him. He consoled himself with wine and food. And me, of course.

On some occasions even the act of love had appeared a burden to him. In bed as much as in the field he wanted to hunt but feared he could not exert himself to the chase. It had taken all my wiles to arouse him then. And on the last few nights I spent with him I was dismayed at what I had to do to satisfy him.

Yet, sometimes, just sometimes, his blackness seemed to leave and he became more like the man he'd been when first we met. Prickly, selfish, demanding, but also with a certain fleeting tenderness. I was fond of him on these occasions, more fond than I cared to be.

But then his leg would cause him grief once more and the vileness would return with renewed strength.

He once confided in me that he suspected the wound was poisoned, that Anne Boleyn had used some necromancer's art to inflict a slow and hideous death upon him. I had helped him dismiss these strange suspicions soon enough. But now I began to wonder about them myself.

It was as if his heart and soul were being poisoned by the suppurating wound in his leg. Poor man. Poor King. Poor England.

And poor little Katheryn Howard.

I dismissed all concern for her from my mind. From what I gathered she was well able to look after herself.

Or perhaps she wasn't. Perhaps, in fact, this was the meaning for Thomas's request.

My bedroom door was flung open and Sissy hurried in. "Is it true, Alice? Are we going back to Court?"

"This very day. Although I've not been summoned by the King but by the Lord High Chamberlain."

She frowned.

"Sir Thomas Cromwell," I said. "Or should I say the Earl of Essex."

"Of course. I'd forgot his new titles."

"I'm sure you're the only one who has," I said. "I think Sir Thomas's elevation has put many a nose out of joint."

If there was one man in the Kingdom who would be reviled for receiving such honors, it was Thomas Cromwell. And if there was one man who deserved it most for stalwart service to the King, then it was him also. I smiled to myself.

Thomas Cromwell. Ten fingers, twenty pies. No, fifty pies more like, and with his fingers in every one of them, usually without leaving the slightest trace.

We arrived at Whitehall Palace later that day. I traveled there with only Humphrey and Sissy to do me service. Susan had sulked about being left behind. She had no love of the Court but an insatiable desire for gossip. Mary had been quite content to stay at Buckland.

I was ushered into Sir Thomas's office. He leapt out of his seat and clasped me by the hands.

"I am so glad you've come," he said.

I blinked as I looked at him. I had never seen his face so animated.

"A mighty blow has been struck against Gardiner," he said, rubbing his hands with delight.

"Bishop Gardiner?"

The two men were bitter enemies and had given up even the pretense of smiling upon each other with civility.

"A few days ago," Thomas said, "Gardiner's crony, the Bishop of Chichester, was given a marvelous promotion and the two fools celebrated this proof of their ascent in the King's favor."

Thomas chuckled before continuing. "Two hours later, Chichester was thrown into the Tower, accused of treason."

I looked aghast at Sir Thomas. Not at the story, for such callous cruelty had become more common of late. I was aghast at my friend's delight at the news. He had never been a man to pause in dealing out justice or injustice on behalf of the King. But to my knowledge he had never before taken such unbridled delight in it.

"Why are you so pleased?" I asked.

"Because they've been defeated. And because they were first given to believe that they had secured the victory."

I poured myself a cup of wine, mulling over his words.

"I can understand your pleasure at the defeat of your foes," I said quietly. "But I cannot understand your delight at how they had been duped. At how they had been exalted one minute and damned the next."

He shrugged in a casual manner.

Who had duped them, I wondered, *the King or Thomas?* I would never know, of course. But as I pondered this a terrible chill crept over my skin. Like someone walking over my grave.

I looked at Thomas.

"Is this the only reason you have summoned me?" I asked. "To tell me of the defeat of Bishop Gardiner?"

"No, no, my dear. I am holding a feast to celebrate my elevation to the Earldom. I would have you host it. You'll stay here until then, for the King has allowed me to hold the feast here in Whitehall. Another signal honor."

I looked at him in astonishment.

"Host it?" I said. "And what does the King think of this?"

"He did not seem to care much one way or the other."

I did not know what to think of this news. Surprise, relief and hurt in quick succession. And a sense of being abandoned.

I sat down and tapped my fingers on the arm of the chair. "I must confess that I find his indifference rather hard," I said.

"He is the King," Thomas said. He gave me a kindly smile. "Your position has changed now, Alice. The King wishes to be seen distant from you. He no longer needs or wants you. He is quite reconciled to his marriage to Anne of Cleves."

I looked at him in astonishment. "That's not what I've heard. Rumor says that he is besotted by the Duke's little niece."

Thomas shook his head. "And that's exactly what it is. Rumor."

If anybody else had said this I would have thought they were fooling me. Or fooling themselves. But Sir Thomas? He was the master of rumor and intrigue and was once again high in the King's favor.

So the King's infatuation must be hearsay then. But to what purpose?

Such rumors were usually kindled and fed by Thomas himself. I looked at him as he sat there congratulating himself on his victory over Gardiner. Perhaps this tale of Katheryn Howard was a subtle ploy to trap his enemies. Perhaps even Norfolk himself. Proffering Anne Boleyn to the King had gone disastrously wrong for the Duke and it had always seemed strange that he appeared eager to repeat the same mistake.

I sipped my wine. I had thought myself glad that I was no longer at the heart of the Court. Now I wondered if hosting Thomas's feast might be the first step back to it. And how I felt about that, I was not sure.

Chapter 24
Arrested

The feast was planned to take place on the tenth of June.

There was no feast.

I think I shall never erase the memory of that day from my mind. It was a day of great heat and humidity. I felt stifled in my chamber but could not bring myself to leave it and walk in the gardens. The sun seemed too blistering and I feared that the heavy, wet air would do nothing to alleviate it.

"Shall I at least open the window?" Sissy asked. "Let in a breath of air?"

I nodded wearily and watched as she undid the casement. She was right; it did let in a breath of air. But it came from off the river and smelled rank and pestilent.

"It's like rotting meat," Sissy cried, slamming the window shut. "One of our calves went missing last summer. We found it by a stagnant pond, half-eaten by other creatures. The air smells just like that."

"Save me such stories," I said. "I feel sickened enough by this heat."

Sissy marched towards me and placed her hand on my forehead. "You're very hot, Alice. It's not the first time. I hope you're not sickening for something."

So did I. This dank, hot weather was a breeding ground for sickness and disease. I felt my head. It was over-warm and damp to the touch. *Not the sweating sickness*, I prayed. *Please don't let it be the sweating sickness.* This was not the first occasion I had worried about it. I had been out of sorts for a couple of days now.

Or it might be the plague, which loved the heat of summer.

Perhaps we should leave London soon, I thought, *before we get struck down by some contagion.*

"I hope you feel better soon," Sissy said. "You have to be ready for Sir Thomas's feast. It's only a few hours now."

"Pour me some wine," I said. "The white one in the small jug."

I sipped at the wine and pulled a face. It was sharp and sour. I longed for a sip of cool water but did not care to take the oily liquid which was all you could find in Whitehall. I dabbed my neck with my kerchief and longed for winter.

The door opened and Humphrey slipped in, closing the door behind him.

"You've got a visitor," he said. He looked concerned.

"Who is it?"

"I don't know. He's cloaked and hooded."

"In this heat. Are you sure?"

"I've got eyes ain't I?" he said, pointing to them as if I did not know what eyes were.

"And a pert tongue," I said. "Go and ask who it is."

I listened to his footsteps hurrying down the corridor and the muffled sound of voices. A few moments later Humphrey returned, shaking his head.

"He won't tell me his name. Says that I'm to let him in at once."

I frowned at the news. "Bring him in then," I said. "But stay here and keep your eyes on him." I feared it might be Richard Rich or one of his cronies.

I stood up and tried to straighten my gown but it clung to my legs like a dead thing. Sissy bent and shook it, managing to loosen it a little.

A moment later Humphrey returned with the visitor.

He was indeed cloaked and hooded and I marveled at anyone dressing in this manner on so hot a day. He turned and watched as Humphrey shut the door behind him, then pulled back his hood.

"Archbishop Cranmer," I said in surprise.

I did a curtsy. My mind raced, wondering why he would visit me. And in such a fashion.

He held his hand out to me and I kissed the simple ring upon his finger.

"Straighten up, girl, do," he said. He glanced around nervously. "We cannot be overheard?" he asked.

"No, Your Grace." I felt uneasy at the question.

He turned and stared at Humphrey and Sissy.

"They are completely trustworthy," I said.

"Nevertheless," he said, nodding his head towards the door.

"Leave us," I told them. "I'll call if I need anything."

They made for the door, Humphrey giving me a suspicious look as if to wonder at my changing my earlier command. *I'll be outside*, he mouthed.

"On second thought, they can stay," the Archbishop said. "It may be safer that way."

"Safer for who, Your Grace?" I said.

He did not answer.

"Get His Grace a chair," I said to Humphrey. "And bring some wine, Sissy. Not the white. The French red."

Archbishop Cranmer slipped off his cloak and sat down, his hands resting upon his knees. His skin looked sallow and his eyes bulged even more than they normally did. A little tremor rippled across his face and when he reached for his wine his hand began to shake. He took the glass but it slipped through his fingers and rolled across the floor, leaving a trail of red wine to stain the woodwork.

"Your Grace, what is wrong?" I asked anxiously.

"Our friend has fallen," he cried. And his hand went to his mouth as if he sought to stifle more words from escaping.

"Our friend?"

"Sir Thomas. He's been arrested for treason."

I shook my head. "You must be mistaken," I began.

"I was there when it happened, child," he said, leaning forward. "There in the Council. The Duke of Norfolk cried out that Thomas was a fiend and a traitor and the captain of the guard came and dragged him away."

"But it must be some mistake?"

The Archbishop shook his head. "Not a mistake but some long-hatched plot. Gardiner is behind it, I suspect, but Norfolk and Wriothesley are the weapons which have harmed our friend."

I stared at him in disbelief. Cromwell accused of treason? The King's most trusted minister, suspect? The ablest man in Court trapped by men of such lowly minds? My closest ally, perhaps destroyed?

"So where is Thomas now?" I asked.

"On his way to the Tower."

I put my hand to my mouth.

"And did he do nothing to try to prevent this?"

"What could he do? He was arrested in the King's name. He threw his bonnet to the floor in rage and I thought for a moment that he meant to use his fists against the guards. But he saw sense and mastered his fury."

"And the rest of the Council? Did they do nothing to aid him?"

Cranmer laughed. "Norfolk cried out that a traitor should not be a Knight of Saint George and wrenched the chain from his neck. And the Lord Admiral, who had ever been Thomas's friend, bent and untied the garter from his leg. A very Judas he is, a cringing, fearful traitor."

I was not surprised. The Lord Admiral always tacked with whichever wind blew strongest.

"And you, Your Grace? What did you do?"

The Archbishop placed his hand on his heart.

"I protested most vehemently. I ordered the captain of the guard to stand fast but Norfolk overruled me. And when I said that I would complain to the King, Wriothesley sneered and said that they performed this deed at the King's command."

Cranmer licked his lips, as if he still could not believe what had happened.

"As soon as he heard Wriothesley's words the fight seemed to go out of Thomas. He allowed himself to be taken to the Tower."

I closed my eyes as if to shut out this terrible news. I could feel the blood pounding in my head. I felt so ill I thought I might be sick.

"So what will happen now?" I managed to ask.

I opened my eyes and saw an almost insufferable look of sorrow upon Cranmer's face.

"Thomas is doomed, child. He has been arrested on an act of attainder, which means there will be no trial in which he can defend himself."

"So there is no hope?"

"Only if the King decides upon mercy."

He held his head in his hand, moaning softly to himself. Mercy was not a quality familiar to the King.

"And you, Your Grace? Are you in danger?"

I froze the instant I said this.

Of course he was in danger. But he was not the only one.

Everybody knew that I was a friend of Thomas Cromwell. Everyone knew that he was my protector. If he had fallen I would likely be dragged after him.

I imagined my enemies observing my destruction. The Duke of Norfolk smiling just a little, but careful not to seem too pleased. Wriothesley's bloodhound snout sniffing the air around me, almost readying himself to bay. Richard Rich, who'd bided hidden and silent in the murkiest of waters. Floating to the surface. Exalting at my downfall.

How can I avoid this? How can I save myself? I tried to quell the panic from my mind. I knew I had to think and think carefully.

"What did you say, child?" the Archbishop asked.

His words dragged me back to the room.

"I asked if you are in danger," I said.

"I do not know, Alice. I have written to the King saying I am astonished that such suspicion has been cast upon Thomas. He should receive my letter later today."

I looked at him in amazement. The rest of the Court would be swift to disown Thomas. Those who had benefited most from his friendship would be the first to pluck up stones to hurl at him, the better to prove their own innocence. Yet Cranmer stood by him. Writing such a letter was a truly courageous act. I feared the Archbishop had made a grave mistake, and one which would unleash his own destruction.

I must not do the same.

"Was that not unwise?" I asked. "Brave and commendable. But unwise."

Cranmer shrugged. "Thomas is my friend. We have undertaken a great work together. I cannot desert him now." He gave a bleak smile. "Besides, I was careful to condemn the crime of treachery while arguing that I did not think Thomas guilty of it."

"Some might call that mincing words, Your Grace, but I call it wisdom. And so would Thomas. The last thing he will want is for you to join him in the Tower. He needs you outside to fight on his behalf."

"And I intend to. As much as I am able. But I fear that this plot, while instigated by those who wish our reforms undone, is smiled upon by the King."

He shook his head as if he could not believe his own words. "The King believes he was inveigled into the Cleves marriage by Thomas and will not forgive him for it."

"But that's poppycock," I cried. "And surely it's not enough to make him dispense with such an able minister."

"People said the same about Cardinal Wolsey. He was even more powerful than Cromwell, a veritable second monarch in the land. But once he failed the King in matters matrimonial he plunged to disaster. I doubt it will be any different for Thomas."

"The King fears being made a fool of," I conceded.

"But at the same time he is hoodwinked by scoundrels like Wriothesley and Rich."

I shook my head in anger.

"Sir Richard Rich has been swift to change sides," Cranmer said. "Thomas recently told me he suspected Rich was in Norfolk's pocket."

"Norfolk." I gave a snort of contempt. "He's the greatest scoundrel of them all."

"Careful, Alice," the Archbishop hissed. He turned towards the door as if fearful it would be thrown open by armed guards. "It is a peer of the realm you speak of, a man with shrewd mind and devious heart."

"And seemingly one who has finally outwitted Thomas."

Cranmer did not answer save to wipe his brow wearily.

"I thank you for coming to tell me, Your Grace," I said. I had suddenly grown exhausted and, more importantly, I needed to be on my own to think.

"I did not come merely to give you this news," he answered.

He leaned close towards me and touched me on the wrist.

"Alice, I have come to warn you to be on your guard. I fear that all friends of Thomas are now in danger. And you, my child, have more enemies than you imagine."

"That is not news to me, Your Grace."

"And you must not think you can rely on your friendship with the King," he said.

My lips went dry as dust at his words. Did they mean that he might turn his back on me, or something even more sinister? Had the King's suspicions of Thomas widened to include me?

The Archbishop rose and threw on his cloak. And then he took me by the hand, speaking in little more than a whisper.

"Alice, the one thing you must avoid is having any contact with Thomas."

Chapter 25
Cromwell in the Tower

"What madness prompted you to come here?" Sir Thomas cried.

I stared at him in dismay. He had been in the Tower for only six days but he looked twenty years older. His clothes hung loose upon him and his face looked gaunt and hectic.

"I have come because I am your friend."

"Which is precisely why you should not have come. The dogs will be sniffing for your scent even now. Why did you decide to beckon them to you by visiting me? This foolishness may destroy you."

"I know it. Why else has it taken me near a week to gird up my courage?"

He stared at me a moment and then a grateful look stole over his face.

He indicated for me to sit in a chair and then went across to a desk for a stool. I glanced around the room. It was a dozen feet square and comfortably furnished with a small bed, a dining table and several chairs. It would have seemed paradise for many, but for disgraced courtiers it would have appeared mean and belittling.

I was glad that there was a desk; I don't think Thomas would have been able to cope without one. A small pile of papers sat on it. A very small one.

Thomas settled himself on the stool and his eyes grew softer.

"I like your courage, Alice. And I like your honesty. But I do not like your willful folly in coming here."

"Nobody knows," I assured him.

He gave me a disbelieving look.

"You forget that I am friendly with the Beast Keeper of the Tower Menagerie," I said. "Sissy's uncle. He smuggled me in."

"Ned Pepper," he murmured. "I hope his part in this rashness does not cause him difficulties." He gave a little chuckle. "You are certainly resourceful."

"I've brought you some fruit and wine," I said, handing him a basket.

His face lit up as he pulled out the bottle. "Malmsey. You hope to make me sweet, Alice?"

"I am not such a miracle worker."

He laughed and went to the dining table for two cups. He had no means of uncorking the wine so knelt at the fireplace and knocked off the head of the bottle. This sad necessity shook us both and we sipped our wine in silence. I mused on how far and fast my friend had fallen.

"I fear I am a dead man," he said quietly. "There will be no trial so I'll have no opportunity to defend myself. I seem to hear the ax sharpening already."

"That will not happen. The King will show you clemency."

He shook his head miserably, a lover spurned and discarded.

"He has forgotten me, Alice. He has forgotten my loyalty. He has erased from his mind that the ill things I did were only for his greater glory."

"I doubt he has forgotten that," I said.

But I immediately repented these words for I realized with sudden, dreadful clarity that this might be one of the reasons the King had sent Thomas here. Henry found it far easier to blame others than to admit to any failing or wrongdoing.

Thomas was his partner in crime; the former Earl knew all the King's dirty secrets. Henry had been content with this while Thomas had been his humble, agreeable tool. But Thomas had made a terrible blunder in the matter of His Majesty's marriage to Anne. Worse, Thomas had not been able to extricate him from the marriage agreement. This failure had proved the start of the slippery slope.

"It is not only the disaster of the marriage," Thomas said quietly.

I caught my breath for it seemed that he had been reading my very thoughts.

"It's not?" I asked.

Thomas shook his head.

"I have moved too swiftly in the King's service. He had come to believe that my greatest usefulness to him was in the closing of the religious houses. I was blamed and vilified and thereby he was shielded from blame."

He took a sip of wine before continuing.

"Every monastery, nunnery and abbey that I suppressed enriched him immensely. To please him and win more favor, I ordered that the rate of closure be increased. And as this vast well of treasure began to run dry so did his perception of my usefulness. Every monastery closed was but another nail in my coffin."

He shook his head and chuckled. "The Bishop of Rome will dance a jig to hear of my destruction."

"You will not be executed," I said.

Something in my tone of voice made him look up. He stared at me sharply.

"Oh no, Alice. Do not even contemplate it."

"I must."

He knelt at my feet, taking my hands in his. "You must not plead for me," he said. "To do so will put you in deadly danger. I like your company a great deal but do not wish you to join me in this place."

"It will not come to that."

"Won't it? The rumors are true; he has become besotted with the Howard sprite. Your standing is no longer high with the King. So all your pleading will help me not a jot. And it may well prove your undoing."

I wiped away a tear. "Can I not try?"

"I forbid it."

I tapped my fingers upon my chin, thinking what I could do to help him.

"There," he said. "You're doing it again. Christ in heaven, I wish I could remember who used to do that."

"Perhaps it was me," I said. "In your dreams."

He nodded. "Perhaps it was."

Then he reached out and touched my cheek. It was the gentlest of touches, full of tenderness and, I realized, of love.

I moved my head a little so that he was forced to cradle my face in his hand. He closed his eyes and sighed. I recalled how he'd once told me that I was a woman who could not help but capture men's hearts. I recalled as well that, had they lived, his daughters would be a similar age to me.

I leaned forward slowly, careful not to dislodge his hold, and kissed him gently on the cheek.

"Thank you," he said.

The guard came and said that the time allotted for visitors was over.

We rose and looked into one another's eyes. I hoped the King would realize his error and show mercy to Sir Thomas. But I suspected that this might be the last time we would see each other.

"You must leave England," he said quietly.

I stared at him in confusion.

"It will be a place of danger for all my friends for a while. Norfolk will set his hounds to catch the foxes and hares. Make sure they do not catch the little kitten."

"Leave England?"

"You do not realize the depth of your peril. My advice will be to go to France. Seek out Monsieur Bourbon. I know he had soft feelings towards you and I suspect that you may have reciprocated them. He is a man well-placed with King François. You will be safer there than here."

Even the thought of finding Nicholas could not allay my consternation.

"It seems a strange thing to do, Thomas. To flee the land of my birth merely because of my friendship with you." I grasped his hand. "Surely there is not such a threat to me."

"Trust me in this, Alice."

He picked up a document from his desk.

"This is the address of a very good friend of mine," he said. "He is called Derick Berck and is a merchant of the Hanseatic League. You met him once, when he was translating for Duke Philip, the suitor for Lady Mary."

I vaguely recalled a large German with an immense beard, although I doubted that I would recognize him again.

"Berck's office is in the Steelyard," Thomas continued. "I have asked him to make arrangements for you to quietly slip away to France. You can trust him absolutely. He is a man of great honor and integrity. He will do everything in his power to help you."

Before I had time to say anything more, Thomas took me by the arm and led me towards the door.

"It has been a privilege to know you, Alice Petherton," he said.

"And it has been an honor and a joy to know you, dear Thomas."

He smiled and gave a sigh of great content. But as I made to step over the threshold he shuddered mightily and took my hands in his.

I stepped closer, gazed into his eyes.

"I fear the ultimate penalty," he whispered. "I dread being drawn upon a hurdle for my enemies to gloat and spit. I fear the rope strangling my neck. But most of all I fear being drawn. Can you imagine seeing your own innards being pulled from your belly?"

My hand went to my mouth.

"It will not come to that," I said.

"Why not? Other men have suffered this. Why should I be exempt?"

"But you are a noteworthy man. You are an earl. Earls and barons do not suffer such a dreadful death."

"But lesser men do. Norfolk and his cronies will delight to remind the world that I am a commoner and do so by condemning me to the lowest and most vile of all possible deaths."

"It will not come to that," I repeated. And I kissed him once again.

Whatever the risk, I would make sure it did not come to that.

Chapter 26
Pleading for Mercy

My heart hammered so much I thought I might die. I had been sitting in the room next to the King's privy chamber for two hours now. It felt like I was being tortured.

For the thousandth time I looked out of the window towards the river. It would be the work of moments for me to slip away and hire a waterman to carry me away from the Palace. Carry me away from the lion's den which I had chosen to enter.

But I would not. Could not.

I will see the King, come what may.

Gregory Frost appeared at my side, although I had not seen or heard him open the door or approach.

"He will receive you now, Alice," he said.

I rose and followed him towards the door. Just before we reached it he touched me deftly upon the wrist. "He is in good humor," he said. "But do not rely on this to last."

I mouthed my thanks and walked into the chamber.

"Alice," the King cried. He beckoned me over and I knelt at his feet, kissing the hand he proffered to me.

"It has been a long time since last I saw you," he said.

"It has indeed, Your Grace."

I saw his eyes narrow at my use of this more familiar term. A term he always used to insist I use. But then he smiled and gestured me to rise.

"Pour some wine," he said. "It is there on the sideboard. You will like the claret. It is deep and complex."

I smiled, but wondered what he meant by such words. I remembered Frost's warning.

I brought a glass of wine to the King. He took a sip and gave a delighted grin.

"Sit down, child, sit down," he said. "Just there, where I can see you."

I sat in a little chair close by, dismayed by the sight of him. Although not imprisoned like Thomas, he too had aged considerably since I had last seen him. He seemed to have swelled in size and his face had a pasty, bloated look. Each individual feature appeared to be losing its distinctiveness, to be blending into a dough of flesh. I was reminded of a ham on a butcher's slab, one which had grown rancid from too much lying in the heat.

"To what do I owe this visit?" he asked.

I opened my mouth to answer but no words came. I swiftly sipped at my wine to moisten my mouth and to give me courage.

"I come to speak of Sir Thomas Cromwell," I said.

The King's face rippled in astonishment.

"That villain?" he said in the softest of voices. "That traitor? That despicable worm of a man?"

My senses reeled away from me as though I were clinging to the highest branches of a tree in a thunderstorm. I felt giddy and sick and thought that at any moment I would lose my grip altogether.

"Yes, Your Majesty," I said. "The Earl of Essex."

"He is an Earl no longer," he said. "I have stripped him of all titles."

He smiled and I was reminded of a fox which had suddenly spied a henhouse.

"And of all his worldly goods," he added.

And then he frowned. "There were not many goods to be found," he said. His voice was hesitant and wondering. "I was surprised at that. I assumed he possessed much greater wealth."

"He was noted for his deeds of charity," I said. "To the poor of London in particular."

"Trying to buy their favor," he said. "That is one of the things which made Norfolk suspicious of him. Why would Cromwell try to buy the favor of the London mob? It smacks of revolt and insurrection."

His eyes had grown smaller now, fierce and sharp with suspicion.

"I am sure that the Duke of Norfolk will bring you proof if that is the case," I said cautiously.

"Do you doubt it? Do you wonder at my suspicions?"

I swallowed hard. "Not yours, Majesty. But I wonder at the Duke's."

He stared at me for a long while, his eyes cold and searching. Then he laughed and slapped himself upon the thigh.

"You do well to wonder, Alice. I do so myself." He laughed aloud and wiped a tear of mirth from his eye.

"Oh, how my two staunch ministers loathed each other. I know it well, Alice, do not doubt it. They smiled upon one another, true enough, and could even work well together when they had to. But each was busy sharpening a knife to plunge into the other's throat when the time proved right."

I decided to seize the chance offered by these words.

"Knowing that, Your Majesty, I am intrigued at your plans for Sir Thomas. Is this all but a play to lull the Duke? Or to remind them that there is but one King of England?"

He laughed but there was no humor in it now.

"No, Alice. It is no play. I intend to execute Sir Thomas for his crimes."

He said it in such a cool and careless way that I could no longer control myself. I flung myself to the floor and raised my hands in prayer.

"Please, Your Majesty. Spare Sir Thomas's life. He has ever been loyal to you, ever been a true friend and a wise counselor."

"Common men are not the friends of a King," he said. "And how can a traitor be a friend?" He nodded as he said this, as if congratulating himself on the aphorism.

"I do not believe he is a traitor, Your Majesty. I believe he is the victim of malice from his rivals."

"There are no rivals at my Court. And no malice. I am convinced of the treachery of Master Cromwell. And all your bleating will not serve to save his life."

"But Your Majesty . . ."

I did not say more for he suddenly leaned forward and gripped me by the throat.

"Do not say *but* to your King," he whispered.

His voice was low and packed with cruelty. His fingers squeezed ever tighter. I thought he would stop in a moment—*he must stop*—but he continued to squeeze, staring at me all the while. I heard my throat cough and gurgle as if from some far distance.

I'll pass out, I thought. *Or die.*

But then the King released his grip and signaled to me to return to my seat. I struggled to my feet, fighting for breath. It felt as if I had been stabbed in the throat.

"I will hear no more about it," he said. "My mind is made up. Thomas Cromwell will die."

I stared at the carpet, remembering the times the King had stood on that spot and taken me in his arms. Those days were over.

Now he had climbed into bed with the Howard girl, though he did not appear to realize he had also got into bed with the Duke of Norfolk.

The warnings of Frost and of Sir Thomas boomed like cannons in my ears but I brushed them aside.

"But not hanging, drawing and quartering," I gasped. "Please, Your Grace, spare him that."

"It is the punishment for treason," he said quietly. He held my gaze in his and shrugged. "I can do nothing about a punishment decreed by the law."

"But you can, Your Majesty. You can choose to be wise and show clemency."

"It will be seen as a sign of weakness."

I shook my head. "It will be seen as a sign of great strength and nobility. What other King could be of so great a heart that he chooses to intercede on behalf of a traitor who was once his loyal servant?"

The King scowled and swallowed his wine. Then he placed the cup on the table and stared at me with eyes devoid of any friendliness or warmth.

"Get out of here, Alice," he said. "I never want to see you again."

I looked at him in disbelief. I got to my feet, forgot to curtsy and fled from the room, pausing for a moment in the hallway to calm myself. I had failed, and worse, I had enraged the King. I shuddered in terror.

And then I heard a loud tap, tap, tapping. The sound of my teeth chattering uncontrollably.

I took several deep breaths and finally mastered myself.

A young girl approached and stood at the door. A child. She was pretty and her neck was festooned with jewels.

She gazed at me a moment. "You must be . . ." she murmured and her finger went to her mouth as she struggled to remember.

"Your predecessor," I snapped, pushing past her.

Chapter 27
Execution

July 1540

It was a glorious, hot morning. A day to be married; not a day to be killed.

Thomas told me to stay away, I said to myself as I pushed through the crowd. He had let me off that cruel hook. There was no need for me to do this.

But I could not stay away. Thomas was my friend—had been my one true friend at Court.

He had been abandoned by his King and deserted by all his erstwhile friends save Archbishop Cranmer and Ralph Sadler. Ralph had been the only man brave enough to take Thomas's plea for mercy to the King. The King had read the letter and flung it on the floor.

After that, Thomas had begged Cranmer not to intercede, but the Archbishop proved determined. He had tried to remonstrate with the King but, like me, he had been rebuffed and refused. He did not try again; he was far too wary a politician to argue overlong for his friend. His neck, like any man's, was made of flesh and bone.

After his plea was refused, Cranmer had withdrawn to Lambeth Palace, skulking some said, showing his displeasure of the verdict said others. The King did not remonstrate or complain about his churchman. Perhaps to mollify him, he even announced that Thomas would not be hung, drawn and quartered like a common traitor but would die like a noble, under the ax.

The King knew the worth of Cranmer and even he could not afford to dispense with all of his loyal servants.

The wonder of it was that he was willing to dispense with his most loyal one of all.

And today was the final act of the tragedy.

I was in the middle of the crowd. It was huge: a vast, pulsating beast, eager for the sight of blood. Thomas Cromwell had been a deeply unpopular man, save for those who knew him well and had seen his capacity for kindness.

I cared for him very much. And the last thing I could do for him would be to witness his execution.

If that was possible. The crowd was virtually at a standstill.

I could see Tower Hill ahead with the grim platform atop it. But it seemed unlikely that I would be able to get any nearer. I cursed myself for not leaving earlier. Humphrey turned and looked at me with sorrow in his eyes.

"We're not going to be able to get closer," he said. "Perhaps it's for the best. Sir Thomas didn't want you to see it. He thought it would distress you."

"It will distress me," I answered. "And that's the reason I must go. I want to be distressed. I want to be angry. I want to understand deep in my heart how vile a deed is done here today."

A look of anguish clouded Humphrey's face. "I understand that," he said gently. "But it seems like fate won't let us get any nearer."

I turned and stared at the throng in front of me. If I pushed and shoved enough surely I could force my way through. I made up my mind to do so. I began to push, ignoring the angry faces and the curses of the crowd. They were as keen as I to witness the execution and they were not going to lose their place if they could help it.

I felt a hand upon my shoulder and turned, ready to curse back in return.

"What are you doing here?"

It was my old friend Ned Pepper, Beast Keeper of the Tower.

"I've come to see the execution, Ned."

He appeared surprised. "I wouldn't have thought to hear you say that, Alice. Executions are not the sort of thing for you. Not the thing at all." He touched my wrist. "Besides, I thought Sir Thomas was a friend of yours."

"He was a friend." I shook my head angrily. "Is a friend. And because of that I want to be there at his death."

He frowned, as if he did not understand my words. "And what's Sir Thomas's view of that?"

"He didn't want her to go," Humphrey said before I had time to answer.

Ned folded his arms and stared at me.

"That's true," I said. "But that was out of kindness and consideration. Now it is my turn to be kind to him." I began to cry. "But it looks like I won't be able to get close to him. That he won't be able to see I've come."

Ned drew a deep breath and thought for a moment. "Come on then. Up to the Menagerie and then round the back. I'll get you there in a trice."

My heart sank at the thought of the Menagerie. I saw again the image of Ned's daughter in the lion's den. I shook the thought away. Today I had to give my mind and heart entirely to Thomas.

I do not recall the rest of the journey, only that it was a swift one. Ned led us artfully through a maze of tunnels, ramps, walkways and doors. All I could concentrate on was the hammering of my heart and the roaring of the King's beasts.

"Do they always make such a racket?" Humphrey asked Ned.

"No. They sense there's to be a death. They roared pretty loud at Thomas More's death and young George Boleyn's. They roared loudest for Anne Boleyn though." He paused a moment. "Odd when you think that Cromwell was the cause of her execution and now he's going to suffer the same fate at the same place. Comeuppance, some might say."

I did not reply.

We turned a corner and came out onto Tower Hill.

Ten yards in front of us was the scaffold, its floor six feet above the ground. The mob was pressed up against it, hundreds upon hundreds of them. A small platform stood ten yards away from the scaffold. A dozen men sat there. I recognized a few: Rich, Wriothesley, Bishop Gardiner. The Duke of Norfolk was not there but his son the Earl of Surrey was; he was an enthusiastic spectator of executions. I was glad to see that two men who cared for Thomas were also there: his son Gregory and friend, Sir Ralph Sadler. The rest I imagined were not his friends.

The path from the Tower had been kept clear, the crowd held back by a line of heavily armed guards. One saw us and began to march over.

"You can't stay there . . ." he called. But he recognized Ned and let us remain.

Standing in the middle of the scaffold was the block. It looked like a low and sturdy stool and, to my surprise, was covered in rich silk cloth as if intended to make sure that all was fine and comfortable. Standing next to the block was a huge man, the masked executioner, his hand resting on the shaft of his ax.

He stared not at the block, not at the crowd, but at the trees which fringed the river. I guessed he had been chosen not merely for his skill with the blade but for his sense of decorum and propriety.

A drum sounded behind me, making me jump in alarm. It beat a steady, simple sound, like the slow march of a man with much upon his mind. It seemed to capture the hammering of my heart and slow it down to its own mournful rhythm.

I turned and saw Sir Thomas walking behind the drummer, guards on either side and to the rear. He looked pale and exhausted, although his face was set in the icy resolve that I knew so well.

He's terrified, I thought, *but he's doing his best to hide it.*

His path took him within a few feet of me. As he got close, he saw me and paused. He shook his head, like a father who had seen his child do something he had forbidden. I almost wept at the sight of it.

"I told you not to come," he said.

"I had to," I whispered.

He gazed at me in silence and gave a tiny, fond smile. "I shall be brave, Alice, never fear."

And he turned and mounted the scaffold.

Thomas gave a long and clever speech, which did not surprise me in the slightest. He praised the King, as well I knew he would, and said he was the most loving and forgiving friend he had known, the most perfect prince in all the world. Pouring poison in the King's soul I thought, his last piece of revenge and very fitting.

But at the end I was taken aback. Sir Thomas paused and said that he was guilty of all the crimes he had been accused of. I shook my head in disbelief. How could he be so craven? Why would he admit to things he had not done?

And then he looked at his son and Ralph Sadler and I realized. It was his only hope of protecting those he loved. If he groveled enough at the moment of his death he might, just might, prevent the King from doing them harm. And then he turned and glanced at me.

He passed a small purse to the executioner, the traditional wage, and knelt at the block.

The executioner took a swift step backward, swung his ax in the air and brought it down.

I expected it to be a clean death but it was not. The executioner had missed the vital point. Blood spurted from Thomas's neck, and his hands fumbled to try to stem it.

I cried out in horror, reached out towards him.

His body rolled and rocked, his voice crying out like a strangled child. Again the ax swept down and this time it seemed to only bludgeon and not to cut. Once more Thomas cried out and lifted up his hand as if to ward off further blows.

I thought I would throw up, stumbled and felt Ned and Humphrey try to pull me away.

"No," I cried. "No. I must see."

The priest at Thomas's side made the sign of the cross, his face distraught.

A third time the executioner raised his ax, much higher. It plunged down and this time it severed my poor friend's neck, putting him out of his dreadful torment.

I took a deep breath, realized that I would not, after all, be sick. I pushed my friends away, not wanting to be touched by anybody.

I had watched Thomas's execution dry-eyed.

I'd feared I'd be incapable of watching but it was a thing I had to do for him. I had to see the King's crime clearly, had to watch the courage of my friend.

At length I felt Humphrey and Ned's arms go around me once again, and I did not push them off this time. But I did not bow my head and I did not weep. Tears could come later. Now was the time for courage and for steadfast loyalty.

The executioner picked up the head and brandished it for all the crowd to see. They bayed with delight.

To my surprise Thomas's eyes were still open. For a moment, I thought they still held his life within them; they looked at me with his usual ironic calculation.

This will never happen to me, I vowed. *I've had enough of Kings and ministers and courtiers and nobles. I've had enough of politics and tiptoeing around the paranoia of the King.*

I stared into those eyes a moment longer. They had always been clever, so wise, so farseeing. Except that he never foresaw this end, poor dear.

I began to weep, very quiet and very soft.

Ned Pepper took me in his arms and hugged me. I felt like a little girl.

"We must go," Humphrey hissed. "We haven't got time to stay here."

I broke free from the embrace. "Give my love to Amy and to Edith," I said.

"I will," Ned said. "But why don't you come back to the house and see them for yourselves? This must have been a shock for you. I know how fond you were of Sir Thomas."

I shook my head. "Humphrey's right. I have to leave London."

Ned's eyebrows rose into his hairline. He did not say anything but I could see his shrewd mind working fast. "Leave London?"

I nodded. I did not want to say more and he was wise enough not to ask.

"Have you got money, child?" he asked.

"I lack for many things, Ned, but at the present not for money."

"Then my blessings be with you. And transport?"

I nodded. Humphrey tugged at my sleeve. I could feel the anxiety in his touch.

I kissed Ned on the cheek and headed into the crowd. I thought it would be safest if we were lost in the throng.

The crowd was every bit as dense as when we'd tried to push our way to the scaffold. But now it seemed even more ungovernable. Many people were trying to force their way homewards; others, even more determined, were intent on thrusting forward to gloat upon the corpse. The noise was unbearable. Some laughed, some sang gutter songs abusing poor Thomas, others howled with bloodlust. It was more terrible than the clamor of the beasts in the Menagerie.

Humphrey glanced back, cried out and seized my hand. "Richard Rich," he hissed.

I turned. There, sure enough, was the reptile. He had clambered on the scaffold, so close that drops of Thomas's gore dripped on him as the executioner flourished the head. At that moment he turned towards the frenzied crowd, his face wide with pleasure.

He stiffened suddenly. He had seen me.

He yelled to some guards, who hurried to join him. Then they leapt into the throng and began to push their way towards me. I stood there quaking in terror, unable to move.

Humphrey pulled at my arm. "Run, Alice, run."

Chapter 28
A Foreign Friend

Humphrey thrust forward, one hand gripping like iron on my wrist, the other pushing wildly in front of him. He did not care how he did it. He put his head down, using it to batter his way through the crowd. He pushed people away, punched some, made wild chopping movements as if he were a second axman. And all the time he screamed and cursed at the top of his voice: "Make way, make way."

I glanced behind. Richard Rich was closing on us, the tall guards securing a speedier passage than we could.

"We'll never make it," I gasped.

Humphrey turned to see how close our pursuers were. Then his eyes opened wide and he pointed towards them, bellowing at the top of his voice. "That's Richard Rich, the worst thief in England."

Only those close to us were able to hear. They turned and looked towards Rich. But it was one thing to see a hated figure, quite another to do harm to one so powerful. The crowd wavered for a moment and then turned back to stare at us.

"Stop, thief!" Humphrey cried, pointing wildly at Rich. "Stop, thief!"

It did the trick. The cry so long familiar, so long a part of London life, had an instant effect. The crowd turned again and surged towards Rich. The guards looked terrified and drew their swords.

Humphrey yanked on my arm and dragged me through the now thinning crowd.

His ploy had bought us enough time to make our way onto the streets below the Tower. But as I glanced back I saw the guards had beaten back the mob and were forcing their way towards the edge of the throng. Rich was in the middle of them, brandishing his fist in fury.

"Come on," Humphrey cried.

He led me at breakneck speed down narrow streets. I was soon hopelessly lost but Humphrey ducked and dived down lanes and alleys without a moment's hesitation. Every so often, when we made a turn, I heard Rich's voice yelling out my name. It served only to make us force our legs still faster.

At last, when I thought my heart would burst, Humphrey slackened his pace.

"Time for a breather," he gasped.

I nodded in relief, but in moments he pulled once more at my arm. "I think we've lost them but I can't be sure. Must get going."

He led the way once again, although not with such reckless haste.

At last we left the fetid little alleys behind and came out onto Eastcheap. I knew where we were at last. It was here that the brothel keeper's men had tracked me after I escaped. Here where they had almost recaptured me. But they had failed and the recollection of my escape gave me renewed strength.

"Come on," I yelled to Humphrey.

We raced into Offal Pudding Lane where Susan, Mary and Sissy were waiting for us.

"We thought you'd never get here," said Susan. She glanced at my face. "You look exhausted."

"Richard Rich," I gasped. "He's after me."

"What will we do?" Mary said.

"We must get on," said Humphrey. "It's no good chuntering about how dangerous things are while we're stuck in the middle of them."

I patted him on the shoulder. "Lead the way, Humphrey. Take charge."

He needed no second bidding, heading off down Offal Pudding Lane. The rest of us followed his swift steps. He did not pause but strode purposefully along.

"Do you know the way?" Mary asked nervously.

"Course I do," he answered. "I came here yesterday. Always best to know your way."

I breathed a sigh of relief at his foresight. *Trust a Page*, I thought. I would have to trust all of my friends if we were to escape the attention of my enemies.

We turned to the right, into a warren of alleys heavy with the stench of rotten fish, overrun with feral cats. The lanes were slick with fish guts.

We came out onto a wider street overlooking the river and drew breath.

Mary took my hand in hers. "Are you all right, Alice?" she asked.

"I think so." I wiped my face. "Being chased by Rich was bad. But the execution was worse. Worse than my worst fears."

"You shouldn't have gone, Alice," Sissy said. "You should have paid heed to Susan."

I shook my head. "I had to go, Sissy. I know you all mean well and I know you wished to protect me. I'm very grateful for that. But I just had to go. I owed Thomas that."

"Come on," said Humphrey. "We're nearly there but we ain't safe yet."

The Steelyard was a couple of hundred yards further west. It was not a yard but a large trading post, almost a town in its own right. There were a multitude of houses, a church, two or three halls and many large storehouses. But Humphrey bypassed these and led us down an alleyway close to the river. The alley grew narrower with every step until I thought it must become a dead end. But then Humphrey stopped at a passageway and beckoned us to follow.

It opened out into a little court with three doorways. The walls above showed half a dozen windows staring down like the eyes of blind men. Humphrey headed for the furthest door and led us up two flights of stairs. If there was a better place in which to trap us I could not imagine it.

"This here's Mr. Berck's office," Humphrey said. "We'll be safe now."

At the top of the stairs stood a narrow door. Humphrey knocked three times in quick succession and put his ear to the woodwork.

I heard the sound of footsteps and then the door opened to reveal a tall, stout man dressed completely in black save for a white undershirt with an extravagantly worked border. His cheeks were smoothly shaved, though he had a sparse moustache which drooped down until it joined with a bushy, dark-brown beard flecked with grey. His nose was large and bulbous like that of some gigantic mole.

He was an imposing figure. With my nerves strung out as they were, the sight of him might well have terrified me.

Perhaps it would have done had he not spoken to me.

"You must be Alice Petherton," he said with a heavy German accent.

As soon as he spoke I realized that he was indeed the man who had translated for Duke Philip. The man who Thomas trusted absolutely. I felt faint with relief.

I nodded and he stood aside, his hand outstretched to show the way into the room.

"My name is Derick Berck," he continued, "and I am here to help you."

Because of the tiny stairs and the narrow door, I expected the room to be cramped and mean. It was anything but. True enough, one of the grimy windows looked out onto the stairwell and gave little light. But there were two more windows and they were bigger, cleaner, and they looked out over the Thames, making the room light and sunny.

It was a large room and very comfortably furnished. It was obviously a place of business and wore a businesslike air. In front of the windows stood an immense oak desk, with neat little piles of papers arranged just so along the right-hand side. In the middle there was a well-worn leather wallet bulging with papers. Next to this this were two inkwells, one containing black ink, the other red, a collection of half a dozen quills and a penknife with an open blade. On the left side of the desk was a large map, held flat by four paperweights. I glanced at it and saw that it was of northern Europe, with ports underlined in neat red ink.

To one side of the room were three large locked cupboards and in front of them a small table and four comfortable chairs. Mr. Berck directed us to take a seat.

Humphrey stood by the door with Sissy while Susan, Mary and I sat and waited for Mr. Berck to join us. He did so after a moment, bringing with him the heavy leather wallet.

"It is a most grievous day," he said, shaking his head. "Sir Thomas Cromwell was always a supporter of the Hanseatic merchants. And he was a good friend to me."

He shook his head once again and fell silent, staring at the table as if he would find there some answer to the wickedness of the world.

Then he sighed, repeatedly, and rubbed his hand across his hair. At last, he gave over and looked at me gravely.

"Sir Thomas told me that you would come to me before now," he said. "A few days ago at the latest."

"I know. But I wanted to be there to witness his . . ." I closed my eyes, unable to bring myself to say the word.

"His departure," Mr. Berck said kindly.

I nodded.

"I understand. But I wish that you had followed his instructions more precisely. Sir Thomas was a most punctilious man and always planned things to the best possible conclusion."

"Except for his own life," I said.

"No man can guard against every eventuality. And, especially, no man can guard against the whim of such a prince as King Henry."

Never had a truer word been spoken.

Berck laid the wallet on the table and flicked it open.

"This is a letter containing directions to our offices in Paris. Jurgen Rink, one of my colleagues there, will be pleased to give you every assistance."

He then reached inside his jacket and produced a leather bag.

"Sir Thomas also asked me to give you this."

I took it cautiously. "What is it?" I asked.

"Open it."

I did so and gasped. It was full of gold coins.

"There is one hundred and twenty pounds in value," Berck said.

"I don't understand. Where has it come from?"

"It is a bequest," he answered. "From Sir Thomas."

I stared at him for a moment, the room charged with silence.

"I cannot take this," I said, pushing it back across the table.

"What would you have me do with it then?" he asked. "Put it into Sir Thomas's poor, dead hand? Or give it to King Henry, who would pocket it without a qualm?"

I did not reply but gave a little shake of my head.

"Then take it, Alice Petherton, in the kindly spirit in which it was given. As was this."

He gave me a roll of documents. I opened them and stared in amazement. They were the deeds of several properties bequeathed to me by people I'd never heard of.

"Who are these people? I don't know any of them."

"Nor will you," Mr. Berck answered. "They have been dead for many years and they received their property from others who died even earlier."

I stared at the papers in confusion.

"For the past three months," Berck continued, "Sir Thomas has been putting his affairs in order. He must have suspected that his position was in jeopardy. He quietly gave away much of his wealth to men long dead who could not communicate news of this surprising generosity. All he asked of them was that they gave it to other dead men, who passed it on to yet more corpses.

"A number of the deceased saw fit to bequeath their wealth to you, Alice Petherton, all legal and correct with any path leading back to Sir Thomas too tortuous for anyone to follow." He gave a chuckle. "Now wasn't that a kind act by men who never knew of your existence?"

He pushed across the purse of money.

"For such an amount I would normally require your signature as proof that you have received it. But these are not normal times and besides, I do not wish for any evidence of our arrangements. As far as I am concerned this meeting has not taken place."

"I understand entirely, Mr. Berck."

He climbed to his feet and held out a paw of a hand. "I had originally intended you to travel on one of the League's trading ships but my colleagues felt it best if that did not happen."

He said no more. I presumed that his fellow merchants were wary of helping me, unwilling to be involved in acts which might jeopardize their privileges.

"So instead," he continued, "I have booked a berth for you and your friends on the first ship out of Dover the day after tomorrow.

"Because you delayed, it is the third-such booking I have made. Please make sure that you catch it."

France, I thought. My heart soared. I would go to France and find my dear Nicholas.

Chapter 29
France and Finch

August 1540

The port of Dover was awash with all manner of ships and boats. One of the King's warships rode at anchor at the far end of the quay, a huge threatening watchdog. It dwarfed the rest of the vessels, which were mostly small cogs designed for making swift dashes across the Channel.

"That's the one for us," Humphrey said. He pointed out a boat which was little bigger than the Royal barge.

"You can't be serious," I said. "That little thing isn't big enough to sail on the sea."

"Size is not important," said a voice behind me. "It's whether she can do the job or no."

I turned and stared into the most villainous face I'd ever seen. *A cutpurse*, I thought in alarm.

I surreptitiously reached for the little dagger I'd hidden in my purse.

"No need for blades, Miss Petherton," he said.

He knows my name, I thought. *How does he know my name? And how does he know I have a knife?*

"Who sent you?" I said, backing away. "Richard Rich? The Duke of Norfolk?"

"Don't know any of they fine gentlemen," he answered, taking a step towards me, making sure that he kept as close to me as possible.

He tilted his head and gave me a strange, crooked look, like a little bird might, perhaps. Or a wolf considering prey.

"Not that they sound like gentlemen if they worry a lovely maid like you," he added.

He was lean and wiry, the sort of man who could well look after himself. He had a confident, almost insolent air and a sharp, intelligent glance. He spoke pleasantly, in very friendly manner. It was this which alarmed me more than his looks.

I felt an icy fear. He was an altogether dangerous man.

Out of the corner of my eye I saw Humphrey moving towards me. I had to do something or the little idiot would try to help me and likely get hurt.

"I'll give you money," I said to the cutpurse.

"No need for that," he said with a grin. He reached inside his tunic and showed me a purse. "Mr. Berck has paid everything up front."

I stared at the purse in confusion.

Susan responded more quickly.

"What do you know of Mr. Berck?" she demanded. "Is he dead in the gutter somewhere? Have you murdered him?"

The cutpurse gave a wide, slow grin.

"If you thought killing Mr. Berck were that simple you doesn't know him very well."

"Come on, man," I said, not believing a word he said. "Out with it. How much do you want?"

"You're every bit as brave as he said," the man answered. "You're not afraid at all."

I didn't feel brave at the moment but I wasn't going to let him see.

"I've dealt with worse scoundrels than you," I said.

"Expect you have, being as how you lived at Court and all." He took off his hat and turned it in his hand, kneading and squeezing it like it were dough.

"We should leave," Susan said. "Run for it."

Mary nodded in agreement.

But Sissy leaned close and whispered in my ear. "I'm not so sure, Alice. I've seen uglier men and he seems gentle-enough behaved."

"The littlest one's got the truth of it," the man said.

He gave a low bow. "My name's Barnaby Finch. I've been engaged to watch out for you." He thrust a letter towards me.

I looked at it as though it were a warrant for my arrest. But I swallowed hard and reached out for it, my hand shaking in fear.

I turned it over in my hand. "It bears Mr. Berck's seal," I said.

Finch nodded and rubbed his nose furiously, as though it itched him.

"You might have stolen that!" Susan said sharply.

"You're right to be suspicious, miss," he said. "But the truth of it will only be found out by breaking the seal. My old mother always said you can't eat the meat till you've cracked the pie lid."

He leaned forward conspiratorially, which made us all step back in alarm.

I broke open the seal. As he had said, the letter was from Derick Berck.

I read it swiftly, twice, and sighed with relief.

"It's as he claims," I said. "Mr. Berck has engaged this man to act as our guide and guard."

"You don't need no guards," said Humphrey hotly. "You've got me."

Finch laughed. "True enough, young 'un. But have you got one of these?"

He twitched back his coat to reveal a long, thin sword such as I'd never seen before.

"What's that?" Humphrey said with a sneer. "A sewing needle?"

"A rapier," Finch said. "And I could split you from gizzard to cock with it."

His hitherto pleasant manner had gone completely. Now he seemed hard, harsh and dangerous. This, even more than Berck's letter, made up my mind.

"I'm glad to have you in my service, Mr. Finch," I said. "Now let's hurry and get on this poor little boat."

I glanced over my shoulder as we climbed on deck. If Barnaby Finch had found it so simple to find me, others less well-disposed might be able to do the same.

The voyage across the Channel was not as bad as I feared. The boat felt little bigger than a bucket but it was seaworthy and the captain and his crew knew what they were about. There was a strong wind coming from the north and in only three hours we pulled up at Calais quayside.

"Are there foreigners in France?" Sissy asked, looking sick with nerves.

"I hope so," I answered. "Or we've wasted our time in traveling here."

"Frenchmen?"

"In the main. Apart from the Frenchwomen and French children."

She shook her head dolefully. "I've heard terrible things about the Frenchies, Alice."

"Come on, Sissy," I said. "Monsieur Bourbon was a Frenchman. You liked him didn't you?"

She gave a little smirk and colored slightly. "Not half as much as you did, Alice." Then she grabbed me by the arm. "Is that why we're here? Are we going to find Mr. Bourbon?"

I gave an enigmatic smile. I had come to France chiefly because Thomas and Mr. Berck thought I'd be safe here. But always, at the back of my mind, I had intended to look for Nicholas. In fact, I recalled that finding Nicholas was exactly what Thomas had advised me to do.

"France is a big country, Sissy," I said. "Nicholas Bourbon could be anywhere."

"You know what they say about true love," she said. "It will find a way."

And she hurried away to get my bags.

I shook the thought of Nicholas from my head as I walked down the gangway. He could indeed be anywhere. He had returned to France to tutor the niece of the King. But the promises of kings seemed to count for little.

Barnaby Finch was already on the dockside, his eyes scouting everywhere for possible signs of trouble.

"I don't like him one bit," Susan said, gesturing towards him.

"I think I do," I said slowly. "I believe he may prove himself over time." I turned to watch him as his head moved this way and that, like a hound sniffing for a fox.

Susan snorted and went off to organize Humphrey, Sissy and the luggage. I usually trusted her intelligence and common sense. Why, then, did I doubt her mistrust of Mr. Finch?

Perhaps it was because I had found that the most handsome people were often the most despicable, and the ugliest the kindest. By that measure, Barnaby Finch should be a very angel. His face was as creased and well-worn as an old shoe.

As if he read my mind he suddenly turned and headed towards me. He did not hurry but his loose-limbed gait covered the distance in an astonishingly short time.

"There's no danger here, Miss Petherton," he said. "Let's find a carriage to get us to Paree."

"Very good, Mr. Finch."

He shook his head. "No need for such nicety. Call me Barnaby. I don't always pay heed when folk call me Mr. Finch. And you may have need of my quickest response. So just yell out Barnaby, if there's need."

"Well, I'm sure I can trust you," I said. "Whatever I call you."

He nodded. "I'm pleased at it. Though there's some in your party who don't like the look of me." He turned to Susan and Humphrey and chuckled.

"It's only because they're concerned for me."

"That's all to the good then. No matter how brave you are, the more eyes that watch for you the better."

I shook my head. "I don't feel brave—quite the contrary."

"Brave and fiery, were his words."

"Mr. Berck said that?"

"It weren't Mr. Berck," he said, shaking his head. "It were Thomas Cromwell. He approached me three months back and said he had an important job for me."

He gave a grin. "He also said you might not be easy to manage."

Chapter 30
Paris

Nicholas Bourbon had told me so many wonderful tales about France that I expected it to be the most beautiful of all lands, a kingdom of wonders. I could not wait to leave the English territory around Calais and felt a thrill of joy when, after a few miles of travel, Barnaby told me that we had now entered the Kingdom of France.

He had procured a carriage large enough for Susan, Mary, Sissy and me to ride inside. The seating was firm and strewn with cushions for comfort. There was a pile of blankets and shawls on the floor in case of unseasonably cold weather. Humphrey climbed on the top of the carriage with the coachman. He was full of excitement at the prospect, although Sissy was anxious in case he fell off.

"I'll get a wonderful view," he said. "I'll be able to spy all the pretty milkmaids." He grinned at Sissy, who slapped him on the arm.

"You keep your eyes to yourself, Humphrey Buck," she said. "Tell him, Alice."

"Keep your eyes to yourself," I said.

He did not answer but gave me an even cheekier grin before winking at Sissy and squeezing her arm.

"Are you riding with the coachman, Mr. Finch?" Susan asked.

"That I'm not, Miss Dunster. I'm riding horseback. I need to keep my eyes sharp you see, but not for milkmaids."

She snorted in derision.

"I expect he'll gallop off to alert some brigands," she muttered before climbing into the carriage.

I peered out of the window as we headed south, filled with anticipation and curiosity. If my lover said France was wonderful then wonderful it must be.

In my imagination, France was a realm of gentle green meadows, each one covered in banks of wild flowers, their scent as subtle as the most costly of perfumes. Little woodlands would speckle these meadows, with herds of deer and fawns peering out from the trees, a solitary stag standing guard over them. In dells and valleys there would be pretty villages with happy villagers toiling in vineyards to the sound of music and song. The women were all pretty, the men handsome and the children chattered like birds in the tree. And the countryside would be dotted with little brooks leading to mighty rivers with fabulous castles towering over them.

It was nothing like that.

The country I gazed upon was flat and drab. Huge forests brooded in the distance and near at hand were not pleasant meadows but vast fields of unrelenting wheat and barley. The villages we passed through were not the joyous and pretty places Nicholas had promised. They were similar to those we had seen on our journey through Kent, small and higgledy-piggledy, with tiny houses patched up in haste against the rigors of the weather.

There were castles in sight, true enough; but they were small and grim, heavy with battlements and dour of aspect. They had been built to fence the English within their last stronghold in France. There would be no princesses in such places and no handsome princes either.

The first night of our journey we slept in a foul inn. The walls and ceilings were festooned with spiderwebs, huge hornets made play across the fetid air and scores of rats slunk across the floor with little fear of being noticed or dealt with. The next morning I awoke with a sick feeling in my stomach. I managed to reach the washbasin and vomited into it. I wasn't sure if it had been caused by the vile food we had been served the previous night, by the terrible lurching of the carriage or by some horrible French ailment.

I could not face breakfast and we set off on the next stage of our journey. So far I had not seen anything to like about France. But every step took me nearer to Nicholas. Or so I hoped.

I insisted to Barnaby that from now on he find us only decent inns. He gave me a doubtful look as if this were an impossible request. But all credit to the man, he found a much better establishment that evening. The rooms were light and airy; the beds were sprung and had clean sheets. The meal was excellent: roast lamb with little green beans and onions. The only thing to mar it was that I was sick again the next morning.

"It must be the carriage," I said. "Perhaps I should ride horseback."

"You'll do no such thing," said Mary. "It's safer in the carriage. We don't want prying eyes to see you."

I sighed. I had fled here to find safety yet we were all still nervous and on edge.

"I don't think anyone in France could possibly be interested in me," I said in a more cheerful tone than I felt.

"Well, Sir Thomas and Mr. Berck must have thought different," she said. "Why else would they have engaged Mr. Finch to protect you?"

I nodded miserably and climbed into the carriage.

The next few days were a blur. On the second day the weather turned decidedly hotter. A breeze blew up from the south but it was not a cooling breeze—quite the contrary. It was dry as dust and the whole land began to bake. No clouds remained in the sky and the sun blazed fierce and relentless.

The roads grew a little better the closer we got to Paris, which meant we could go at a faster pace and in a little more comfort. It was with great relief that one afternoon Barnaby cantered up beside the coach and peered in to announce that he could see Paris in the distance.

At last I found something to impress me about France.

Paris was an astonishing place, larger than London and more populous. Although most of the streets were as narrow and as crooked in our own capital, there was a big difference. Many of the houses had plots of land behind them where crops could be raised. And not just crops. There was a constant racket from cows and sheep and horses. Pigs roamed the street, gobbling up rubbish.

"Street cleaners," Barnaby said with a grin. "They should have 'em in every city."

"It doesn't stop the stench though," I said.

Indeed the city stank like a cesspit. The heat from the sun acted like an oven, intensifying every smell.

But the buildings which lined the streets made up for it. There was every type of dwelling imaginable, from tiny places little bigger than sheds to merchants' houses with countless windows, fine leaded roofs and gateways large enough to admit horses and wagons. There were churches and inns and scores of shops. Every so often we came upon little open spaces, many of them containing wells round which old people sat and gossiped, a few crowded with stalls selling meat, bread, fruit and wine. Men strolled, women hurried, children raced, beggars limped. It was as if the whole world had been poured into Paris. The hubbub was tremendous.

Barnaby led us across the river to a small island crowded with churches, palaces and fine mansions. He pointed out a large palace to the west of the island. "That's where the King lives when he's in Paris. Not that he's often here, mind. Too much dirt and disease for the fastidious François. He prefers to spend his time in the valley of the Loire."

"I've heard of that," I said. Perhaps that was the magical place which Nicholas had described to me. "Have you been there, Barnaby?"

"That I have, Alice. It's a wonderful, warm and gentle place. Green and lush with lots of vines and excellent wines."

"And castles?" I asked. "Are there castles there?"

"Châteaux they're called in France. And there's more in the Loire Valley than anywhere else in the world."

"I can't imagine there are more than in England," I said. "The King alone owns fifty or sixty palaces and countless other halls and houses."

"And a few more now that he's taken Master Cromwell's properties into his hands," Barnaby said.

I nodded and wondered how long it would be before the King snatched up my manors. I still held Luddington and Buckland, but they had been his gifts to me and he would likely take them back. It would also, doubtless, take little time for him to sniff out the four properties which Sir Thomas had so cunningly bequeathed to me. Thomas had been at pains to hide the fact that they had come from him, not that they belonged to me. He had not foreseen that a time might come when I would be so out of favor with the King that I might be at risk of losing them.

"Nevertheless," Barnaby continued, "I'll wager there are more palaces in the valley of the Loire than in the whole of England. You have no idea of the size and wealth of this Kingdom, Alice. It makes England look a poor, shadowy thing in comparison."

I doubted his words, particularly after seeing the country on the journey from Calais. Surely nothing could compare to the might and glory of England. Nor match her colossus of a king.

"So King François is not likely to be in Paris?" I asked.

"At one of his palaces, I guess. He may be at Fontainebleau, which is close to Paris. But we haven't come to Paris to see the King. We've come to see Jurgen Rink."

He climbed off his horse and helped me down from the carriage. Mary let him help her down but Susan refused his offer of a hand and leapt down to the ground herself, narrowly missing what Barnaby's horse was depositing on the ground.

I took a deep breath but without much effect. It felt like I had descended into a potter's kiln. I touched a wall and it felt hot as burning wood.

"This is Master Rink's place," Barnaby said, guiding us up a narrow alley which led towards the south side of the island.

At the very end of the alley a tall town house perched on the riverbank. I glanced up at it and imagined it likely to shortly topple into the river.

"Herr Rink's on the third floor," Barnaby said. I noticed that he checked for his dagger as he led the way up the narrow stairs.

He knocked once upon the only door on the landing.

"Come in," came a voice so high-pitched I was not sure if it came from a man or a woman.

I followed Barnaby into a very comfortable office with the finest of furnishings.

The owner of the voice was a slim, old gentleman who was seated at his ease behind a desk. His face was as wrinkled as an old apple and his rheumy eyes peered out behind a pair of eyeglasses secured around his head by a silk ribbon. Upon his head he wore a little round cap, decorated with bright colors.

He struggled to his feet and came around the desk to greet us. He must have been very tall in his youth for he was still of good height despite his obvious years. He seemed to have wallowed in a field of lavender, for the scent of the herb enveloped him like a cloud. It was so strong it caught my throat and I coughed.

"You're not sick are you?" he asked anxiously. "I'm old and I will not have sick people come too close to me."

"It's just a tickle," I said. "From the dust on the road."

He gave me a dubious look, fiddled fussily with his eyeglasses and after a moment or two stepped closer and examined me carefully.

"You are a beautiful young lady," he said, as if he were confirming something in his own mind. "Young Berck was quite right." He bent to kiss my hand, obviously no longer worried about any lack of health on my part.

"I don't have occasion to do that very often," he said with a gentle smile. "Not now. But in my youth, ah, that was a different story."

"And one we have no time for, Jurgen," Barnaby said.

The old man waved his hand as if in displeasure, but he smiled as he did so.

"Jurgen is so old he cannot recall his age," Barnaby continued. "But he can recall every woman he has ever slept with and if he were to recite the list we'd be here until this time tomorrow."

"There are not so many," the old man said in a quiet tone.

"Don't you believe it," Barnaby said. "He's had more lovers than King François and that takes some doing."

"And five wives," Jurgen said. "Don't forget my wives."

"You seem to have done, you old dog. They must have had a lot of forbearance to put up with your philandering."

The old man looked at me and shook his head as if to deny Barnaby's words. But from the way he appraised me I was sure that every word was true. He was a handsome man still, despite his wrinkles. And his gentle, courtly ways were very consoling.

"Derick Berck said that you'd have information for us," Barnaby said.

The old man nodded. "Please, sit."

He folded his hands and regarded me thoughtfully. "You have heard that the marriage of King Henry to Anne of Cleves has been annulled?"

"I knew this in the middle of July," I answered. "It is common knowledge. The English courtiers and churchmen did amazingly well to produce enough evidence for the King to dispense with the poor woman. They claimed that she had been betrothed already, that she was not a virgin and that the King never had intimate relations with her."

"Well that knowledge seems decidedly common," Barnaby said with a chuckle.

"But what is not common knowledge," Rink continued, "is that the King has married once again, in secret, to a very young woman."

"Katheryn Howard," I said.

Rink looked mildly surprised. "You know? Yet Ambassador Marillac says that it is only rumor."

"I guessed; I did not know for certain. I am not surprised and I am grateful for your telling me."

He bowed his head with great politeness. In truth the only thing which had surprised me was that this mild old man had received news of events so swiftly.

He felt inside his jerkin and retrieved a little key which he used to unlock one of the three strongboxes on his desk. He searched through it, muttering to himself as he did so. The scent of lavender wafted towards me with each movement he made.

"Ah," he said at last. He locked the box and secreted the key once again. He handed me a sheet of paper folded over and sealed with red wax.

"It is from one of your King's principal secretaries," Herr Rink said.

"Not Wriothesley?" I said in alarm.

"No. I have no dealings with such as him. This is from Sir Ralph Sadler."

I gave a sigh of relief. I liked Ralph and he liked me.

I especially liked him because he had risked life and liberty by taking to the King a letter in which Thomas had begged for his life. It was a courageous thing to do, some said an insane one. It was certainly to no avail.

But the King had apparently admired Sadler's ability. Far from punishing him for his loyalty to Thomas he gave him his master's former post. Or, rather, part of it. He had split the Principal Secretary's responsibilities between Sadler and Wriothesley. Perhaps it needed two men to fill Thomas's shoes. Or maybe the King feared anyone ever again becoming as powerful as Thomas.

But at least it meant that I had one friend still left at Court.

Sadler's letter was short and terse. It confirmed that the King had married Katheryn in secret. Presumably the secrecy was because he did not wish to show unseemly haste between wives. The haste must have been due to either Katheryn's insistence or to his lust.

Yet this information was not the main reason that Ralph had written to me. It was to give me a dire warning.

He stated most insistently that all of Thomas's friends were in danger, myself included. Gardiner and Norfolk were hunting down every one of their old adversary's friends and that not even Archbishop Cranmer appeared safe.

Ralph begged me to seek the sanctuary of a powerful monarch. "And given the King of France's well-known predilections," he wrote, "I strongly advise that you seek this particular sovereign's friendship and protection."

I put down the letter. So my friends were right. I was still in danger. I took a deep breath to try to calm myself. Would I never be safe? I picked up the letter once more, read it more carefully. I wondered what

Ralph meant by the last sentence, about seeking the King of France's friendship. And about his predilections.

Herr Rink was unlocking a second box. He grunted as he pulled another item from it. It was a small bag, which he pushed towards me.

"Sir Thomas Cromwell left this money for you," he said.

"More money?" I cried. "He has given me so much already."

"I have learnt in a very long life that one can never have too much money," Herr Rink said softly. "Not unless you are a king or pope, in which case your head is turned and your appetite grows insatiable.

"In this particular case, Sir Thomas feared that you might have had all your money taken from you and that you would arrive at Paris penniless. He wished to provide for you."

He opened the bag and poured out the contents.

"Three hundred marks. Enough, if you are sensible, for seven or eight years. Less, if you are foolish."

Tears filled my eyes. Even though in utmost distress and danger my friend had planned so carefully for me.

"Now," Herr Rink said briskly. "I have two pieces of advice for you. One is that you seek the protection of King François. If one king becomes angry with you, your best recourse is to seek sanctuary with a second king who dislikes the first."

"That is what Sir Ralph Sadler advised as well," I said.

The old man pursed his lips and nodded. "I know young Sadler. He is that most unusual of creatures, a man of integrity. You do well to follow his advice, especially when it concurs with mine. The King, by the by, is presently at Chambord. I have here a letter of introduction for you to give to him."

I took a deep breath and asked as casually as I could, "And do you know, Herr Rink, if the King's sister will be at Chambord? And his niece?" I prayed that they were, for if so I would find Nicholas.

He shrugged. "I doubt it. The King has gone hunting, a pastime that has no fascination for his sister."

I sat back, a little deflated by his comment.

He began to hum as if pleased with himself. He scooped up the coins with practiced skill and poured them back in the bag before opening a ledger and passing it towards me.

"Please sign here," he said, indicating a line.

"And your second piece of advice?" I said, passing the ledger back to him. "You said you had two pieces of advice."

"Second piece? Oh yes. Trust Barnaby Finch completely. With your fortune, with your honor, with your life. He may be as ugly as a toad but he is a man of sterling worth."

I turned and looked at Finch, who shrugged his shoulders.

"As ugly as a toad?" I asked when we had left the office.

"I've no idea what the old man meant by it," Barnaby said. "His mind must be wandering. My mother always said I was the most beautiful boy in all creation."

"And of sterling worth?"

He shook his head and chuckled. "My mother was never that misguided."

Chapter 31

King François of France

I spent the journey pondering all that I had heard about King François. Some of this came from King Henry and was, therefore, a strange mixture of fascination, admiration, spite and envy. Most of it came from Nicholas, who saw the King as a great man, though an all-too-human one.

In many ways François was very like King Henry. Neither man was born to be king but the death of older heirs propelled them into the throne, in both cases before they were twenty years of age. Most young men would have been happy to have received a suit of clothes and a sword at that age. Henry and François were given kingdoms.

François was educated by the finest scholars and considered himself a patron of art and letters. He bought many books and even read most of them. And he loved and wrote poetry. Very useful I thought this last piece of information.

Like Henry, he was astonishingly profligate and spent vast amounts on building and decorating his palaces.

And like Henry, he had a taste for women. Henry was circumspect and somewhat restrained. François was none of these things. No one could quite be sure what type of woman he favored. This was because he seemed to favor all. Young or old, plain, pretty or ugly, clever or stupid: all were welcome into the Royal bed. The only quality these hundreds of women shared was in being willing to enter it.

And so, as the journey wound on, I began to think that my hopes to find Nicholas might have to wait. Instead I made plans to be François's newest conquest. Or rather, to conquer him.

I had grown used to marvelous palaces, having lived at Hampton Court, Greenwich Palace, Windsor Castle, Whitehall and Knole House. But none of these prepared me for the Château de Chambord.

It was one hundred miles south of Paris, in the center of the valley of the Loire. It was built of white stonework, dazzling in the bright August sunlight, a sumptuous creation, looking more like the ice statues which grace royal tables at feasts than a place to dwell.

At first sight it appeared to have a perfect symmetry, each tower and window a mirror of another. But on closer inspection I saw there were subtle differences. It was as if the architects were worried that too much perfection would weary the eye and soul.

Floating above these walls was a fantasy of roofs and turrets, an airy vista where fairies and fabulous beasts might delight to sport. As with the walls below, these were both like and unlike each other, every roof and turret a near echo of another but unique unto itself.

It was all utterly and completely beguiling.

As our carriage approached the Château we heard the sound of music in the air, sweet and joyful melodies to gladden the mind. And then one lone singer raised his voice high to the heavens and sang a haunting, bittersweet song which made my heart ache with its beauty.

My eyes filled with tears at the sound, at the sight, at the glory and delight of Chambord.

"I've never seen anything like this," I whispered.

My friends did not answer. They were speechless.

The carriage drew to a halt and Barnaby leapt from his horse to hand me down. At his suggestion I had worn my finest gown and most precious jewelry. But as I approached the entrance I saw groups of ladies of the Court and felt that my loveliest clothes were cheap and tawdry in comparison.

"Them French ladies look gorgeous," breathed Sissy, her eyes wide and staring.

"But not as beautiful as your mistress," Barnaby said. "No costly gowns and glitter can remedy that."

He passed Herr Rink's letter of introduction to a servant, who bade us follow him into the Château.

We waited for almost an hour before the servant returned.

"The King will see you," he said. His face wore a faint look of surprise at this message. "He is in the gardens."

We started to follow the servant but he stopped and held up his hand.

"The King desires to see Mademoiselle alone. Her servants are to wait here."

And he turned on his heel and hurried off, leaving me to keep up with him as best I could.

He led me through corridor after corridor, each one with many windows giving a view of the landscape outside. Eventually he stopped and indicated that I go through a door. Then he turned, and without another word, strode away.

After the wonders of the Château, the gardens were a disappointment. The ground was laid to lawn but the only flowers were in pots and they looked rather sad and bedraggled. I learnt later that the Château was merely a hunting lodge, a magnificent hunting lodge, which King

François rarely visited. And, like with all of his Châteaux, when he was not present it was stripped of everything and left empty save for a handful of servants.

When he made another visit, every item in the vast edifice had to be brought here on wagons. The wonderful furniture, the wall hangings, the kitchen equipment, the food, wine, silverware, drinking vessels and crockery: all traveled by ox-drawn carts ahead of the King in order to be set up in good time for his arrival. This included the flowers. They were woebegone because of the great heat and they were the only things in all the Château which did not look permanent and wonderful.

Perhaps most wonderful was King François himself.

He stood half-turned away from me, staring out at a forest beyond a river which ran to the south of the Château. It gave me a chance to examine him.

I knew that he was three years younger than King Henry but in physique he looked twenty years his junior. Henry had aged dreadfully these past few years and was now a vast bloated wreck of the man he once was. François still retained the look and vigor of youth.

He was tall and well made, with no excess weight. He looked strong, with broad shoulders, and I could well imagine how the two young kings had wrestled with each other at the Field of the Cloth of Gold. I was not convinced of the truth of this but I knew that the rivalry between the two men had simmered as constant and as bitter as any between two brothers.

He turned at that moment and regarded me. He was not handsome; his face was long and with few fine features. He wore a beard and moustache, but the latter was not enough to hide his mouth, which was small, ugly and with a rather self-satisfied look. Most striking of all was his extremely large nose. It was the shape of a boat's tiller, long and questing, and it dominated his face. There was something shocking about it, something which made me catch my breath. But then my gaze was caught by something else.

King Henry's eyes were a cornucopia of emotions, as changeable as the weather in April. Sometimes they were gentle, sometimes harsh, sometimes amused, sometimes stern, and all within moments. The last time I had seen him, when I pleaded for Thomas's life, they had raged with madness. But they were never as disconcerting as I thought François's eyes on that first meeting.

The French King's eyes were hooded and watchful, as if he were suspicious of everyone and everything. They seemed particularly well suited for snooping, for weighing things up, for peering into one's heart, mind and soul.

I felt sorry for him when I saw this. It made me consider that maybe Henry was not so unusual, after all. Perhaps becoming a King had made these men mistrustful and wary. They possessed the greatest wealth and blessings of anyone in their realm, but maybe this very bounty filled them with anxiety, made them terrified of losing everything.

And then François smiled and his eyes took on a different look entirely. They were warm and beguiling and seemed to say, *you will come to bed with me this minute and I shall love you to your core.*

"You must be Mademoiselle Petherton," he said. His voice was quiet yet with a deep resonance. *Probably on account of his nose*, I thought.

I curtsied. "That is my name, Your Majesty."

He stepped towards me and lifted my hand to his lips. His eyes stared at me a moment longer, scrutinizing me, recording. But they did more. They seemed to be binding me in invisible cords.

Well, two can play at that game, I thought.

"You are every bit as beautiful as I have been told."

I tilted my head in question. "You have been told of me?" I asked. "The King of France told of a simple little English girl?"

He nodded and kissed my hand. The heat of his breath washed over my fingers.

"By Charles de Marillac," he said. "My ambassador to London."

I nodded. "I am acquainted with Monsieur Marillac," I said.

He allowed my hand to drop to my side but he did not relinquish hold of it.

"Marillac told me that you were the most beautiful woman in England and that he knew of none finer in France or in the realm of the Ottomans." He paused and then smiled. "I think he may well have been correct."

"I am flattered, Your Majesty."

He shook his head, as if to say there was no need to acknowledge his praise.

"And I hear that you have been flattered by my dear cousin Henry," he continued. "That you have been his mistress for a number of years."

I pretended surprise at the casual way he mentioned this.

"Oh, do not worry, Alice," he said, squeezing my hand. "May I call you Alice?"

I nodded.

"We French are sympathetic to the power of love. You need feel no concern or doubt about your relationship with Henry. All kings have mistresses. In France most commoners have them as well."

"Are there so many women to go round?" I asked.

He smiled. "Of course there are. A man has, let us say, one wife and one mistress. His wife is the mistress of another man and that man's wife the mistress of yet another. It is all quite equable—some might say, quite mathematical."

"So of all the branches of mathematics," I said, "it lends itself best to multiplication. Now I know why there are so many French folk in the world."

He looked surprised at my comment and then laughed.

"You have wit as much as beauty, Alice Petherton," he said. "I marvel that Henry let you go. Marvel even more that he allowed you to come to my Court."

He gave a self-satisfied smile. If he had been a cat his lips would have been white with stolen cream.

I lowered my eyes bashfully, looked down at the ground for a moment. When I looked up I gazed into his eyes, demure yet challenging.

And then I leant close to him, put my mouth to his ear.

"He did not allow me to come to you," I murmured. "I came because I chose to."

At that moment, with those words, I saw that even the great King François, the man of lovers and mistresses beyond compute, had been captivated by me.

Thomas had once told me that no man could stop himself from falling under my spell. A natural gift he called it. Sometimes I thought it was not a gift at all.

The King stared at me in silence for a moment longer. Then he raised my hand to his lips once again.

"You are welcome at my Court," he said. His voice was lower than before, the sound slower, almost slurred. "You are more than welcome, and you may stay as long as you please."

I put my hand to my breast and curtsied low. I felt rather than saw his eyes watch me. The pretty young English girl, so fresh and uncompleted, so naive.

I hid a secret smile. I would become the King of France's lover. Henry would hear of it soon enough and he would become angry and jealous. The constant rivalry between the two kings would fester even more.

And so I would avenge Sir Thomas's death.

I allowed the King to help me rise from my curtsy.

"I have been honored by the King of England," I said. "I feel even more honored by the kindness and good opinion of the King of France."

I smiled upon him and I swear I heard a little groan of anticipation and of trepidation issue from his throat. *Caught*, I thought to myself. *And I shall be avenged.*

King François left the Château that day. Rumor had come that there was a white stag in the forest to the west. Everyone agreed that this was a wonder, a marvel. And as such it must be hunted, must be slaughtered and its head brought back to hang from a wall rather than from its own fine shoulders.

The King spent two days hunting in the forest. He was either chasing after a myth or he was incredibly unlucky. He returned to Chambord empty-handed, no wonderful white stag as trophy. Or perhaps it was the stag that had been lucky.

Thwarted in one pursuit, he made certain that he was not thwarted in another. He dined with his closest friends and then sent a message for me to join him in his private quarters.

On the perilous journey once again, I thought. *Shall I take a book of poetry as I had with King Henry?* I glanced in the mirror. Away with such subterfuge. I would take only myself.

The King was waiting for me in his Evening Room. It was huge, large enough to accommodate an audience. But screens had been placed in one corner, creating a smaller, more intimate space. It was here that I found the King, sprawling on a couch, his legs resting on the arm, kicking slightly as if he were a bored little boy.

"Ah, Alice," he said. "Come here. I wish you to entertain me."

I stepped towards him. "And how do you wish to be entertained, Your Majesty?"

He looked at me in surprise and then smiled. "Come now," he said, sitting up and patting the spot beside him. "No English coquetry please. We both know you have been the mistress of King Henry. We are not children." And he kissed me on the lips.

It was a gentle kiss, at first. It soon became more passionate, more insistent. I had intended to hold myself a trifle aloof, to make sure that

I was in charge of this game. In a way I was, for the King was evidently enraptured by me. But at the same time, he seemed determined to seduce me, to conquer me. The strangest thing was that I was aware that he was attempting to cast a spell over me. If I had not been so intent on snaring him, who knows if I would have succumbed? Hundreds of others had. But there was only one man I had let capture my heart.

What a game, I thought, lying back a little and pulling the King onto me. *What a game.*

Chapter 32
Bauble

"I cannot believe it," Susan said. "You've hopped out of the bed of one king only to leap into the bed of another."

"May I remind you that it is none of your business," I said icily.

"I'm your friend," Susan snapped, "not your servant."

I stared at her in fury. I would not be talked to like this. I would tell her to leave.

"I can poke my nose into your business," she continued, folding her arms in a belligerent manner, "precisely because I am your friend."

I was astonished at her temerity. And then I put my hands to my lips. But it was not enough to prevent the laugh escaping from them.

Susan blinked in confusion. My laughter got more and more intense. Tears flooded my eyes and I had trouble breathing. I reached out for her arm, holding on to it for dear life.

"Oh Susan," I said. "You cannot believe how right you are." I continued to laugh for a while longer. Eventually my laughter subsided and I wiped my eyes. "And you cannot believe how much I shall ignore you."

"On your own head be it," she said.

Then her hand went to her mouth. She looked crestfallen. "I didn't mean to say that," she said. "Not after what happened to Sir Thomas."

I patted her arm. "Sir Thomas is the reason I'm sleeping with King François," I said. "Partly because he would have advised me to find a new and powerful protector. But there's another reason. I've become François's lover in order to infuriate King Henry and make him boil with jealousy. That will be my revenge for the execution of Sir Thomas."

There was a stunned silence in the room.

"Do you think King Henry cares for you so mμch, still?" Mary asked. "When he has Katheryn Howard as his new wife?"

"Oh yes," I answered. "I know the nature of King Henry."

For I did know it. I knew that there was nothing more likely to arouse him than being thwarted in an attempt to possess a bauble which had caught his fancy. And I was one bauble I knew he could never completely relinquish.

"Well, promise us you'll be careful," Susan said. "We love you."

"I will be careful," I said. "But I have less cause for fear. I do not think François is as keen a lover of the ax as is our King."

But he was every bit as susceptible to my charms.

King François intended to stay only a few more days at Chambord; he was as restless as King Henry. But there were other reasons why he had to move around so continually. His Court was as large as Henry's and, like locusts, would strip a locality bare of every sup and morsel if it stayed there too long. Even the vast resources carried to a Château began to run out, and so, whether he wished to or not, the King must continually move and batten upon other places. And he always wished to.

We were going to Fontainebleau, his favorite palace, forty miles south of Paris. And, he told me, I would meet there the woman he loved most in all the world, his mistress, Anne de Pisseleu d'Heilly.

"She had to stay in Fontainebleau when I left," he said. "There is constant dispute between the Constable of France and the Admiral. It wearies me to despair so I thought it best to leave Anne to deal with them."

"But what about your Queen?" I asked.

François snorted. "Queen Eleanor? I see her as rarely as possible. I do not care for her."

I gave a curious look. "Then why did you marry her?" With the exception of Anne of Cleves, King Henry of England had always married for love or lust.

"Do not seek to judge me regarding this, Alice," he said, sharply. "It is not Kings alone, nor men, who take new lovers."

He gave me a thoughtful look, and not a particularly pleasant one at that.

"You have had two Kings as lovers in your short life," he continued. "You are fickle in your affections and will continue to be so, no doubt. Women are creatures of constant change, perhaps more so than even men."

He leaned back in his chair, his arms behind his head.

"Kings marry for reasons other than love," he continued. "My predecessor arranged for me to marry the heir to the throne of Brittany in order to gain the Dukedom. He was right to do so. I would marry in such fashion whenever it is necessary.

"Why, I've even thought about marrying Henry's daughter, Mary, and thereby ruling England. But Henry would never allow it."

He gave a wide grin. "If Sultan Suleiman had a daughter, I'd marry her."

"A Turk?" I asked in astonishment.

"Why not? The Ottoman Empire is the most powerful in the world and it is very close to my borders. The only lands separating it from France are Venice and the Swiss Confederation. I doubt they'll stop Suleiman for long if he chooses to march his legions westward. The Sultan could prove a very dangerous enemy. I have chosen to make him a very dear friend."

He gave a little clap of his hands, applauding himself for his cleverness.

I pondered this information. François was beginning to seem even more scheming than Henry.

"And what lands did you gain when you married your present wife?" I asked.

A look of distress clouded his face.

"I did not gain any lands," he said. His voice grew sharp and curt in an instant and he gnawed fiercely on his bottom lip. "I married Eleanor of Austria for the sake of my sons."

I frowned with confusion.

His face had become cold and blank and when he spoke again it was in a voice even colder.

"I had been captured by my enemy, the Emperor Charles. My horse was killed under me, you must understand, and I was powerless to fight on. I was imprisoned for almost a year. In the end, at the plea of my poor people, I was allowed to return to France. But my courtiers had won my liberty by exchanging me with my two eldest sons."

I looked at him swiftly. I could see that he was lying about something. But I decided not to pursue the reason for this dissembling.

"But your sons are free now?" I asked.

"After three long, dreadful years. And at an almost intolerable price."

I frowned, wondering what the price might have been. And then I realized.

"You married a woman you did not love in order to secure their release?" I said quietly.

A look of relief flooded his face and he reached out for my hands. "That is what happened," he said. "I married Emperor Charles's sister. I bought my sons' freedom at the expense of my own."

He nodded at his own words, as if chewing them over, to taste how they fitted in his mouth.

Chapter 33
Fontainebleau

It took four or five days to travel from Chambord to Fontainebleau; I do not recall exactly how long for the journey was a blur to me. The weather was so hot I could barely breathe and every morning I was sick. I wondered if it was the French food. The meat often tasted rancid, presumably because of the heat. Fortunately fruit and vegetables were plentiful so I ate more of these and less of the meat.

The change of diet seemed to have little effect on me, however. I was still sick most days. *Maybe it's the constant traveling*, I thought. I groaned, wondering how long we would be allowed to stay at Fontainebleau.

I was growing heartily sick of carriages and decided to go the rest of the way on horse. The Royal officials insisted that I ride side-saddle, but this made me feel queasy so I asked for a man's saddle. They were astonished by this, some outraged, others amused. All put it down to my strange English ways.

I felt great relief that we finally entered the well-tended parkland which surrounded Fontainebleau and an end to traveling was in sight.

And then, at last, we approached the Château. I gasped in astonishment when I saw it. I had been impressed by Chambord. I was overwhelmed by Fontainebleau.

I had never seen anything so vast, so grand, so wonderful. It made even the Palaces of Hampton Court and Greenwich appear mean and paltry. I gazed at King François as he rode on his fine white charger at the head of the retinue. What wealth he must command to have created such a magnificent palace. What power. What confident grandiosity.

I looked once again at the Château. The mere sight of it made me feel giddy and humbled. Humphrey rode up to me.

"Can you believe this, Alice?" he said. "Have you ever seen anything so grand and eye-watering?"

"Never," I said, still dazed.

"I bet old Henry would die of rage and envy if he could see it. There's no place in England to compare."

I smiled. Even Humphrey could see it. I wondered at the pretension of King Henry. Perhaps he was not the magnificent, all-powerful monarch he believed himself to be.

That evening I met the King's mistress, Anne de Pisseleu d'Heilly, Duchess of Étampes.

Anne was one of the great powers in the land, so powerful that she would defer to only the King and his sister, and then only in public. Anne certainly had no need to defer to François's wife, Eleanor, who she eclipsed in every sphere. Or almost every sphere.

Eleanor, who had been offered in marriage to virtually every monarch in Europe, including King Henry, still had one great diplomatic advantage. She was the sister of Emperor Charles of Germany, the most powerful monarch in Christendom. Whenever he had need to, François would trot her out to act as intermediary between them. At all other times he ignored her. She might well have not existed. In all the time that I was at Fontainebleau I never saw sight of her.

So the Duchess of Étampes ruled as queen in everything but name.

I was very much in two minds about meeting her. Nicholas had told me exactly how ruthless she could be. Apparently she had engaged in a furious two-year battle to usurp the position of François's first mistress. Since then she had consolidated her influence with a steely determination.

I certainly had no intention of putting myself forward as her rival. I had only slept with François to gain a measure of security and to spite King Henry. I had no desire to wield any power at the French Court. In fact, the only desire I had was to try to find Nicholas.

But I did want to make the acquaintance of the Duchess. Women have ever had to use subtle means to make their way in the world: their charm, their beauty, their wit, their grace. Some, such as Anne, added other qualities in order to attain their ends. Until now I had found advantage without really planning it. Now I wanted to learn from a master. Or rather, from a mistress.

Anne was no great beauty, although her twinkling eyes and vivacity made her seem very attractive. I found out later that she was thirty-two years of age. I could never quite make up my mind if she looked older or younger. She was one of those women who seemed to live forever on the cusp: between plain looks and beauty, between one age and another, between ruthlessness and benevolence.

The King introduced me as a friend of King Henry, as casual and offhand as if I were a second-rate diplomat. No suggestion of our recent liaison as much as flickered over him.

Anne did not reply but looked at him with a gaze which I found quite unfathomable.

She turned to me after an eternity and gave a tight little smile.

"You are very beautiful, child," she said. "You are welcome at Court. I hope that the King has already given you a good and warm welcome."

"He has," I said, feeling a blush rise in my cheeks.

She smiled more luxuriantly, as if my words had confirmed her suspicions and, in some mysterious fashion, augmented rather than diminished her standing.

What do I call her? I wondered. I had been mistress of a King so I should have known, but under Anne's cool, cool stare I could not remember how I had been titled at Court.

"Call me Anne," she said after a moment, almost as though she had read my mind. "And I shall call you Alys."

"Alice," I said. "It is pronounced Alice."

She pursed her lips and shrugged her shoulders. It was as if my preference in the pronunciation of my own name was of little importance.

I was relieved when François steered me away.

"And now let me introduce you to my sister," he said.

Marguerite had been watching my introduction to Anne with interest and some amusement. I had the suspicion that she knew exactly what had transpired between her brother and me and wished to see how Anne would react. It was not a comfortable feeling. It was as if I were a kitten being watched by two cats, each pondering whether I would grow to become more like herself or like her rival.

Marguerite was a few years older than her brother and bore a strong physical resemblance to him, especially in the size and shape of her nose, poor woman.

But she bore even more resemblance in her personality. She was as energetic and inquisitive as her brother, fascinated by everything new, whether in the arts or in ideas. But she was steadier than François, less mercurial. I liked her from the moment I met her.

Marguerite gave me a warm smile and, taking me by the arm, escorted me to one side of the Hall.

"You are welcome here," she said. "I have heard a lot about you."

"Have you?" I said. How on earth would she have heard about me?

"We have a mutual friend," she said. "He is over there, by the door."

I followed her gaze and gasped. Leaning against the wall was Nicholas Bourbon. The whole world seemed to fall away from me. All that I could see was my lover.

I felt a tap on my shoulder and saw Marguerite beaming down at me. "Go, child," she said, then turned and walked across the hall to her brother.

A moment later a familiar voice was whispering in my ear.

"You look beautiful, my darling. I have been expecting you."

I turned and gazed into his eyes. I had forgotten how beautiful they were. Dreams were not the same at all.

"You're here," I said.

He chuckled. "It appears so."

I swallowed hard and said the first words that came to mind. They were amazingly banal. "And how do you like tutoring the King's niece?"

Nicholas looked a little astonished at my question, as well he might. Then he appeared to decide to play along.

"It keeps the wolf from the door. And I have time to write and think. It is, on the whole, a most pleasant existence."

I held his gaze for a moment.

"As long as you are content, Nicholas." I could not believe how stiff and stilted I sounded.

"I am," he said. He gave a deep sigh. "And I am even more content now that you are here."

He bent and kissed my hand. "Come to my chamber."

"But King François?" I said.

"He has forgotten you already."

I looked across at the King. Nicholas was right. He was sitting between his sister and his mistress, listening avidly to them, wide-eyed with pleasure. He had no need of me.

Nicholas led me to his chamber. We walked for what seemed a mile through endless corridors, past countless windows and numberless doors.

After a while we found ourselves holding hands. My heart felt light as a breeze. I giggled a little and then a little more.

We walked still further, silent and content.

"How big is the Palace?" I asked at last.

"I'm not sure anybody knows," he answered. "And if a computation were made it would be out of date almost immediately. King François is constantly adding new bits to the Château."

"In that, at least, he is like King Henry."

"Only that?" he asked.

I did not answer but I could see that he was a little hurt. I did not doubt that news of my liaison with King François had come to his ears as well as to the rest of the Court.

I bit my lip. "It was expedient," I answered. "I had need of a protector."

The English Court was a morass of sexual favors, liaisons, bargains and broken promises. The French Court appeared little different, if perhaps a fraction more discreet and sophisticated. Nicholas would not have been surprised to hear the King had bedded me. In fact, he would have been more surprised had the King chosen not to.

But that did not mean he had to be happy with the situation. And judging by his glance it appeared that he was not. He was hurt by my liaison, wounded, a little jealous. My heart danced at the thought, both happy and sad. Sad that I had caused my lover grief. Happiness because that grief meant he loved me.

He did not answer for a moment but then he nodded. "I have heard about the downfall of Sir Thomas." He stopped and took me by the hand. "I am sorry for it. I liked the man and I know that he was a good friend to you."

He raised my hand and gave it a tiny kiss. "But most of all I am glad that you are safe, dear Alice."

He opened a door and led me into his chamber.

"I did not think I would see you again," I said. My eyes began to fill with tears and I did not know if they were of sorrow at the thought of losing him or joy at finding him again.

"The stars have set our course," he said. And he raised my chin and kissed me.

It was wonderful to be in his arms once again. He kissed and caressed with the combination of strength and gentleness which I had almost forgotten. Now I realized that some part of me would remember it forever.

He kissed me so deeply I thought my heart would grow wings and fly out of my chest. My head felt light and giddy and I heard my sighs as if from some distant forest. His fingers stroked and petted me and they were soft and tender, playful and frolicsome, inquisitive and determined. My skin tingled at every touch.

"I love you, Alice," he murmured in my ear and then kissed it with the utmost delicacy.

"I love you too," I said. "I've missed you so much."

I felt his smile rather than saw it, felt it grow upon his face until it swept all his body and then encompassed me. We were one vast smile; bigger than ourselves, larger than Fontainebleau, greater than all the kings and kingdoms of the world.

We made love, real love. It was tender and passionate, giving and taking, sharing and sighing. All the time we gazed into each other's eyes, as if we could not get enough of the sight.

At last, after time had long disappeared, we climaxed, him first in one long paean of delight and me after, wave upon wave of warm, sweet ecstasy, the purr of a kitten sounding from me, the nets of love entangling us utterly.

I lay upon the bed and held Nicholas tight. *This is what I was born for*, I thought. *This is where I was meant to be.* Not with kings and supercilious courtiers but with a real man, simple, honest, caring—a man who loved me rather than himself, a man who made me feel not a mistress but his love.

But as I drifted into sleep I found myself wondering, *is this enough?*

When I awoke Nicholas was sitting up and gazing at me.

"You are even more beautiful than before," he said, reaching out and touching my cheek as if to make sure that I was real.

"As are you," I said. "And the kindest, strongest, loveliest man in all creation."

He laughed at my words, a delightful, kindly laugh. I felt he did not believe them, even though I did. But I think he was flattered, nonetheless.

Chapter 34
With Child

The very next day I woke with my stomach wallowing even more than usual. I only just managed to reach for the chamber pot.

"Are you unwell?" Nicholas asked, sitting up in bed. He looked very concerned, something I had rarely seen in a man.

"I have been like this for a while now," I said. "It must have been something I have eaten."

"For how long?"

I shook my head. "I don't know. Since we came to France. About three weeks, I suppose."

He frowned at my words and then his eyes went to my stomach.

"Don't worry," I said, "I'm not fading away. In fact, if anything, my clothes are getting a little tighter."

He pulled up his knees and rested his elbows on them, regarding me thoughtfully.

"And how long is it since you last had your monthly bleed?" he asked.

I glanced at the window, thinking back to the last occasion.

"Do you know, I can't quite recall." I tapped my fingers on my chin, trying to remember.

"It was some time ago, I think. Before Sir Thomas was executed." My mind delved back further and then I nodded. "I remember now. It was the day after he was arrested."

Nicholas nodded. "And when was that? Exactly?"

"The tenth of June," I said. "Not a date I'll easily forget."

Nicholas did not answer for a moment. When he did, his voice was serious and thoughtful. "It is now the twenty-first of August. Does not the length of time between your last bleed and now tell you something?"

I looked at him in confusion for a moment. Then my heart went to my mouth and my hands to my stomach.

"Oh no," I said.

"Did you have no idea?" he asked in astonishment.

I shook my head. If my mother had been alive she would have told me, my Grandmother even. But who else was there to school a child in the nature of women? I had been left alone to face the world, an innocent.

We stared at each other in silence. At last Nicholas spoke. "Who is the father? Do you know?"

I was hurt by the question. It made me seem a girl of easy virtue, some whore who sold her favors for the smallest coin. My face blazed with heat.

"You and I were lovers in the spring," I said.

"That is true. But what of others?"

"There were no others."

He tilted his head a little, regarded me quizzically.

"Well," I faltered. "I was summoned by the King. Once, in June. The day after you left for France."

He put his hand to his mouth as if to stop himself from speaking.

"So it could be your child, Nicholas," I said in a little voice.

I stared at him desperately, wanting him to shout out that it was his child, that he was the father. That he was ecstatic to learn that I was the mother of his child.

But instead he shrugged.

"We will know in the new year," he said.

His words made me feel utterly alone, abandoned.

"I will speak with the Court Physician," he continued. "We are good friends and he will keep it confidential."

I gave him a wan smile, terribly hurt by his reaction. But maybe this was the way of men. He was thinking practically rather than romantically.

I suppose I should have been grateful. I needed a physician who was skillful and circumspect. I feared what might happen if people suspected I was carrying King Henry's bastard. For all I knew my life might be in grave danger. *Not just mine*, I thought, my hand going involuntarily to my belly.

And then I smiled.

I was with child. I was going to be a mother.

The Court Physician confirmed that I was expecting. He thought I had probably fallen pregnant in May or June. That was no help to me. It meant that the child might be Nicholas's. Or it might be King Henry's.

Nicholas was outwardly solicitous of me and appeared pleased at being a father. But I sensed that inwardly he doubted the paternity of the child.

Nevertheless, he decided to petition King François to allow us to marry.

"Is it usual to ask the King such a thing?" I asked.

"It is as I am one of his servants," he answered. "And even more so when asking to marry a woman such as you."

"You mean a foreigner?"

"I mean someone who was once the favorite of the King of England. One who was also favored by François himself."

Nicholas spent the whole of the next day awaiting audience with the King. When he returned to me in the evening he looked tired and resigned.

"The King has refused my petition," he said.

I felt cold and hollow at his words.

"But why?"

Nicholas poured himself some wine and threw it down his throat.

"I suspect that he may not wish to antagonize King Henry. But there are other reasons."

He came and sat beside me.

"The King is getting increasingly intolerant of religious reformers. There have been imprisonments, torture, even executions. He does not wish his niece's tutor to be married to a follower of the new religion."

"But I'm not. Not really. I'll become a Catholic."

"Nobody at Court would believe it. You are known to be a friend of Thomas Cromwell and Archbishop Cranmer. You would be considered suspect, someone who might contaminate Princess Jeanne."

I felt sick at his words. It seemed that François was becoming as despotic and callous as Henry. I had no wish to fall foul of another King intent on beating people's souls into the pattern he preferred.

I wished that Nicholas would say he'd marry me and give up his post as tutor. But no man dare defy the King. And nor would I let him.

"So what is to become of me? Of us? Can we be together no longer?"

He gave a wry smile.

"We cannot marry but we can live together."

"King François has allowed this?"

"Not the King. Anne, the Royal mistress. She has persuaded him to agree to it."

"Anne? But why?"

Nicholas laughed and took my hands. "Gaze in a mirror, Alice. Anne has no wish for such a beauty to be close to the King. The sooner you are out of the way and settled with me the better she will like it. I think she would have tried to persuade the King to allow us to marry if she thought there had been a chance of it."

"But there isn't?"

Nicholas shook his head. "François may choose to turn a blind eye to our relationship but he will never countenance our marriage."

He paused and gave me a peculiar glance. "Anne asked me to give you a message. Concerning some news from England."

"What news?"

"The King has married Katheryn Howard. Anne thought you should know."

"I knew this already," I said. "But how very kind of her to let me know." Though I suspected it was not.

I poured Nicholas and myself some wine. "Let us wish the royal couple every happiness," I said.

I was not sure if I wished this or not, to be honest. And I was not at all certain that such wishes would come true.

Nicholas had to go south at the beginning of September. His pupil, Jeanne d'Albret, was a flighty and impetuous child of eleven years and her inquisitive ways and impertinence had become increasingly annoying to the King. And, more to the point, to his mistress.

The child was packed off to the Château de Plessis-lèz-Tours, one of the most distant châteaux of the Loire. Nicholas went with her and so did I.

I could not quite make up my mind whether I wanted my child to be as independent and self-assured as Jeanne. Perhaps to others, I concluded, but not to me.

Nicholas was in high good spirits at being sent away. He did not find the Court as beguiling as I did. He was given an extra allowance for the journey and the time we would be away. It was sufficient for him but not for me. Fortunately I still had money and was able to support myself and my friends.

"You have your own entourage," Nicholas said. "You are almost a queen."

"Don't say that," I begged. "Please. The mere thought of being queen terrifies me."

"Then it is good that you shall not be one," he said. "Better, by far, to be a humble scholar's mistress."

The journey was more pleasant than the ones I had taken hitherto in France. The weather was still hotter than anything I had ever experienced, but I must have been getting used to it, for it bothered me less.

The morning sickness stopped the day we began our journey, which was a great relief. Because the King was not leading the party we moved at less frantic a pace, stopping every night at a Château or, if we could not reach one in time, finding a secluded location to pitch tents.

I must admit I preferred it when we did this, for it meant a cooler night and better sleep. Sometimes Nicholas and I would sleep under the stars, watching them wheel across the heavens.

He taught me the names of the constellations and told me the stories and legends which had given rise to them. I loved Orion most of all for in my heart I imagined that ancient hunter must have had the qualities of my lover: bravery, intelligence, kindness and wisdom.

We journeyed through Pithiviers and Orléans and then made our way along the River Loire. The long period of hot weather had made the water level drop alarmingly and in some places people were able to wade far out into the stream. Shoals of fish washed up upon the banks, dying from the heat and want of water. The people who lived nearby rejoiced in this bounty, cooking vast quantities of fish on fires set up along the river, smoking those they could not eat that day and salting those they lacked the fires to smoke. It seemed like a carnival atmosphere.

We stayed at Chambord, Blois, Chaumont and Amboise. The Châteaux were wonderful, each one different in design and appearance. There were so many they became a blurred memory in the main. I seem to recall that I liked Chaumont most for it was the smallest and prettiest and looked like a castle that King Arthur and his knights might well have dwelt in.

This was not the case with the Château de Plessis-lèz-Tours. It was quite the ugliest Château I had seen, a huge straddling edifice with sweeping great wings. It was surrounded by high ramparts bristling with cruel-looking spikes.

We clattered across a drawbridge, through a heavily fortified gateway and into the great central court. The Château servants attended us with courteous efficiency, whisking everyone away to their chambers.

Somehow they had even received word about the relationship between Nicholas and me. We were given adjacent apartments with a private door between the two.

His rooms were larger, with a library and study, paneled in dark oak. Very masculine, appropriately serious for a tutor to royalty.

Mine were smaller but more pleasant, with a plaster frieze depicting the four seasons.

"I prefer your rooms," Nicholas said with a smile. "I think I shall have to spend much of my time here."

I went over to the window and gazed down at the courtyard. "It feels like a prison," I said.

Nicholas put his arms around me and held me tight.

"This was a favorite residence of King Louis XI," he said. "He grew more suspicious as he got older and ensured that this place was a haven of security. It's as much a fortress as a palace."

"But why have we come here with Jeanne?" I said. "It seems a strange place to lodge a little girl."

Nicholas did not answer for a moment. "Let us just say that King François has also grown more suspicious."

"Surely he has no fear of his little niece."

"Probably not. But perhaps he fears that his enemies will try to make use of her."

"What enemies?"

Nicholas gave a swift glance round.

"I think that François doubts his son and heir."

I looked at him in surprise. "Henri?"

Nicholas nodded. "Every King wants the Dauphin to succeed him in order to keep the monarchy strong and the Kingdom safe. But every King of France comes to loathe and distrust his heir. They remember how much they thirsted for the Crown when they were young, you see, and assume that their sons feel the same. So, inevitably, every King sees plots where there are none. But often, too often, such plots exist."

"But would Henri rebel against his father?"

Nicholas gave a tight little laugh.

"With this King and this Dauphin, I think it highly likely. Henri bears no love for his father, blaming him for his childhood incarceration. Perhaps he even hates him. And some may think it understandable."

"Be careful of what you say, Nicholas."

"I would not say this to anyone except you. But you're right. The Court is full of spies and eavesdroppers. I should learn to be more circumspect."

The weather cooled off at last and winter settled on the Château de Plessis-lèz-Tours.

But it was a glorious winter, unlike any I had ever known. The days were not grey and damp as they were in England; the winter sun shone joyfully and the air was cool but not cold. Winter began to bite only at the beginning of January and it was then that we were summoned to Paris.

I had not wished to go on such a journey for by this time I was big with child. But Jeanne, who had become attached to me, burst into tears at hearing this and sulked and stamped amazingly. This display would not have persuaded me, however. It was the reason for our journey that did so. For Jeanne was journeying to her wedding, to Duke William of Cleves, the brother of King Henry's previous Queen. He was in his mid-twenties and a shrewd and grasping man. Jeanne was only twelve years of age.

We arrived in Paris with Jeanne throwing tantrums more fitting to a child half her age. I had every sympathy with her.

She was bitter at the marriage and pleaded with her uncle not to go ahead with it. For a few days François indulged her. Then he grew weary of her intransigence. His mistress, Anne, grew even wearier and in the end poor Jeanne was given a fierce beating to make her learn the error of her ways.

On the morning of the wedding she was dressed in a rich and sumptuous manner. She wore a golden crown upon her head to show her Royal standing. A silver-and-gold skirt was encrusted with precious stones, so heavy that the poor child could hardly take one step in front of another. Above this she wore a crimson satin cloak trimmed with ermine.

But although she looked like a princess, any hopes that she would act like one were soon dashed. As she walked down the aisle she caught a glimpse of her future husband and began to howl and shriek. She tried to run out of the church but was caught before she made her escape.

She was carried up the aisle by Constable Montmorency. And every step of the way she beat him upon the head and shoulders and screamed so loud that the guests held their hands to their ears.

Fortunately for Jeanne, her mother was able to persuade the King that she was too overwrought to fulfil the more intimate of wifely duties. The Duke of Cleves returned to Germany with a rich dowry but without his wife. It seemed he thought he had got a better bargain than he could have hoped for. Jeanne returned to the Loire Valley and we went with her.

And then, in the middle of February, I gave birth.

The midwives told me that it was an easy birth, all things considered. *It might have been for you*, I thought, but it had not been for me.

The "all things considered" were that I gave birth not to one baby, but to two. A little girl and a little boy. I fell in love with them the instant I saw them.

The little girl I called Lily, after my Grandmother. The little boy I called Thomas, not after my father so much as after my friend, Thomas Cromwell. But the moment I named him I heard a little voice in my head telling me to call him Tommy. I was relieved. It sounded a much luckier name.

Nicholas was very loving to them, cuddling them, showing them off to friends with fatherly pride. Yet sometimes, when I came upon him alone with them, I found him peering at them closely. I did not ask him, but I felt that he was scrutinizing them to see if he could detect any features they might have inherited from him.

Of course, it was far too early to tell. Babies are babies and change as rapidly as the weather. All I knew was that they belonged to me and I loved them more completely and more fiercely than I had loved anything in the world. More even than Nicholas.

Sometimes, when the evenings were quiet, and when Nicholas was busy tutoring Jeanne, I would allow myself to wonder aloud who the father might be.

"It doesn't matter who he is," Mary said. "Nicholas will be a father to the children and who could ask for a better one."

Susan nodded in agreement but I could not help but detect a dubious look upon her face.

I hoped fervently that Nicholas was my babies' father, was terrified that he might not be.

If Henry was their father then their lives might be in danger.

Having excluded his daughters from the succession, Henry now had only one legitimate heir, Prince Edward. If Edward were to die then Tommy might well be considered next in line to the throne. I had no desire for my children to become puppets in the hands of the ambitious and devious men of the English Court.

"Please look like Nicholas," I pleaded to them sometimes when no one was near. "Please, oh please."

"We'll know who the father is in a year," Humphrey said one evening. "When the babies start to talk. If they speak French then their father is Nicholas Bourbon. If they speak English then it's King Henry."

I looked at him in astonishment. I opened my mouth to ask if he was serious but caught Sissy nodding gravely as if he had just spoken the wisest of words. I decided it was not worth responding.

But maybe there was some wisdom there after all. As long as I remained in France, Lily and Thomas would grow to live and speak as if they were French. It would make little real difference if they were the children of King Henry. But at least it would make them appear less so.

Chapter 35
The Loss of Tommy

April 1541

Spring came early to the Loire Valley, and Nicholas was summoned to Fontainebleau to discuss Jeanne's education. It seemed that King François had a new scheme to make his niece a more suitable young woman than she was proving to be.

My babies grew fat and healthy. By the beginning of April the weather was warm enough for Sissy and me to walk with them in the grounds of the Château, basking in the sunshine.

I marveled at them still, barely able to take my eyes from them. I had never felt more at peace. Nor more hopeful for the future.

And then, on the tenth day of April, Mary came running into my bedroom. My heart fell like stone when I saw her. Something was wrong.

"Come quickly," she said.

"The twins?"

She nodded and hurried from the room.

I raced after her down the hallway. Sissy was standing with Tommy in her arms.

"He's burning up, Alice," she said. "And Lily as well."

I took him from her. He felt as hot as a coal.

Mary went over to the crib and held her fingers against Lily's forehead. "Sissy's right," she said. "Lily's hot as well, though cooler than Tommy."

"Send for Doctor Arnaud," I said.

"Get wet towels," said Mary. "We can use them to keep the babies cool."

I lost count of how many towels and linens we used. They seemed to keep Lily cool, but they did little or nothing to combat the heat which gripped Tommy. Where Lily cried loudly at her discomfort, he grizzled ever more softly. His arms and legs started to twitch and spasm and he began to struggle for breath.

"Whatever can I do?" I cried. "When will the doctor come?"

If only Nicholas were here, I thought desperately.

The long minutes crept by. I stared at my son as he writhed in torment. My mind was so overcome with horror and distress I could barely think. My friends continued the work of pressing damp towels upon the bodies of both babies. They worked ceaselessly. All too soon, the water in the basin would grow warm from the heat of the fever and Humphrey would snatch up the basin and race to the well to draw cooler water. It was to little avail.

Doctor Arnaud arrived within the hour, although it seemed like I had sent for him a week before. He took one look at the babies and shook his head.

"The girl may survive," he said. "Girls are often stronger."

"My boy?" I asked bleakly.

He shook his head again. "I'm sorry."

I brushed him aside and reached down for Tommy. He was burning up, yet had started to shiver as if with terrible cold. He made weak sucking noises and, without caring who saw, I pulled down my chemise and put him to my breast. I felt his tiny lips brush against my nipple, felt them pucker and try to fasten on. And then he seemed to sigh and I felt the life fly from him.

My eyes became lakes of bitter tears. I pulled Tommy from my breast and nuzzled him softly, murmuring words of gentle love into his unheeding ears.

Dimly I saw Mary and Sissy continuing to bathe Lily. Dimly I saw the doctor peering over her cradle, feeling gently at her body. Dimly I felt a part of my life ebb from me as the whole of Tommy's had ebbed from him.

I stood alone, rocking my poor dead child, crooning little songs, heedless of the world.

And then I felt Humphrey near. "I'll take the little fellow," he said. "I'll look after him while you tend to Lily."

I turned to him in astonishment.

Lily. Of course.

I pushed Sissy aside, snatching the towel from her hand. I bathed my darling girl's face with the cloth. She felt hot, yet not quite as hot as before.

"More water," I cried. "More water."

Sissy picked up the basin and clattered down the stairs. Out of the corner of my eye I saw Humphrey standing with Tommy in his arms, moving back and forth as if he were rocking him to sleep.

He's asleep now, I thought with one part of my mind. But with most of it I concentrated on Lily. I would fight to keep her alive, fight and die myself if necessary.

I have no idea how many hours we tended to my baby. The doctor left and returned bearing cooling liniments and a gentle tonic. "You should give it to her if she recovers," he said.

"If?" I said. "Don't say if to me. I warn you, don't say if."

I returned to my task, wiping and cooling, wiping and cooling. I had no time to wonder where Humphrey had taken my son. He returned a little after to resume his task of taking away the warm water and replacing it with cold.

The evening came and still we worked. The doctor took his leave saying he had other patients to attend to and that Lily was in God's hands.

"She's in our hands," I cried savagely. "Mine and my friends. It was God who took my son from me. I'm not going to let him take my daughter."

Mary tried to get me to leave the nursery to take some rest but I refused.

Susan and Barnaby had spent the day at a neighboring town but at last they returned to the Château. Susan took in the scene at once and immediately joined the others in the constant laying on of towels.

Barnaby stared at Lily for one brief moment and took my hand. "I've heard of a healer," he said and hurried from the room.

A little later he came back with a tiny bottle of dark liquid. "The healer says to brush one drop on Lily's lips," he said. "One drop only."

I nodded and he dripped a tiny amount on his finger and gently rubbed it on Lily's mouth. She seemed startled at the touch and then her little tongue popped out and licked her lips.

"It's enough," Barnaby said. "The old woman said one drop would be enough."

I do not know if the strange liquid had any effect or whether it was our hours of constant struggle to keep her cool. But within a little while, Lily's fever began to calm. I stretched to relieve the tension, went and took a sip of water.

When I turned back I saw she had suddenly grown more still. I put my hand to my mouth, thought she was being taken from me as Tommy had been.

I doubt I ever did a braver thing. I stepped over and felt her head. I breathed a prayer, although I do not know who I addressed it to. Without a thought I picked her up and held her close. She gave a prodigious yawn and cooed as if with pleasure.

I placed her on my breast. For a moment I felt nothing and then her little lips fastened on my nipple and gently she began to suck. There was little strength in her, I could tell that. But there was enough and soon she drew down some milk. She yawned once again and fell into slumber.

"It's the best thing for her," Sissy said. "My mum always said that. Sleep's the best thing for folk that's ailing."

"We must watch over her," I said. "Throughout the night."

"I'll take the first watch," said Susan. "You all look exhausted."

"I will stay here," I said.

Sissy pulled up a chair and helped me into it. Susan pulled up another and together we sat until the small hours when Mary came and took over from Susan. Sissy and Humphrey arrived in the hour before dawn.

I do not know whether I slept at all in that endless night. My eyes felt as if hot irons had pierced them. But then, just as the sun rose, I felt myself drift off. My head slumped, no matter how much I tried to stop it. And I joined my darling daughter in a blessed healing sleep.

Chapter 36
Rejection

We buried Tommy the next day. I felt so used up I could no longer weep. I followed the tiny coffin as silent as a mute. The service was short and beautiful, that I knew. I watched the coffin being lowered into the ground and swayed at the sight. Humphrey and Barnaby took hold of me and held me safe.

I did not speak for two days, tending only to Lily. On the day after the funeral, Mary came and sat beside us and played gentle melodies. That and the gurgles and smiles of Lily began to ease my soul.

I wrote to Nicholas to tell him. As the courier rode out I hoped that he would find him swiftly. The Court could be any of a dozen places.

Lily made a surprisingly quick recovery and was soon thriving once again.

"You need to take her out," Susan told me. "She needs fresh air and sunshine. And so do you. You cannot sit in the nursery all the time."

"But Tommy . . ." I began.

"Tommy has gone," she said. "You have to bend all your heart to Lily."

And I did.

That cruel April drew to a close. My friends celebrated my birthday in gentle mood, encouraging me to look to the future and not to the past.

I will do so, I determined. *For all our sakes.* But I knew that a part of me would always linger by the little grave beyond the Château walls.

Nicholas returned in the second week in May. The letter had only found him a week before and he had asked permission of the King to hurry to me.

He was considerate and loving. The death of Tommy did not hit him as bitterly as it had me. Perhaps it was because he was a man. Perhaps it was because he had not been here to see the little mite's struggle to survive. Perhaps there were other reasons which I did not care to know.

Two weeks after he returned I awoke to find my bed empty. I put on some clothes and found Nicholas alone in the sitting room. An untouched cup of wine was by his side and a hard crust of bread uneaten.

"Why are you up so early, my love?" I asked.

He started as if I had woken him from some deep reverie. Yet it could not have been a pleasant one for his face appeared anxious.

I sat beside him and took his hands in mine.

"What troubles you?" I asked. "Tell me and perhaps we can put it to rest."

He smiled but I thought it was a sad and weary one.

"What troubles me," he said, "is what may happen to you."

"What do you mean?" I was confused and surprised by his words.

Nicholas took a deep breath and turned his face away from me.

"I begin to think it is folly for you to stay in France any longer. I think you should consider returning to England."

I stared at him, bewildered. "Your words make no sense. I wouldn't feel safe in England."

"You're not safe here," he said. He reached inside his jacket and pulled out a letter. "This is from Charles de Marillac. He warns me that English agents are in France searching for you."

"What nonsense. How can English agents work in France?"

"They're here at this very moment," he said. "They're everywhere in Europe. As King Henry's paranoia grows so does his army of spies and kidnappers. Several of his victims have been captured on French soil and taken back to England. A few have been murdered here at his command."

I snatched the Ambassador's letter and read it swiftly. My hand began to shake and I had to place the paper on the table in order to continue reading it.

"Why does the King seek to harm you?" Nicholas asked at last.

I swallowed hard. Perhaps it was because of what I had done. Fleeing the country without his consent. Sleeping with François in order to anger him. What a fool I'd been. But I would never have imagined such a ferocious response. It was something he might mete out to courtiers who betrayed him. But not to me. Surely not to me?

"Perhaps it is not Henry's doing," I said after a moment more's reflection.

Nicholas shot a glance at me. "If not King Henry, then who? And why?"

"The reason why is probably because of my friendship with Thomas Cromwell. His enemies dread the man even though he's in his grave. Perhaps they fear that the secrets he held about them were not buried with his corpse."

"And who are these enemies?"

"I suspect the Duke of Norfolk most. But others are in league with him and some of these men bear me personal grudges. Richard Rich, for example. And Thomas Wriothesley."

"Powerful men," he said. "Powerful enemies."

"So if you think that's the case," I said, "why on earth are you advising me to return to England?"

"It's not my advice. It's Marillac's." He tapped the document a couple of times. "Charles says that your flight to France has cast suspicion upon you. It makes you appear to share the same guilt as Cromwell. Suspicion was enough to destroy the man. What chance that you will escape if Cromwell could not?"

"Then I shall seek the protection of King François."

Nicholas shook his head. "What are you to François? He likes you well enough but if Henry asks it and it suits him he would send you back in chains, or worse."

"What is the worse?"

Nicholas turned away, stared at the floor. When he looked up his face was twisted in grief. It was answer and more than answer enough.

"Then I am doomed whatever I do."

Nicholas squeezed my hands.

"It is because of this danger that Marillac advises you return to England. Show that you are not a traitor who has fled to protect yourself. Show that you do not fear to walk on dangerous ground. And throw yourself on the King's mercy."

I gave a bitter laugh. "I have had no success in such ventures before. Why should I hope for it now?"

"You were pleading for the lives of others then, Alice."

"And now I will be pleading for my own." I grew suddenly angry, not with my persecutors but with Nicholas. "I suppose you think I did not plead for Sir Thomas with as much vigor as I will plead for myself."

"I did not say that. But Henry wished to have done with Cromwell. I doubt he bears you no such malicious intent."

"But if he fears I am tainted with the same treason?"

"That is why you must seek an audience with him. To persuade him of your innocence and your loyalty. To persuade him of your love for him."

My heart lurched and I glared at him in fury.

"So you would have me whore myself with him."

He pulled my hands towards his lips and kissed them. "I would, Alice. If it was the only way to save your life. Then I would."

My eyes had been hot and dry until this moment. Now they filled with tears.

"I have done nothing," I said. "Save to walk like a giddy fool in a den of savage beasts."

He gave me a look of pity. Found no more words to say.

I walked to the window and cudgeled my brains. *Think, think, think.*

Perhaps, after all, Marillac's advice was sound. Perhaps I should return to the den of the savage beasts. But this time I would not walk there like a giddy fool. I would be like Theseus when he entered the labyrinth. I would arm myself with cunning. I would not be prey to the Minotaur.

"Perhaps you could seek out friends who will support you," Nicholas said, giving a more hopeful look.

"What friends do I have now at Court?" I said. "My greatest friend lies rotting in his grave."

"Then find others. And never forget that the King can be both the deadliest enemy and greatest of friends."

I nodded. He spoke truly. But he did not speak altogether wisely.

The King had grown too suspicious, too wayward and savage to rely upon. If I did throw myself on his mercy I would need to have friends already primed to support me.

My mind ran over the men with influence over the King. I bit my lip as I recalled them. Most had little reason to love me; some actively sought my undoing. And then a familiar face came to mind.

"Cranmer," I said. "Archbishop Cranmer. He has always been kind to me."

"But he was a friend of Cromwell," Nicholas said. "Does that not make him a suspect ally?"

"Not at all. He is one of the few men that the King trusts. Cranmer is completely loyal, you see. More than that, he has integrity as well. The King may have dispensed with his but he can still recognize the quality in others. And still value it."

Let's hope that Cranmer will be my Ariadne, I thought. *And that he has plenty of thread to help me make my escape from the monster.*

"I shall return to England," I said.

"Will you take Lily with you?" Nicholas asked.

"I shall."

"Is that not dangerous? For her?"

"It's better than leaving her here to be found by English agents. Besides, I will take Barnaby Finch with me."

Later that day I went alone to where my baby Tommy slept and said farewell to him. His little grave was well tended but I wondered how long this would remain the case.

I could not bear the thought of deserting him.

"It's for your sister's sake," I whispered. I bent and laid a solitary flower upon the turf, a bluebell.

The next morning I decided to go to the market at La Riche to buy provisions for my journey. In particular I wanted to buy some leather bags so that I could hide as much coin as possible.

Nicholas had been concerned at my leaving the Château. I waited until he had gone to tutor Jeanne and slipped out. But to be on the safe side, I took my friends with me. I had not thought of a way to tell them the news from Ambassador Marillac nor that I'd decided to return to England. I guessed they would try to dissuade me from doing this, so the less they knew for now, the better. I told them that the bags were for Jeanne's jewels.

"What about these?" Mary asked, pointing out a pile in a stall.

"Too heavy," Susan said, weighing them carefully.

"Those seem better," I said, gesturing to some small but well-made bags near the back of the stall. The merchant passed them to me so that I could examine them.

Suddenly, I heard Sissy scream. I turned. A ruffian had grabbed her, wrenching her arm behind her back. Barnaby was on him in an instant, knocking him down with one swift punch to the throat.

I had no time to see more. I was hauled off my feet and carried down an alley over the shoulder of an assailant.

Like when Thorne took me.

I screamed for all I was worth.

The man clamped his hand over my mouth and threatened to smash my face if I made any more noise. I continued to scream, kicking out at him with my feet.

Three more men joined him and all four ran swiftly, dodging down various twists and turns. In a moment, I was hopelessly lost.

In the distance I could hear the cries of Susan and Mary. Far in the distance and getting fainter.

"You're coming back to England," my attacker said in my ear.

I gasped. I had not noticed before but now I did. He was English.

"I can give you money," I said.

"Not as much as we got for this job," he said. "Your purse would never be able to match that."

By this time we had reached the River Loire. Close to the bank was a small boat, with two men waiting aboard it.

"You got her?" cried one of the men.

"Safe and sound," my captor yelled. "Raise the sail."

And then a figure leapt in front of him and he suddenly doubled up.

I tumbled to the ground but got to my knees in an instant and looked round wildly.

Barnaby Finch stood over the prostrate man. He kicked him with deadly accuracy and then spun around. The other three men were on him, one with a cudgel, the others with drawn swords.

Barnaby turned to one side, drawing his rapier as he did so. I saw it flash and one of the men dropped his sword and looked aghast at the deep cut which appeared on his body. The man with the cudgel leapt forward. The rapier jabbed into his eye, slipped out and sliced off half his cheek.

The third swordsman took up position. He was more skilled with a sword and managed to make two lunges at Barnaby. He did not make a third.

Barnaby's blade pierced his heart and he fell to the ground beside his fellows.

The man who had seized me decided his best course of action and was even now halfway to the riverbank. Barnaby raced after him and threw him to the ground.

"Who are you?" he cried. "Who sent you?"

"Mercy," cried the man. "We're on the business of the Privy Council."

And then he leapt up, pulled a knife and plunged it towards Barnaby's chest. He cried out in triumph, then in agony. Barnaby had caught his wrist and broken it.

A moment later, a man leapt from the boat, bearing a bow and arrow. He raced towards his injured companion. He came to a halt and drew the bow.

"Watch out!" I screamed at Barnaby.

But instead the man released the arrow into his companion's chest. Then he fled back to the boat and pushed out into the river.

I raced over to Barnaby.

He clasped me in his arms. "Are you all right?" he asked. "Are you harmed?"

"Not at all," I said. "Only frightened."

I looked at the man with the arrow in his chest.

"Why did they kill him?" I asked.

"To stop him talking, probably," Barnaby said. "Seems they were keen to keep who ordered this a secret."

He gave me a thoughtful look. Very thoughtful. Very shrewd. I had a notion that Barnaby had made up his mind concerning who had ordered the attack. As had I.

We stood like that for a little while longer. And then I was aware that my friends had found me. Humphrey's back-street skills had stood him in good stead.

Susan stared down at the dead men. "Who were they?" she asked.

"English agents," Barnaby said. "Someone wants Alice back in England."

"Then she must not go," said Mary.

Barnaby glanced at me. "Possibly not," he said. "But maybe it's the wisest thing to do."

I wrung my hands in anguish. Would I never be safe? Even if I returned to England and sought aid and sanctuary from Archbishop Cranmer? Would I ever be safe again?

In the end, it was not Archbishop Cranmer who was to prove my savior. It was Henry's new Queen, Katheryn Howard.

The day after the attack, I received a letter from her. She begged me to return to Court, saying that she had always liked me and desired me to call her sister.

I was at a loss to understand this. We had met only the once, when I had fled from the King's presence. *Always liked me. Desired to call me sister.* I heard that she was shallow-minded, but surely not this much.

I doubted her words, thought something was amiss.

I showed the letter to Nicholas. He seemed confused as I was at first, but then he seemed relieved.

"The Queen of England," he said. "What better ally could you have?"

He took me by the hand. "I urge you to take this message to heart and return to England at once." He glanced towards the cradle where Lily was sleeping. "I am sure this means that now you will both be completely safe."

I gave him a doubtful look. The letter made me feel the opposite. *Perhaps we might be safe with Barnaby beside us,* I thought. But I was not sure otherwise.

We spent the next few days discussing the risks and advantages of returning to England.

Finally, on balance, we all decided that we should leave.

Nicholas tried and failed to get permission to go with me. The King was adamant that he remain as Jeanne's tutor until she was a few years older and could be shipped off to her husband.

Nicholas acquiesced. It appeared that he had no wish to antagonize François on my behalf.

"I thought he'd have more gumption," I overheard Susan say to Mary that evening.

I did not make my presence known to them. Part of me thought the same myself.

And lurking in the shadows of my mind was the thought that this may be the last time I would see him.

On the first day of June I set foot in Dover and climbed aboard the carriage which Queen Katheryn had sent to convey me to Hampton Court. My friends rode behind me on horses which Barnaby had procured.

Full circle, I thought as the horses began the long journey back to Court.

Chapter 37
A Plea from Queen Katheryn

Summer 1541

I was surprised at how much Queen Katheryn had changed. She was said to be sixteen or seventeen years of age; it was testimony to the negligence of her caretakers that no one knew her exact date of birth, not even the girl herself. But as I looked at her, I thought how one year of marriage to the King had been a terrible burden to her. She looked far older than her years. If I didn't know better, I would have thought she was in her mid-twenties.

She was still extremely pretty but she had lost that childlike quality which had so attracted the King to her. There was a new hardness about her face which I found unattractive. When I had seen her last, her mouth had worn a petulant pout. This now seemed to be a permanent feature, and not an attractive one. Her cheeks had lost their childlike fullness and bloom. Her chin seemed more set, more forceful, as if she knew her mind and was determined to follow it.

But then I noticed her eyes. They were nervous and watchful, like a deer which had found itself on the edge of the forest and was forced to graze away from the safety of the trees. I well recalled similar feelings and I experienced a tide of sympathy and compassion.

She took me by the hands and kissed me on the cheek. "You've come," she said. "I knew you would."

"You are the Queen of England," I answered more lightly than I felt. "Your wish is as a command to me."

She giggled. "I am the Queen, aren't I?" I felt certain she meant it as a statement but there was something in her tone and in her gaze which made it seem more like a question.

"And how is His Majesty?" I asked. "I trust he is in good health."

Her face clouded over, became almost bleak. "Not in good health, I'm afraid. His leg hurts him such a lot."

And his mood, I wanted to ask? His behavior? Was he as suspicious and raging as the reports which had crossed to France? I knew from experience that the pain in his leg would build and worsen until he lashed out at anything and anybody. Perhaps this explained why Katheryn looked as she did. I felt sympathy for her.

But my real concern was how the King would receive me and news of Lily.

"I could weep when I see how much his leg hurts," she continued. "And how brave he is for my sake. He tries to hide it from me but I know how much it hurts. I see him wince whenever he moves. And then I'm the only one able to comfort my grumpy old bear."

I nodded. It seemed that her troubled look was not caused by any anger he directed to her. Or, at least, she was not going to admit it to me.

"I do hope that he will be able to manage the journey to the north," she said.

My eyebrows lifted at this. The King's constant travels usually took place in the south. A journey to the north was astonishing, especially given that there had been a recent rebellion there.

"He's going to the north?"

"Yes. I think he's calling it a progress. To show himself to the people up there. The poor things have never seen him, you see."

"But there has been insurrection there."

"Has there?" she said airily. "I didn't know."

I wanted to ask if it might still be dangerous for him to travel to where rebels had demanded his overthrow and the reintroduction of the old religion. But it seemed pointless to press her further.

"Come, sit beside me," Katheryn said, "and take some wine." She led me to a settle and signaled to a maid.

The girl seemed nervous as she poured the wine and spilled some on the table. She bit her lip and wiped it up so swiftly that Katheryn did not see. But the Queen did notice that the girl had taken time in serving the wine and scowled before snatching up her glass.

"You may leave us now," Katheryn said. She spoke more loudly to the maid than her normal tone, almost harshly. The girl curtsied and hurriedly withdrew.

Katheryn waited until the maid had left the room before turning to me with a thoughtful look.

"You must be wondering why I asked you to come back to England," she said. Her voice was its normal self once again. Childlike and wheedling.

"I have wondered, Your Grace," I answered.

"You used to be dear Henry's girlfriend," she said.

I nodded cautiously, wondering where this conversation might lead.

"He talks about you often," she continued lightly. "He is very fond of you. Not only for your beauty but because you're clever. You can read books and talk to him about poems and things. He even said you write songs."

"I do," I said. "Well, poems rather than songs."

Katheryn's words reminded me of the way Sissy enthused about my talents.

"Songs, poems—what's the difference?" Katheryn said. "You're clever and can talk clever and funny. He loves that; he told me so."

Her head drooped a little and the pout of her lip seemed to soften, almost as if Katheryn had suddenly discovered sorrow and disappointment. She turned her big eyes to me and they glistened with moisture.

"I'm not clever, Alice. I know I'm pretty, everybody tells me that. But I'm not clever like you are. The King would so love me to be clever but I can't be. It's rather sad isn't it?"

I took her hand in mine. "We can't all be the same," I said. "The King loves you for the person you are, for your sweet and gentle nature. And because you love him."

It was what I thought Katheryn would expect me to say. I was used to telling falsehoods to the King so why would it be any different for his Queen?

But even as I said the words I felt moved to believe them. Moved, I suspected, by the vulnerability of the foolish girl sitting beside me.

"I do love him," she said thoughtfully. "And he does so love me."

She looked out of the window. "That's why you're here really."

My skin suddenly crawled.

"Why I'm here?" I asked.

"Yes," she said, still staring out of the window. "You see, Henry is so very demanding. And I'm afraid that I can't always meet those demands. Not on my own."

A charged silence fell on the room. I heard the cracking of the logs in the flame, saw one catch light and blaze up with sudden gusto, saw the others diminished by its power for a moment before they too began to burn more fiercely. Then, brief moments later, the stack collapsed upon itself and black smoke belched from the grate.

"You can't meet his demands?" I repeated.

"Not on my own."

Katheryn turned; her face wore a plaintive, pleading look.

"I need someone else to distract him sometimes, to deal with his ardor. I need you, Alice. Especially when we're going on such a long journey north and he won't have any other entertainments."

She paused and stared at me, her face now bold.

"I need you to sometimes spend the night with him."

"I can't believe you are asking this of me," I began.

"But I'm desperate," she said. "He's such a big, heavy man and I'm so small. And he wants to love me so much and so often. I've tried my best, as Jesus is my witness. But I'm getting worn out by him and need your help. I need you to help ease his desire."

I grew furious at her and then even more furious at myself. For, although I felt scandalized and cheapened by the proposal, I was also more than flattered. And more than interested. Not in the man himself. Any affection I had for him had long since vanished. But I missed the excitement of being his mistress. And I had seen how the Duchess of Étampes had wielded such power and influence in France. It was exciting; it was beguiling.

And, to my astonishment, I was more than tempted by Katheryn's proposal.

But then I thought of the risks. The King had always been more indulgent of his mistresses than of his queens. Was this the case still? It seemed that nowadays his tyranny brooked no bounds. His malice and cruelty had grown as vast as his bulk. The peril for those closest to him must also, surely, have increased.

I remembered how Thomas Cromwell had been treated so cruelly despite all his love and loyalty for the King. I tried to swallow but could not.

To be the mistress of King Henry was not the same as being the mistress of King François. Both men loved themselves to an inordinate degree. But Henry's heart had grown so dark and shriveled I feared there was barely room for any other creature to dwell there safely.

I knew I must resist temptation.

"You are his wife, Katheryn," I said. "You made this decision and you must live with it."

"But he took you as his lover when Queen Jane was still alive," she said.

Barely alive, I thought. If she were ever alive except to her own ambition.

"And when the Flanders Mare was Queen," Katheryn continued. "He took you back to his bed, he told me so. And you went willingly. So why not now when I'm begging you?"

"Because you are so newly wed," I replied. "And because it's known that he loves you more than any other of his wives. Because you are sweethearts. And because, young and pretty as you are, you chose to love and cherish him despite his age and infirmities."

"I did not choose," she said.

My mouth opened in astonishment. I was not certain I had heard her right.

"I had no choice in it at all," she continued. "My uncle made me do it."

"The Duke of Norfolk?" I breathed.

"Yes. He said I must marry the King or he'd have me thrown out on the street. And that I had to do it for the good of the family."

My heart softened and I reached out to her.

"You poor child," I said.

"I am a child," she said. "I don't know for sure, but I think I may be even younger than I've been told."

I sighed. My heartstrings grew raw from such anguished plucking.

"I can't promise you," I said. "And I don't think it's right or fair of you to ask." I wiped my brow, realized a lock of hair had strayed out of my bonnet and pushed it back.

Katheryn seized my hand and brought it to her lips to kiss it.

I looked at her face. *She is a child*, I thought. A poor, manipulated, ruined child.

"I promise I won't tell anybody about our conversation," I continued, "and I beg you, for your sake, to do the same."

"But you will consider it?" she asked eagerly.

"I cannot promise that," I said. I pulled my hand out of her grasp.

She gave a rather mournful, wistful smile and nodded her head. My sympathy for her felt overwhelming at that moment. I was aware that my eyes were wet and turned away to hide it.

Yet when I glanced back, I saw that Katheryn's dejected look had been replaced by a momentary look of triumph. She hid it in an instant, so quickly that I thought that I might have been mistaken. But a sense of unease fluttered up and down my spine like spiders.

"Will you stay and dine with me?" she asked.

"If you so desire," I said.

"I don't necessarily," she answered. "If you wish to dine then we will. But I have little appetite for food of late."

"In that case, if you will allow, I'll take my leave. My child will be missing me."

"Oh yes, your lovely little boy."

"My lovely little girl," I said. "My baby boy died."

"Oh yes." She gave a little giggle and tapped the side of her head. "I'm so forgetful."

And she rang a bell to summon a servant to escort me from the room.

Chapter 38
The Great Northern Progress

On the last day of June, King and Court set out from Whitehall Palace on the Great Northern Progress. I was part of the throng.

It was a glorious day with clear skies and warm sunshine. The King was in extremely high spirits, excessively exuberant and loud. Most of his courtiers seemed ill at ease with his behavior, although the Duke of Suffolk joined in with loud jests and guffaws of his own. Queen Katheryn sat upon a little palfrey, her face set in a fixed smile. The King seemed to have forgotten she was there.

He had been delighted at my return to England. His anger when I had pleaded for Thomas Cromwell's life seemed quite forgotten. I was, of course, well aware that this may have been pretense on the King's part and I avoided all mention of my friend.

He was fascinated to hear about France and most of all about François. He listened to me avidly, sometimes asking me to repeat an account of his rival's doings. I was careful of the words I chose. I had to intimate that, though François was a magnificent king, he was not as magnificent or wonderful as Henry.

It was a delicate trick. Henry did not wish for comparison with a man who was not a titan, a demigod. I had to make plain that François was a colossus of a king. And that Henry, of course, outshone him.

He was most interested in the Royal Châteaux. I was slightly dismissive of them, implying, though without saying so, that their reputation was finer than the reality. Chambord, I told him, was merely an empty hunting lodge, Fontainebleau as vainglorious as its master.

"And François's nose?" the King asked. "Is it still as ludicrously huge?"

"Every bit as much," I answered.

If he had any inkling that I had slept with François he did not show it. I found this unnerving, remarkably so.

In fact I became so alarmed I wondered if I should confess. But how to broach it? To casually mention the differences in their bedspreads or nightshirts, to compare the throatiness of their snores, to say that François did not have a rancid, stinking leg but that his toenails could do with a little more attention.

Now that I was once more in his presence, I was relieved that my plan to anger him by sleeping with François seemed to have failed. I could only pray that it never came to light.

The King did, however, take a very great interest in Lily. He never asked me who her father was. It was as if he did not want to hear an answer he might not like. To have fathered yet another girl might well have been galling to him. Yet for a commoner to have fathered her would have been more galling yet.

If Tommy had survived? Well, a son would have been a different matter.

But often, when I was not looking, I caught him peering at Lily with a thoughtful look.

There were only half a dozen Maids of Honor on the journey. I did not know any of them and thought they all looked dull and plain faced. A few I would have called downright ugly, and the Queen shone in comparison with them. Perhaps this was why she had chosen them to accompany her.

I knew full well why she had chosen me but put the thought to the back of my mind. I had no intention of going where she wanted me to.

I knew I would miss the company of Susan and Mary. I sent them to Buckland, close to Dover and the crossing to France.

Sissy and Humphrey came with me, a concession ordered especially by the King so that they could help take care of Lily. I was fretful of her coming on such an arduous journey but I did not wish to be apart from her and would not countenance her having a wet nurse.

She did not share my concerns. She slept through all the noise and bustle of the multitude assembling, only wrinkling her nose when a donkey relieved itself close by.

I gazed at her for a moment, smoothing back her hair and praying that she would not take ill on the journey.

"Shall I take her, Alice?" Sissy asked. "While you get into your carriage?"

The carriage was another thing the King had commanded. I climbed inside and sighed with pleasure. It seemed well made, was well upholstered and contained everything which Lily might need. Everything I might need.

Sissy handed Lily up to me. The movement woke her and she gazed around. Her hand reached out and prodded at a cushion, then she dozed off once again.

I looked out of the window and saw the King trotting his stallion towards the carriage. I opened the door to step out but he waved me to stay inside.

"Keep your seat, Alice," he said. "You have a precious bundle to look after." He reached in and touched Lily gently on the cheek and gazed at her for a time.

"Is there not a trace of gold in her hair?" he murmured.

I felt my stomach churn.

"There is, Your Majesty. I think the sun picks it out."

He glanced at me, was about to answer, then decided not to. Instead he gave me an indulgent little smile.

Every day I had scanned Lily's little face for a sign of Henry's features. I was never sure whether I desired or dreaded to discover it. Some days I thought she looked like Henry, others that she favored Nicholas. It was infuriating. Once I even found myself considering Humphrey's nonsense, wondering if her first words would be French or English.

The King reached out and kissed my hand.

"We have wonderful weather," he cried. "And I go to see my people in the north. Do you not think they will be delighted to see their sovereign, Alice?"

"They will be overjoyed, Your Majesty."

"That's exactly what I think," he cried. "Overjoyed and ecstatic."

They've waited long enough to see him, I thought. Thirty years on the throne and he'd never been far north of London.

He waved his hand in farewell and trotted off. I gnawed my lip a little as I watched him depart. His wild exuberance unnerved me. I hoped he was not harboring the same hopes about me as Katheryn was.

The first few days of the Progress were very pleasant.

Everyone was very jolly, even the King's eldest daughter, Mary. She seemed to have shaken off her usual taciturn manner and, on a few occasions, was even heard to laugh with her companions.

On the second morning of the Progress I stood by a pond with Lily in my arms, pointing out the ducklings. She gurgled with pleasure, although, as she was only a few days over ten weeks, I doubted it was at the sight of the ducks. I felt the familiar pang of losing Tommy. In a few years Lily would be able to chase after ducklings, but she would do so alone.

"Can I see her?" called a voice from behind me.

I turned and did the best curtsy I was able to with Lily in my arms.

"Of course, Your Grace," I said.

Mary reached out for her and, with a little reluctance, I gave her over.

"She's beautiful," she said. "Just like her mother."

I found myself blushing.

"And her father?" she asked. "Does she take after him?"

She glanced up at me as she said this, her eyes sharp as needles. Not unpleasantly sharp but clever and questioning.

I hesitated for a moment and a little smile crossed Mary's face, as if my hesitation had answered the question.

"A little," I said. "But babies change so rapidly it's difficult to know."

"Sometimes it is difficult for the mother to know the father." Her smile grew tighter now.

I thought it best not to respond to this.

"And how is Your Grace?" I asked. "Are you enjoying the Progress?"

"I am," she said. "I was surprised that my father allowed me to come on it, but I am gratified."

I wondered whether she was being honest when she spoke of her surprise. It seemed to me obvious why she was accompanying the King. He had just put down the worst rebellion of his reign.

The rebels had promised to overturn his religious reforms but that was not the end of it. They denied the legitimacy of Prince Edward and proclaimed Mary the sole legitimate heir to the throne. Some went further and demanded that the King be forced from the throne and that Mary take his place.

Mary was now the greatest threat to his safety and he had no desire to leave her behind. If I surmised this I imagined that Mary must also have done.

"And how is Duke Philip?" I asked. "I gather that he has been a frequent visitor to England."

She passed Lily back to me. "I have only seen him the once," she said. "When you brought him to Hertford Castle."

"He seemed to me to be a kindly man," I said for want of anything better.

"It appears that I have less acquaintance of him than you do." She folded her arms and gazed in the direction of the King's pavilion. "My father keeps Duke Philip on a string, Alice. As he keeps me on a leash."

Lily began to grizzle a little, almost as if she were saddened by Mary's words.

"There is no hope of any marriage to Philip," she continued. "For the moment it suits my father to let the world believe that I may soon marry. Next month it will likely be another suitor. I am merely a tool of diplomacy, a threat or a promise to the kings and emperors of the world."

Her voice sounded melancholy and resigned.

"I am sorry to hear it," I said, unable to hold my tongue.

"Thank you," she answered, glancing at me in surprise.

"Women are ever the playthings of powerful men," she continued. "You know that every bit as much as I do, Alice."

She straightened up suddenly and looked over towards the tents. Queen Katheryn was being helped onto her horse by a young courtier. Even from this distance we could hear her laughter carrying on the morning air.

"And what about that plaything?" Mary said in a more bitter tone. "She's a child, younger than I am. It's distasteful.

"My father is ruled by his lust once again. As he was with the witch, Boleyn. At least Katheryn is no witch; she lacks even that talent. There is nothing between her ears, you see. Her only quality lies in her pretty young face."

I struggled to find words to answer. "She is a loving wife to your father," I said at last.

Mary considered this for a moment and shrugged.

"What do I care anyway? As a child I loved my father, very much. He was fond of me, although I always sensed his disappointment that I was not a boy. But then I think he came to hate me."

"That's not true," I said.

"My mother's death meant he could no longer vent his spite on her. He did so to me instead."

I swallowed. I knew well the dreadful vindictiveness of the King.

"I know he loves you," I said. "And your sister." I regretted mentioning Elizabeth the instant I did so.

"Poor little Elizabeth," Mary said. "She is much like our father. I pray she is not like her mother, Boleyn."

She reached out and stroked Lily on the cheek. "I do love Elizabeth," she said. "I loathe her as well, of course. Love and loathe. Just as I do my father."

She gave me a smile I could not read. "Just as I may come to do with you, Alice Petherton. For who knows what our future holds? Only God above."

And with that she turned and walked away.

We stayed three days in Enfield, for the hunting here was very good and the King spent almost every hour in pursuit of game. Not that he hunted in the field anymore; his physicians forbade that. Instead somebody had contrived a most unusual manner of hunt.

Servants drove the deer into a temporary enclosure and, when the King and his courtiers were comfortably seated, set greyhounds on the poor imprisoned beasts. I saw this hunt once and never again. The deer were terrified and the hounds relentless. Many of the courtiers looked on with ill-disguised distaste. A few, such as Sir Thomas Wriothesley, appeared to enjoy the gory spectacle; indeed he seemed positively to delight in it. But any emotion they showed was outdone by the behavior of the King. He reveled at the carnage, gripping white-knuckled on the fence, shouting encouragement to the hounds and clapping and yelling wildly when a huge stag was brought to its knees and savaged to death.

What has happened to him? I wondered. What has made him so wantonly cruel?

I was joined by Ralph Sadler as we set off towards St. Albans.

I was glad to see him well. Despite his loyalty to Thomas Cromwell, Ralph had been promoted to the post of Principal Secretary by the King. But the royal favor had not lasted long. Within six months he had been arrested and thrown into the Tower. Poor man, he must have believed that he was going to follow Thomas not only in office but also in the manner of his death.

But whatever the reason for his imprisonment, he was released soon after and restored to his former position. The King must have realized that he was in danger of running out of good servants.

I had always liked Ralph, finding him a man of integrity and good humor, a very rare blend in King Henry's Court.

"The King's wound must be causing him less pain," I said to him. "I suspect the good weather helps."

"You think the pain makes him choleric?" he asked.

I nodded. "It would anyone. And, as you and I know, the King's virtues do not include composure."

"Then let us hope that this good weather continues," he said.

Within a few days the good weather ended and the rain began. At first we all thought nothing of it but then it began to pour without cease. The roads became quagmires and we inched along at an agonizingly slow pace. My carriage got stuck so often I feared we would never get any further. The enthusiasm and good humor at the start of the Progress was forgotten, the jollity of the participants quite extinguished.

This was particularly the case with Queen Katheryn. She looked more despondent with each mile.

Her humor was not helped by the people who surrounded her. In particular, two unsavory-looking men hung round, dogging her every movement. Both looked sly and ill at ease, but that was the only thing which united them. They treated each other with contempt, bristling like street dogs whenever the other approached. Both continually ingratiated themselves with the Queen, and when they were successful seemed delighted not so much by her favorable reaction as by the scowls of their rival.

Both men had been employed by Agnes Howard, the Dowager Duchess of Norfolk, when Katheryn was her ward. Francis Dereham had been employed as one of the household secretaries, a fact he boasted of continually.

The other man, Henry Mannox, had been Katheryn's music teacher. I could not help but contrast his oily, sly demeanor with my honest and upright Nicholas.

Only the Duchess could have been fickle and negligent enough to employ such disreputable-seeming men. Why they were here now I could not imagine.

But the person who was closest to Katheryn was Jane, Lady Rochford. She had been wife to George Boleyn, brother to Queen Anne. I despised and loathed the woman.

She had accused her husband of sleeping with his sister Anne and thereby ensured the execution of both of them. Nobody was ever sure of her motives for doing so. Was it spite, jealousy or a desire for her own advancement?

I was always watchful when she was around. Her eyes and ears were everywhere, observing and recording everybody's doings. Her face was pinched and sour, mirroring her mind, I thought.

She was always pleasant to me, calling me the King's dearest friend. So friendly a phrase made my blood run cold. It was easy to trip and fall at the King's Court. Jane Rochford was ever ready to assist such a fall with a spiteful, furtive push. Gossip was food and drink to her, malice her religion. I was always careful to smile graciously at her and speak as little as humanly possible.

We arrived at Ampthill on the eighth of July in the most terrible thunderstorm. Then the rain began to lash down even more relentlessly. It seemed as if someone had opened the heavens and refused to close them again. Fields became ponds and we could barely keep our feet in the slick wet mud. The poor servants struggled to erect the tents and it was with some relief that word was sent to me that I would be given a room in the Castle.

"You'll be nice and snug in there," Sissy said. "And this rain won't last forever, so I'll be all right soon enough."

I think she repented her optimism over the next few days. The tents for the servants were the last ones to be erected and they gave poor shelter from the unseasonable torrents. I have never seen her look so woebegone. She never seemed to be dry, poor thing, and as the weather also turned chill I began to fear she would fall ill.

Thankfully the rains eased after five days of sodden misery. The stewards took heart and we made our way west towards Watling Street. It was a sad reflection of our times that the best road in the Kingdom had been built a thousand years ago by the Romans. The road ran straight and true across firm ground and we made good progress, arriving at the River Ouse at the end of a long day's travel.

It was then that I saw him clearly for the first time, the young man who Princess Mary and I had watched help Katheryn onto her horse, causing her to laugh so much and so loud. Thomas Culpeper.

Chapter 39
Thomas Culpeper

The great River Ouse was sluggish, deep and very wide. It was too deep to ford, and there was only one narrow bridge. This had been recently rebuilt but was still only wide enough to accommodate a couple of horses at a time.

I glanced at the hordes of people behind me. It would take most of the day for the hindmost to cross. Perhaps even longer.

But the steward knew what he was about. He ordered the tent erectors and cooks across the bridge first, ahead of even the King and his friends. The din as they crossed was deafening. The donkeys were laden down with food and were reluctant to take their first steps onto the bridge. The mules behind bellowed in complaint at the delay. The only sound louder was that of the drivers, who cursed and yelled in fury. They kept casting anxious looks towards the King, fearful that his patience would snap at the delay.

Eventually the poor pack animals were whipped and cajoled across and the relieved drivers hurried away to build the campsite.

The mules and donkeys were followed by a dozen ox-drawn carts containing the cooking pots and tents. The oxen were too docile to resist crossing the bridge but their slow gait meant that they took even longer than the donkeys.

I stood and watched them, all the while admiring their strength and fortitude. There was something noble about them, as though they had decided to weather all storms and whatever adversity the world threw at them. Great beasts with great hearts. And strong odors, it must be said.

The oxen were followed by a small herd of bullocks and cows, who trotted across with great enthusiasm. Then came a vast flock of sheep. They ran this way and that along the riverbank, bleating with stupidity and terror, reluctant to go where they had to. *Just like Henry's courtiers*, I thought, and found myself smiling at the notion.

I turned away and then I saw him, cantering on a black stallion with fine bridle and well-groomed coat.

He was without hat, his long hair unkempt from the ride. It was his hair which first attracted my attention: so long and thick, golden red in color, rich and luxurious.

He swept his leg above his horse's head and slid off its back like an acrobat concluding his display at a Royal feast. He patted and fondled the horse, a caring gesture, shook his head with a flourish and gave a long stretch like a cat. Not a household cat but one such as Ned Pepper keeps in the Menagerie. He massaged his head a moment, then raked his fingers through his locks, slowly and with evident pleasure. Two or three times he did this, his eyes closed as he did so, his mouth open a little as if with pleasure.

A shiver of excitement went through me at the sight of him.

I shook myself sternly. What was this? Had I become a giddy girl again? I was a young woman, a mother, and should have been Nicholas's wife had King François not forbidden it. Nevertheless, I stole another glance at the young horseman.

And at that moment he saw me. He stopped beautifying his hair and allowed his hands to drop to his side. He did not move, although his eyes did. They swept over me in a twinkling, from my head to my feet, then lingered longer on my face and my middle regions. Practiced eyes they seemed to me, unabashed, unembarrassed and wanton.

He smiled and gave me a little bow before turning on his heels and striding off in the direction of the King.

I felt a little disheartened by this. I was not used to men ignoring me. I half expected him to come over to introduce himself. But no, he had examined me and then left without further sign of interest.

"He's full of himself," said a voice behind me. "As usual."

I turned to see Sir Ralph Sadler, holding the reins of a horse. His eyes were thoughtful and pensive as he stared at the retreating figure.

"The young man?" I spoke in as nonchalant a tone as possible.

"The young man," Sadler said. "Do you know who he is?"

I shook my head.

"Thomas Culpeper. A great favorite of the King."

I turned to watch him as he strode into the distance.

"I have not seen him before," I said. "Apart from, in the distance, when he helped the Queen mount her horse."

"He has been away from Court for a long while. He is adept at finding beautiful and precious things and the King sent him off with Rich's hounds to sniff out wonderful objects to adorn the royal palaces. I don't doubt that you have some of them in your possession."

"Other people's property," I said, stiffening at the thought. "That's theft."

Sadler chuckled. "Is it not true that everything in the realm is ultimately the property of the King? We all believe we own our money, our homes, the clothes on our backs. Yet this delusion is shattered when the King demands them."

I glanced at him. His words were close to treason but he spoke with a bland, innocent tone.

"Do you really believe this to be true?" I asked.

"Why not? If our lives belong to the King, why not our cloaks and gowns, our ornaments and jewelry?"

I did not answer. I thought it dangerous to do so.

"You have your horse with you, Sir Ralph," I said lightly to change the subject.

He turned and patted the creature, a beautiful bay mare with a white diamond on her forehead.

"Yes, and I think she is one possession I shall keep hidden from the King." He smiled. "I return to London to sit on the Council there."

My face fell at the news. Ralph was one of the few people I liked on the Progress.

"You see the wisdom of my words, Alice? The King commands me to go and I go. My life is merely on loan to me."

He climbed into the saddle and leaned down towards me. "Remember this, Alice. While our lives are on loan we must do the best we can with them. So keep safe. And keep away from Thomas Culpeper."

I bade farewell to Sir Ralph and took my turn in crossing the river. We continued along the Roman road for a few hundred yards and then headed off on a smaller road which led northeast towards our next stop at the village of Grafton.

The King possessed the manor house here. It was small by his standards but comfortable and beautiful. There was an old park to the side of it and the tents for the courtiers were erected there. A larger park to the west housed the thousands of servants. The people of the village stared open-mouthed as this strange new town of tents rose up like mushrooms after autumn rain.

It was not a moment too soon. The storm clouds began to build and the torrents of rain started once more. A message came from the King that I was not to stay in my tent but come to the house. I obeyed with alacrity, sheltering Lily under my cloak.

A servant showed me to a chamber at the back of the house. It was tiny, with only a slit of a window, but it was dry and relatively warm.

I sat down on the bed with a sigh of relief, rocking Lily gently on my lap. I looked around the room and smiled. It reminded me of my little bedroom at Hampton Court Palace. The room I had loved so much before Richard Rich came to haunt me.

I banished the memory from my mind. It had been a long time since I had seen that villain. I guessed that he was too busy trying to fill the shoes of Thomas Cromwell. He was far too small a man to do so. I hoped that they would cause him to trip and fall.

We spent the next few days in the manor, while the rains continued to hammer without relent.

I grew intrigued by Culpeper, the more so because he seemed to pay hardly any attention to me. He was courteous enough whenever we bumped into each other but he made no attempt to linger or engage me in conversation. The more he ignored me the more I grew disgruntled.

I was not the only woman whose attention was caught by the handsome Mr. Culpeper. Wherever he walked he was followed by wistful female eyes. Servants, Maids of Honor, the wives and daughters of officials and great lords: all were entranced by him. Only the Queen seemed indifferent to him, her attention fixed solely on her husband.

Or at least until she fell ill. She took to her chamber and it was rumored that the Progress might be abandoned. Most of us, drenched as we were by the torrential rain, would have been delighted to see this happen.

The King, however, was adamant that he would journey to York. This was not only because he wished to finally visit the north of his Kingdom. He was alarmed at the growing friendship between Scotland and France and wished to make overtures to his nephew, James, King of Scotland. Although reluctant, James had finally agreed to meet him at York. Henry was determined to put on a huge show there, though one intended more to overawe the young King than to welcome him.

And, in truth, the whole country had been turned upside down to host the King, so it seemed impossible to abandon our plans. Come what may we would grind our way onward.

But not for a few more days, I hoped. The manor house in Grafton was delightful, warm and cheery with lots of little nooks and crannies where one could escape from the noise and bustle. I found a favorite spot, a narrow window seat beside a minstrel gallery. It was partially hidden by a wooden screen and people would pass by without realizing I was there.

I, however, could look down into the Great Hall, amused to watch the play of the courtiers while not, for the moment, being part of it.

It was there that I first noticed how attentive Thomas Culpeper was to the King. He was assiduous in the care and attention he gave, more so than everyone else, if that were humanly possible. Wherever the King went, there went Culpeper, a few steps behind him, a constant shadow.

I sat in my little hideaway on the third afternoon after we had arrived. Lily was sleeping in my room with Sissy to watch over her. I had taken a book to read but could not settle to it, preferring to stare out of the window at the trees, which swayed like dancers in the buffeting wind. It was beguiling, a pretty and enchanting show.

My reverie was broken by the sound of laughter in the Great Hall. I turned my attention there and saw the King. His head was thrown back in wild pleasure, his face red from the explosion of mirth.

Culpeper was beside him, his face also full of amusement. He said something more to the King, causing him to roar with laughter once again. I thought suddenly of Will Sommers, the King's Fool. *Where is he?* I wondered vaguely, for I had not seen him for a long time. Not that I minded, as I did not care for the man. In any case, the King seemed to have found alternative means of entertainment. I watched as he listened once more to Thomas Culpeper, wiping the tears of mirth from his eyes.

"He is witty as well as handsome," came a voice from behind the screen. I nearly slipped from my seat, so startled was I by the sound.

"Don't you agree, Alice Petherton?" the man said, sliding into view beside me.

I tried to hide my sigh but failed. It was Wriothesley, Sadler's fellow Secretary, the man rewarded most richly for his treachery towards Thomas Cromwell.

I gazed at Wriothesley's cold, hard face, his eyebrows arching far above his eyes as if he were constantly surprised by the world.

"Who are you referring to, Master Wriothesley?"

"To young Culpeper there. The young man you are watching." He gave a little chuckle which was chill and without humor. "Oh, how we all watch that young man."

He took a step closer and his face took on a more kindly expression, one I had never seen it wear before.

He bent and peered out of the window.

"We are all of us the playthings of the weather," he said. "It is so very changeable. One day we are in bright sunshine, the next plunged into gloom. You have found this, I know, dear Alice. The weather has changed more for you than for many others, has it not? The sun that is our King is attended by a bright young moon now. I imagine you must feel quite eclipsed."

"A new young moon, Sir Thomas? To whom do you refer? The Queen or Master Culpeper?"

Wriothesley smiled but chose not to answer.

"Perhaps the rain will end soon," he said. "And then we will all see our way clear."

He made to move but then paused. "And how is your child, Alice? I trust Lily is thriving."

"She is. I thank you for asking."

He slipped away and I was left wondering. Wondering about everything. About Thomas Culpeper, about my relationship with the King.

Wondering what the future would bring.

Chapter 40
Poetry, Please

What the future brought next was a summons from the King.

We had been stuck fast at Grafton for four days. The rains continued worse than before and the fields around began to fill with water. There was no possibility of continuing north.

"He's in a real foul mood, apparently," Humphrey said when he told me of the summons. "Let's hope you can cheer him like you used to."

I looked at him sharply, wondering if he really meant what I suspected. I had no desire to play the bedmate of the King ever again. I recalled Katheryn's request for me to do exactly this and wondered if she was behind the summons. A dread seized my heart.

"Where is the King?" I asked.

"In his bedchamber."

I closed my eyes and groaned. I could not believe it.

I knocked upon the door of the King's bedchamber and was met by Gregory Frost. He gave a little smile of welcome when he saw me.

"He is not in good humor," he whispered. He ushered me in, stepped out of the chamber and shut the door behind him.

The King was sitting in a chair by the window, papers strewn around his feet. He glanced at me and beckoned me closer.

"I'm glad to see you, Alice," he said. "I'm sick to the stomach. Sick of this weather, sick of the puerile questions of my Council, sick of being stuck here."

He poured a cup of wine. "Do you know, we should have been in Lincoln today? And where are we? Stuck here, not even reached Northampton." He drained the cup with one swallow and poured himself another.

"Because of this intolerable situation," he continued, "I thought I would bring you here to entertain me."

My stomach sank. "I am more than happy to do so," I lied.

It had been over a year since I had last slept with him. That occasion had been a trial. Since then he had grown even more immense and found it difficult to move. I could not imagine how I would manage him.

"I'd have the Queen do this," he said. "But she has not been at all well and, in any case, is not very skilled at it. So I thought that you could take her place."

"As you command," I said, astonished at his words. Not skilled?

I made my way towards the bed. As I did so the King looked at me with surprise and then slapped his thigh, laughing out loud.

"I did not mean that, Alice." He picked up a book. "I merely want you to read to me."

"Read to you?"

"Yes. Read." He smiled contentedly. "I am a happy husband, Alice. I am a well-satisfied husband. I desire you only to read to me."

I swallowed my sigh of relief.

"But can't the Queen read to you?"

His face clouded a little. "I told you, she is unwell. She has retired to her chamber since we arrived here."

"I hope she does not ail too long."

He shrugged. "One of my physicians thinks we should return to London and many of my councillors are happy to agree with him. Another physician argues that the northern air will be good for her. It's more bracing, so he claimed. I can never get a straight answer from anyone. Not anymore."

He fell silent and it seemed to me that he was remembering someone who could give at least the semblance of a straight answer. Sir Thomas loomed over us all, even in his grave.

"Whatever the advice," the King continued, "I am determined to continue with the Progress."

Even at risk to the Queen's health, I thought.

He held the book out to me. It was *The Canterbury Tales* by Geoffrey Chaucer.

"I thought this would be appropriate," he said. "We too are going on a journey, or at least we would be if this blasted weather relented. So while I am stuck here I would, at least, hear about another journey."

He gestured to a chair nearby. "Bring that closer. Pour us both some wine. And start at the beginning."

"It begins with April showers," I said. "How appropriate."

He nodded his head. "I pray that these floods turn to mere showers. Then I could be on my way once more. But in the meanwhile, read."

The rain hammered on the window and the fire crackled in the hearth. But the words of the poet transported us back to a more pleasant spring day a hundred and more years ago.

I read for a couple of hours and, as I did so, the King visibly relaxed. He stopped swilling his wine, sipping at it occasionally as I described the pilgrims and all their characters. At length, I finished the Prologue and glanced up at him.

"That will do for today," he said. "Tomorrow you shall read one of the tales. I think 'The Knight's Tale' comes first."

"It does indeed, Your Majesty. But maybe the Queen will be well enough to read to you tomorrow."

He looked at me thoughtfully, pursing his lips, then shook his head.

"As I said, Katheryn is not the best of readers. She was not properly tutored in it. That vile old crone, the Dowager Duchess, seemed to think that the only things a young girl need learn are needlework, dancing and music. She was not a good choice for guardian. Not of such a precious flower as Katheryn."

"She is a flower," I said.

"My rose without thorns," he said. "That's how I think of her. So many of my wives had more thorns than petals." He sighed and then gave me a wistful smile. "I do not speak of you in this way, Alice. You were all petals and buds."

"Thank you, Your Majesty."

"Your Grace," he said. "I said long ago that you could call me Your Grace."

"You did. I recall it well."

"Then I would have you call me this again."

"Thank you," I said. "I am honored. Your Grace."

My heart began to hammer. Was this prelude to the next act in the entertainment? Had I allowed myself to be lulled into thinking that poetry was all that he was interested in?

He turned to look at me most intently. I wondered if the same thoughts were in his mind. His eyes did not blink but studied my face as if he were Master Holbein about to sketch me.

"Tomorrow," he said. "Return to read to me tomorrow."

"Perhaps we will be on our travels again tomorrow," I said, hastening to rise. "Unless you decide to return to London."

He shook his head. "I must go north. There has been too much preparation to call things off now. And I plan to meet the King of

Scotland in York. Miserable little wretch that he is. He has precious little of my dear sister's blood in his veins, of that I'm certain."

I curtsied and stood a moment beside him, staring down at his huge bulk. Would I climb into his bed if he commanded?

Of course I would, for he was the King and I dare not refuse. But I also realized that a little bit of me, a tiny little bit, would have been pleased to do so. Excited at the thought of being his favorite again, though dismayed at thought of the act.

"Tomorrow," the King said. "We'll have 'The Knight's Tale' and perhaps the Squire's."

"Your Grace," I said, bowing and beating a hasty exit.

Chapter 41

Enemies and Friends

I read Chaucer to the King for the next few days, which seemed to console him a little at his forced inactivity. At last the rains began to ease and on the twenty-first of July we resumed our journey north. The vast company had been over a week in Grafton and the villages and farms for miles around had been picked bare of every last morsel of food, every last drop of liquid.

The Queen appeared to have recovered from whatever had been ailing her. She was in the highest of spirits as we began to make our way towards Northampton. Her mood seemed contagious; everyone appeared to be in similar good humor. Or maybe it was merely because of the change in weather.

Katheryn was dressed in a gorgeous white satin robe with sprays of cornflower fastened to it like jewels. I was surprised at this, for cornflowers were normally worn by young men to proclaim their love. Perhaps the King had given them to her, imagining himself made youthful by his Queen.

She sent her carriage on its way, insisting on riding a dainty little palfrey. I thought she would be precarious riding side-saddle on such slippery paths, but a careful old horseman was entrusted to lead her slowly on the road.

We stayed at Northampton only a few days before moving north.

At Pipewell we were overtaken by Nicholas's friend, Ambassador Marillac. He sought me out soon after arriving but unfortunately he had no news of Nicholas.

"I am pleased that you have come all the way from London to join the Progress," I said. "I hope that you find the journey worthwhile."

He gave me an enigmatic smile. "It is important for King François that his ambassador is in contact with your King. Especially as the Emperor has sent only a couple of junior envoys."

"So you have won this round of the tourney," I said. But I guessed there must be a more important reason for him to travel here.

"Will you come all the way on the Progress?" I asked.

"As long as the Emperor's envoys remain," he said, "so will I."

He paused and then said casually, "How is Princess Mary? I hope she does not feel too unhappy that her courtship of Duke Philip has gone awry."

I looked into his face. "Perhaps there will soon be another suitor."

He blushed, but I do not think that it was at my gaze.

We arrived at Collyweston Palace on the second day of August. The house had been rebuilt and refurbished by the King's grandmother and was a real delight. It was small, however, and as the rains had ceased I was accommodated in one of the grander tents in the grounds.

"Isn't this lovely?" Sissy said as she carried Lily out of the tent the morning after we arrived. "A clear sky at last. I thought the sun would never return."

"Get a rug," I told her. "We can put Lily down on it."

I took Lily in my arms and gazed at her, crooning to her and pulling faces.

I began to rock and turn which made her gurgle with delight, little bubbles appearing about her mouth. I took a few steps forward and turned, a few steps further and swung round.

"Do you want to dance, baby?" I said.

And I began to dance, up and down in front of the tent, humming a tune, making up nonsensical words. Lily loved it and I loved it every bit as much. I was transported, forgetting all the dreariness of the Progress, my meetings with courtiers, my dealings with the King. A deep flood of love and affection washed over me. More than this, I felt an overwhelming sense of friendship with my child.

"We're going to be the best of friends," I said, surprised by the revelation. "Mummy and baby, the best of playmates."

I sang out loud again, dancing and swaying with Lily in my arms while she smiled up at me in delight.

"A giddy babe," a voice whispered in my ear.

I stopped in my tracks for I knew the voice. I turned and stared into the dead eyes of Sir Richard Rich.

"Sissy, fetch a bodkin from my sewing basket," I called. "The biggest you can find."

Rich gave a mirthless chuckle, but I saw him flinch at the memory of the bodkin I had once pressed to his eye.

"Such a pretty baby," he continued, reaching out to touch Lily on the chin.

I swung away. "Don't you dare! Keep your paws off my child."

He shrugged and his mouth smiled, like a gash in flesh.

"The child is precious to you then?" he said quietly. "Perhaps the rumors are true. Perhaps she is yet another of the King's bastards."

"Keep away from me," I said.

At that moment, Sissy appeared with a bodkin. "Is this what you wanted, Alice . . . ?" Then she saw Rich and her eyes narrowed. "Oh no," she said. She took a step closer. "Is he bothering you, miss? Shall I send for someone?"

"And who would you send for?" Rich sneered. "Oh, of course, Master Cromwell." He put his finger to his lip as if in thought. "But, of course, he can't protect you now, Alice. He's long dead."

"And you have gained from it, I don't doubt," I replied. "You are aptly named as Chancellor of the Court of Augmentations, Sir Richard. You have spent the past many years augmenting your wealth and standing with the King."

"And both have waxed great, Alice Petherton," he said. "You would do well to remember it." He blew me a kiss and strolled away.

I stared after him, my heart pounding with anger and distress.

"He's a villain," Sissy said. "You should keep away from him."

"I don't need to be told that," I said. "The question is, will he keep away from me?"

Sissy gnawed her lips thoughtfully, glanced quickly beyond the camp and then gave a little smile. "Things will be all right with Richard Rich," she said. "Never you fear."

I decided that I would make sure that this was the case.

I was summoned to read to the King again that afternoon. He had grown despondent, for the Duke of Suffolk had gone ahead to make the final preparations for our arrival at Grimsthorpe Castle. The Duke was his oldest friend, perhaps his only one.

"Make it a light tale," the King said. "Nothing of classical heroes and courtly dupes. Make me laugh."

I saw my chance and seized it. "You like 'The Reeve's Tale,'" I said in casual tone.

"The one about the miller who cheats his customers?"

I nodded.

"Such men are a menace," he said.

"But he gets his comeuppance," I said. "He suffers for his avarice. As should all men who deceive and steal."

I said this with such emphasis that he gave me a curious look.

"Read on, my dear," he said after a moment. "Beguile me for an hour or two."

Partway through the story I giggled.

"Why do you laugh?" the King asked.

"Because the cheating miller reminds me of someone, Your Grace."

"Someone at Court?"

I put my hand to my mouth and nodded.

He pulled at his beard, thoughtfully. "I know of no one who resembles the miller," he said at last.

"Not in looks," I said.

He nodded, realizing that I was talking about behavior rather than appearance. "Who then? Who does the miller remind you of?"

"I cannot say, Your Grace."

He looked at me for a moment and then it dawned on him. "Richard Rich, perhaps?" he said quietly. "I recall there was some trouble between you, was there not? He disparaged you in some way, insulted you?"

I did not answer.

He frowned at my silence. "Come, child," he said. "You can tell your King."

"He tried to rape me."

I looked at him frankly, wondering how he would react to this revelation.

To my surprise, he did not react much at all. "Ah yes," he said. "I remember now."

Then his eyes narrowed to little pinpoints, cold with suspicion. "So what would you have me do about it, Alice?" he said.

This conversation was not going the way I had hoped. Far from it.

"That is for you to decide, Your Grace."

He pursed his lips and nodded again, as if I had spoken the blindingly obvious, which I had.

He leaned forward in his seat. "You would do well to remember that Sir Richard is useful to me. He has ever been useful to me. He ferrets out money which is due me, watches out for enemies, betrays them to me at the bat of an eyelid."

He held my gaze in his.

"I do not need to love someone to make use of them," he said eventually. "Affection is not necessary between a prince and his servant."

"I understand," I said.

I also understood that I had completely failed to raise the King's hand against Rich. In fact, I may well have jeopardized my own position.

"You must understand my situation, Alice," the King continued. "I am bereft of my greatest servant. Sir Thomas. He was the most efficient, intelligent and loyal man I have ever known."

My mouth opened wide in amazement at these words.

Fortunately he did not see this; he was too intent on his own thoughts.

"I miss him, Alice," he continued. "I was betrayed into executing him. Told lies, told calumnies. I was kept ignorant of a plot to foil my Minister and bring him down. I repent daily the duplicity of his enemies."

I could not believe what I was hearing. The complete reversal of his views, the change to his opinion.

But it presented me with a second opportunity.

"Sir Richard Rich was one of them," I ventured.

The King turned his face to me. A face like a mask.

"He was indeed. I know it well."

He picked up a glass of wine, stared into it but did not drink. "Rich has always had a predilection for sensing the way the wind is turning. He makes sure to jump ship if the vessel is in danger.

"But I have need of him, Alice. Now with my dear Thomas gone, I have very great need of him."

The room fell silent. There was nothing further I dared say.

"Christ, but I miss Thomas," he cried, smashing his hand upon the arm of his chair. "I've had to split his duties between three men, damn it. I never truly comprehended how hard the man worked, how patient and painstaking he was. How much he put my interests above his own."

Maudlin tears began to fill his eyes.

"I am angered at how I was deluded about our friend," he continued, dabbing his eyes with a handkerchief. "But let me promise you that no matter how much I may need his enemies now, no matter how highly placed they are, no matter if they are sheriff, earl or bishop, I will bide my time and punish them. No matter if they are even a duke."

There were only two dukes in the Kingdom and one was his greatest friend, the Duke of Suffolk. That could only mean that he had suspicions of the Duke of Norfolk. Norfolk's position was unassailable at the moment; he was needed for his military prowess and diplomatic skills. But I sensed that he would not forever remain in the sun.

"Enough for today," the King said quietly. "Shall I ask someone to have a word with Sir Richard? To tell him to keep away from you?"

"That would be a great boon, Your Grace."

"I shall get Wriothesley to do so then."

I pulled a face.

"What?" the King cried. "You don't like Wriothesley either?"

"It's rather that he and Sir Richard are particularly close."

"Who then? I won't speak to him myself." His voice sounded almost petulant now.

"The Duke of Suffolk perhaps?"

He considered it for a moment and then nodded. "When we arrive at Grimsthorpe Castle," he said.

The Duke of Suffolk had gained Grimsthorpe Castle eight years before, upon his marriage to Catherine Willoughby. She had been his ward, betrothed to his son and only fourteen years of age to her guardian's forty-nine. Suffolk had let none of these considerations impede him in wedding her.

Cupid can strike in the most capricious and sudden manner, his friends said with great earnestness. The fact that the girl was the richest heiress in England had not occurred to the Duke, said others, though without quite the same sincerity. For indeed, how could he have known this, having been her guardian for a mere five years?

He was a philandering opportunist, whispered his enemies, a man who repeatedly slept his way to ever greater fortune and influence. But they were careful not to say it too loudly about the only man the King truly considered his friend.

No matter. The marriage between Suffolk and Catherine appeared to be successful, to almost everyone's surprise. The couple seemed content and affectionate to one another.

Grimsthorpe Castle was only one of the many properties Catherine brought to the marriage. The King had given the couple title to an abbey nearby and Suffolk had wasted no time in tearing it down to use the stone to refurbish the Castle. It was fifteen miles north of Collyweston and we reached it the next day. It was magnificent, but more than that. It bore the charm of a home that was well loved.

I had met Catherine on several occasions and we liked each other from the first. She was a year older than me and was good-natured and level-headed.

I was pleased to find that I was to be housed within the Castle at Catherine's special request. I was shown into a large and airy chamber strewn with flowers and herbs to make it sweet smelling. The window looked to the south over a fine garden. I sat in the window seat and gazed out. The clouds scudded by swift as horses but they were not the heavy, brooding rain clouds of the past month. It seemed that summer had arrived at last.

"Alice," Sissy called. "You've got a visitor."

I turned to see Catherine standing just inside the room. She smiled and came forward, arms outstretched.

"It is good to see you again," she said, embracing me.

"And you, Cathy," I said. "And I'm grateful that you've given me this lovely room."

"I wanted you close on hand." Her eyes twinkled. "All these miserable old men bore me to death. And besides, we have your baby to consider."

She bent over the cradle where Lily was sleeping.

"Oh, she's beautiful, Alice," she said. "Adorable. You must let me hold her when she wakes."

"Of course." I stood beside her and gazed down at Lily.

"And your boys?" I asked. "How are they?"

"They're boys," she said. "Rather too much like boys. They cannot keep still; they run all over the house and scream and fight. Even little Charlie."

"He must be what, three years old?" I said.

"Almost four. And Henry is six. Charlie adores his older brother, who returns that adoration with scorn. Or at least he does when I'm looking. When he thinks he can't be seen he is the perfect, protective big brother."

She suddenly looked distraught. "This is so insensitive of me," she said. "I forgot about your baby."

She embraced me again, a warm and consoling hug.

"We eat in an hour," she said. "We won't be able to talk then, but perhaps tomorrow I can show you the gardens. We'll have some peace there."

The next day dawned fine and bright and I joined Cathy in the gardens mid-morning. There was a knot garden made up of box and laurel and sweet-smelling herbs. This led out to a large terrace with rosebushes in ordered, well-tended rows.

"I love roses," Cathy said. "I planted a few of the bushes myself."

I turned to her in admiration. Not at her horticultural abilities, but at her self-assured nature and her sense of contentment. She seemed happy with the world and with herself. I realized that I was a little envious of this.

"Do you regret returning to England?" she asked, almost as if she had picked up my thoughts.

I started to answer but found myself not sure how to. I bent and breathed in the scent of a rose to give me time to collect my thoughts.

"I miss France," I said. "And some of the people I met there."

"King François?" she asked.

I shrugged. "Not him so much as his sister and his niece."

"And the Frenchman? Nicholas Bourbon?"

I blushed. "I miss him a lot."

She glanced back towards the Castle.

"And who is father of little Lily?" she asked softly. "Monsieur Bourbon or King Henry?"

I blushed even more and reached for her hand. "I'm not really sure. It could be either, for I slept with them both within the space of two days."

Her eyes widened slightly in surprise but then she smiled. "And what does the King think? Does he believe that Lily is his child?"

"I think he may suspect it. I've seen him seek her out to stare at her, as if trying to discern some resemblance to him. I expect he'd be rather more interested if she were a boy."

I bit my lip, thinking of little Tommy. I blinked rapidly for I found that this was the best way to clear my eyes of tears.

"I was so sorry to hear about your little boy," Catherine said.

I nodded and forced a smile to my lips. There would always be a part of my heart just for Tommy.

"Let's walk down by the lake," she said. "I love it there."

It was a short stroll to the lake, which was west of the Castle. Ducks and curlews dotted its surface and two swans sailed close to the bank, giving us an inquisitive look. A goose honked on the far side of the water and slid into it, sailing towards us with intent.

Cathy stared at the lake for a little while and then said, without turning to me, "And what do you think of the King?"

"What do you mean?" I said, surprised.

She sighed and glanced around. "Since you've returned? Since his marriage to the Howard girl?"

I noted the dismissive way she referred to Katheryn but decided not to comment on it.

"He seems happy," I said. "Or at least when his leg isn't causing him too much pain. I think he is very fond of Katheryn."

"He dotes on her. My husband says he's never seen him so besotted. Not even when Anne Boleyn led him such a merry dance. Not even with you."

"She is young and pretty. And she dotes on him."

"Ah, but does she?"

She turned her gaze from the lake and stared into my face.

I shook my head. "What on earth do you mean?"

"I don't know." She took my arm and bent close to my ear. "There are rumors, or so my husband says. About two men, Mannox and Dereham."

"I've met them. There is something nasty and sneaky about them and they despise each other. And they seem to haunt Katheryn's steps. I believe they knew her when she was a young girl."

"Knew her too well, so rumor says."

I gasped in surprise. "But she must have been no more than a child."

She gave me a quizzical look and then burst out laughing. "We are not two to condemn such behavior. Or at least I'm not. I was only fourteen when I was wedded and bedded. And you were how old when you became the King's lover? Fifteen, sixteen?"

"Seventeen," I said. "A mature and worldly-wise woman." I smiled. "Or at least I pretended to myself I was."

And then I said something I did not intend to. "Besides, Cathy, I only became his lover to escape the attentions of a dreadful man."

"Really? I didn't know."

I did not answer for a moment, surprised she had not heard of this before.

"Richard Rich," I said.

"Ooh. That villain. My husband loathes him."

"Your husband was kind enough to warn Rich to stay away from me. I am grateful for that."

She shot a glance at me. I thought I detected a hint of suspicion there. Although they were happily married, there were always rumors that Suffolk's eye was more roving than fixed.

"The King asked him to speak to Rich," I explained.

She nodded slowly and seemed, at length, persuaded by my explanation. I was surprised that her husband had not told her of it.

"Men," Cathy said, taking me by the hand. "They are all like little boys really. Even dukes and kings."

"Your husband and the King have stayed friends for most of their lives."

She shrugged. "For most of it. Although Charles has sometimes presumed too much upon that friendship and felt the King's wrath because of it." She turned and glanced back towards the Castle. "And it's usually because of women."

So her suspicions of me were not completely allayed.

"Men are such children," I said. "If there were any nunneries left I might consider joining one. But I expect I shall return to France instead."

"That may be wise, Alice." She took my hand and smiled warmly. "But before you do, take this advice. Stay away from Queen Katheryn as much as possible."

I gave her a curious look. "What makes you say that?"

Cathy sighed. "Just a feeling. There is something I don't like about the girl. There is an air of secrecy about her, deceit maybe. And stay away from Mannox and Dereham. I don't like what I've seen of them."

She shielded her eyes, looking towards the far end of the lake.

"Who's that fellow?"

I followed her gaze. "I don't know," I said, suddenly alarmed.

I stared more closely. "Yes I do," I said at last. "It's one of my friends."

"Well, he's been following us ever since we left the garden. Are you certain he's a friend?"

"The best of them. He's called Barnaby Finch, my sworn and sure guard. I had no idea he was here."

"So he's followed you from London?"

"He must have done."

"Is he a good guard?"

"None better."

"Then my advice is to keep him close."

She took my arm and led me back along the path.

I glanced at Barnaby and jerked my head towards the Castle. He gave a little wave of acknowledgment and followed after.

Chapter 42
The Sniff of Culpeper

"What on earth are you doing here?" I said to Barnaby as he walked into my room.

He slipped across to my window and peered out before turning to face me.

"It's my job to protect you," he said.

"But you were supposed to stay in London."

"Who says?"

"I say."

"Begging your pardon, Alice, but what's that got to do with it? I'm employed by Derick Berck and my wages are paid by Thomas Cromwell. It seems to me you've not got a lot of say in the matter."

"Oh, very pert, Mr. Finch."

He chuckled and winked at Humphrey, who had followed him into the room.

"So you've had a hand in it as well?" I said.

"Course I have, Alice. We all knew Barnaby was close by."

I turned to see Sissy red faced and chewing her lip. "Sorry, Alice. We didn't think you'd be angry."

"I'm not angry," I said. "Just upset that you didn't tell me." I turned towards Barnaby. "Why didn't you?"

"You might have been alarmed if you thought I was still looking out for you."

"I'm rather more astonished. Who are you going to protect me against? The King?"

He shrugged. "If necessary. Not a hard man to get close to, I warrant. Too full of the bluff, hail-fellow well-met for his own good. Just give me the word, Alice."

"Don't be so ridiculous. I do not need protecting from the King. Or anyone."

"Richard Rich is here though," Humphrey said.

"He'll be no problem," I said. "Not anymore."

"Maybe," said Barnaby, although he sounded far from convinced. "But there's others I'm keeping an eye on."

I poured myself a glass of wine. "And who would they be?"

"Those two friends of the Queen. Skulking, sly fellows; they're said to have been old acquaintances of hers." He gave a slow wink. "Close acquaintances if you take my meaning."

"Mannox and Dereham," I said. "If you were wise you'd keep quiet about them. And you two as well," I said to Sissy and Humphrey.

Sissy nodded but Humphrey merely smirked.

"Very quiet," I repeated.

"And there's that prancing, preening chap," Barnaby continued. "Culpeper."

"There's no danger from him," I said, rather too quickly.

Barnaby pursed his lips and looked doubtful. "I'll keep my eye on him, even while he's busy sniffing around the Queen."

"What?" I said. "Sniffing around the Queen?"

He nodded. "Not many realize it, so don't be surprised you didn't see it either. But there's nobody as shrewd as Barnaby Finch." He tapped his nose. "I've got my suspicions, though I doubt anyone else has."

"You're just a troublemaker," I said. I was disconcerted by his words. I realized that I was a mite taken with the pretty face of Thomas Culpeper.

"On the contrary," Barnaby replied. "I'm a trouble-finder. And my job is to keep you out of it."

I sighed. "And I'm grateful for it, Barnaby. I just wish you'd told me you were, well, following me."

"It's not always for the best, Alice. I didn't want any attention on me."

"So why have you made yourself known now?"

"Because we're getting close to Yorkshire. And it's still a hotbed of rebels against the King. Why else do you think he's come north with what amounts to an army?"

A relatively sparse meal was served at noon because the Duke had organized a feast for the evening. I returned to the chamber, where I found Sissy sitting by the window, dozing in the warm sunshine. She stirred when she saw me and hurried to rise.

"I must have dropped off," she said, her face red with embarrassment.

"It's because you were sitting in the sun. The heat made you drowsy."

"It could only have been for a minute, Alice."

"It doesn't matter. Lily's still sound asleep. Now, go and get yourself some food."

She went towards the door and then a thought struck me. "Sissy, how does Barnaby eat?"

"He stays in inns when he can," she answered, "so he probably eats there or at a farm."

"And if there's no inn close by?"

"He wraps himself in a blanket in the woods. He says he can always find somewhere snug and dry. And then Humphrey sneaks some food out to him."

I sat on the bed, pondering. "I suppose there's nothing else for it," I said at last. "I don't think the King or his officials would take kindly to my having a private guard on the Progress." *Especially one as dangerous and deadly as Barnaby.*

"Go and eat," I said once again. "And tell Humphrey to take something to Barnaby."

"He has done already."

"What an efficient conspiracy," I said, trying to sound annoyed but quite failing. I was glad that Barnaby was here.

"Where's Barnaby now?" I asked.

"Doing some snooping," she said. "He's got wind that Richard Rich and Thomas Wriothesley are meeting in a tavern in the village. It made him suspect they're up to no good so he's gone to find out what."

I frowned. There was certainly something suspicious about them meeting so secretly. Thank goodness Barnaby had gone to discover the reason.

"Thanks, Sissy. Off you go, but come back the minute you hear anything from Barnaby."

I walked over to the cradle and gazed down at Lily. She was fast asleep, her little thumb stroking her chin every so often.

Perhaps she was dreaming. And what would she dream about? Of milk and me? Of Sissy and Humphrey? Of constant traveling along dreadful roads? Of her poor, dead brother?

I smoothed a little strand of hair from off her forehead and blew a kiss at her. My little darling. My world.

I settled down in the seat by the window with a book which Cathy had lent me. It concerned the new religion and how it was different from our former forms of worship, and far superior.

I have to confess that I did not understand most of the arguments it offered and cared even less. I found my head nodding and my eyelids drooping. I lifted the book closer and willed myself to keep reading.

The next thing I heard was the door closing quietly. "Is that you, Sissy?" I asked, drowsily. I struggled to force my eyes open and yawned loud and long.

"Not Sissy," said a voice. "Thomas."

I turned in an instant.

Standing by the window, gazing down at me, was Thomas Culpeper.

"You startled me, sir," I said, struggling to my feet.

He bowed his head. "A thousand apologies, Miss Petherton," he said. "I've been watching you for a while, hoping that you would awaken from your slumbers."

"Watching for a while?" I said. "I was not aware of it."

"It is a gift I have. Watching. While not being seen." He gave a smile which seemed a little too self-congratulatory.

"And is it your habit to enter a lady's chamber without her permission?"

"Only when I think she would give it to me anyway."

I did not say anything, too astonished by his answer. I felt my face begin to glow.

He saw this and smiled once again, a smile even more self-satisfied, even more smug.

"You presume too much," I said quietly.

"Do I, Alice?" he said, his eyebrows rising in pretend surprise. "I don't think I do, to be honest."

He stepped towards me, stood so close he filled my vision. I felt my breath come quicker but was unsure whether from excitement or alarm.

"You are very beautiful," he said. "More beautiful than even the reports of you." And he reached out and touched my hair.

I knew I should have brushed his hand away, knew I should step back or turn away. But I could not. I felt I did not have the power to do so.

He smiled once again. "I see you like me, sweet Alice Petherton." He turned towards the bed. "It is hot is it not? Perhaps you should remove some clothing." He gave another smile. "I think the afternoon is a very good time for making love."

"Now you do presume too much," I said. I was conscious that my tone was not as firm as it might be.

He chuckled. "Oh, I don't think so. You are a woman who knows the meaning of attraction. And you like me, do you not?"

I tried to answer but could find no words.

He placed his hand fleetingly upon my arm. He smiled, revealing sharp little teeth.

"You're a prime filly, Alice," he said. "And I'm a prime stallion." His mouth opened still wider but this time it seemed less of a smile. More a snarl.

He squeezed my shoulder and I felt him begin to turn me towards the bed.

"Oh, I would see you naked, Alice Petherton. And I would have you writhe and moan beneath me. The ecstasy of love, my dear. An ecstasy so close to pain, yet so very, very sweet."

I knocked his hand away.

"Get out," I cried.

He looked surprised, for a moment. The he frowned, looked baffled. He took a step back and then a step forward. His face had changed and now looked hard and threatening.

"You little bitch," he said.

"Get out. This instant. Or I shall call for help." I took a deep breath. "The King will not take kindly to your behavior. Nor the Duke."

He gave a little mocking smile and bowed. "I'm sorry to have been so in error," he said. "But I promise that I will not make the same mistake again. Not even if you beg me."

He strode out of the room and I slammed the door behind him.

I slumped on the bed, held my head in my hands and wept.

Not again, I thought, *not again.* What did I do to inflame men so terribly? I wept and wept and felt so alone and frightened.

When Sissy returned she found me still weeping. She got the story out of me in moments.

"Don't you worry," she said, taking my hand. "Humphrey and I will watch out for you."

"I don't want Humphrey to do anything silly," I said.

"Don't fret yourself," she said. "He's too sensible for that."

She gave a tiny smile. "Won't be a minute, Alice," she said, hurrying from the room.

What is she about? I wondered. But when she returned a little later I had no energy to inquire.

I spent the rest of the afternoon curled up on my bed while Sissy watched over me.

I thought back to the words Thomas Cromwell had said when I first returned to the King's favor. That I was a woman who could turn the heads of a multitude of men, beguile them, enthrall them. He said it was a talent, a gift if you like. That I had no more say in the matter than I had say in the color of my hair or eyes. That I must not blame myself that some men would be captivated by me while others would be inflamed.

I yearned to believe that he'd been right in saying it was no fault of mine. I feared that he was wrong.

I knew that I could entice men. Had I done so with Thomas Culpeper?

I thought over every time I had seen him, the few words we had ever exchanged. I could think of nothing I'd done to make him believe I was interested in him.

The fault did not lie with me.

Culpeper was one of those men who love themselves so much they assume that every woman feels the same towards them. Foolish, pitiable even, but nothing worse.

But there was a worse. Some men believed they deserved a woman's adoration, that it was theirs by right. Some demanded proof of it by sneers or threats or blows.

Barnaby had been right to be suspicious of him.

I sighed. *What a lucky escape.*

And what luck to have found a man like Nicholas. Even if I never saw him again, at least I would always know that there was at least one man worthy of love, and capable of giving it.

Barnaby Finch slipped into my chamber a few hours later. He had no news to alarm me. He had located Richard Rich and Thomas Wriothesley in an unsavory tavern. A fitting place for them, I thought. They had spent all the time talking about Katheryn's old servants, Mannox and Dereham. Why they were taking such an interest and doing so in secret was beyond me. Something malicious and petty no doubt.

Despite this, Barnaby seemed more than usually solicitous towards me. When I asked him the reason he hastily denied it. Then, with a strange little smile, he excused himself and hurried out of the room.

Towards evening a messenger came from Cathy to say that I was to sit with her and the Duke at the feast. I was surprised, and not a little horrified. I had no desire to go to the feast at all, still less to sit in a seat so visible and public. But I could not deny my friend and hurried to get ready.

I put on a red petticoat and a light-blue kirtle. There were any number of gowns I could have chosen, but in the end I decided on one of dark green with an even darker border. *Nothing too showy*, I thought, *nothing too glamorous.*

I finished off by choosing a gable hood rather than a French one. It did not suit my looks at all well, which is exactly what I intended.

The Great Hall was filled to capacity when I arrived and made my way to the Duke's table.

Cathy indicated a chair next to hers and I took it with relief. I did not relish light conversation with anybody, especially not the Duke of Suffolk. He was far too loud, and if I were honest, far too attentive to pretty women.

A fanfare sounded. The Duke appeared at the far end of the hall and made his way down it, acknowledging the applause as he did so. Walking by his side was the Duke of Norfolk.

I was surprised to see Norfolk. He had not been on the Progress and was said to be far to the north. He looked tired and not in the best of health, but his sharp owl eyes glinted around the hall, noting everyone who was there. He gave a disdainful sniff when he saw me and took his seat close to the King's chair.

And then the fanfare sounded once again, louder and more prolonged, and the assembly rose to its feet. Slow and stately, the King paced through the Hall, holding the Queen's hand high in his own. It looked to me as if they were tiptoeing along a muddy path, an old man being guided by his granddaughter.

They took their seats; the applause quieted and then dwindled to a close.

The Duke of Suffolk rose, cup of wine in hand, saluted the King and Queen and bade all enjoy the feast, put on especially in honor of the Duke of Norfolk.

"And to thank him," he concluded, "for his hard work in organizing the King's Progress."

Norfolk tried to look pleased but could not quite manage it. He knew a put-down when he heard it. Suffolk had intimated that the more senior Duke had been little more than a steward and lackey in matters of the Progress.

In actual fact, both men had shared the duties. I did not doubt that if it had been left entirely in Suffolk's hands it would not have been so well organized. The Duke of Norfolk was not a man I trusted but he could be relied upon to be effective.

The feast began, a lordly and rich repast. It was designed with the utmost care to be almost as wonderful as those of the King. But not quite so wonderful. No man dared upstage Henry Tudor, not even in matters of venison, roast beef and game pies.

Partway through the feast the King suddenly banged upon the table.

"Let's have a look at you, Thomas," he cried.

A figure rose with seeming reluctance from one of the lower tables and pushed his way towards the King. It was Thomas Culpeper.

Queen Katheryn gave a startled look. I soon saw the reason.

Culpeper's face was black with bruises. One eye was closed, the other red with blood. His lips were huge and torn, and his chin badly swollen.

"What on earth happened to you, lad?" asked the Duke of Norfolk.

"Set upon by ruffians," Culpeper answered. His words were thick and hard to distinguish.

"How many?" the Duke asked.

"Four or five, Your Grace," he answered.

Not true, I thought. Not four or five assailants.

Barnaby Finch needed no assistance in such matters.

Chapter 43
Lust in Lincoln

We made our way to the city of Lincoln on the ninth day of August but halted at a tiny village some miles away from it at an hour before noon. I wondered why we had stopped here, but the sight of Richard Rich nosing round the church and dwellings told me. Temple Bruer had been a House of the Hospitaller Knights of St. John and one of the wealthiest in the Kingdom. Although the House had been suppressed eighteen months before, there were still a few old soldiers and retainers in residence.

Not for much longer. Rich and his minions scurried over the buildings like rats in a hay-barn. By the time we sat down for dinner, the last remaining treasures had been located and piled onto mules, the old men sent on their way with a few coins in recompense.

The King, of course, pretended not to see any of this.

Kitchens and tables had been set up beside the church. There were sweeping views across a wide, flat landscape, and far to the north I could see the high hill of Lincoln crowned by its cathedral and castle.

The meal was a hurried affair and we were soon on the road again. It was almost as if the King felt a little uneasy at being present at the destruction of a religious order.

Lincoln was the first large city we had visited since leaving London and the preparations for our arrival were elaborate.

The Royal pavilions had been set up a mile south of the city itself. We endured a lengthy welcome in Latin from the Archdeacon of the cathedral and then retired to the tents to make our preparations for entry to the city. The King had arrived wearing a costume of Lincoln green in honor of the shire. The Queen wore one of crimson velvet.

I thought it diplomatic for the King to honor the shire in this way, but the moment he arrived he took steps to reassert his own majesty by a change of clothes. We were all kept waiting while he and Katheryn retired to their tents. They emerged in the most gorgeous of costumes. The King wore layer upon layer of cloth of gold, the Queen a beautiful gown of silver; veritable sun god and moon goddess indeed. They mounted their horses and led the way to the city.

I saw Thomas Culpeper amongst the gentlemen of the Court, his face now more blue than black. He scowled at me, either because I had rejected his advances or because he suspected that his beating had been the price of his attempted seduction. All the Court ladies made much of his injuries, save the Queen. She did not once look at him, indeed seemed to avert her gaze whenever he was near. Some might have put this down to an aversion to looking at his damaged face. I wondered if there were not another cause.

I had no idea why I had been included in the Royal party, although I was towards the rear of the Queen's retinue with only the guards behind me. I thought I would be riding alone until the French ambassador, Monsieur Marillac, rode up beside me and doffed his hat.

"I would like to escort you into the city," he said. "If I may."

"Why would you want to do that?" I asked.

"Because you are the companion of my friend, Nicholas Bourbon, and I can speak French with you." He gave a gallant smile. "And because you outshine everybody here in your beauty and grace."

"Surely not the Queen?" I said, hastily concealing my pleasure at his words.

He smiled once again but made no answer beyond a raising of his eyebrows.

"You are most courteous, Monsieur," I said. "I welcome your company."

We reached the edge of the city and were greeted by the assembled worthies of Lincoln. We listened to a speech, thankfully in English and half the length of that of the Archdeacon, watched the mayor fumble a gift of sword and mace to the King, and finally entered the city to the wild pealing of bells.

I felt strangely uplifted by the sound of them and of the crowds of people waving at the King and Queen. Little children rushed forward and offered flowers to the cavalcade and I garnered more than a few admiring glances from men both young and old.

"You see now that my reputation is enhanced," said Marillac. "Just riding beside you makes me look grand and lordly."

"You talk nonsense, sir," I answered, but I was glad of the compliment.

Such talk seemed typical of the man, all light and frothy. The English diplomats thought Marillac naive and easily duped. I suspected, however, that he played the innocent for his own purposes and found that foolish questions gave him more useful answers than shrewd ones. At any rate, he always seemed to know what was going on in Court, sometimes before the King's own officials.

At the west end of the cathedral were set a wonderful Ottoman carpet and stools and cushions of cloth of gold. The King knelt and was blessed by the Bishop, clouds of incense as thick as fog wafting over their heads. Then the King, Queen and the most eminent members of the Court entered the cathedral for a sacrament.

"Will you not go in?" I asked.

"I cannot," said Marillac. "I am sensible that our religions differ now and it is wisest for me to remain aloof from your practices. We are near our lodgings. It would be an honor if you allowed me to escort you there."

I thanked him and followed him towards the Cathedral hostel. As we did, I saw the Master of Horse, Anthony Browne, collecting the stools, cushions and even the great Ottoman carpet.

"You safeguard these for the King, Sir Anthony?" Marillac asked.

"For me," he answered with a grin. "They are my fee for leading the King's horse into the city."

They were of more value than a real groom would earn in a lifetime. By far the greatest effort Sir Anthony had made was when he busily exerted himself to make sure that every item due to him was collected.

Browne was cheered by the poor folk of the city as he led his burdened servants towards the Castle. No doubt some of them thought he was the King.

That night I was awakened by lights going past my chamber. I rose from my bed, fearing some alarm of fire or danger, and opened my door. Jane Rochford was standing in the corridor, lamp in hand, her eyes wide and darting.

"What are you doing?" she hissed.

"I saw lights," I answered. "I thought there might be an alarm."

"Foolish girl," she said. "There is nothing happening. Go back to your bed."

"But what are you doing?" I asked, pointedly.

"Nothing. None of your business. Now go to your bed."

I withdrew into my chamber. I sat up in bed for a little while, staring at the light coming through the crack of the closed door. And then it was snuffed out. *How peculiar*, I thought and then snuggled under the sheets and into a dreamless sleep.

We stayed in Lincoln for another day before starting on our journey once again.

Ambassador Marillac often sought me out to ride with me. I did not worry about this; he was far more gallant than most Englishmen. At first I thought he traveled with me because he liked my company. But I soon found out there was rather more to it than this.

"Your baby is delightful," he said one morning. "She is a pretty little thing, which is not surprising considering who her mother is."

"Thank you, Monsieur. As always, you flatter me."

"Has she any of her father's looks?" His voice sounded casual but he could not entirely hide his interest.

"I don't know," I said. "What do you think?"

He laughed uncomfortably, wrong-footed by my reply. "I could not say, Mademoiselle. After all, I do not know who the father is."

"But who does my daughter look like, would you say?" I glanced towards the coach where Sissy was watching over Lily.

"She has very blue eyes," he said, "unlike her mother. But eyes are not settled things in a child so young, so they may well change. Her nose is rather fine like yours, I think, although yours turns up most delightfully. But there again, my friend Bourbon has a fine, straight nose so Lily's could come from him."

"Then we must wait upon her nose as well as her eyes."

He nodded. He was silent for a few heartbeats and when he spoke again it was in a very quiet tone. "But the color of her hair? She is *rousse*, which you call a redhead, is she not?"

"But that also may change with age."

"True. But the King, he is a redhead and I think he has been since childhood. And Lily's hair is very similar to the Princess Elizabeth's."

He said no more but turned a quizzical eye on me.

"Babies are an enigma," I said. "Are they not, Monsieur? Especially to men. And, it must be confessed, that this uncertainty extends even to their fathers."

He chuckled. "I find the English language difficult enough without your use of ambiguity." He gave a little bow. "I will not pursue this topic any further, Alice. Although I do have my suspicions as to Lily's father."

"And you will keep these to yourself? For fear of getting it completely wrong?"

I said it lightly but I did not feel light at heart. Questions concerning Lily's paternity were already being whispered at the English Court. I had no desire for the same at the French one.

"I will keep them to myself. The child herself, as she grows, will begin to answer the question more fully. And then, *ma chère* Alice, you may wish to remember that I am your friend and have your best wishes at heart."

I did not answer, more worried by this statement than by anything else he had said. It seemed to me a clear sign that Lily and I might have to seek French protection at some time in the future.

We rode in silence for a time, with Marillac humming a little song from his homeland. If he thought this silence would prompt me to answer his question he had another think coming. Even I was not sure who Lily's father was. Sometimes when I looked at her I could see a resemblance to Nicholas. At others, I would discover a similarity to the King.

I still could not make up my own mind whether the latter was a cause for alarm or for rejoicing. There might be opportunity if she was the King's daughter. Or there might be terrible danger. I did not know what I feared most: that Lily was not the daughter of the King or that she was. My thoughts returned to their well-worn tracks concerning this.

"And what do you think of the young Queen Katheryn?" Marillac said at last, a welcome intrusion from my musings.

"She is very pretty," I said, grateful to change the subject. "And full of spirit."

He gave an arch and knowing look. "That may prove a problem for an older man such as King Henry. It is why he was attracted to her in the first place, of course. But a pretty face and vibrant spirit are attractive to younger men as well as older."

"What do you mean, Monsieur?"

"Those two sneaking fellows who used to work for the old Duchess. Their eyes follow her all the time like wolves stalking sheep." He paused. "And the other man. The one whose handsome face has been so disfigured recently."

"Thomas Culpeper," I said. "But you talk foolishly there, Monsieur. Culpeper barely looks at the Queen and she ignores him completely."

"Precisely my point," he said. "Illicit lovers always think they can hide their affection by pretending indifference to each other. But most feign poorly. They ignore their lover too much, too obviously. By doing this they delude only themselves. And it makes others begin to grow suspicious."

He said nothing further but gave a little chuckle to himself, which I found more disconcerting than any other comments he might have offered.

Now that he had mentioned it, the half-formed questions in my own mind coalesced into doubt and misgiving.

"I think that no man would be foolish enough to become the lover of the Queen of England," I said.

"You are probably right, Mademoiselle," he said. "Probably right."

Then he leaned closely to me.

"But how do you think Culpeper got so badly beaten? And who is that ugly fellow who follows our company and keeps such a close eye on you?"

"You ask too many questions, Monsieur," I said tartly. I was alarmed that he had noticed Barnaby, who had promised me that he would be so discreet as to be invisible.

"Forgive me," Marillac said. "It is my job to ask questions. And part of my job is to keep my eyes open for strange events and strange people. But fear not. Knowledge of your secret friend is safe with me. And I am very glad that you have such an efficient guardian."

I did not answer beyond giving a feeble attempt at looking confused. I felt certain it did not fool the Ambassador for an instant.

"And now let us speak of different things," he said. "Nicholas tells me that you write poetry. Please let us talk about that."

Chapter 44

Pontefract Castle

We spent a pleasant week journeying north. The weather kept fine although it felt a little chiller than I was used to. The winds blew sharp and strong across the flat landscape to the east but thankfully the rain kept away.

When we reached Yorkshire something most peculiar happened. A vast throng of people awaited us in the distance. A change came over our party. Men looked tense and most of the guards hurried to take up position closer to the King.

"Stay close to me," whispered a voice in my ear.

I nearly jumped out of my saddle. Barnaby had arrived silently at my side.

He had flung his cloak back over his shoulders, revealing his armory of weapons.

"Why do I have to stay close?" I asked. "What's wrong?"

"The northern rebels," he said, pointing ahead.

"Rebels," I said in alarm. "Are they a danger?"

"Possibly. Judging from the guards' reaction I fear it likely." He turned towards the coach. "Sissy, give Lily to Alice."

Sissy passed her through the window and I wrapped her under my cloak.

Humphrey appeared on horseback, leading a second one.

Barnaby ordered Sissy onto the horse. She jumped out of the carriage while it was still moving and climbed into the saddle.

"On my word," said Barnaby, "head south. I'll ride behind." He drew his sword and tested the sharpness of its edge.

But at that moment, to my relief, the rebels threw themselves on their knees and cried pardon of the King. I relaxed at once and turned towards Barnaby. He did not react but scanned the horizon. My heart went to my mouth. *He must still fear danger.*

One man stepped forward from the throng and delivered a lengthy speech to the King. I could not hear what he said, but evidently it went down well for the King returned an answer and the men of Yorkshire gave three loud cheers. Then they climbed to their feet and dispersed.

"All safe," said Barnaby at last. He pulled my cloak aside a little and smiled at Lily. "And look, the brave child has not even awoken."

Then he turned and cantered away.

"It's a good job we've got him on our side," Humphrey said. "I hadn't even spotted the rebels when he galloped towards me and told me to fetch a horse for Sissy."

"It's rare for you to praise anyone other than yourself," I said with a laugh.

"Well he's a rare 'un, that Barnaby Finch. Very rare."

"I'll be glad when we're back south," said Sissy. "I'm sick of all these travels and goings on."

"Me too," I said. "But we've got to go to York before we can head home again."

"Is it far?" she asked. "And will we be safe?"

"A long way," I said. "But of course we'll be safe with Barnaby to look after us. In any case, we're going to stay in a castle on the way."

We journeyed for a week more before reaching Pontefract Castle. It stood on a high hill and was a mighty structure, not pleasant looking as were the King's Houses near London, but designed and maintained for war. High walls ran between a vast keep and a further six towers. The walls enclosed a large bailey, which contained fine lodging houses and an imposing Chapel. To the southeast of this central part of the Castle ran a long curtain wall, which enclosed two more baileys where tents had been set up for our party. The guards, however, were housed in the keep.

The Queen professed she was frightened by the look of the keep and said she'd heard tales that terrible ghosts and ghouls walked there. Fortunately for her, or perhaps because of her complaints, she was housed in a tower opposite to it, close to the Chapel. The King and his friends were lodged in a second tower, nearby.

The first few nights in the Castle were spent indulging in huge and lavish feasts.

"The King can relax now that he is safe in this mighty stronghold," Marillac said rather cruelly. "He must still fear that the men of Yorkshire seek his death and a return to the old religion."

I wondered at his words. I had always thought the King a courageous man; surely Marillac was in error to think he had been afraid. Now he was behaving as if he hadn't a care in the world. Yet perhaps this was a masquerade; the King was putting on a show of insouciance. There was definitely an air of nervousness amongst his courtiers.

I thought it best not to tell Sissy. I told Barnaby, of course, but he said that we were quite safe in the Castle. Nothing untoward had ever happened here.

I felt slightly queasy after the second feast. The food had been astonishingly rich and lay heavy on my stomach. For a moment I wondered if the dishes had been poisoned by one of the rebels but I dismissed the thought from my mind. The King always used his own cooks and they were amongst the best paid of his servants. He demanded only the finest food and did not stint to ensure he got it. The cooks would sooner have cut their own throats than try to poison their master.

I lay tossing and turning for hours and, in the end, decided that I would go for a breath of fresh air.

"Isn't it dangerous?" said Sissy. "Going out, I mean."

"We're in the strongest castle in England," I said. "What on earth could harm me?"

"Ghosts," she said, climbing out of bed. "Ghouls. I'm coming with you."

So, candle in hand, we ventured out into the darkness. A few minutes later we found ourselves standing in the bailey.

I should have been alarmed at the sight of the vast walls towering above us but I was not. In fact, it seemed quite beautiful with stars twinkling in the sky and a crescent moon climbing above the gateway. I could just make out the shapes of guards strolling on the turret at the top. They should have been marching, I thought, but who could begrudge them their more relaxed gait.

"That's where all the ghosts walk," Sissy said, pointing to the keep.

"Well we're a long way from them," I said, "so we're quite safe."

"If you say so. It gives me the shivers." She pulled her cloak tighter.

We strolled a little way, past the Chapel, then turned and made our way back to the tower. The staircase looked far more sinister than I had noticed walking down. We were walking up into a dark and constricted space, the only light coming from a few torches which flickered and guttered, sending shadows leaping before us. Sissy shrunk closer to me and grasped my hand tightly.

We reached the third floor and then I paused. There were more lights just along the corridor, towards the Queen's chamber.

I put my fingers to my lips and took a few steps into the corridor. Jane Rochford was sitting in a chair placed close to a door. The Queen's bedroom door. Jane's head lolled in sleep.

I watched for a few moments and then I heard it. The sound of laughter from inside the room. And then another voice, that of a man, a teasing yet emphatic tone. A voice I thought I recognized. And, after a short silence, more laughter and squeals of pleasure. Squeals and unmistakable groans.

I turned and gestured Sissy to make a move. I tiptoed after her.

I turned in the doorway for one last glance. I could not see well, but I thought that Jane Rochford had woken. And she appeared to be staring straight at me.

Chapter 45
Misgivings

"Oh no," I said as I shut the door behind me. "Monsieur Marillac was right."

I sat on my bed, my thoughts running as wild as kittens being chased by a child.

"What's happening, Alice?" Sissy asked in alarm. She bolted the door behind her and sat beside me. "What was Monsieur Marillac right about?"

I bit my lip, wondering whether to tell her or not. Such information could prove perilous to anyone who heard it.

"Nothing," I said.

"I don't believe you," she said. "I don't believe you one little bit."

"It doesn't matter, Sissy. There's no need for you to worry about anything."

"There is though," she said, squeezing my hand so strongly it hurt. "If you're worried then so am I. I don't want anything to happen to you."

"Nothing will happen to me. Hush now, for goodness' sake. I need to think."

She pulled back and looked at me with the greatest scrutiny.

"So there is something wrong," she said at last. "Why else would you need to think?"

"It's good to think," I said sharply. "You should try to do it more often."

I regretted my words immediately for Sissy's bottom lip wobbled and I saw her eyes fill with tears. I stroked her hair away from her face. "There's nothing to worry about," I said gently. "Nothing to trouble your mind about at all."

She nodded, although I could see I had not convinced her.

She was right. My mind filled up with more troubles than I could count.

I managed a fitful sleep for a few hours only. I woke just after dawn and sat at the window looking out over the vale below the Castle.

It promised to be a beautiful day, as such days often are on the cusp of August and September. The air was warm and mellow, drowsy with the accumulated heat of summer. The sun was neither too hot nor bright, and cast a gentle, golden glow over fields that had themselves grown gold with ripening wheat. Even the trees seemed to catch this promise of harvest, some of their leaves streaked with an ocher which looked like fairy dust.

What a glorious day on which to be so troubled, I thought bitterly.

All of the things I had witnessed and half witnessed, the behavior of Katheryn towards Culpeper, the swaggering arrogance of the man, the smug way in which Jane Rochford behaved, all now made more sense to me. And Barnaby's words came back to me, his suspicions of Culpeper.

I thought of what Ambassador Marillac had said about lovers trying too hard to hide their guilty interest in each other. Heavens, if he suspected then who else did?

I went over in my mind all that I had seen last night. Jane Rochford standing guard. The laughter, the voice of the man. I recalled how Culpeper had tried to force himself on me.

And then I gasped. Katheryn had asked me to give sexual favors to the King because she said she found it too burdensome a task. Could this instead be the real reason? That she wished the King to bed me and so give her the opportunity to do the same with Culpeper?

I rested my chin upon my hands and gazed at the distant view. I was now privy to dangerous information and my position was perilous. My stomach sickened at the thought. I realized that the King should be told, of course. But who would dare to tell him?

Not I, certainly. I had more than enough experience of telling him things he did not want to hear. I had suffered terrible consequences for doing so. And those things were nothing compared to this news.

If I kept it quiet I would be complicit in the crime. If it were discovered, and my silence likewise, there would be no power on earth which could protect me. I realized I would have to tell somebody.

There were a great many members of the Privy Council on the Progress. I ran through them in my mind. Richard Rich, Thomas Wriothesley and the new Lord Privy Seal FitzWilliam I dismissed straight away. They only ever acted in their own best interest and were strangers to honor, decency and the truth. Odious though he was, the Duke of Norfolk was a better man, but he disliked me intensely. I did not know the other members of the Council well enough to form an opinion of them. Most were too busy clinging to position and life to lend a helping hand to the likes of me.

If only Archbishop Cranmer or Ralph Sadler were here. I could trust them to act sensibly and in the King's best interest. I believed I could trust them to protect me, as well. Not that this would prove an easy task. I shuddered at the thought of the King's ungovernable rages. Those who sought the best for him sometimes suffered as much as those who sought the worst.

I wondered about telling the Duke of Suffolk. He was a kindly man and had already warned Richard Rich to keep away from me. And I was good friends with his wife. Eventually, though, I dismissed the idea. Charles Brandon had never been known for deep thought or subtlety. He had tried the King's patience more often and more spectacularly than any man still alive. If I chose him to be my messenger it would be like being carried on a tightrope by an exuberant ox.

No, I decided at last. It would be wisest to keep the secret locked away until we returned to London. Once there I would unburden myself to Archbishop Cranmer. After all, since the death of Thomas Cromwell, he was the most adroit juggler still left performing in the King's circus.

Chapter 46
Investigation into Adultery

November 1541

Of all the months of the year, I liked November least. It was dank and drear, full of fogs and fumes and smoke from autumn burnings. There was a bleakness about the days, as if they were disappointed with themselves. The bright colors of autumn leaves had blown away, leaving the trees and bushes to rattle miserably in the wind. The harvest had been gathered, the farm animals slaughtered and salted, ready for the winter. But it was not yet winter. There was no snow, no sign of frost, no stark, bright skies to gladden the eye. November was the invalid of the year, sickly and languishing.

It was with such jolly musings that I stared out of my window at the gardens of Hampton Court Palace. On the journey south I had been anticipating arriving here with some relief, leaving behind a Progress which had become increasingly wearisome and worrying.

I had so many happy memories of the days I'd spent at Hampton Court. But now it was strangely different, indeed disconcerting.

In the past, the Palace had always seemed a place of great light and fanfare, the beating heart of the Kingdom. Yesterday, as we approached, it appeared to squat like a toad upon the riverbank, brooding and discontented with itself. I put it down to my weariness at traveling for so long a time and the fact that it was All Hallows' Eve, a day I never liked for it reminded me of my departed family.

Usually I awoke the following morning with such sad thoughts quite forgotten.

But today brought no relief. This morning I awoke with the same feeling of disquiet, wondering what the weeks ahead would bring.

It had been over two months since the night I had heard the sound of frolicking coming from Queen Katheryn's bedchamber. Because Sissy had not relented in questioning me about my worries, I had finally told her my fears and sworn her to secrecy. She was the only soul I could trust to tell. I had spent the rest of the Progress on tenterhooks, wondering what on earth to do.

I became obsessed with the thought of Katheryn's liaisons, wanted to discover more, yet dreaded doing so. The less I knew the less I might be thought complicit in the crime. So I tried to shut my eyes and ears to what went on.

I was not able to do so. Whenever I saw the Queen she looked either guilty or smug. She seemed to be perpetually exhausted, as well she might be after such vigorous romping. Her servants Mannox and Dereham appeared to dog her every step and I began to wonder if it was they who were pleasuring her.

But Thomas Culpeper ignored her to such an ostentatious extent it verged on rudeness, a folly which only served to suggest that, as Ambassador Marillac hinted, it was he who was her secret lover.

Every day we drew closer to London my anxiety had increased. I felt certain that Katheryn's dalliance could not remain secret. Then woe betide any suspected of actual involvement.

Jane Rochford had seen me that night in Pontefract, when she had guarded Katheryn's chamber. I knew with certainty that if she were condemned, she would hesitate not a heartbeat before incriminating me. Out of vengeance for my friendship with Anne Boleyn, partly. Out of the malice in her nature, chiefly.

I had made up my mind to tell my suspicions to either Ralph Sadler or Archbishop Cranmer. The only difficulty was that I could not make up my mind who. I would probably get a more comforting response from my friend Ralph. But the Archbishop would be a more powerful ally. That is, if I could persuade him of the truth of it.

And now, here I was at Hampton Court, in easy reach of either of them. The more I delayed telling them the worse it would look for me. Yet I could not make my mind up how to approach them or what to say.

Every time I rehearsed the interview in my head it seemed astonishingly pathetic. What concrete information did I actually have? That I had seen Jane Rochford sitting outside the Queen's chamber? That I had heard Katheryn laughing and thought, but could not be sure, that an unknown man was in her bedroom? I could almost see the puzzled look on the Archbishop's face before he gently told me that it must have been the King's voice I had heard.

And then he might grow suspicious, thinking that I was jealous of Katheryn and wanted to discredit her in order to resume my place as the King's favorite. That I sought her destruction, itself an act of treason.

"You've got a lovely room, Alice," Sissy said, breaking my train of thought. I glanced up and found her tidying my bed, humming to herself as she worked.

I was grateful for the interruption to my ceaseless ruminating.

"It is lovely," I said. "I'm very lucky."

"Are you going to have breakfast?" she asked.

I shook my head. "I have no appetite this morning."

She placed her palm against my forehead. "You're not feeling poorly are you? I could send for a doctor."

"There's no need, Sissy. I'm not unwell." I turned and glanced out of the window. "Just out of sorts."

At that moment there came a knock on the door and Humphrey entered.

"You've got a visitor," he said. There was an unusually serious look upon his face. Perhaps this miserable day was dampening his usual high spirits.

"A visitor? At this early an hour?"

He nodded.

"Is it Susan?"

He shook his head. "It's a gentleman."

"And did he say what he wanted?"

"Not a word."

I frowned, having no patience for such talk. "Who is my visitor, Humphrey?"

"The Archbishop of Canterbury."

I stared at him in surprise. What on earth would Thomas Cranmer want of me that he would come to my bedchamber?

I hurried to the looking glass to examine myself.

"You'd best show him in," I said, fiddling to make myself look more presentable. "Hurry yourself."

Humphrey disappeared, returning moments later with a cloaked and hooded figure.

"Your Grace," I said, curtsying. My stomach was roiling like I had swallowed a snake. The last time he had visited me like this was when he came to tell me that Sir Thomas had been arrested.

He held out his hand for me to kiss.

"Good morning, child," he said. He pulled back his hood and looked about him with a vague, preoccupied air.

I waved my hand to Sissy, who hurried over to take his cloak.

"Would you like some wine, Your Grace?" I asked.

"A cup of wine would be welcome," he said.

He took a seat and gave a heavy sigh. For a moment he bowed his head towards the floor and I wondered if he might be praying. But then he sighed again and shook his head as if all the troubles of the world were on his shoulders.

Sissy stood beside him with the cup of wine, not sure what to do. I nodded to her fiercely, indicating that she should give the cup to him.

"Here's a cup of wine, Your Archbishopness," she said, her voice trailing off in uncertainty.

He looked up and stared into her face, as if perplexed to see her there.

"Thank you, my dear," he said at last, with an attempt at a smile. He took the cup from the tray and sipped it, though he looked so deep in thought I doubt he tasted anything.

After a moment he cleared his throat, gave me a searching look and stared pointedly at Sissy and Humphrey.

"You may leave us," I told them. "And see that we are not disturbed."

"By anybody," the Archbishop said. "Anybody at all."

They fled from the room.

"I will get straight to the point," the Archbishop said once he heard the door shut behind them. "Do you know anything of the Queen's friends?"

It felt like the very knell of doom.

"I know that Lady Rochford is a close friend," I said feebly.

The Archbishop waved his hand, dismissing my words.

"I don't mean women friends," he said. "I mean men friends."

He did not say anything more, merely watched me.

My heart fell like a stone. I was such a fool. So my suspicions had been right all along. Katheryn's dalliance with Culpeper was more than mere courtliness.

And now I found out that the Archbishop already knew. That I had lost the chance to prove my innocence by telling him of my fears.

My innocence, I thought wildly. *My innocence is now in question.*

The blood beat in my temple so fiercely I thought my skull would split open.

Thank God I had refused her request to sleep with the King. I would have been considered an accomplice to her deceit, distracting the King so that she could couple to her heart's content. Some kindly spirit had saved me from such reckless behavior, at least.

The Archbishop's voice intruded into my thoughts.

"I repeat," he said. "Do you know anything of the Queen's men friends?" His voice was hard and unbending.

My stomach lurched still more.

Perhaps he did suspect me of complicity in Katheryn's actions. Was this why he had come here so early and alone? I cursed myself. I should not have delayed voicing my concerns.

"I know nothing, Your Grace," I stammered.

He regarded me in silence. His eyes had always looked distant to me, as if he were thinking of some place he would rather be or struggling to remember something just out of reach of memory. Now they had taken on a different look. They had grown heavy with suspicion, and shrewd, too shrewd.

How had he found out? I wondered. Who had told him?

"You know nothing?" he said. He shook his head, doubtfully. "But our late good friend, Sir Thomas, told me that you are quick and intelligent. Remarkably so." He took another sip of wine. "In which case how do you expect me to believe you know nothing of the Queen's indiscretions?"

"I may have had suspicions," I faltered.

"Suspicions?" He pursed his lips. "And yet you did nothing? Told no one?" His words were even harsher now, edged with iron.

I felt my cheeks grow hot. I had walked into a trap.

I stood up and went across to the sideboard. I poured myself a cup of wine and then walked back to offer more to the Archbishop. He had drunk almost the whole cup. I was a little relieved by this. Perhaps he was also finding the interview difficult.

"There was no one I could trust to tell," I said. "Who should I have spoken to? The Duke of Norfolk?"

He took a deep breath but did not answer. He disliked the Duke almost as much as the Duke loathed him.

"There were others of the King's advisers."

"But you were not on the King's Progress, Your Grace. I decided to wait until I could seek out your wise advice."

He looked shocked at that, and then a little alarmed. He knew that such words could easily be misconstrued, that they might be used to implicate him.

"Who else could I trust?" I continued. "Men who snatched at Thomas Cromwell's titles as soon as he fell? Wriothesley?" I placed my hand upon my bosom. "Sir Richard Rich?"

The Archbishop raised his hand as if to calm me. "I know something of the dealings between you and Richard Rich," he said.

There was only one man who would have told him such things. I decided I would have to play this card.

"And our very dear friend, Sir Thomas, is no longer with us," I said, dabbing at my eyes. "If he were then I'd have gone to him with my suspicions. Immediately."

My words hit home; a pained look crossed his face. The Lord Privy Seal and the Archbishop had been close, unlikely though that seemed. Indeed, they had been friends.

"It is a great pity that Sir Thomas is no longer with us," he said, clenching his hands. "He would have known what to do for the best. He would have taken this onerous task from off my shoulders."

"And what task is this, Your Grace?" I asked. I felt sorry for him suddenly, so doleful did he seem.

"Investigating the Queen," he answered. "Asking questions of people as I have to do of you." He put his hand against his mouth. "It is very distressing."

"Then why are you doing it? Have you been commanded by the King?"

Cranmer recoiled in his seat. "Of course I haven't."

He turned and stared fearfully at the door a moment before continuing with lowered voice. "The King knows nothing of these rumors, nothing at all. He is still besotted with the Howard girl."

It had come to such a pass then. The Archbishop of Canterbury was beginning to think of Katheryn not as the Queen but as merely one of the Howard clan. A tool of the Howards. Anne Boleyn in miniature.

"Then who, Your Grace?" I said. "Who has commanded you to pursue this investigation?"

He had appeared distressed before; now he looked wretched. He jabbed his finger at his chest.

"It is I, Alice. I who have set this dreadful business in motion."

I did not hesitate. Saw my chance. I was out of my chair and kneeling at his feet in an instant.

"You do right, Your Grace," I said, taking his hand. "You do right for the King and for the realm. No matter how painful and onerous it may prove to you, always remember that you are doing right."

I don't suppose that archbishops are much accustomed to being given blessings; he lapped up my words as if I were offering him eternal salvation.

"Thank you, dear Alice," he said. He closed his eyes and sighed.

"You look exhausted, Your Grace," I said, quietly. "Have you eaten this morning? I wager you have not. Let us breakfast together and think what to do for the best."

He opened his eyes and his former look of misery was replaced by one of cautious hope.

"And you promise that you will be frank with me?" he said. "You have been close to Queen Katheryn. I need more than the tittle-tattle and innuendo I have been fed with until now."

"Tittle-tattle," I said, breathing a sigh of relief that I had not, after all, come to him first with my insubstantial tales. "You must think it more than tittle-tattle or else why would you have come to me?"

"The rumors are compelling," he answered. "Quite compelling."

"And who has told you these rumors?"

He gave a little cough and lowered his voice. "I have been told that Katheryn's behavior was a scandal when she lived in the household of the Dowager Duchess."

"But that was before she was married to the King."

"I know." He lowered his voice still more. "But she is said to have had relationships with her music teacher, Mannox, and with another, Francis Dereham."

"But before her marriage to the King," I repeated. "And she was little more than a child, Your Grace. Surely the men were more at fault than she?"

He shrugged. "But she was still at fault. And the latest incidents have taken place within these past few months. Incidents concerning Thomas Culpeper."

So it was he. I made myself look a little shocked, just enough, so that the Archbishop could not be certain of my knowledge one way or the other.

He ran his fingers through his hair and gave me a pointed look. "That is what I came to ask you about, Alice. And yet I find that you have done all the questioning of me. How has this turned out so?" He gave a little, self-deprecating smile. "Thomas was right about you, it seems. Quick and intelligent. Too quick for an old churchman like myself."

"But of one mind with you, Your Grace. Loyal to our sovereign lord, King Henry."

The Archbishop nodded.

Cranmer is a survivor, I thought. So many others took the wrong path and fell, but he had survived. Despite his many enemies, despite the plots against him, he had survived. Perhaps he was not as politically naive as he pretended.

I rang the bell for Sissy and asked her to bring food to the room. She returned with plates of bread and honey, some cheese and fruit.

"Is there anything else?" she asked. It was clear that she was agog to find out what was happening.

"Not for the present," I said. "I shall ring if I need you."

All this while I had been observing the Archbishop. He seemed a little less fraught but he was still obviously troubled in mind. He muttered under his breath as if disputing with himself some arcane point of theology. It was with a palpable look of relief that he found the plate of food set beside him. He muttered grace and began to pick at some cheese.

"Tell me all you know about the Queen's liaison with Thomas Culpeper," he said. "Spare no details. I am not easily shocked."

I took a deep breath and told him all I had seen of their behavior. That most of the time they had appeared to be unaware of each other's existence. Manifestly so. But then, on occasion I had noticed knowing smirks and glances between them.

I told of how I had heard that Culpeper had instructed Katheryn with playing of the harp and, on more than one occasion, made haste to help her mount and dismount from her horse.

"The actions of a gentleman, perhaps?" the Archbishop said, almost hopefully.

"Possibly so," I answered in a tone which suggested they were not.

I peeled an apple and wondered if I had said enough. Enough but not too much.

It was time for me to find out a little more from him.

I cut the apple into slices and arranged them on the plate. "Who else knows of these accusations, Your Grace?"

"Baron Audley of Walden, the Lord Chancellor."

That weathercock. A fair-weather friend indeed, one quick to support anyone high in the King's favor and adroit at jettisoning them the moment they fell from it. Catherine of Aragon, Anne Boleyn, Anne of Cleves and Thomas Cromwell had all thought Audley their friend until they realized it was he who had gathered up the evidence which would destroy them.

"Only the Lord Chancellor?" I asked.

"And the Earl of Hertford," the Archbishop answered.

I picked up a piece of apple and nibbled at it to preclude further conversation while I pondered this.

The Earl of Hertford, Edward Seymour. He was no friend of the Duke of Norfolk and had been somewhat sidelined over the past few years. But he was intelligent and patient. Two attributes which had served him well. Almost as well as the fact that he was the uncle of the heir to the throne.

I could see several reasons for Hertford seeking Katheryn's downfall. One was to dismay and best the Duke of Norfolk. Another was to try to hinder the Duke's growing influence on religious matters. Hertford kept quiet about his own views on religion, a sensible move since the execution of Sir Thomas. But his fool of a brother had been heard to claim that Hertford was more Lutheran than Martin Luther.

And then a third motive came to mind. If Katheryn gave birth, her child would be second in line to the throne. This was not a problem if Prince Edward lived to succeed to the throne. But if he did not, a member of the Howard family would rule the Kingdom. Which meant, of course, that the Duke of Norfolk would be in control and the Seymours' power eclipsed. Perhaps even their lives placed in peril.

All in all, more than enough reason for Hertford to be comfortable with the destruction of Katheryn.

And Archbishop Cranmer? He shared several of the motives of Hertford. He was certainly not a friend of Norfolk. Yet I thought there was something more. He was loyal to the King above all else.

I suspected that he was also cursed with those most deadly of afflictions for those who lived in our times. A conscience and a belief in truth.

His loyalty to the King and his scrupulous conscience might prove the deadliest danger to Katheryn Howard.

Chapter 47
Rich and Wriothesley

But there proved a deadlier threat yet.

Humphrey hurtled into my room a few days after the visit of the Archbishop.

"They've set Richard Rich and Thomas Wriothesley to find the truth about the Queen," he said.

"Don't say any more," I cried.

I raced to the door, opened it carefully and looked out. There was no one near.

"Walls have ears," I told him, "and corridors have ears and eyes. Now sit down and tell me what you've heard, quietly. Who has set Rich and Wriothesley on?"

"The Privy Council," he said.

I shuddered. So the Archbishop had found out enough to launch a full-scale investigation.

"It's like a bonfire beginning to smolder," Humphrey continued. "The Queen's old lovers have been rounded up."

Susan and Mary hurried over.

"What do you mean, old lovers?" Susan asked.

"Mannox and Dereham," Humphrey answered. "They seduced her when she was a child."

I stared at him, astonished at how this hearsay appeared to be fact. The cat was out of the bag now. There could be no putting it back.

"That must be idle gossip," Mary said.

I did not answer though I felt there was truth in it.

"Idle gossip, poppycock," said Susan. "The Howard girl reeks of lust."

I had a sudden image of Katheryn Howard blithely unaware of what was about to descend upon her.

"In any case," Susan continued, "it doesn't matter whether the gossip is true or false. "Rich and Wriothesley will twist the facts to suit their purpose."

"But the King can't believe it, surely," Mary said. "He loves Katheryn so much."

"That's true," I said. "And it's all the more reason his wrath will be uncontrollable if she is guilty."

"But what does it matter?" Mary said. "These liaisons happened before Katheryn even met the King."

I was a moment too long in answering.

"You know something else!" cried Susan.

She ran to my chair and knelt at my feet.

Things half-said are as dangerous as the whole story. To end speculation I would have to tell my friends more.

"You must swear not to repeat what I'm about to tell you," I said. "Not to anyone."

I looked daggers at Humphrey, who crossed his heart. "I warn you, Humphrey, I shall unleash Mr. Finch on you if you betray me."

"Gawd help us, Alice," he cried. "Credit me with more sense."

"I'll make sure he keeps his tongue," Sissy said.

So I told them about the Queen and Culpeper on the Progress. I told them about what Sissy and I had seen and heard. I told them about the steely indifference of the Queen towards Culpeper and how strange this appeared.

"But that is proof of nothing," Mary said.

"Rich and Wriothesley don't need proof," Susan said. "They'll twist what little they find and convince the King. And putting witnesses to the rack will help furnish something for them to work on."

Mary's eyes widened in horror, Humphrey's in excitement. I slapped him on the arm.

"What about you and me, Alice?" Sissy said. "Will Rich and Wriothesley question us?"

I turned to her open-mouthed. I had not thought of that. But the moment she said it I could not banish the thought from my mind.

Rich and Wriothesley must have found out enough to convince the King there was something amiss. He would not have authorized proceedings otherwise. Of course, they would need still more proof to convict her.

"Let's pray that they find nothing amiss," said Mary.

"Amen to that," I said. But I suspected that this investigation would come to a terrible conclusion.

While Rich and Wriothesley spread their net wide, the poor old Archbishop was commanded to conduct the interrogation of Katheryn herself. Terrible for him, I thought it, but better for Katheryn. At least she would avoid the attentions of Rich and Wriothesley. Bloodhounds sniffing out the evidence, I thought them.

And then I shuddered. Blood is a very telling word.

The process went on for weeks. Katheryn was moved to Syon House and kept under close guard. She lost her title and all her possessions.

The investigation grew ever larger, dragging in people who had known Katheryn since she was a child.

I had never known the Palace like this. Most people seemed to be caught in a dream, moving with legs of lead and reluctant to talk. Others, members of the Privy Council, hurried everywhere in the most extreme haste, their demeanor intense and heated.

The Duke of Norfolk appeared most implacable of all. He had publicly washed his hands of Katheryn, more ostentatious than Pontius Pilate, determined to deflect all suspicion from him and his immediate family. I was not surprised by this perfidy. I was, however, astonished when he announced that he wished her to be burnt at the stake.

Thomas Wriothesley was found around every corner. The energy of the man was prodigious. He appeared elated by the investigation, exalted and enlarged, his reputation enhanced beyond all measure. I shuddered whenever I saw him. He appeared more like a bloodhound with every passing day. At the moment he was held on a leash but I suspected that soon he would be set free to hunt wherever he saw fit.

"I fear Katheryn Howard may well be guilty," the Archbishop confided in me.

He had come to me late that evening. He looked distressed and exhausted. I could not understand why he was visiting me so late and why he was telling me such a thing. A terrible sense of foreboding came over me.

"You fear she may be guilty?" I asked.

He put his hands together as if praying. "I am certain she is guilty. She has said as much herself."

"Poor child . . ." I began. And then I paused. "Why are you here, Your Grace?" I could barely get the next words out. "Am I implicated in any way? Am I in danger?"

"Of course not," he said. "I wanted to tell you the news myself, the horse's mouth so to speak. And I wanted to allay any troubles in your own mind."

"Thank you, Your Grace."

"I have found out everything I need from you," he continued. "In any case Richard Rich and Thomas Wriothesley have uncovered an astonishing amount from a veritable host of witnesses."

"A host?" I said. "Do you think this likely? Why would the Queen be so foolish as to conduct her affairs so publicly?"

He opened his hands as if to show he was as surprised as me. We both knew how untrustworthy such witnesses would be. How they would be swift to sell Katheryn for reward or to ensure their own safety.

"So what will happen next?" I asked. "To Katheryn?"

"She will continue to be examined."

"It sounds to me that she has already been found guilty."

"Oh no, no, no," he said hastily. "That is not the case at all. There will be due process, a proper trial."

I did not answer but I stared him straight in the eye. He looked away after only a few moments.

"And what about the men who are said to be her lovers?" I asked.

"Doomed, if they confess."

"And doomed if they don't?"

"That is unwise talk if you don't mind me saying, Alice."

I nodded. "Thank you for your advice. I will make sure I guard my tongue more carefully from now on."

And I think I shall prepare to return to France.

He took my hands in his. "You did well in this matter, Alice. You must not reproach yourself in any way. You did well by the King and by your conscience. You can rest easy."

But the very next day Thomas Wriothesley came to see me.

Chapter 48
The Majesty of the Law

December 1541

"You have heard the news?" Wriothesley asked.

"What news, Sir Thomas?" I replied. "There is so much news to listen to. I don't know how to choose what to give ear to."

He gave a smile so greasy I could have cooked a pork chop on it. "Always the quick one, aren't you, always pert and confident." He pulled at his beard. "I do not mean these words as a compliment."

"I do not take them as one."

"That is unaccustomedly wise of you." He closed his eyes for a moment as if savoring some delicious titbit.

I took a deep breath. I would have to guard my tongue very carefully.

"The news," he continued, "is that Dereham and Culpeper have been found guilty of treason. They will be taken to Tyburn tomorrow."

He leaned closer to me and I felt the taint of his breath in my nostrils. "Have you seen an execution, Alice?"

I had witnessed the death of my friend Thomas Cromwell but had no wish to speak his name today.

"I have never been to one," I lied.

"Oh, but you should. It is most instructive, most educational."

"I leave such pleasures to my servant. I am sure he will beg to go."

Wriothesley gave a humorless laugh. "The lower orders are such savages are they not? They delight to see an execution, especially of those found guilty of treason.

"They spit and curse at the traitor as he is dragged along the streets. They watch agog as he is hanged until he's blue in the face for want of breath. And then comes what they most delight in. The traitor is cut down, his legs and arms severed."

He paused and watched me to judge my reaction.

"You'd think this would be enough to kill a man," he said. "But it is not. Most live long enough to see their bellies slit open and their entrails plucked out. And how the common crowd loves it. Some stand as close as possible in hope of some blood or entrails landing on them. They think it lucky."

He shook his head like a schoolmaster admonishing a child.

"But it is all too clear that you are distressed by such a sight," I said.

He frowned, uncertain of whether I was being ironic or not.

"Both traitors are to suffer this fate," he continued. "Some argue that Culpeper should be given the ax, as he is a gentleman. But His Majesty commands the more hideous death for him as well as Dereham. To encourage loyalty."

His hands clenched and unclenched as he said this. I imagined he would like to be the one removing the entrails.

"Is this all you have come to tell me, Sir Thomas?" I asked. "I have a busy morning ahead of me."

"I have a few questions," he said. "Concerning what you did and did not know about the relationship between the Howard woman and Culpeper."

"I have told the Archbishop all that I know."

He gave another greasy smile. "Isn't the Archbishop a lovely old gentleman? So kind, so considerate, so good to his friends?" Then his face hardened. "So easily fooled."

"I do not think the Archbishop is a fool," I said.

"I did not say that," he responded swiftly. "I said that he is easily fooled. It is a failing of the gentle hearted."

"And are you easily fooled, Sir Thomas?"

"Never, Alice Petherton. Never."

I gave a little cough. "Would you like some wine? Something to eat? You need to sustain your health and well-being."

He shook his head. "All I require from you is the truth. Tell me what you know of Katheryn Howard and Thomas Culpeper."

"But what do you need to know? Thomas Culpeper is to be executed. Surely you have all that you need."

"I need still more," he said. "And I think that you may well provide it."

"For what purpose do you desire such intelligence?"

"To ascertain the full extent of the Howard woman's guilt. To encompass the degree of her perfidy."

I took a breath. I would have to tread very carefully indeed.

I recounted all that I had seen of Katheryn and Culpeper's behavior in Lincoln and Pontefract. I kept to the facts and did not tell him that the way they behaved together had aroused my suspicions.

"That has been most helpful," he said when I finished. "I do not think I have need to trouble you again."

I was relieved and astonished. Then he produced a blank piece of paper.

"But for our records I would ask you to put what you have told me in writing." He pushed the paper towards me.

"Do you want me to do so now?"

"If you would be so kind."

I went across to my writing table. I had to write exactly what I had already told him. I must write baldly, succinctly, putting nothing in the account which might vary from what I had said already, nothing which would give Wriothesley any excuse for questioning me again.

I spent twenty minutes writing my account, acutely aware that he was watching me all the while. *So must the serpent have watched Adam eating the fruit in Eden*, I thought. Unblinking eyes, flickering tongue, icy heart.

I finished at last and took the document to him. He read it carefully, asked me to sign and date it and then added his own signature before putting the document in a leather wallet.

"One last thing," he said.

My heart plummeted to the floor at his tone.

"Knowing all these things, why did you not speak of them?"

I went to lick my lips but managed to restrain my tongue. He was watching me with pitiless eyes.

"I had no one to tell."

He feigned surprise.

"No one? But you were surrounded by members of the Privy Council. By the Lord Privy Seal, the Master of Horse, the Duke of Norfolk." He tapped me on the knee as if in gentle admonishment. "You could even have come to me."

"I thought about it," I said. "But I did not wish to upset the King. I worry about his health, you see."

"As we all do," he said.

He glanced at what I had written, as if seeking there for some answer to a puzzle.

Then he asked, "But did you not consider that the Howard woman and Culpeper were committing treason? And that your keeping quiet about it might also be construed as treason?"

I shook my head.

"Does the shake of your head indicate no to my first question or to my second?"

I began to tremble with fear. "Neither," I whispered. "I mean both."

He pretended to look perplexed although I doubt very much that he was.

"Neither? Both?" he said. "Are these the words of an honest woman or of a dissembler?"

"An honest one, Sir Thomas, and a loyal one."

He nodded. "But loyal to who, I wonder? The King or Katheryn Howard?"

My mouth tried to reply but no words came.

Wriothesley put the document wallet in a bag. "I am sorry, Alice Petherton, but I am not happy with your answers."

"I don't much care if you are happy or not, Sir Thomas," I said. I instantly regretted my words. "It is the truth, as God is my witness."

He stared at me in silence, his face inscrutable. Then he gave a little sigh and stood up.

"I do not think the King's Justice will trouble God to plead on your behalf," he said. "You may need to have recourse to other friends. If you can still find any."

And then he swept out of the door.

I spent the rest of the day mulling over Wriothesley's words. I cursed myself for saying that I did not care whether he was happy or not.

He was a man of little worth and such men are often the most prickly when their dignity is hurt. They cannot bear to contemplate the truth, especially when their noses are rubbed in it. Well, it was too late now. He would take a place near the top of my list of enemies.

I developed a dreadful headache and went to bed. But I got little rest there. My sleep was troubled by hideous dreams: of being chased through streets by dogs dressed as men, of Thomas Wriothesley calculating on an abacus made of bone, of approaching the King as he sat reading and seeing him glance up at me with the head of Richard Rich on his shoulders. I reached out to the empty place beside me and began to weep for the lack of Nicholas.

Because my sleep had been so disturbed I woke next morning as if from a stupor. My head felt stuffed with the wool of a dozen sheep. I went over to Lily's cot but it was empty. *Sissy must have taken her*, I thought, stretching to try to wake myself fully.

I washed and dressed hurriedly for it was cold in my chamber. Even colder in my heart; the visit of Thomas Wriothesley had left a dead, drear hand upon it. The fire in the sitting room would warm and cheer me, I hoped.

I was almost knocked over by Mary rushing out as I walked in.

"I can't listen to any more of this," she muttered, more to herself than to me.

I entered the room and saw Susan sitting at the table open-mouthed. Sissy had her hands to her ears. Barnaby was eating a plate of eggs and sausages, half listening to Humphrey, who stood in front of them, excited and breathless.

"And then they took him down, gasping and choking," he said, "and they cut off his arms and legs."

Susan gasped at his words.

Oh no, I thought, glancing at Sissy, her eyes clenched tight, shaking her head to try to drown out the words.

"And then," Humphrey continued, "the executioner slit open his stomach and dragged out his guts. Before his very eyes."

Sissy gave a little scream; Susan closed her eyes then opened them immediately once more. Barnaby stabbed a sausage and put it in his mouth.

"Humphrey Buck," I cried, "stop this at once."

He turned to me with a look of surprise.

"I was only telling them about the execution of Francis Dereham. A good show of it he made."

"You disgusting creature," I said. "How could you go and gape at such a thing?"

"There were loads of people there," he answered, his voice hurt and defensive. "Ordinary folk, gentry and lots of clergymen and courtiers. Why I even saw the Earl of Surrey there."

"That doesn't matter a jot. You shouldn't have gone. I'm surprised at you."

"I told him not to," Sissy said. "I begged him."

"And you sit there listening to him," I said to Barnaby. "And calmly eating your breakfast as you do so."

"I've heard worse," he answered. "Seen worse. Done worse." He dunked his sausage in his egg and swirled the yolk around a little.

"Anyway," Barnaby continued, "Dereham was a mean, despicable figure. He deserved his fate. I for one am glad to see the back of him."

"He never did us any harm," I said.

Barnaby shrugged. "That's true, he didn't. But that rogue Culpeper did."

"I think you did more harm to him when you beat him black and blue."

But then I faltered in my words and turned to Humphrey. "I suppose Culpeper was hanged and quartered as well."

"No," he answered, in a disappointed, churlish tone. "He was just about to be when a messenger arrived and stopped it. The King had decided to be merciful to him, on account of him being a gentleman."

"Typical," Barnaby said with surprising vehemence. "It's one law for the poor and another for the rich. He's far more guilty than Dereham yet he's got off scot-free. I wouldn't be surprised if he doesn't walk into the Palace this morning and start up his old tricks."

"He'd have difficulty," Humphrey said. "Not without his head."

Barnaby mimed a cutting motion to his throat, a questioning look on his face.

"Yes. He had his head chopped off but nothing worse. What a shame. I wanted to see if he was as brave as Dereham."

"I can't believe we are calmly sitting here discussing the death of these two poor men," I said. I gave Susan a withering look.

"It's fascinating," she said. "Horrible. But fascinating."

I shook my head in disbelief.

At that moment the door was flung open and Mary appeared, her face white and drained.

She was pushed out of the way by Sir Richard Rich.

He took in the scene with a mocking smile.

"Quite the little picture," he said. "Domestic tranquility. Ah well."

He took a step towards me, pulled a piece of paper from his pocket.

"This is a warrant for your arrest, Alice Petherton. You shall go to the Tower. You'll be relatively comfortable there and may even take your maid with you. There are guards outside to escort you."

The heat seemed to drain from me. I thought I might faint.

"I've done nothing wrong," I said.

He gave a ghastly grin. "Then you have nothing to fear."

"I've done nothing wrong," I repeated.

He did not answer but took out a second document.

"This is not what this honest witness testifies to. Under oath. He says that you actively helped Katheryn Howard engage in lascivious and treasonous acts. He says that you boasted of this."

"And who would this witness be?" I asked with contempt.

"One who your judges will, with heavy heart, believe."

He paused and gave a huge, pretend sigh.

"The witness is myself, Alice."

His face lit up with pleasure.

Chapter 49
Imprisoned in the Tower

I stared out of the window onto Tower Green.

It was New Year's Eve and the old year was ending on a black, unquiet day. A shrill wind howled and every so often a sudden squall would spatter viciously upon the pavements below. Even the fire sputtering in the grate did not dispel the dank and chill airs.

I wondered if I should write yet another letter to the King. I had written half a dozen already, each one more desperate than its predecessor. Pleading for my freedom, for an audience with him, for some communication from him. The only reply had come from Richard Rich. He told me that the King had washed his hands of me, that he did not wish to even hear mention of my name. My fate was to be decided by officials and he took no interest in it.

The King, in fact, no longer took any interest in me.

I had been abandoned.

I went across to the little table and pulled open a drawer. There, hidden within, was the drawing of my beloved Nicholas. I placed it against my lips. Why had I left him? Why had he allowed me to return to England? Why was I in such a terrible predicament? I dabbed away a tear.

At that moment the door was unlocked and an all too familiar figure stepped into the room. I replaced the drawing hurriedly, praying that he had not seen it.

"Sir Thomas Wriothesley," I said. "Come with fresh accusations?"

"We do not accuse you of anything," Wriothesley said.

"Then why have you arrested me?" I asked. "And why am I in the Tower?"

He looked around as if surprised. "You cannot complain, surely? This is a pleasant chamber, well-furnished and with a window overlooking Tower Hill."

"I would call it an arrow slit rather than a window," I said.

And Tower Hill was where Sir Thomas Cromwell had been executed. My room had been chosen with great care. Or rather, with great malice.

"All you need to do is answer some questions," Wriothesley said. He pulled over a chair and settled himself in it.

"I have answered them. Repeatedly. Over the last three weeks."

"But you have not answered to our satisfaction," he continued. "We remain perplexed why you did not tell anyone of your suspicions of Katheryn Howard."

"I remain perplexed myself, Sir Thomas. And I repent greatly that I did not do so."

"You say you wished to wait until you returned to London and could seek guidance from the Archbishop of Canterbury. But the Bishop of Durham was with us. Could you not have opened your heart to him?"

"I've told you already, I did not know the Bishop."

"Whether you were acquainted with him or not is immaterial. Whether you knew anybody is immaterial. A loyal subject of the King should have confessed her suspicions."

I caught his use of the word *confessed* and could have wept. One thing I had learnt over this last month is that Thomas Wriothesley did not use words heedlessly. He selected every one as carefully as a soldier chooses his armament.

I turned away from him in despair.

"I will return," he said at last. "Though not for a while. I have work more vital to the Crown than wringing the truth out of you."

I was glad to see the back of him. His visits left me drained and furious. Over the next month I was to hear exactly what this vital business was.

Chapter 50
Paying to Survive

February 1542

Katheryn Howard was executed on the thirteenth of February, 1542. I remember the date vividly, partly because of this terrible event but chiefly because Lily had her first birthday on this day. She had been taken from me on the day I was arrested, two endless months ago. My only consolation was that the Archbishop had interceded and arranged that she be taken to a place of safekeeping.

And now I was not even able to celebrate her first birthday. I spent the rest of the day weeping for Lily and for me. I was still doing so when the door opened and Richard Rich appeared.

"Leave us," he said to Sissy. "The kitchen has need of an extra pair of hands."

Sissy looked worried at this command but I told her to obey. Any argument would have been futile.

"You've been crying," Rich said in mock surprise. "Are your tears for the death of the treasonous adulteress? Or for her accomplice, Jane

Rochford? Despite her recent display of madness Rochford joined her mistress on the block this morning. The sight of the ax appeared to cure her raving for she became quite composed. Odd how people react to their own demise."

I felt terribly vulnerable. I was sitting on the rug in front of the fire for warmth. It had given me some small comfort during the day, but all such thoughts had vanished with Rich's arrival.

He sat at his ease in a chair and regarded me. "Or are they tears because you fear that you will share their terrible fate? You'll find the ax much sharper than a bodkin."

And then he laughed.

"But of course, there will be no ax for you. Such a death is reserved for ladies. You'll be hanged like a common whore."

He put his finger on his chin and stared at me. "So beautiful a creature and so misguided. What a waste of a young life. And how terrible for your child to be brought up an orphan."

My stomach lurched at his words but I resolved not to give him the satisfaction of seeing any weakness.

"You have my death warrant?" I asked. "Yet I have not been tried."

He gave a hollow laugh. "Trials are for the innocent," he said. "The guilty need no trial. Such niceties have been dispensed with."

I was horrified by his words. So there would be no recourse to the law, no hope of pleading with the King?

I could not move; I was struck dumb and immobile.

My poor darling, Lily. She would spend her life never having known me, never having had a mother. *Mary and Susan will look after her*, I thought. *And Sissy.*

Dear, dear Sissy. I would ask her to take Lily back to her parents' farm in Stratford. My baby would grow fit and strong there. But an orphan. Without me.

Rich's words intruded on my thoughts.

"No, I do not have your death warrant," he said. "But I do have another warrant." He pulled out a piece of paper and showed it to me. I scanned it with disbelief. It was a full pardon, signed by the Duke of Norfolk and countersigned by the Lord Chancellor.

I looked up at him, my heart beating wildly with hope.

"I've been pardoned."

He pursed his lips and shrugged. "Almost. Quite possibly. Perhaps."

He took back the document and put it in his pocket.

"But there is one certain way of ensuring that this document goes to the King for final signature."

I frowned, not understanding what he meant.

"The certain way, dear Alice, is for me to take you. Here, now.

"You don't need to get up from the floor if you don't want to. But the bed may be a little more comfortable."

The skin tightened on my body, grew hard and cold as though it sought to protect me. I shuddered inwardly but my flesh would not let it show.

My first impulse was to scream at him. *Never in ten thousand years would I stoop so low*, I wished to cry. But the words died on my lips.

I craved my freedom. I craved life. I yearned for my baby.

My heart was cold as stone as I got to my feet and approached the bed. There was no question in my mind now. And I knew I had better play the part in excellent fashion.

I stripped off my clothes and lay down, positioning myself to look most beguiling. I could not bring myself to appear welcoming to him but I stared as if to say, *I am wanton, I am available. I am yours.*

And he took me.

Oh, he was every bit as awful as I had suspected. Clumsy, oafish, crude and violent. A gutter sexual predator such as haunted the filthiest brothels of Southwark. He scratched my breasts, bit my chin and dribbled on my face. I do not know which sickened me most.

At last he had his fill of me and climbed off.

He rose and dressed swiftly, whistling contentedly all the while.

"The pardon," I said clutching the sheets to my breast. "Now give me my pardon."

He pulled it from his pocket, tore it in half and flung it on the fire.

I screamed in horror and rushed over, vainly trying to snatch the paper from the flames.

"I have my vengeance, little whore," Rich said. "I have my vengeance."

Night was falling when the door opened once more.

It was Sissy.

"Are you all right, Alice?" she cried. "You look terrible. What did Rich do to you?"

"I cannot say," I answered. I felt ashamed, filthy. It was worse than being in Crane's foul brothel.

I had chosen to do this, knowing that there had been no choice. But I had chosen, nonetheless.

Sissy was too sensitive to question me further.

"You poor thing," she said. "Whatever he did."

"If he harmed you, he'll regret it," came a voice from the shadows.

I nearly expired with shock. Barnaby stepped into the light.

"What are you doing here?" I asked. "How did you get in?"

"I've climbed higher walls in the midst of battle," he answered.

"But the guards . . ."

"Guards come," he said, "guards go."

I saw the look on his face and did not press for further explanation.

"What are you doing here?" I repeated.

"I wish I could say I've come to rescue you," he said. "But though I can scale the Tower walls and climb back down, neither you nor Sissy could."

He placed a leather wallet on the desk. "But I've brought something which Ralph Sadler said was of vital importance."

"Ralph Sadler?" I murmured. I looked at the wallet with blank eyes. I was exhausted and used up by my ordeal. I could barely focus.

"Thank you for bringing it," I said. "I shall have to look at it later."

Barnaby stepped closer. "Then take some rest, Alice. But make sure that you do as Sadler asked. There are documents inside. He would not have sent me with them unless they were important."

"I will."

He kissed me on the hand and left. I slumped onto the bed. As my eyes closed I wondered what on earth Barnaby could think so important he would risk his life to bring it to me. But it was too late. I had given up all hope and did not care.

I was woken by the sound of Sissy calling.

She was sitting at the table. The wallet was open and documents were strewn upon the table. She held up a sheet of paper and waved it frantically at me.

"Alice," she said, "Alice, Alice. You must read this. I think it's really important." She began to cry. "I can't understand it all but I think it's really important. Really important. That's why Sir Ralph sent it."

She leapt from her seat and thrust it into my hands.

"It's from Sir Thomas Cromwell," she said.

Chapter 51
The Trial

I looked around at the assembled men. I could read my death in every face.

Not without a fight, I thought. *Most definitely not without a fight.*

I unclenched my hands and placed them palm down upon the table.

A few of the men in the room seemed sorrowful: Archbishop Cranmer, the Duke of Suffolk, Edward Seymour. Some appeared smug and pleased with the thought of the work ahead. Richard Rich and Wriothesley, on the other hand, hugged themselves with delight.

I felt sick at the sight of Rich and shuddered. But I held his gaze, held it so long that he eventually looked away.

Ralph Sadler gave me only the most fleeting glance before bending his full concentration to the task of recording events.

The Duke of Norfolk made himself appear detached and far above events, like God in his heaven. But a hair's breadth below this facade I suspected that he exulted to see me vanquished.

"Alice Petherton," the Duke said. "You have been summoned to hear judgment upon you." He arranged a handful of papers on the table.

"So it seems," I said.

He looked at me as though I were a creature so despicable she should not deign to utter words in his presence.

He turned to the Lord Chancellor, Thomas Audley.

My heart sank. Audley's turncoat history was unparalleled. A man's best friend one moment, the worst of his enemies the next. A pitiless judge who filled up graveyards to win favor with the King.

"There is little to discuss in this matter," he said. "There are numerous dispositions alluding to the guilt of this disreputable young woman."

"Numerous?" the Archbishop ventured to say. "May we examine them?"

Audley gave a dismissive wave of his hand. "That is not necessary. Believe me when I say that the case is beyond question."

"Who has condemned me?" I demanded. "I have a right to know."

Audley sneered. "You have no rights in this matter," he said. "But let me tell you that many servants of the King have condemned you, including friends who were reluctant to confirm your guilt."

"Which friends?" I asked. "False friends."

"Enough of your insolence," said Norfolk. He took a deep breath. "This case has gone on long enough. It must be concluded today. It is, of course, for the Lord Chancellor to decide, but I would recommend the utmost penalty."

Ralph Sadler paused in his writing for a moment but did not look up.

"The ax?" asked Seymour with a frown.

"Certainly not," responded Audley. "Petherton is little more than a strumpet. The rope is more usual although I have not ruled out death by fire."

I nearly swooned. But then I mastered myself. I had only the one chance left to me.

"It were a pity," I said, "if I am to be condemned on mere hearsay and whispers."

With trembling hands, I produced one of the papers which Ralph Sadler had secretly sent to me.

"This," I continued, "is a document full of just such hearsay and whispers. I would deem it a tragedy if the noble names listed in it were besmirched by this voice from the grave."

"A voice from the grave?" said the Archbishop in serious tone. "Whatever do you mean, child?"

I gave him a doleful look before continuing.

"As your lords know," I continued in stronger voice, "Sir Thomas Cromwell and I were good friends. I visited him in the Tower the day before his death and he gave me this."

I produced the document wallet.

"It contains letters to me," I said. "From Sir Thomas."

I gave a sweet and innocent smile and was rewarded by a few indulgent ones in return.

"It also contained a number of other documents," I continued, "written in the hand of Sir Thomas."

At those words the atmosphere of the room changed. A sudden stillness gripped my accusers.

Yes, even though long dead, the hand of Thomas Cromwell could reach out and freeze men's hearts.

I had brought only one document with me. I held it up, tapped it lightly on the side of my hand, beat a rhythm with it, like the knelling of a distant drum.

"What is that document, Alice?" asked the Archbishop.

I took a deep breath.

"As you all know," I said, "Sir Thomas was a cautious man. He was well-placed in the business of the King and he knew everything. He made sure that he knew everything."

I paused to let this point go truly home.

"This document, for example, is full of hearsay and innuendo. Very like that which you have heard concerning me. It is not the only such document in my possession. There is barely a person at Court who did not merit the attention of Thomas Cromwell, who did not merit his writing a record of their words and deeds."

If the room had been silent before it was like nothing to the dread stillness that gripped it now. Every man stared at me with horrid fascination, aghast at what I might reveal about them. Every man bar Ralph Sadler.

"And this particular document, Alice?" asked the Duke of Suffolk, at last. "To who does this refer?"

I did not answer save to pass it to him.

He unfolded it and leaned towards the Archbishop so that they both might read. Their faces grew astonished as they did. I saw the Archbishop's eyes slide towards the Duke of Norfolk and then Suffolk's eyes did likewise.

Norfolk straightened in his seat and leaned over in an attempt to read the document. "Does that concern me?" he asked.

"Some of it," said Suffolk, moving the document beyond Norfolk's gaze. "It shows what Cromwell thought of you. And a list of his suspicions concerning various of your deeds."

"And what is the purpose of the document?" asked Seymour. His nostrils twitched. His enmity towards Norfolk was no secret.

"It is addressed to His Majesty," said the Archbishop. "It is dated the day before Cromwell's death."

"So it did not reach the King?" Suffolk asked.

"There was no one to take it," I said. "Sir Thomas had time only to place it in the wallet intended for me. This document and several others."

"Let me see it," Norfolk said. He held out his hand and I saw that it shook a little.

Sir Richard Rich rose, hound-like, and reached for the paper.

"You are mentioned in this, also, Sir Richard," I told him lightly.

He started at my words and glanced at the document. And then he gasped.

"But this is not in Cromwell's hand," he cried. "It is very similar but it is not his hand."

He turned to me with a triumphant smirk. "This is a forgery."

The atmosphere in the room changed at his words. The feeling of disquiet eased and was replaced by a nervous hope.

He hurried over to Norfolk and gave the paper into his hand.

We all watched closely as the Duke read it. He attempted to hide it, but anxiety and alarm chased each other in quick succession.

I swiftly appraised the rest of the men. They saw this too.

"It is a forgery," said Norfolk at last, in a tone of utmost relief.

"Not a forgery, Your Grace," I said. "A copy. The original documents are quite safe. Well beyond the reach of anyone implicated by them."

This was not true but the men in the room did not know it. The originals were hidden in Sissy's undergarments.

Rich's hand clenched and unclenched, writhing like snakes.

The Duke stared at me in horror. Then a dreadful rage seized him.

"You will tell me where they are, you whore, or I'll rack you until your joints burst asunder."

"Your Grace," cried the Archbishop angrily. "You will not utter such threats in this court."

And with these words, and those of the angry Duke, the sentiment of the other nobles began to slowly tip towards me.

Or, more likely, the shift was due to their fear of what I had learnt from Thomas Cromwell.

"Where are the original documents?" the Duke repeated. "Every man here has an interest in them, you say. Every man is condemned by them."

"But Your Grace," I said, holding my hand to my breast in all innocence, "they are hearsay merely. I would not wish any man condemned by wicked lies."

I lowered my eyes but not before giving the tiniest little glance towards Rich and Wriothesley. It did not go unnoticed.

Silence fell on the room, then was punctured by Ralph Sadler's quill scratching once more upon parchment.

All eyes were on me, waiting for what I would say next. I waited for a few seconds more before continuing.

"Just as, I feel certain, my noble lords would not wish me condemned because of hearsay."

"Where are the documents?" Norfolk thundered.

Everyone turned to him, surprised that his usual self-control had deserted him.

"With Anne of Cleves," I said. It was a lie but they had no reason to believe it so. "I gave them to her for safekeeping."

Every eye turned from Norfolk to me. It was as if, until this moment, they had been playing a game of chess they thought they would easily win.

Yet now they saw that they had been lured to their own destruction.

"The documents are irrelevant to the case," the Lord Chancellor said, desperately. "If Alice Petherton will not admit to her guilt here we must find more pressing ways to make her confess."

"You cannot rack her," I heard Seymour murmur.

There was silence at his words. And then every head turned back towards the Duke of Norfolk.

What happened next was remarkable.

Never underestimate the Duke, Sir Thomas had told me long ago. He was right.

Norfolk licked his lips and took a deep breath. I guessed that he was remembering all the deeds which Thomas might have recorded, deeds he would be desperate the King should not learn about. That he next considered countless stratagems to get himself out of the situation he now found himself in. That he dismissed them all as impracticable.

And all this in mere moments.

The Duke composed his features and gave me a kindly smile. He glanced at Ralph Sadler and waited until he had dipped his quill in fresh ink.

"This document contains disgraceful accusations, Miss Petherton," Norfolk said. "False accusations. I doubt they were even written by Thomas Cromwell. False, scurrilous hearsay, nothing more. I am grateful to you, Alice, for bringing them to our attention."

He slowly began to tear the document into pieces.

"They are not fit to be read further," he continued. "And, as you say, dear Alice, hearsay and lies are not fit evidence for a court such as this."

He turned towards the others.

"It is unseemly," he said, "for men such as us to have our conduct questioned by innuendo and rumor. I wish to emphasize that Alice Petherton has performed good service in drawing the existence of these reprehensible documents to our attention. I for one am glad that Anne of Cleves keeps them safe from prying eyes."

He turned towards the Lord Chancellor. "Do you agree with me that we should not similarly judge this honest young woman on the basis of equally false and malicious evidence?"

Audley pretended to give this suggestion the full attention of his legalistic brain.

"I think you have summarized the judicial position admirably," he said. A bead of sweat trickled down his brow.

"Then in that case," Norfolk said, "I am sure that you will all join me in dismissing the case against Alice Petherton."

There was heartfelt and unanimous agreement.

And only then did Ralph Sadler risk looking at me. But he kept his face inscrutable.

Chapter 52

A Message from the Past

I spent the next few days with Ned Pepper and his wife, Edith. Susan and Mary had been staying there with Lily all the while that I had been in the Tower.

I was astonished to find this out. They had been only yards away but I had no knowledge of it.

I hugged Lily, weeping, laughing and weeping some more. I never wanted to let her go.

Now my friends proved themselves valuable indeed.

Although I had been freed and all charges against me dropped, I was still in a very vulnerable position. The King had purloined all my properties, Luddington and Buckland, even the four that Thomas had been at such pains to give to me. Sissy wanted me to go to her parents' farm in Stratford. Barnaby thought I should go back to France.

"I cannot afford to travel overseas," I said. "Richard Rich and Thomas Wriothesley have stolen all my money. I don't even have enough to pay Ned and Edith for my food."

The next day a visitor appeared at the Peppers' house. It was the Hanseatic merchant, Derick Berck. I made him welcome and he asked after my health. And then, with a happy smile, he passed to me a box. It was made of oak, plain and simple with two metal bands running around it. He reached around his neck, undid a cord and handed me a little key.

"Sir Thomas Cromwell gave me this box ten years ago," he said, "and bade me keep it safe at my home in Cologne. I forgot about it and it seems that Sir Thomas had as well."

He beamed at me, waiting for my response.

"And you sent for it?" I said. "All the way to Cologne?" I had no idea why he was so keen to show me a box.

"I went there myself to collect it. I thought it too important to entrust to a messenger."

I stared at his face, which was intent and serious.

"But why have you brought it here?" I asked.

Herr Berck smiled. "Because on the morning of his execution Sir Thomas sent me a message to do so. He believed the box belongs to you."

I shook my head, wondering at these strange tidings.

"Well, open it then," Susan said.

I sighed and placed the key in the lock. It was stiff, as if it had not been used for many years, but I managed to turn the key and heard a little click.

I opened the box, peered inside and gasped. Lying in it were three beautiful necklaces, hanging with jewels. One was made of opals, topaz and ruby, the other, pearls. The third had three little starlike gems which I had never seen before. I held it up to show the others.

"Diamonds," said Berck, leaning close to look at them. "They must be worth a fortune."

There was also a little purse which contained gold and silver coins to the value of fifty pounds or more.

And underneath was a bundle of documents, perhaps half a dozen in all. The topmost was a parchment tied up with red ribbon and stamped with a red seal.

It was addressed to Elsbeth Petherton. My mother.

It read: *To be given to our daughter, Alice.*

I opened it with trembling hands, straightened it and began to read. I gasped aloud, my hand flying to my mouth. "It's not my father's hand," I said. "It's not his handwriting."

I stared at the parchment once more, unable to comprehend it.

If it was not written by my father, then who had written it? Who was claiming that I was his daughter?

"Are you going to read it?" Susan asked.

I shook my head. "I cannot." My hand went to my breast. I could not breathe. All that I had believed about myself was crumbling around me.

She looked at me, puzzled at my reaction.

Mary leaned forward and took the letter from my hands.

"Let me, Alice," she said.

She straightened out the letter and began to read:

> *My dearest Elsbeth, I am most heartily relieved and overjoyed to hear that you have recovered from the sickness and are again in good health. I am equally pleased to hear that our daughter is thriving.*
>
> *Despite the pressure of rumor I am relieved that Master Petherton still continues to name the child as his. I am most grateful for his discretion in this.*

Mary paused and glanced up at me a moment, her eyes puzzled. I could say nothing, still shocked by the revelation. She gave a little cough and continued.

I enclose some little trifles for you and, if you choose, for our daughter when she reaches womanhood. I know they will look very well on your neck and am confident they will do the same on Alice's if she has half the beauty of her mother.

I trust that the land and monies I have settled upon your husband continue to be more than sufficient to support your family. Alice should want for nothing as she grows. In particular I would have her educated. For this purpose I send you seventy pounds, which I calculate should be enough for you to engage a tutor for the next fifteen years.

I am also taking mind for Alice's more distant future. I have, therefore, enclosed the deeds of various properties, here and abroad, in the name of the child. She will want for nothing when she reaches the age of twenty-one.

I continue in excellent health and good spirits. I continue to enjoy the full confidence of His Majesty in all spheres.

With fond regards, Thomas Wolsey. Dated 1 August 1530.

Mary put down the letter. Silence settled upon the room. None of my friends looked at me.

So I was a Petherton in name but not in blood. My father was not the man who had brought me up.

My father was Cardinal Wolsey.

The poor man's son who had risen to be the most important of King Henry's servants. Who wielded so much power he was considered almost the second monarch of the land. Who had accumulated riches beyond compare, even building Hampton Court Palace, a place so wonderful the King could not hide his craving for it. A man who seemed unassailable until he failed the King and was destroyed.

Sir Thomas Cromwell's mentor and idol. My father.

A sudden memory came to me of Sir Thomas puzzling at the way I tapped my chin when deep in thought. One of the last things he said to me was that he had finally recalled who it reminded him of but would pursue the matter later. I had thought he meant pursue it with me. But instead he meant pursue it by tracking down the box.

Ten years before, Thomas must have guessed the box contained things of an incendiary nature and asked Berck to take it out of the way to Cologne. And in his last days he must finally have remembered that the box contained a letter of a highly personal nature.

I had a sudden thought and picked up the letter again.

"But this letter has not been opened. Why didn't it get to my mother?" I said. "Why didn't the other things get to her?"

Derick Berck glanced at the letter. "Look at the date, Alice. The Cardinal wrote it just a little while before the King condemned him. Perhaps he had no time to send it to your mother but put it in this box and gave it to Thomas Cromwell for safekeeping."

A tear came to my eye. Sir Thomas may now be denigrated as a demon but he had always acted like a guardian angel to me. And he did so even now, when he was long in his grave.

Berck picked up the necklaces and examined them intently.

"How much do you think they're worth?" asked Humphrey.

Berck shrugged. "A fortune, I imagine. A King's ransom." He gave a little dry laugh at his own wit.

"And what of the deeds?" Susan asked.

I pulled them out of the box. Three of the deeds related to manors in England, one in Suffolk, a second in Cornwall, a third a few miles south of Nottingham.

The other three gave me title to rather more.

The first was the deed to a small château in Normandy, together with a thousand acres of land. The second gave me extensive lands and river rights on the River Loire near Tours. The last one gave me a holding on the Mediterranean Sea in the Republic of Genoa with ownership of five hundred acres of orange and lemon fields.

"You're rich," said Humphrey.

"Maybe," Berck said. "But we need to check that all of the Cardinal's lands did not go to the King when he was disgraced."

He reached out for the deeds, reading them with the utmost care.

"Clever old man," he murmured at last.

He looked up and his face glowed with pleasure.

"These deeds expressly settle the lands upon you," he said. "They were the Cardinal's to give to whom he pleased and he gave them to you. The fact that he ended his days in disgrace makes no difference to this particular legacy. The King has no legal claim on them, Alice. The properties remain yours."

That might be the case legally, I thought. But in England the King was the law. If he wanted to take them from me then he would.

But he could not, I felt certain, steal my foreign properties.

I picked up the letter from Cardinal Wolsey once again. My father. I seemed unable to believe what it said and what it meant. What I had learnt. My heart was all aflutter and my mind whirling at this news.

And then I heard a noise behind me, a scraping and bustle and a voice quietly cursing. The door was kicked open and I leapt to my feet in alarm. I glanced at Barnaby and was horrified to see that he had not moved, that he was standing quite relaxed with his arms crossed, staring at the figure beyond the door.

The man entered and I gave a sigh of relief. It was Hans Holbein, struggling with an unwieldy object wrapped in linen.

"What are you doing here?" I asked.

"That is not the nicest welcome," he said, although he smiled as he spoke. "I have brought you a gift."

"A gift?"

He nodded. "I have labored on it for a long while. I hope it meets your approval."

He used his foot to drag over a chair and placed the parcel on it, propping it up against the chair back. He looked around as if to make sure he had the full attention of everyone in the room. Then he turned to me and, without taking his eyes from me, pulled off the linen cover.

It was a portrait of me. A smaller one than the one he had painted for the King; a portrait intended for me and me alone.

"I found the very first sketch I made of you," he said. "I decided that I could, after all, use that."

My heart went into my mouth. A strange mixture of emotions flooded over me. Thanks that he had labored to produce a second portrait, curiosity to see how it looked and acute anxiety lest it was as unflattering as his first one.

"Come closer," Holbein said. "She won't bite."

I stepped towards it and gasped. It was the absolute likeness of me. But me as I wished to be.

His previous portrait, the one the King had commanded, made me look cold and disdainful. High-and-mighty, Humphrey had thought. Implacable, Susan said.

Now, here I was, relaxed and quiet, with no airs and graces, no holding in, no keeping something hoarded to myself.

The portrait was of me, a young woman. Smiling, light in heart and lovely.

"Thank you, Hans," I said.

"Thank you," he said. "It has been a delight to know you and a privilege to paint you."

And now? I thought. Where should I go for safety? Where should I go with my daughter and my dear, loyal friends? Where else, of course? To France. And to Nicholas.

I found that I had no need to worry about making the journey.

"I've booked places on a boat bound for Calais," Barnaby said. "And I can promise that France is beautiful even at this time of year."

"I shall leave it to you then, Barnaby," I said. And I burst into tears.

Character List

Historical figures are in bold.

Alice Petherton. A former Maid of Honor to Queen Anne Boleyn and Queen Jane Seymour. Alice is the lover and favorite of King Henry VIII. She is nineteen years old at the start of the novel.

King Henry VIII. King of England. He is forty-seven years old at the beginning of the novel and has been on the throne for thirty years.

Hans Holbein. Court Painter.

Anne of Cleves. Henry's fourth wife.

Katheryn Howard. Henry's fifth wife.

Sir Thomas Cromwell, Lord Privy Seal. The King's First Minister and one of his most important advisers. He is instrumental in the Dissolution of the Monasteries, in enriching the King and consolidating the power of King and State. During the course of the novel he is further ennobled as Earl of Essex.

Susan Dunster. Alice's good friend.

Mary Zouche. Alice's good friend. She is a skilled musician.

Gregory Frost. The King's Groom.

Humphrey Buck. Alice's young servant.

Sissy Cooper. Alice's maid and friend.

Barnaby Finch. Former mercenary, now Alice's bodyguard.

Charles de Marillac. Ambassador of France.

Nicholas Bourbon. Marillac's friend. Writer, philosopher and tutor.

Sir Richard Rich. Cromwell's assistant. Said to be the second-most-hated man in the Kingdom, after his master.

Sir Ralph Sadler. Cromwell's protégé, who succeeded Cromwell as one of two Principal Secretaries to the King and was determined to be avenged upon his old master.

Sir Thomas Wriothesley. Together with Sadler, joint Principal Secretary, following Cromwell's death.

Thomas Howard, Duke of Norfolk. Premier noble of the Kingdom. A useful servant to the King though perhaps a grudging one.

Sir Edward Seymour, Earl of Hertford. The brother of Henry's Queen Jane Seymour. As uncle of the young Prince Edward, he remains high in the King's favor.

Charles Brandon, Duke of Suffolk. The only man who could truthfully be considered a friend of the King.

Catherine, Duchess of Suffolk. Formerly Brandon's ward, now his wife. A friend of Alice.

Thomas Cranmer. Archbishop of Canterbury.

Thomas Culpeper. Convicted of being Queen Katheryn's lover.

Francis Dereham. Former servant of Katheryn. Convicted of being her lover.

Henry Mannox. Former music teacher of Katheryn. Accused of being her lover.

Ned Pepper. Beast Keeper of the Royal Menagerie.

Edith Pepper. Ned Pepper's wife.

Robert Cooper. Edith Pepper's brother.

Hannah Cooper. Robert's wife.

Edward Cooper. Their eldest son.

Derick Berck. A senior merchant of the Hanseatic League. Based in the Steelyard in London.

Jurgen Rink. A representative of the Hanseatic League in Paris.
King François I of France.
Anne de Pisseleu d'Heilly. Mistress of King François.
Robert Bench. Steward of the King's Palace in Knole.
Mary. Elder daughter of King Henry.
Philip, Duke of Palatinate-Neuburg. Potential husband of Princess Mary.
Elizabeth. Younger daughter of King Henry.
Kat Champernowne. Elizabeth's governess.

Acknowledgments

I would like to acknowledge and thank the researchers of past and present who have endeavoured to give us a better understanding of these complex times. This book would not have been possible without them.

I would also like to thank Jodi Warshaw and her team at Lake Union Publishing for their support, encouragement and creative ideas not forgetting the behind the scenes work of Gabriella Dumpit and her colleagues. Thanks also to Kathleen Lynch for the cover design. My wife, Janine, has been, as always, a thoughtful reader of the book and an astute adviser.

Finally I would like to thank my editors, Marianna Baer, Irene Billings, Michael Townley and their associates. As with *A Love Most Dangerous*, Marianna worked with me to fine-tune, polish and improve this book, bringing to the task the creativity, imagination and sensibility of a writer as well as an editor. Irene and Michael have been marvelous in their roles as copy editor and proofreader, thorough, thoughtful and with a precision and attention to detail which I can only marvel at.

Everybody has helped polish and hone *Very Like a Queen*. Any mistakes that might remain are, of course, mine.